Unfinished Business

By

Angela Scott

ISBN:**979-8-9860333-4-1**
ISBN-13:

To Romance lovers everywhere

1

Valentine's Day diners packed Lou's Restaurant. For the first time in a year, silverware clinked on dishes, ice rattled in glasses, conversations hummed, and Amy Taylor had to work to speak above the din.

The post pandemic world struggled to regain its footing, but on this night set aside for lovers, life couldn't contain itself.

Out of the corner of her eye, she glimpsed the hostess, Briana, seating a couple at one of her few reserved cozy booths.

Briana provided the couple with menus, which they studied without speaking. The woman, who sat facing Amy, didn't raise her eyes from her menu but stretched her arm across the table, an invitation to take her hand. The man studied his menu and didn't respond. After a few moments, the woman withdrew her hand as though nothing happened.

That couple has been together too long. Still, Amy didn't have time to pay much more attention.

Forgetting where she went, she stopped to grab her receipt book. Oh yeah, the couple at table fifteen.

"Head's up!" Kara swerved to avoid a collision. Amy ducked as a fully laden tray whooshed overhead.

"What the hell, Amy!" Kara hissed on her way by.

"Sorry."

Amy got moving again. Stopping in traffic only led to disaster. She handed the couple their bill and started to move off, expecting them to linger a bit, but the man held out his credit card.

"Oh, perfect." Amy smiled. "I'll be right back."

She went to the computer and returned a few moments later, placing the folder at the edge of the couple's table. "Thank you for coming, tonight. Happy Valentine's Day."

All this she did without conscious thought. As a point of pride, she always approached new diners within a minute of their being seated, so she approached the new couple with a welcoming smile on her face.

"Happy Valentine's Day," she said, but when Jeremy Austin turned her way, her breath lodged in her throat and her stomach twisted into a hard knot. The blood drained from her face, and she struggled not to faint right there. With effort, she squeezed two words out of her constricted throat. "Hello, Jay."

The warmth in his brown eyes died. The smile she assumed he meant to offer a nobody waitress disappeared and his mouth dropped open in an O of surprise.

Gripping her order book in both hands like a protective shield, she wished for a place to hide.

"Amy!"

She flinched at the horror with which he said her name.

"How are you?" Her pulse pounded while the sight of him drove a stake through her heart.

"I'm…fine. Surprised. I wasn't aware you worked here." His tone suggested if he was, he never would have shown up.

The last time she'd seen him, he'd screamed disgusting insults at her from her father's front lawn while his brother tried to hold him back. Her father screamed threats of his own about calling the police.

She'd barricaded herself in her bedroom before he broke her heart any worse. She'd deserved every word.

His brow furrowed as he slid from the booth. To his credit, he managed to plaster a neutral smile on his face and behave like a gentleman. "God, no one's called me Jay…" Faltering, he offered an apologetic wave, shrugged, and opened his arms.

Stepping close, she leaned in for a clumsy hug and he patted her shoulder like Superman touching kryptonite before pulling away.

"Since me?"

He gave her a quick, acquiescent duck of the head. "You look wonderful," he said as though at a high school reunion, talking to someone he'd been friends with back in the day but now struggled to recall their name. "How long has it been? Ten years at least."

"At least."

They stared at each other, and Amy chewed her bottom lip, trying to think of something to say. "So how's Emma?"

The familiar smile melted her heart as his face lit. The skin around his brown eyes crinkled with his grin. He'd be the proud owner of crow's feet before the age of thirty-five. They would be handsome on him too.

"Oh." A flip of his hand. "Emma's doing well. She and her husband are attorneys, and they live and work in Philadelphia. She's the mother of twin boys."

Amy's brows rose. "Twins. Why am I not surprised?" She tilted her head and cocked a brow. "And you?"

"I teach math at Arrowhead High."

Milton! All these years he's been in the area. How have I never seen him around? Well, I do live in an ever-decreasing sphere of work and home.

"A math teacher, eh?" A smile pulled her lips as she recalled the hours spent trying to help her with her homework.

Jay chuckled and jabbed a finger at her. "No smartass comments from you!"

Giving her a sideways teasing glance, he resumed his seat.

Amy snorted and held her hands out to her sides. "What?" Eyes round in feigned surprise, and with a grin on her lips, she tried to sound innocent. "I would never!"

"Sure you wouldn't." Their gazes locked as the humor died, each recognizing the stop sign in this conversation, and she slapped her notepad on her palm.

Jeremy indicated the woman sitting across from him. "This is Maggie Hayes."

Amy bobbed her head at the woman who acted less than pleased over the encounter. "How do you do?"

"Pleasure." Maggie sounded anything but pleased, and Amy decided she best climb back on her professional horse as the woman's hazel-eyed gaze shot daggers.

"Well, I'm Amy." She turned to Jay, "as you know."

She turned back to Maggie. "And I'll be your server tonight. Can I start you off with drinks and an appetizer?"

You gotta be kidding me! Jeremy's gaze followed Amy as she walked away with their orders.

She'd cut the shoulder-length brown hair he'd always loved running his fingers through, but the style was attractive, and her round blue eyes still shone with the easy humor he remembered, though tempered with a somberness he didn't recall in high school.

The quick way they fell into their old banter dismayed him. Why didn't he give her the cold shoulder and act like a stranger? Instead, he laughed and teased, remembering the old days like they occurred yesterday. Dammit! He leaned on his elbows and pressed his hands to his mouth as his gaze returned to Maggie. *I couldn't bring myself to call her my girlfriend in front of Amy. What a jackass!*

Sighing, he opened his hands. "Sorry."

"For what?" Maggie cocked an eyebrow. "Obviously you didn't expect to encounter her. Am I to assume she's an old girlfriend?"

"No," Jeremy said. "She was Emma's best friend. She dated Charlie for a while too."

Maggie shot him a doubtful glare. "Charlie is gay." With a jerk of her head toward the dining room, she indicated Amy. "Was she slow on the uptake?"

Anger flared, but Jeremy refused to take the bait, recognizing when jealousy turned her waspish.

A male waiter appeared with their drinks and plunked a Heineken down in front of him and rye and ginger in front of Maggie.

"Enjoy!" The waiter spun on his heel and departed.

Jeremy picked up his beer bottle. "Well, happy Valentine's Day, Mags." Raising his bottle in salute, he tried to put the evening back on track.

Maggie stared at him, unsmiling. With narrowed eyes, she glared and didn't pick up her drink. "Why does she call you Jay?"

Jeremy thumped his beer bottle down as his shoulders drooped. The damned woman went from zero to sixty in no time flat and for no reason. "I don't recall. I forgot she called me Jay."

He lied about the second part of his sentence, but Maggie didn't need to know. He sighed. "Come on, Mags, you can't be mad at me because an old flame works in this restaurant."

Maggie leaned forward, gripping her drink. "You said she wasn't an old flame."

With a sigh, he sat back. *Why do I bother?* He stared off into space, gathered his wits, and when he returned his gaze to Maggie, he narrowed his eyes.

"You're right. I didn't. I apologize. She dated Charlie for a year until he came out. When they broke up, I asked her out because I crushed on her the entire time she went out with him."

"And the 'No smartass comments from you.' thing? Do you mind explaining?" Maggie toyed with the black linen napkin, inside of which silverware clinked.

I mind a lot. "Our geometry teacher assigned me to tutor her."

Despite knowing he threw gas on the fire he couldn't keep the grin from his face. "Man, she sucked at math."

Amy wasn't faking regarding geometry to his everlasting frustration. But when their study groups became make-out sessions, they became a hundred times more fun for him. With effort, he pushed his memories away and bit the inside of his lower lip, hoping the pain would drive the goofy grin from his face.

Maggie gulped her rye and ginger. "From the expression on your face, I judge her better at sucking other things."

Jeremy shot forward. "Marguerite! How dare you?" From his peripheral vision, he caught the couple at the next table glancing over. He lowered his voice, which lent more menace to his words. "Why must you be so disgusting?" He slammed his back into the cushioned bench and glared as he picked up his beer and took a swallow.

Instant contrition shone from her eyes. Regret pulled her mouth down. "You're right, Jeremy. I'm sorry. I talk crazy sometimes and say stupid things."

She offered a helpless shrug but didn't fool him. "As far as you're concerned, I have a protective streak." A suggestive gleam lit her eyes. "I don't understand why you're still surprised after all these years." With a half-teasing smile, she stretched out a hand across the table again. "Please, sweetheart, let's start over. Please. We're here to celebrate Valentine's Day."

We were here to celebrate Valentine's Day. Jeremy took several deep breaths, grasped her hand, squeezed her fingers, and let go.

He cocked his head. "May I ask a question?"

She nodded.

"What about my behavior sparks jealousy in you?"

"Nothing. I don't…I just…" She stopped, sighed, and dropped her gaze to the wood tabletop. "I don't mean what I say. Seriously,

Jeremy. After four years together, you haven't figured out I say shit I don't mean?"

Like a teacher to a pupil, he asked, "And why do you?"

Her mouth opened and closed like a landed fish.

Despite his best effort, the familiar sensation of the evening's fun draining away didn't surprise him. Over the past year, the sensation had become a familiar companion.

"Jeremy, I said I'm sorry," Maggie said, the death grip on her drink giving away her level of defensiveness.

"We need to talk about this jealous streak of yours. We've discussed this before. You drive me up a wall. You're telling me you don't trust me."

"Yes, I do."

Her wary gaze wandered the room.

He shook his head, leaned close again, and lowered his voice to a harsh whisper. "No, you don't. Because if you did, you would accept the fact an old girlfriend works here—someone I haven't laid eyes on in ten years—without lashing out at me or saying something disgusting and gross about her."

He sat back chewing his lower lip and leaned close again. "I didn't live in a vacuum before I met you."

"I'm aware."

"Are you?" His gaze dropped to the small candle, and he studied the flame dancing in the glass. So much for the romantic ambience.

He raised his gaze as Amy breezed past their table to take a new couple's order. She was still sexy as hell. Curvier than he remembered. Her hips were fuller, and her breasts bigger, or was that a trick of the light? He mentally shrugged and acknowledged he was no longer the beanpole his father used to call him. One last growth spurt added height and widened his chest and shoulders. He kept in shape, but since breaking his leg in high school, no more baseball, except coaching.

Maggie cleared her throat loudly and when he cut his gaze to her, she put on what Jeremy referred to as her Best Apology Face, eyes round and innocent, a slight tilt of her head to her right shoulder, lips parted and pouty. "You're right, Jer. I can't stand the idea of you ever having feelings for any other woman but me."

Resisting the urge to stare as Amy walked past again, he leveled Maggie with a long steady I'm-not-buying-it glare before changing the subject to one of his struggling students.

As Jeremy nattered on about Britney's difficulties, he tried to ignore every time Maggie's gaze darted about as if checking for Amy's whereabouts. She half listened too, which irritated him more, but he shoved his annoyance down and tried to ignore it.

She sipped from her drink. "Did you try a project-based learning program?" She set her drink down and her gaze found Amy who approached but stopped at a nearby table.

He followed her gaze. Turning he faced her with a glare of warning and a lowered brow. "What kind of a teacher do you take me for? Of course, I did. But when we discuss quadratic equations, I half expect her head to explode."

He lifted his beer bottle. "I can't figure out how to break through her confusion. I'm running out of ideas. Tomorrow, I'm going to start working with her after class. Find a way to drag her through the remainder of the school year."

"You better," Maggie said. "Because if you don't, she'll repeat tenth grade next year."

Startled, Jeremy gawked. "What about the rest of her classes? Is she doing so poorly?"

Irritation filled her hazel eyes, shading them greener. "She's doing passably. Her English grades are through the roof, but they're not enough to help her. She is a solid C+ to C- student everywhere else except for math where her average is D- to F. Must we discuss work?"

"We do now. How are you going to help her?" Jeremy stared hard at her. "You're the guidance counselor."

Maggie sighed and thumped her empty glass down. "I'm in consultation with her parents."

She signaled for the waiter as she pushed a perfectly coiffed slip of hair behind her ear. A diamond earring sparkled in the candlelight and the rings on her fingers flashed and danced. "But if she needs to repeat, she needs to repeat."

Heartless.

The waiter returned and Maggie asked for another rye and ginger.

Turning to Jeremy he asked, "Another Heineken for you, sir?"

Jeremy never took his gaze off Maggie. "No thank you, I'm fine."

"Excellent." The waiter moved off.

Amy returned a short time later with their food, ending the discussion. She served first Maggie's salmon and her drink before

Jeremy's steak. She took the empty glass and plunked it on the tray.

"Please cut your steak and tell me if you approve."

He did.

The corners of Amy's lips jerked up and down. "Enjoy your meals."

She walked away and he craned his neck until she moved out of his sight range.

Maggie's lip curled and she lifted her drink. "Sure you don't want another go?"

He snatched up his fork and knife, as his eyebrows lowered over the bridge of his nose. Stabbing his fork into his steak, he sawed his meat and dropped his knife on his plate with a clatter. "Where does this insecurity come from?" He lifted his fork but didn't eat. "When have I ever given you a reason to think I'm the kind of man who cheats?"

He stuck his fork into his mouth and yanked it back. The delicious food was now like ash in his mouth.

Maggie drained her glass before picking up her knife and fork. She held her glass up in a signal for another before offering him a conciliatory smile. "You didn't." A shrug. "I become irrational."

Which has to stop. He ate in silence. To avoid thinking of Amy who kept moving in and out of his sight, he focused his attention on Britney Foster. He didn't want her to repeat the tenth grade.

The waiter returned and refreshed Maggie's drink. Jeremy arched an eyebrow. "How many of those are you planning to have?"

She shrugged. "How many will I need?"

Amy returned. "Can I interest either of you in dessert?"

"Not for me," Jeremy growled.

Maggie hesitated. Shrugged. "Me neither, I guess."

Amy shot him a questioning glance. Heat rolled up his neck and his armpits grew slick. *My former girlfriend, who I thought was the love of my life, served me dinner while my present girlfriend drinks herself silly. Someone shoot me now.*

"I'll be back in a few." With another quick glance at him, Amy pivoted and left.

This time, Jeremy made sure not to glance in the direction she went. Instead, he concentrated on finishing his meal.

Amy returned and without a word set the bill folder on the edge of the table and left.

He lifted the folder and pulled out the bill. A folded sheet of paper with the letter J on the front slid out. Using the folder as a cover, he unfolded the note and his breath caught in his throat: *My shift ends at eleven. Can we talk?* Beneath it she wrote her phone number. He glanced at Maggie through his lashes, but she continued to eat her salmon.

Forcing himself to remain calm, he kept his head down as though calculating the tip amount in his head.

Can we talk? About what? What an idiot she took him for? She'd provided her contact information, so he supposed he need not respond right away.

"Everything okay, Jer?"

He jerked his head up. Maggie sat forward.

"Fine."

Refolding the note, which he shoved into his pants pocket, he signed the bill, added a tip, and reached for his wallet. He removed his credit card and dropped it into the bill holder before sliding the book to the edge of the table. His heart pounded and his hands grew clammy. Amy wanted to talk.

What if she'd made a huge mistake? She wasn't asking for a week in Paris.

Slipping him a note under the nose of his obvious girlfriend was gutsy, but Amy wanted an opportunity to apologize. Nothing more. Girlfriend or no, she needed to make things right.

Their napkins lay crumpled on their plates as they talked. She finished up at another table and headed toward them.

Jay sat back and met her eyes with a cold but unreadable stare, and she yearned for an inkling of his thoughts.

She stopped, picked up their bill holder, and glanced inside, as though checking for completion. She didn't find the note and snapped the holder closed. "Great," she said. "I'll be right back."

While she waited for Jason to finish at the computer station, she peered out the front window. Sometime during the evening, snow had started falling and now came down hard, covering the brick walkway outside Lou's. She sighed. "I'm not looking forward to the drive home tonight."

He rolled his eyes. "Just when you think spring is coming."

He flapped a credit card in her direction. "I'll be done in a sec.

How was serving the happy couple?" His glance indicated Jeremy and Maggie and his voice dripped with sarcasm.

She snickered. "Interesting. I'll have to ask him sometime what the attraction is."

"You know him?"

"Yup. We dated in high school."

To change the subject, she covered her mouth and yawned. "What a crazy busy night, with another four and a half hours to go."

Jason finished up. "You love being here as much as I do," he said, and with an airy wave of his hand, he moved off.

Chuckling, Amy stepped up to the computer and completed Jay's transaction. As she removed the bill, she confirmed he took the note. Her hands shook and her heart pounded.

What if he hands the note back in front of his girlfriend? What if he laughs in my face or tells me where to get off, which is nothing less than I deserve?

She slapped her cheek. *Stop playing mental gymnastics. The time for doubts was before your dumbass study hall note.*

She returned to the table. "Drive home safely. The snow's falling hard. And thank you for coming to Lou's. I hope you enjoyed your dinner." Not knowing how she dared, she lay her hand on his upper arm. "It was a pleasure to see you again, Jay."

"Same here, Amy." He spoke in a monotone and busied himself stuffing the receipt into his wallet, refusing to meet her eye.

He leaned far over to slip his wallet back into his pocket and her hand fell away. Understanding the intent, she didn't take offense. Instead, she reached for their plates. "Let me take these away for you."

Maggie said, "The food was delicious."

Amy smiled. "I'm glad. I'll tell the chef."

She pivoted and headed for the kitchen, stopping at a table where the diners asked for ketchup. She nodded and told them she'd be right back. They thanked her and she moved away. After depositing the ketchup bottle, she moved to the computer station where she tallied her tips to appear busy.

Jay and Maggie made their way to the front of the restaurant. Maggie walked ahead of him, her expression sour. Did she possess little sense of humor or did Amy's serving them throw a wrench into what she thought her Valentine's Day might entail? If she was her natural self, what did Jay see in her?

As he passed, their eyes met. His expression remained cool, almost angry, as he shoved the door open and stalked out. He grasped Maggie's hand and they disappeared into the snowstorm without so much as a backward glance.

Amy sighed and forced a smile on her face. Her earlier pleasant mood walked out the door with Jay Austin.

2

The only sound in the car on the long, silent drive home was the snap of windshield wipers and the radio with the volume down. A few times Jeremy started to speak yet realized he would sound defensive, and dammit, he had nothing to defend against. Instead, he concentrated on driving through snowy, slippery roads.

"I'm sorry about tonight, Maggie. Things didn't go the way I wanted either."

She said nothing, her eyes fixed on the dash.

Jeremy glanced at her. "Do you remember last year? Presidents' Day weekend?"

Maggie studied him in the dashboard light. "I do." She slid her hand along his forearm.

"What do you recall from our weekend?"

She smiled her sultry smile. "I remember a beautiful ski condo, skiing, making love in the Jacuzzi." Her voice grew dreamy with the memory. She rolled her head to gaze at him and squeezed his forearm. "Why? What do you remember?"

He nodded. "I remember a beautiful ski condo, skiing, making love in the Jacuzzi." His stern glance wiped the smile from her face.

"But I also remember going to the bar on Friday night to wait for you because you took forever applying your makeup and making sure your clothing and jewelry made a perfect complement."

He released a deep sigh. "I remember striking up a conversation with a couple from Vail who came to Vermont for a comparison of the ski experience."

"Why are you bringing this up now?"

"I remember her husband left to use the men's room and you walked in while I was sitting at the bar talking to a beautiful woman. His wife."

Maggie sighed. "Jeremy, I apologized. How long are you going to hold that incident against me? Do I need to apologize again?"

"No. You apologized. Several times, in fact, but only after putting me through hell for the entire weekend. By Saturday afternoon I was ready to leave because I couldn't stand the nagging and picking anymore. For the first time since we'd started going together, I planned a weekend to celebrate your birthday before you turned thirty, but your angry, outlandish accusations drove all the joy from a gift I spent months organizing and saving for."

"What do you want me to say?"

He shrugged one shoulder. "Nothing. I don't want you to say anything. I'm remembering a time, much like tonight, when you accused me of things without merit and I want you to understand, or at least try to understand, how your behavior affects me. You've done this to me for years, like you have a pathological need to push me away, to push away anyone who tries to make a close emotional connection. You shut me out all the time."

He pulled into her driveway, put the car in park, and faced her. "Lack of trust in a couple is a deadly thing, Maggie, and I'm tired of your distrust. I can't help the fact an old girlfriend works at the restaurant. Our relationship didn't end well and if I'd had an inkling she worked at Lou's, I would have chosen a different place. But I'm not going to pay the price. I'm tired of having to."

"Fine, okay. I'm sorry for my behavior tonight." She peeked at him through her lashes. "I love you."

Jeremy sighed and tapped his fingers on the steering wheel. He had the distinct impression she'd listened to his words but didn't understand them. He ran a hand through his hair, grabbed a handful, and released.

After a moment, she drew in a deep breath. "Do you want to come in?" She slid her gaze to the side to study him.

He shook his head and stared straight ahead. "It's late, I'm tired, and the snow is coming down hard. I think I'd better go home."

"Fine." This time she spat the word and exited the car, slamming the door behind her.

Maggie made tracks through the deepening snow to the front door, and Jeremy let his headlights illuminate the way. When she fit the key into the lock, he put the car in reverse, backed out of the driveway, and drove away, expecting a day or two of the silent treatment. Maggie always struggled with the truth, and he sighed at the thought.

He pulled into his driveway and entered a cold house. After removing his coat and boots, he fiddled with the thermostat. Beneath his feet, the furnace rumbled awake.

With a glance at his wristwatch, he grabbed the remote and turned on the TV. Almost nine o'clock.

Wandering into the kitchen, he took down a cup and made some coffee. While the hot liquid poured into his mug, he stared at the lesson plans he still needed to complete. The brewer hissed the last of his coffee and he picked up his cup. He sipped, wandered back into the living room, and sat down.

Lifting his left hip, he reached into his back pocket and pulled out his phone. He swiped the screen with his thumb as he sipped his coffee and scrolled until he found what he sought: Magpie.

After tapping her nickname he put his cup down and texted. *Sorry about tonight. I don't want to argue with you.* He raised his thumb to hit the send button, but instead deleted the message and put his phone down.

Not this time. He would not be the first to apologize again. She needed to apologize first. Deep in his heart, he realized he might wait forever. Maggie seldom apologized unless forced to.

Taking another swallow of coffee he flipped through the channels, stopping for a moment first on CNN, then MSNBC, to find out what went on in the world. He surfed some more and landed on ESPN.

After he settled on the sofa, he dropped the remote beside him and propped his feet on the small table, listening as they discussed football and possible baseball trades. The Red Sox had traded their starting pitcher— glory hallelujah.

He glanced at his wristwatch again. Because of the storm, the trip home took an hour and forty-five minutes to make a twenty-five-minute drive from Burlington to Milton. If he went back, he needed to leave soon. Went back? What was he thinking?

Jeremy slid his hand into his pocket and drew out the note.

My shift ends at eleven. Can we talk? About what? He was completely uninterested in anything she had to say. Still, he admitted she'd made a gutsy move. What if Maggie had picked up their bill? Not like she would, but what if? Amy took the chance. What did she want to talk about? The truth? What a fool she thought he was? Ten years made a difference in a person's life. Perhaps maturity motivated her request.

She pitched a fastball right down the middle. Should he swing or not?

Bored with ESPN, he turned to the local news. The lead story was about another rape incident in Burlington. Last night. The anchor, a blond woman, gave the details.

"This made the fourth attack in the past week," she spoke to the camera. "Incidents began in October, but since the beginning of the new year, the attacks have picked up in frequency and violence. The Queen City Rapist is becoming bolder. Police ask anyone with information to please contact their local law enforcement agency." She stood on the corner of Church and Cherry Streets, Lou's Restaurant a backdrop behind her as she scrolled on her phone reading aloud from her text.

He jerked his feet off the coffee table and grabbed the remote.

"Goddammit!"

Jeremy snapped off the TV, grabbed his phone, and moved fast before changing his mind. Snatching his jacket off the coat tree, he stepped into his boots and headed back out the door.

Lou's closed at last. Amy couldn't wait to go home and put tonight behind her. She wanted to crawl into bed, pull the covers over her head, and remain hidden for the rest of her life.

As she moved about cleaning, her feet screamed at her, and her legs wobbled like a pair of swimming pool noodles. Her mind constantly replayed her dumb note. She should have left well enough alone, but the minute she set eyes on him, she realized she couldn't.

"Who is he? Does anyone have a clue?" Frank Mitchell, the owner, held a glass in one hand and a dishtowel in the other as he stared out the window, suspicion creasing his brow.

"Who?" Amy finished wiping her table.

"Frosty the Snowman sitting on the bench outside."

Jason, Briana, Kara, and Amy gathered at the window.

"Oh my God!" Amy's hand flew to her throat. "He came back!" Her fingers toyed with the chain of a small necklace. "I didn't think he would."

Kara nudged her. "Isn't he the man you hugged earlier like he was a dirty wet mop? If you don't want him…"

Heat rose in her neck and suffused Amy's face, and she covered her mouth. "I can't believe he came back." Her heart pounded. Why had he?

Briana grinned. "Too bad I'm already married."

"Well he's obviously not for me," Jason said, sounding disappointed.

Amy tsked at all the comments swirling around her head.

"Well, we're almost finished here." Frank gave Amy a shove toward the back of the restaurant. "Go, before he freezes to death."

"Thanks, Frankie. You're a peach." Amy ran to the locker room.

She exited out the front door and Jeremy rose as she approached. He pushed his hands deep into his coat pockets as snow dampened his hair and mounded on his shoulders. When he shook his head, the accumulated snow flew in all directions. His wet hair plastered itself to his head.

Amy's breath stuck in her throat as a vision of him swimming in her father's pool, his wet tanned shoulders and chest glistening in the sun, tore at her insides and left her knees weak. The memory of him emerging from underwater and shaking his head, whipping his hair free of excess water rocked her senses and she stopped several paces away from the bench.

"Hello."

"Hi." He shuffled his feet. "Where are you parked?"

She pointed behind him. "On Bank Street. In the garage."

He half turned and offered his elbow, but she didn't move.

"Where's…?" The woman's name escaped her. "Your friend?" she finished. "Wouldn't she mind you being here?"

"I dropped her off at her condo and yes, she would mind a lot. But you said you wanted to talk." His stern tone and honesty caught her off guard, as the familiarity of his direct style reassured her.

"I did."

She approached and slipped her mittened hand into the crook of his arm. They walked in silence. So many things she wanted to say, but now her brain went on lockdown.

"I shouldn't call you 'Jay' anymore, should I?" *I shouldn't call you anything but ancient history.*

A frigid gust of wind screamed off Lake Champlain behind them, swirled snowflakes, and slithered down Amy's neck wringing a shiver from her. She glanced behind them.

"No. Jay's fine. You came up with the name." His brow lowered over the top of his nose. "How did you come up with Jay, if I may ask?"

Amy smirked and turned her face away to hide her embarrassment. "In those days, when I was in a hurry about everything," she said, rolling her eyes at her own silliness, "'Jeremy' took too long to say, so I shortened your name to the first letter."

He smiled. "Funny," he said but didn't laugh.

She offered a conciliatory nod. "I won't call you Jay anymore if you don't want me to."

Her head swiveled on her neck and her eyes stayed in constant motion.

"I don't mind." He stopped walking and faced her. "Coming from you." His gaze slid away and returned. "Jay sounds…right. Comfortable."

Snow gathered on his shoulders and landed on his eyelashes.

"You need a hat and a pair of mittens," she said, letting her gaze roam his face, refamiliarizing herself with his almond-shaped brown eyes and thick lashes, dark full brows, and long nose.

He was taller than she remembered. They used to stand eye to eye, but now, the top of her head came to his chin. She met his eyes. They were dark, guarded, almost unfriendly.

He turned away and his breath puffed in a white cloud. "I'm fine."

She glanced toward the lake before grasping his elbow again to steer him to the garage. The silence stretched.

"I took Maggie to dinner tonight for Valentine's Day."

Her brow furrowed. "What?"

"Maggie." He said her name almost savagely. "She and I have been together for some time. I took her to dinner to celebrate Valentine's Day. I didn't realize you work at Lou's."

"Oh." Message received. They had nothing to talk about. But if true, why return? She would have reached the same conclusion if he had never come back.

Her mind whirred so fast, she struggled to contain the noise. "I hope I didn't piss her off with my teasing. Teaching fits you. Of course, what I think doesn't matter, I suppose." Amy glanced at him.

His nose stood out on his rigid face. She plowed on. "Far more realistic than your dream of replacing Dustin Pedroia."

Though she didn't intend it, he laughed, and the rich deep sound sent a corkscrew of pleasure twisting down her spine.

"I forgot about that!" He raised a finger. "And for the record, if not for breaking my leg stealing home in the state championship game, I might have given Pedie a run for his money. I'm just sayin'."

She chuckled. "I'm sure you would have."

Funny, how she remembered his dream of playing second base for the Boston Red Sox. How he recalled struggling to teach her geometry. And to his credit, he kept trying one technique after another, such as pulling out his old wooden building blocks as teaching tools.

They drew parallel to an alleyway and Amy glanced past him toward the entrance.

She hesitated. "I'm sure you're an excellent teacher."

Jeremy also peered down the alley. "Thank you. I coach varsity baseball too."

"Not surprising."

As they rounded the corner and approached the garage, her gaze swept the intersection.

Jay turned as well. "What are you looking for?"

Embarrassment warmed her cheeks and she shrugged. "I try to be aware of what's around me."

He grew solemn. "I don't blame you. The news is full of some creep running around."

"Is he why you're here?" Amy cast a quick glance at him but feared to meet his eyes. "I figured never to lay eyes on you again."

He didn't answer but tugged her back into movement.

Amy had parked her Toyota near the exit ramp on the third level. As they approached, she removed the fob from her coat pocket and pushed the button. The headlights flashed and the horn gave a small honk. They stopped at the back of the car.

"Thank you, Jay."

"You're welcome."

She feasted her eyes on him. He wore his dark brown hair short, shaved close around his ears and temples and the back of his neck, but full on top. The spikes he sported in school were a thing of the past. He wore tan dress pants, and she remembered an Oxford shirt and sweater earlier.

A wet strand of hair fell over his forehead, and she fought the urge to brush the lock back and smooth his dark arched eyebrows. His eyelashes were long and spiky from melting snow. She wanted to lean into him and lay her head on his chest the way she used to.

His gaze roamed her face, and her heart seized at the pain, confusion, and anger in his eyes.

She pretended to search the garage. "Where are you parked?"

"Cherry Street."

"Hop in." She gestured. "I'll take you to your car."

"Thanks."

As she drove down the road, Jeremy pointed out his Honda, and she pulled over and put her car in park.

"No more Jeep." Her heart pinged and she pushed away memories of their make-out sessions in the backseat. Unbidden came the remembered pressure of his lips on hers, and her stomach spasmed.

"Nope," he said. "Sold it years ago."

His nonchalant answer stung as perhaps he'd intended.

Though he reached for the handle, he made no move to open the door. Now that her chance to speak had arrived, her tongue riveted itself to the roof of her mouth.

He dropped his hand, contemplated her for an eternity, and sighed. "You said you wanted to talk. What about?"

Try as she might, she couldn't ignite her brain and she stared at him for so long that he grew disgusted. He pushed the door open letting in a blast of cold air and swirling snow. "Good night, Amy."

He means goodbye, Amy. The floodgates crashed and words flowed like a torrent.

"I'm sorry, Jay. I'm so sorry for everything I did to you. I hurt you and I hope someday you can forgive me. If I could take any minute of those days back I would, and if you still can't forgive me, please understand how profoundly sorry I am." Her throat tightened choking off more words.

He hesitated, closed the door, but didn't speak and he kept his gaze fixed on her glovebox.

"You didn't do anything wrong," she answered his unspoken question. "The fault was mine."

He lifted his gaze. "If I didn't do anything wrong, tell me why?"

"I can't. Please don't ask."

"That doesn't help!" He turned on her fast, and she flinched, thinking he might strike her.

He stared, alarmed and questioning, and ran his hand through his hair. “I thought you loved me. I thought you wanted…” He let his hand drop. “I thought you wanted the same things I wanted. I wanted to marry you. Young as we were, I never doubted you…us.”

Nothing would make her happier, but he’d changed everything for her, and she couldn’t share that with him. She raised a meek face to Jeremy. “I had no choice…”

He challenged her with a steely glare. “Bullshit. We always have choices.”

She averted her eyes. “I don’t want you to hate me more than you do now.”

Rage contorted his features. “Oh, sweetie, not possible.” He squeezed his eyes shut and made a growling noise in his throat.

Amy ran her mittened hands around the steering wheel and glanced at him from the corner of her eye.

Their conversation went off the rails fast, and a sudden urge to confess everything overwhelmed her, but he would press for details. The extreme hurt if he discovered the truth would be too much for her to bear.

“Amy.” The sound of her name was fraught with discouragement and impatience, and she almost gave in. She met his eyes and her heart lurched at the profound sadness in them. “Tell me. After so much time, what difference does it make?”

She raised an eyebrow and with a tilt of her head, acknowledged the truth, yet he wouldn’t believe her if she told him the truth and swore on a stack of Bibles.

Instead, she hid her fear behind a surge of anger. “You’re right, Jeremy. I’m sorry for what happened. I’m sorry I hurt you all those years ago. I’m sorry I asked you to talk to me. I’m sorry you were compelled to leave your girlfriend and drag your ass back here this late at night and in this weather. Forget I said anything. I wanted to apologize, and I did.”

She slashed a hand through the air.

He leaned his arm against the door and stared at her as if trying to solve a complex math problem.

Amy cringed, unsure what he might do or say next. This is where Peter, her ex-husband, would take the time to come up with the worst, most hurtful thing he could dredge up, and she steeled herself.

"What do you want from me?" Anger, frustration, and hurt, laced his harsh whisper.

Drained and exhausted, she shrugged, still running her hand around the steering wheel. "Forgiveness. Nothing more."

His sudden intake of air sounded loud in the enclosed space despite the heater blowing full blast. "Okay," he slapped his thigh. "Fine. Done."

Her temper flared. "What the hell? Meaning what?" She pounded her fist on the steering wheel. "What the fuck is 'okay, fine, done?'" She dropped her voice an octave, mimicking and mocking then flicked off the heater. The cabin was suffocating.

"Exactly what I said," he snarled. "Fine. You want my forgiveness. No clue why I should grant you forgiveness but granted. I forgive you. You're sorry for what happened. Terrific! I'm sorry too. I'm sorry you turned your back on me. I'm sorry you wouldn't tell me what I did wrong. I'm sorry you turned out to be such a…a…" He bit off his words and turned away. "Fuck!" Smashing his fist into the door, he pressed his palm against his eyes.

Amy cringed at his outburst.

Drawing in a ragged breath, he said, "I don't want to do this. I don't want to argue with you." He grabbed the handle and opened the door again, letting in another blast of cold air. "Enjoy your life, Amy Taylor."

He slammed the door shut and rapped on her rear window indicating she was free to leave.

Instead, she pushed the button to roll down her window. "Jay?"

She choked his name out through her constricted throat.

He turned a frustrated glare on her.

Her sad smile communicated her regret for the way things turned out. "Thank you for coming back. In spite of everything, happy Valentine's Day."

His shoulders dropped and he turned away. "Yeah, same to you," he said in an uncharitable way and unlocked his car.

She rolled up her window and drove away, crying.

3

Lou's bustled worse than last night, and Amy ran herself ragged. Despite how her meeting with Jay had ended in anger, her hopeful heart kept her glancing at the door every time someone entered.

Near the end of the night and needing a break, she went to the employees' bathroom. She left the water running as she scrubbed her hands, then let the hot water pour over them. As she squeezed the rough brown paper towels, she stared into the mirror, drew in a deep breath, and exhaled. *Don't let the idiot customers annoy you. You need this job. Smile, nod, and give them what they ask for. Deep breath in, slow breath out.*

By the time Amy returned to her station, the restaurant had cleared. With a few customers left, she inquired after their needs, went to the bar, and began wrapping silverware into black linen napkins, Frank's signature color. His uniforms were also black.

Frank approached. "Amy." He jerked his chin toward the door. "Tell him to come inside. He must be frozen sitting outside."

Amy backed up to peer out the front window. Jay sat huddled on the same bench beneath the streetlight, his hands deep in his pockets. He appeared so cold a shiver jerked her body.

Her heart leaped into her throat. Why had he returned when he'd made it clear she would never lay eyes on him again? And why not come in? The restaurant was still open. She set down the wrapped napkin and went to the front door. A frigid blast of air hit her like a physical slap.

"Jay!" She waved him over, unable to keep the pleased surprise from her tone.

As he approached, she stepped aside and held the door open for him. “Frank says to come inside.”

“Thanks. I’m freezing.”

His face was red and raw, his eyes watered, and deep in his jacket pockets, the outlines of his clenched hands bulged.

“Don’t you have gloves or mittens or something? And what about a hat? Your ears are bright red. You’ll have frostbite.”

“Who are you, my mother?”

He moved past her and into the restaurant.

She chose not to respond, unsure if he teased or offered sarcasm. “I didn’t expect you to come back.”

“Yeah, well, neither did I.”

He started to say more when Frank appeared and extended his fist. No handshakes. Only fist bumps.

“Frank,” he said, introducing himself.

Jeremy pressed his knuckles to Frank’s. “Jeremy.”

“Have a seat, Jeremy. Care for a coffee? Why didn’t you come in?”

Jay removed his jacket and made himself comfortable on a barstool. He wore an olive green Oxford shirt beneath a rust-colored sweater and black dress pants. A thin black belt encircled his narrow waist. “Thanks. I didn’t think I should since I’m not dining.” He tried to settle his jacket on his knees, but it slipped off.

Amy extended her hand. “I’ll hang your jacket in my locker.”

Yanking the metal door open, she studied the picture taped to the inside door. She never tired of looking at the photo Dad took of three-hour-old Ricky sleeping in her arms.

No smiling father stood beside her or leaned into the picture. Amy beamed for two. Terrified at the prospect of raising a child alone, her smile was extra exuberant.

She got revenge on her ex by giving Ricky her maiden name and listing his father as unknown on his birth certificate. Ricky would ask someday, but she’d cross that bridge if the time came. She tore her gaze away from the photograph.

Before reaching into her locker, she brought the garment to her face and inhaled his aftershave. *God, he still smells like Old Spice.*

“Checking what he uses for laundry detergent?”

Jason spoke behind her.

Amy jumped, slamming into her locker door.

"Holy crap, Amy!"

"Jason." She hung the coat and rubbed her arm. "You startled me. Stop sneaking up on me."

"Talk about an understatement." Jason leaned his shoulder against the bank of lockers and crossed his arms as if imparting a lecture. "And for the record, I wasn't sneaking. Your customers are ready to leave."

She closed her locker and snapped the padlock into place. "On my way."

Amy attended to her customers, aware of Jay on the barstool. He cradled a cup of coffee in one hand while chatting with Frank who no doubt was getting the particulars on Jay's bloodline and financial history.

After seeing to her customers, she returned to the bar to wrap more silverware and place it all in the tub while she listened to the two men chat.

"Well, God bless you." Frank refilled Jay's cup and pushed a small dish of creamers at him. "I don't understand how you can deal with all those hormone-overdosed adolescents all day long."

Jay chuckled at Frank's description. He took a creamer and poured the liquid into his coffee.

"I love teaching. I always loved math. For a while, I thought of becoming an accountant, but sitting behind a desk all day crunching numbers is not my idea of exciting. Preparing kids to go out into the world is…" He shrugged as if unable to think of the words.

"A noble cause," Amy said, remembering how he liked noble causes.

Meeting her eyes, he smiled back. "A noble cause."

When he took a sip, the smile disappeared behind the mug, but his eyes warmed as he gazed at her.

Her heart pounded. She smiled back.

Frank thumped a cup down on the counter and Amy jumped. "Amy, I think table seven is ready for their check."

She glanced over to the couple sitting, not eating, and not talking.

She gasped. "Oh, shit. Sorry, Frank."

She moved away from the bar and gave herself a mental kick for letting his presence sidetrack her. After last night's angry exchange, she figured never to lay eyes on him again. So why was he here?

As Amy bustled off, Jeremy sized up her boss. "Frank, if my coming here is a problem, tell me now. I don't want to cause her trouble."

Sipping his coffee, Jeremy tried not to squirm under Frank's hard scrutiny, doing his best to keep eye contact, understanding if he broke first, that would be game over and to his surprise, Frank's goodwill mattered to him.

Frank set his coffee cup down. "Well, not so much a problem, as…"

Jeremy waited as Frank pulled the white cloth off his shoulder and wiped a spot on the bar as though using the motion to collect his thoughts.

He judged Frank to be in his mid to late forties. His short dark hair showed gray at the temples and though he had an open and friendly face, he gave off a sense of being someone you didn't want to meet in a dark alley.

He met Jeremy's eye. "I think of Amy as my little sister, and I don't want her hurt. Her life is hard enough, she's had more than her share of heartache, and she doesn't need any more."

Jeremy straightened up. So she got some of her own back, did she? "I understand."

Frank leaned an elbow on the bar and leveled his stern blue-eyed gaze straight at Jeremy's eyes. "Do you? Because I recall you were here last night with a rather fancy-looking woman on your arm." He held Jeremy's gaze with a hard stare and he did his best not to squirm.

"Don't trifle with my Amy, son." Frank straightened and moved away to serve a patron who had entered and taken a seat at the far end of the bar.

Jeremy's gaze followed him. Frank glanced back and locked eyes, a warning in his look before he returned his attention to his customer.

As eleven drew near, Amy stopped by his stool with his coat in her hand. She had her jacket on and her mittens and hat in her other hand. He slipped the garment on and turned to Frank.

"Thank you for letting me in, and for the coffee and advice." He reached for his wallet. "How much do I owe you?"

"Nothing." Frank waved a hand. "On the house for walking Amy to her car. She told me."

They studied each other once again, each taking the other's measure. Jeremy nodded. "Well, thank you."

Frank shot him an irritated glance. "In the future, Jeremy, come in and sit down. No need to freeze your ass off outside," he scolded and walked away.

Amy chuckled and called over her shoulder, "G'night, Frankie."

"Later," he called back.

"Frank's a likable guy. A little intimidating, though," Jeremy said as they made their way to the garage.

She smiled. "He's a teddy bear."

They walked to the end of Cherry Street in silence and at the intersection with South Winooski Avenue, Amy glanced all four ways.

"You don't have to worry. I'm here."

Her breath huffed a white cloud and her teeth flashed in a quick smile. "Habit."

On the street, piles of snow from yesterday's storm made a waist-high barrier between the street and the sidewalk. The hard-packed snow from so many feet and plummeting nighttime temperatures made the sidewalk a skating rink. Amy's grip tightened on his forearm, and he braced himself. If she fell, he would go down too.

They crossed the street and headed south toward Bank Street and the parking garage.

"Lou's isn't my only job," Amy broke an uncomfortable silence.

"What?"

She glanced at him. "Lou's isn't my only job. I also work at the hospital, but I need the extra income. I don't want you to think I'm not smart enough or ambitious enough to be anything other than a waitress. I need the money."

Okay. I didn't ask. "I never thought anything of the sort." He paused. "What do you do at the hospital?"

She tsked and made a face. "I check people in for their appointments and schedule their next ones. I hate the job, but I need the money."

"You like dealing with people." At least he remembered her as a person who liked people and always thought the best of them. What changed?

Amy sighed. "I used to like dealing with people. I used to think most people were kind, but I gotta admit, as I grow older, I've come to the conclusion most people are assholes. And the older they are, the more…assholey."

Jeremy gaped at her.

She studied him. "If you're wondering where the girl is who used to think the best of everyone," she said, reading his thoughts, "I have a short but efficient list of men who've gone out of their way to disabuse me of such a notion. The naive child in me no longer exists."

The bitterness in her tone shocked him and he continued to stare.

She offered a small smile and tugged his arm. They continued walking.

The hard edge to her words, combined with Frank's warning, gave him something to think about and left him sad to find the girl he remembered had changed. But the trusting kid he used to be disappeared too and she was to blame. Well, she and Maggie.

When he'd arrived in town, Jeremy had driven through the garage until he found her Toyota and pulled into the adjacent spot.

A smile lit her face when she noticed his car and she glanced at him. "I guess I'm not giving you a ride to your car."

He snapped his fingers. "Damn, I didn't think of that."

She chuckled as she pushed the button on the key fob and her car flashed and beeped.

"Besides, this way I don't have to wait for the windshield to defrost or swipe snow."

"Smart thinking." Amy stopped at her car and studied him. She squeezed her lips together as though squeezing words back into her brain.

To his utter disbelief, he asked, "Would you like me to come again tomorrow night?" Tonight he gave in to the impulse growing in him all day. For better or worse, he had to go back, and now that the time had come to part ways, he wanted more.

Her eyes narrowed as she stared at him. "I don't want you to think I'm ungrateful, but I don't understand why you came tonight. You were adamant last night. I had my say and that was that." Her brow furrowed. "So…why?"

He scowled and turned away.

"Listen, Jay." Her mittened hands found her hips. "I don't understand what game you're playing but I'm not participating. You were never the cheating sort, so you can count me out."

"Cheating? You're the one who asked for an audience knowing I was with someone. What do you call that, if not an invitation?"

"Only an invitation to a conversation. For years, I wanted to apologize to you. I regret what I did and, yes, I wish I could take it all back, but I can't. When you came in last night, I thought…here's my chance to make things right."

His jaw tightened and he stared at the filthy concrete flooring of the garage. The cold made him shiver. He stuffed his hands into his pockets.

"Well," he said, glaring into her determined face. "Congratulations. You accomplished your goal." He stepped up to his car door and fumbled with his keys.

"Jay," she said as he opened the door.

He slammed his door shut and turned on her. "Why do you get to make things right and I pay the price?" He came around the car and stepped almost face-to-face with Amy.

Her blue eyes widened, and her mouth worked, but nothing came out. She stepped back.

Jeremy advanced. "You broke up with me. Remember? No explanation, just 'Go away, leave me alone.'"

He made a sweeping motion with his hand. "I mean, one day we're talking about going to the same college so we can stay together, we're planning our future after college, marriage, everything. And the next thing I know"—he slapped a hand to his chest— "you're running from me, which was easy for you." He thrust his hand toward her.

She flinched and part of him was aware of her shrinking into herself as her shoulders rose and her neck lowered.

"I was on crutches and couldn't move fast. You wouldn't talk to me, wouldn't look at me. You ducked into a girl's bathroom or a classroom every time I appeared. I considered following you into a girl's bathroom so I might have my say!"

At last, he stopped shouting, but he glared, breathing hard.

Now Amy stared at the filthy concrete. Her shoulders slumped and she kept her head down as though used to being shouted at and hunkering down to wait out the storm.

With a sigh, he backed off. "You're right. I was angry last night. I'm angry now. Last night I was ready to say, 'Okay, Amy, you got your apology in, no problem.' But you made me wait a long time too. I waited—not for an apology, but for an explanation, a chance for some payback—and I decided I'm going to hound you until I obtain what I want, and your feeble excuses will no longer work."

4

Snow had begun falling again, so Amy kept the car at a steady thirty-five miles per hour with quick glances at the speedometer. If she strayed too far above, she removed her foot from the gas pedal. He was going to hound her. What did that mean? Had the years changed him?

Was he more like Peter than the Jay she remembered? The sweet boy who held her hand every chance he got. Who made out with her, and protected her from those who teased and bullied her when Charlie came out? Who protected Charlie too?

Few people understood the truth about her relationship with his older brother besides Jay and Emma. She gave their brother shade until he was brave enough to declare himself.

Both boys were sensitive but in different ways. Jay wore his heart on his sleeve, which she glimpsed in his anger. He had reason to be angry with her, but it was more. In the two years, she'd worked for Frank, she'd learned to read people. The woman he was with last night made him unhappy.

Well, if he moved past his anger, perhaps she might be a catalyst. Amy hadn't realized, until he walked into Lou's with the other woman, how much she wanted him back, but she had one problem. How to tell him the truth.

Images flashed in her mind and with effort, she pushed them away, squirming at a familiar ghost pain she hadn't experienced in years, but still, her rape had the capacity to strike terror when she least expected.

She'd taken tae kwon do classes to defend herself from physical attacks and earned a blue belt, but the psychological wounds still debilitated her.

Without quite knowing how she arrived, she pulled into her parents' driveway. Well past midnight, the house was dark, but Dad would still be awake, with Ricky asleep next to him.

She left the engine running to keep the car warm, and sure enough, the front light came on. She moved with care up the sidewalk, and as she approached the steps, he opened the door and let her in.

Dad kissed her cheek. "Hi," he whispered. "Cold night!"

She nodded. "How was he?"

"Perfect. He ate a decent supper, played for about an hour, and went right to sleep." He moved to the couch and lifted the sleeping boy to his shoulder. Dressed in his snowsuit, the poor kid was sweaty all bundled up.

As they made the transition, Ricky twitched but didn't wake. Amy settled him on her left shoulder while Dad handed her the diaper bag, which she draped over her right shoulder. "I'm home tomorrow night," she said.

She told him this every Monday and Wednesday night and it became part of the ritual between them. "I hope you realize how much I appreciate your help."

He waved her away. "Nonsense. We did the same thing for Lindsay when we took care of Jessica." He touched her arm. "Life hasn't been kind to either of you girls, but I'm sure you'll find your way same as she has."

Amy shifted Ricky. "Well, I'll let you go to bed now. I'm sorry I was late. We had a busy night." She shook her head, unsure why she said what she did. Dad didn't expect an explanation. He often said his generation worked until given permission to leave.

Again, he waved a hand. "We'll see you in the morning."

"Which is in a few hours, so I want to go to bed myself."

He followed her outside and held one of her arms while she navigated the front steps, before going back inside.

After Amy buckled her sleeping son into his car seat and closed her door, the front light went off. She backed out of the driveway and drove around the corner to the house she rented from her father, which he bought for her shortly after her divorce. Somehow, she managed to unlock her back door, hold Ricky in her arms, and not drop the diaper bag or her purse.

She closed the door but didn't turn on the light to avoid waking him. There were enough night-lights plugged in around her small kitchen to give her plenty of illumination.

Dropping her bags, she laid the toddler on the kitchen table. As she pulled him out of his snowsuit, she caught a whiff and turned her face away. Would she ever be able to stop putting him in nighttime diapers? They were the largest part of her grocery budget. What she wouldn't give to spend those thirty dollars on something like…meat…vegetables…food.

Gingerly, she lifted her son and carried him upstairs, hoping to change him without waking him. Otherwise, she'd never fall asleep, and she was exhausted.

Five thirty came early, but Amy didn't need an alarm clock. She had Ricky. She lay half-awake staring at the crib across the room. Perhaps this morning he would sleep beyond five thirty and give her an extra half hour. She switched her gaze to the clock. Five twenty-nine. When the numbers changed, as if an electrical current connected the clock to the crib, Ricky sat up.

He grasped the edges of the crib and pulled himself to his feet. "Mommy, I get up now," he said, and like a little gymnast, he tried to climb out.

She rubbed a hand over her face. "Okay, buddy. I'm coming." Amy threw the covers back and made her way across the room to lift him from the crib before he crashed to the floor. He needed a bed. Time to ask Dad for her old one.

Downstairs, she fixed a breakfast of oatmeal with blueberries, orange juice in a sippy cup, and a coffee for herself.

After tucking Ricky close to the table so he wouldn't fall out of his booster seat while he ate, she ran into the bathroom for a five-minute shower, something that always filled her with anxiety. What if he choked or fell? But what choice did she have? She needed to prepare for work.

Wrapping a towel around herself, Amy checked on him. Oatmeal goo stuck in his hair and smeared his face.

"Gracious, kid. Can't you locate your mouth?"

His bright blue eyes gazed at her as he chewed. With an inexpert hand, he dipped the spoon and using both hands, aimed for his wide-open mouth. The tip bumped the corner of his lip and most of the oatmeal plopped on the table. He picked it up with his fingers, which he shoved into his mouth. Despite the mess, Amy laughed. She went back into the bathroom and got a warm, wet washcloth.

Returning to the kitchen, she held the cloth spread on her palm. "Incoming!" she called and shoved the cloth over his face.

Beneath her hand, his muffled child's laugh reached her heart. The sound gave her strength and helped her put one foot in front of the other each day. She laughed too and made motor noises as she swiped the cloth across his face and into his hair.

"Remind me you need a bath tonight."

He tried to spoon more oatmeal and missed his mouth again.

"Okay, sport, enough. Grammy can feed you more if you're still hungry."

After kissing the top of his head, she wiped his hands and face again, lifted him off his chair, and set him on his feet. As he started for the TV room, she called him back. "Come on, let's go upstairs and dress."

He braced his feet and clenched his fingers, a sure sign of a tantrum, which she tried to forestall with an announcement. "We need to go to Grammy's, Rick. Jessica's coming to play today."

Her five-year-old niece was his only playmate and the poor little girl wandered lost these days after COVID took her father.

Unclenching his fingers, he stared as though unsure he should believe her but reversed course and ran for the stairs.

Amy held her breath as he breezed by a small desk, his temple missing the corner by mere inches. All boy, he went nowhere without running and Amy couldn't imagine her life without him.

5

Jeremy graded quizzes but his mind wasn't on his task. The classroom was quiet at the end of the day, the ringing shouts of students in the hallway long gone, as was the clanging of locker doors and the intermittent buzz of what passed as a bell.

He liked this time of day to do schoolwork and to have time to concentrate without the distractions of TV or the internet.

Amy's face loomed in his mind. He regretted his harsh words, the way she cowered at his anger. He couldn't recall a time when he'd lost his temper with her. Sure, he'd been annoyed from time to time but never furious with her. That is, until the time she dumped him and last night.

Why did he go back to Lou's? Excellent question. He supposed his anger spoke a truth he hadn't realized lurked in his heart. He wanted an explanation—needed one. If, as she said, he'd regret knowing, he didn't care.

Jeremy tilted his head back, closed his eyes, and made his brain refocus on the task at hand. In his left hand, he held the edge of Britney Foster's quiz while in his right, his red pen.

Britney struggled no matter how much he explained, and his heart hurt for her. Try as he might, he couldn't figure out how to break through her confusion. Yesterday he began working with her for an hour at the small table in the back of his classroom.

Britney was almost in tears. "Why should I learn algebra if I don't intend to use it?"

"Do you intend to graduate?"

He regretted his snark, which he supposed stemmed from concern she might have to repeat her sophomore year and the suspicion little would happen if he didn't step in.

He finished grading her quiz and with a sad sigh, wrote "F" in red and drew a circle around it. Ten questions and she got two right. He lifted the sheet and studied her quiz, marred by eraser marks and round puckers on the page. Were those tearstains? Had she cried throughout quiz time? Jeremy racked his brain trying to come up with something, some way to break through to her. Needing to think, he pushed the rest of the quizzes aside and opened a textbook.

For the next twenty minutes, he worked on math problems, but no immediate solution came to him. He'd recently downloaded a Sudoku app on his phone. Tonight he'd try one. Working numbers often helped him clear his mind.

Part of his problem was Amy. His mind filled with her, and he couldn't shift their conversation out of his head. Sunday night she apologized, tears streaming down her face, but she didn't explain her reasons in the first place. She only said he'd hate her more. What information did she have to make him think such a thing?

What about Maggie? He cared for her. He did or he wouldn't have spent the last four years with her, but did he want to commit the rest of his life to her? Much as he hated to admit the truth, the idea of ending their relationship had lurked in the back of his mind since the pandemic forced them to quarantine almost a year ago. What stopped him never crossed his mind, but perhaps the time had come. He needed to take the step, but he didn't like the idea of hurting her.

"Hey, soldier." Maggie's greeting jerked him back to reality. She leaned against his doorframe looking all chic and sexy in mustard-colored woolen slacks and a white silk shirt. A long gold chain graced her neck and gold hoop earrings dangled from each lobe.

He sat back and extended an arm. "Hey yourself."

Hips swinging, Maggie entered and perched on his desk, swinging a foot clad in a fashionable brown leather boot with a long spiky heel. "You appeared lost in thought. What's going on in your head?" She shuffled through the papers on his desk as though looking for something and gave him an exasperated glance when her gaze landed on his open textbook.

"Nothing important." He pointed to her feet. "How do you negotiate the ice and snow without landing on your keister in those boots?"

She sighed. "I don't wear them outside, silly man. I have other boots for outdoors."

"I see," he said, ignoring the "silly man" reference, an unintended insult.

Her earrings caught the winter sunlight from the classroom windows and gleamed. Her light brown curls tucked tight behind her left ear, and her rings flashed and gleamed on her manicured fingers. She'd even covered her thumbs in metal.

By comparison, he wore simple dress pants and plain button-down shirts. No adornments except for the occasional necktie required on game days.

"I almost called you last night," he said and chose to ignore her exasperation. "But it was late and snowing again, and you don't like to drive in bad weather."

Maggie raised a brow. "Well, I appreciate your thinking of me, but you might have come to me."

He closed the textbook. "Well, like I said, it was late."

She slid off the desk and sat in his lap, forcing him to push his chair away from his desk.

He slid his hands in a loose grasp around her waist. "What are you doing, woman? Some student might report us for inappropriate PDA."

He teased but only half. A quick glance toward the door to discover if anyone lurked outside didn't go unnoticed.

A frown pulled her mouth down as she played with his light blue collar, giving him a suggestive smile as her fingernails scraped his jawline. "That would be terrible."

"Terrible," he whispered. He leaned in for a kiss, but when he got within inches of her lips, she drew back.

His sigh was loud. She was still pissed and not finished making him pay.

"I said I was sorry about Sunday night." He stared hard into her hazel eyes, now shaded to green, a sign she was annoyed.

"I know you did, and I know you are." She got off his lap and perched on the edge of his desk again.

"So?"

Maggie shrugged. "So I'm thinking you're not telling me the entire story about your waitress."

"Oh, c'mon!" Jeremy snapped. "First, she's not my waitress. I told you. We dated in high school. Nothing more."

"Yes, but you were quite undone when she stopped at our table. Am I wrong to think more went on than dating in your relationship? You cared for her more than a little?"

Would telling the truth hurt? He studied her, assessing, and walked straight into her trap. "You're right. Amy was my first love." A negligent shrug. "We were young and stupid and besides, everyone has a first love in high school."

She arched a brow. "Not me."

He flinched at the vehemence in her voice and rubbed his forehead with his fingers.

"Well." He dropped his hand and let it dangle. "What can I say to convince you? I hadn't seen, or heard, or thought of Amy in ten years and her sudden appearance took me by surprise." He peered up at her. "You've never been surprised by someone you haven't seen in years?"

Shrugging, she refused to meet his eyes. "I have."

"So why am I not allowed to have the same reaction?"

"You're right," she said at last. "I'm sorry."

She lay her palm against his cheek. Her long fingernails brushed his skin, and he tensed half expecting her to rake his face with the daggers at the ends of her fingers.

"I don't understand what comes over me sometimes."

For the sake of peace, Jeremy dropped the discussion with a pat on her knee. "Atta girl," he said and changed the subject. "I thought we'd check out the new Italian joint up the street."

"Can't. I'm going out with Alyssa and a few friends. For her engagement party." She drew out the last two words. "I told you." Raising a scolding brow, she flipped open the textbook and riffled through the pages. "Besides, you're in one of your philosophical moods, which is never fun for me. I'm surprised you haven't found a Sudoku to work."

He grinned. "I have an app on my phone."

She wrinkled her nose and closed the book with a snap. "Of course you do."

He closed his eyes and drew in a breath. *Why did he take the bait?* "I'm trying to figure out what to do about Britney Foster. Working math problems is how I think, like compulsively cleaning your condo is how you think."

His reward was an ugly glare. His lips pulled up in a satisfied smile.

"What's on your mind, Jeremy?"

"I told you. I'm trying to figure out how to help Britney."

"She'll have to repeat tenth grade. I'm sorry, but." A shrug. "I have a conference with her parents tomorrow. Why don't you join us?"

Leaning his elbow on the arm of his chair, Jeremy cradled his head in his palm and stared at her. "You're a guidance counselor. Don't you think you should have more concern than shrugging her off and placating her parents?"

"I'm not shrugging her off, and I'm not placating her parents. I'm trying to do my job, but you have to admit, it's too late in the year for her to turn things around. You should have shown this kind of concern last semester."

"I did," he growled and slapped the arm of his chair. "And got no support then either. As I recall, you were one of those advocating I await developments. Well, I'm done waiting. She will not repeat tenth grade, not if I can help her."

"So dramatic." She rolled her eyes. "I love when you go all drama queen on me." She tried to press her palm to his cheek, but he jerked his head away and in a fit of pique, swatted at her arm. Her eyes widened and she sat back.

With a scowl, he stood. "High school is hard enough for sensitive kids like Britney." He gathered up his papers and the math book. Grabbing his backpack off the floor next to the desk leg, he shoved the items inside and gave the bag a shake to settle the contents.

Maggie uttered a humorless chuckle. "You are nothing if not predictable, Jeremy Austin."

At once, he stopped loading his backpack and blinked. "Meaning what?"

She hunched her shoulders in a small shrug. "Meaning I can depend on you to be what you are."

"And what am I?" His defenses rose, as he searched for the insult.

She stretched her chin, pouting her lower lip. "I realize what you're not. You're not my father."

This again. He drew in a deep breath, tried for levity, but landed on sarcasm. "Thank God. Because if I were, sitting on my lap and kissing me would be all kinds of inappropriate."

She huffed. "You understood what I meant." A scowl marred her brow.

"No, Mags, I didn't. Your parents divorced when you were a teenager. Bad things happen to people but they move on. You should try to do the same."

"Thank you, Jeremy," she sneered.

Pursing her lips, she lay her palm against his cheek. "I'm sorry. I don't want to fight, and we do nothing else these days. We need to discuss why some time, but for now, I've gotta go home and prepare for tonight." She placed a light kiss on his cheek and with her thumb wiped away the smear of lipstick.

"Have fun with your Sudoku puzzles. I'll call you tomorrow." Maggie strode from his classroom, hips swaying.

On the way home from work, he stopped at the new Italian restaurant and ordered himself take-out. Once at home, he plated his food, which he warmed in the microwave and carried to the living room.

Making himself comfortable on the sofa, he grabbed the remote, his fingers catching Amy's note, which he'd left next to the remote. He stared at the number, and without allowing time to change his mind, he called her.

The phone rang, once, twice, a third time. If he got to five rings, he was hanging up.

"Hello," a sleepy voice drawled partway through the fourth ring.

"Oh, shit! I'm sorry," he said. Then, "Amy?"

"Yeah…Jay?"

He uttered a soft laugh. "Well, we've now established our identities."

She chuckled. "I'm sorry. I don't mean to sound stupid. I had a few minutes and thought I'd sneak in a catnap. Sleep deprivation is the cornerstone of my life."

Jeremy picked up a pen. Under her number, he wrote *catnap*.

"I'm so sorry. I thought you'd be on your way to Lou's. I never thought you might be sleeping." He glanced at his kitchen clock. Five o'clock. "Shouldn't you be on your way to work?"

"No," she said, sounding more awake. "You wouldn't expect someone to be asleep at five in the afternoon. I don't work on Tuesday or Thursday nights, so I'm not being delinquent, I assure you."

Shuffling noises on her end and, he thought, whispering made him quirk his brow. Perhaps she was shifting into a sitting position.

"Well, I'm glad. I was calling to find out if you needed an escort tonight." *Liar, you wanted to hear her voice.*

Again he thought he caught a whisper and a shh. He was about to ask who she was talking to when she spoke.

"I appreciate your thinking of me. How sweet of you."

"I had another more honest reason for calling."

"Oh?"

He sighed and rubbed his forehead with his fingers. "I wanted to say how sorry I am for my abominable behavior the other night. You didn't deserve my shouting at you. I meant what I said about hounding you for the truth, but you didn't deserve the other angry things I said."

"Huh," she said. "Yes, I did. I came from out of nowhere and caught you off guard. The fault was mine, so no need to apologize."

He couldn't think of anything to say to that. The silence lengthened.

"Jay?"

"Yeah."

"I am sorry for the way things turned out. Not only for the other night but all those years ago. I was young and immature and didn't understand how to handle…things." A pause. "I realize this isn't what you want from me, but I'm doing the best I can."

Please tell me what you didn't understand how to handle. What did I do? His mother liked to say, "Put a smile on your face and you'll change the tone of your voice." He forced a smile and ignored a sudden searing pain to his heart. "No problem."

He dropped his fork on his plate, no longer hungry. "Well, we've both done our duty. You to apologize for the past, me for the present." The smile did perk up his voice but did nothing for his hurt. "As well as forgive and forget. I'll let you go back to sleep. I'm sorry I woke you."

"No worries and I hope you don't think me a duty."

"I don't." He sighed. "I think you're a pleasure."

"Will you come to the restaurant tomorrow night?"

"Do you want me to?"

"Yes." A pause. "But what about Maggie?"

"Don't worry about her."

A long silence ensued in which her breathing rasped through the phone. "Maybe you shouldn't come," she said. "I don't want to screw things up for you."

"You won't." *They're screwed up now. You can't make them any worse.*

"Hmm. Well, thanks for calling, Jay."

She clicked off. He programmed Catnap into his phone, slipped her note into his wallet, and got to work on lesson plans.

6

After the call with Amy ended, he rubbed his head in confusion. He wanted more from her than an explanation. She remembered him well. He was always a one-woman man. When she and Charlie were over, he broke up with Melanie and waited two weeks as an appropriate "cooling-off period" before asking Amy out.

Jeremy stretched and yawned. His wristwatch showed ten thirty. No wonder he felt exhausted. Where had the evening gone?

He prepared enough lessons to take him to April. They were his least favorite task of teaching. He liked being at the chalkboard, writing problems, explaining quadratic equations and how and why they were important. But enough for one night. Part of him was glad he didn't have to be in Burlington tonight. The late nights were taking a toll and he wanted to go to bed.

His phone rang and Magpie flashed on his screen. She was out with her girlfriends, so why was she calling this late? He considered ignoring her, but what if something had happened? He grabbed the phone.

"I thought you were out with your friends," he said and grimaced at his annoyed tone.

"Is this Jeremy Austin?"

He didn't recognize the voice. "Maggie?"

"My name is Alyssa Green, a friend of Maggie's."

"Hello, Alyssa," Jeremy frowned. "What's the matter?"

"Well, I hate to inconvenience you so late, but I was wondering if you'd come pick her up. She's soused and behaving like a crazy person."

Jeremy yanked the phone away from his ear as Alyssa shouted, but not at him. "We got kicked out of a bar because of you!"

He clapped a hand over his mouth to stifle a laugh. *Holy shit, Mags, what did you do?*

Returning to the call, she sighed, then spoke in a calm and measured way. "She's ranting about going to some restaurant and telling some woman off because of something. I have no idea what she's talking about, but at this point I don't care. I want her gone. The police are here."

"Oh, Jesus."

No longer amused, he began putting away his things with angry movements. So much for going to bed.

"Where are you?" He got off the stool and walked to the back door. Pressing the phone between his ear and shoulder, he listened to the directions while he put on his coat and slid his feet into his shoes.

"Okay," he said when she finished. "I'm on my way." Grabbing his keys off the hook by the door, he ran to his car.

Once in Burlington, Jeremy drove up Main Street looking for Maggie. A cluster of women had gathered in front of the entrance to the Flynn Theater, where police officers had them corralled giving away her position.

"Must be them," he said out loud and pulled over. Cutting the engine, he got out and approached a police officer. "She belongs to me," he pointed out Maggie in the center of the cluster, in a shouting match with a female officer. "What's going on?"

The officer squared up. "We're citing her for drunk and disorderly." He handed Jeremy a copy of the citation. "She's to appear in Superior Court tomorrow morning, nine o'clock. We're also considering citing her for making threats against certain individuals, though we haven't ascertained who."

"Well, most often when she's drunk, she rages about her father, but he lives in Texas. They've been estranged for years."

Jeremy studied the citation. "Can I move this appearance to Thursday? I'll need tomorrow to make arrangements for time off for both of us."

"Tomorrow morning," the officer said, his face deadpan.

Jeremy sighed. "Can I take her home now?"

"Please do." The officer cleared a path to Maggie.

"At last!" she shouted, throwing her arms open and staggering forward. The female officer reached out in case she toppled.

"My dear sweet…boyfriend." She giggled and threw her arms around his neck, splaying her body flat against his.

His breath left him with an oof, and she forced Jeremy to grasp her waist and shift his feet to keep from being yanked to the pavement. He'd seen her drunk before, but not like this.

After laying a sloppy kiss on his cheek, she hung one arm around his neck and addressed her girlfriends. "Isn't he cute, ladies? Absotively the most handsome man in the world?"

He wiped his palm across his cheek.

"But…" As if giving a lecture she raised a finger. "Too bad he's afraid of commitment. I should know. I've waited four long, frigging years for him to pull his shit together."

She grasped his chin, her long, manicured fingernails digging painfully into the skin around his mouth as she tried to shake his head.

Stiffening, he pulled his face away. "Okay." He shook her. "Enough! Let's go."

Alyssa handed him Maggie's purse. "Thank you for coming. I'm sorry about this." She gestured at her friend hanging off Jeremy's neck.

"I'm sorry too." Jeremy tried to extricate himself from Maggie's grasp. "Someday you'll have to tell me what happened."

"I'll tell you now." Alyssa's green eyes blazed. "She said you two argued, something about you flirting with some woman in a restaurant last Sunday." Her tone suggested Alyssa took her friend's side against his alleged flirting.

Jeremy blinked. "Not. True." Fury bubbled in his gut. "I took her out to dinner and an old high school girlfriend served us. Someone I hadn't seen since graduation."

"Whatever," Alyssa said, with obvious disinterest. "Anyway the more she drank the louder and more obnoxious she got until the bartender told us to leave and she got mad."

"Hey!" Maggie shouted.

Jeremy jerked his head away, but his ear rang. He jabbed his pinkie finger in and waggled.

"I was not mad. I calmly told him to stick his bar where the sun don't shine," Maggie said, sounding proud of herself.

"And then, you tossed your drink in his face!" Alyssa yelled, gesticulating with wild arm movements, miming the drink throw. "You told him to go fuck himself!"

The visual of prim and proper Maggie not only flinging a drink in the bartender's face but telling him to go F himself struck Jeremy as funny and he laughed. "Wa-was he a burly kinda guy or l-l-long and stringy?" He wheezed, and an image of Frank's long, lean frame hauling the likes of Maggie out of his restaurant made him laugh harder.

Maggie lashed out. "Of course you'd take her side. You don't love me." Her hazel eyes glittered with tears, and she tried to punch him in the shoulder, but her aim was off, and the blow glanced off his shoulder. The smack of her fist against his jaw silenced everyone.

Maggie stared at him, silent and wide-eyed.

The punch didn't hurt, but it sobered him, and after assuring the hovering police officer he had everything in hand, he thanked Alyssa again.

Alyssa sighed. "Take care of her, please."

Jeremy nodded. Grasping Maggie's elbow, he hustled her to the car. "Come along, Marguerite, time to go home."

She pulled away. "No! I don't want to go home. Not with you!"

She yanked away from him and staggered to the curb, talking at five hundred decibels for everyone's entertainment. "I want to go to the restaurant we went to, and we'll have a drink, and you can talk to your other girlfriend some more. She can sashay her ass around the restaurant to your heart's delight. I won't care. I promise."

He grabbed both her arms and gave her a none-to-gentle shake. "Knock it off!" His brows crowded his nose and his mouth turned down while his gut churned and a vein in his forehead began to pulse.

He checked himself at the sight of her frightened eyes. A quick glance at the cop assured him he witnessed their interactions. He lowered his voice and adopted a calm, cajoling tone.

"You're gonna regret appearing in court tomorrow, so I'd suggest we go home now."

He let go to open the door for her and Maggie spun around to face her friends.

"G'night everyone! Congrats again, Lyss." Drawing in a deep breath, Maggie waved to the police officer. "Adios, Mr. P'liceman. See you tomorrow morning."

"Maggie, shut up." He grasped her elbow and pulled her to the car.

She wriggled and fought him so much he struggled to sit her in the car, reminding him of his freshman year at college. He'd packed his car to leave, struggling to squeeze in every last item he thought he'd need and shutting the door before the contents exploded.

Once seated, he pulled the seat belt and buckled her in. Nose to nose, he glared into her face. "Don't you dare puke in my car. I'll make you fucking clean it." He retreated, slamming the car door.

Most of the drive home was sullen and silent. Jeremy fought his fury as he drove back to Maggie's. Yes, she was drunk, but she didn't need to embarrass and humiliate him in front of her friends.

He drove with his right hand on the wheel, his left arm propped on the door, knuckles pressed into the side of his head. She was mad because Alyssa was getting married. Her friends were marrying, and she feared being left behind.

She was turning thirty next week, and she often joked about her ticking biological clock, but when they discussed the future, children were never an option for her. Her common refrain was if they were to divorce, she didn't want to traumatize innocents. He understood her point, but why assume your marriage would end in divorce? Because her parents' marriage had? Each marriage was different, unique.

He sighed, knowing he was going over well-cultivated ground. He wanted a solid, loving marriage not always under threat of divorce, a marriage of give-and-take. And he wanted children.

His parents were together and still happy. Dad complimented Mom every chance he got. Told her he loved her and that she was beautiful. He listened to her complaints and ideas and treated her as an equal partner in their marriage.

If he made mention of a meal he hadn't eaten in a long while or a book he wanted to read, she cooked the meal or bought the book. Give and take. That's how they did things, and it was what Jeremy was looking for.

He glanced at her. She was slumped over, her head pressed against the cold window. Her eyes closed, and her breath came in huge draws raising and lowering her chest.

"You okay?" he asked, glancing at her again and refocusing on the road. "Tell me if you need me to pull over."

She didn't answer.

"Maggie! Are you in there?"

"Jeremy, do you love me?"

"What?" His jaw clenched. Not this discussion again. He pressed his fingers to the spot where she hit him.

She lifted her head and tried to focus her gaze on him. "Do. You. Love. Me?"

He shook his head. "What kind of ridiculous question is that?" he countered, pressing the gas pedal.

Glancing out her window, he drove past his darkened house. *I could be snug in bed by now.* From the corner of his eye, he studied her, ready to jerk the car to the side of the road if she showed any sign of turning green. Why did she do this to him?

"The kind that deserves an answer and 'What kind of a question is that?' is not an answer."

He drew in a deep, calming breath. "Well," he hedged. "I don't understand where this is coming from. Probably because you're drunk." He lowered his voice to a whisper. "Not for the first time."

If he was being uncharitable, he didn't care.

"I am drunk. Not as much as I was, but being drunk lowers the…" She waved a ring-laden hand. "Whatever."

"The wall?"

"Yeah, the wall, so now I can ask you what I've been wondering for a while, and I suspect even without your waitress, why you don't ever propose." She shifted in her seat and pulled at the seat belt. "I think you don't love me anymore. I think you never did."

He drove in silence, squeezing his lips as his heart pounded in his chest. Her eyes on him made him want to squirm, but he refused to glance her way.

"Don't be ridiculous," he said again, but his words held no power.

"No. I'm not being ridiculous. I'm being honest. I should get drunk more often. Honesty is liberating. I was talking with the girls."

Oh, okay, here it comes.

"And all we do is argue. About everything. We haven't made love in…I don't know how long. Months? Why?"

He remained silent. He didn't want to hurt her with the answer, but he hadn't touched her since Presidents' Day weekend last year. That was the last time he'd wanted to.

Crossing the bridge over Lake Arrowhead, he entered the town of

Georgia. Past the bridge, he turned left and proceeded up the hill toward her condominium.

"You've been faithful," she went on, almost musing. "At least, I think you have. And you did act surprised when your waitress appeared. So…you haven't been skanking her on the side."

"Maggie! Jesus!" He glared at her. "What is your problem? She's not my waitress. Why are you fixated on her? I told you I haven't had contact with her since high school. So climb off your horse about her!"

He scrubbed his forehead and reined himself in. There was no point in yelling at a woman who wouldn't believe him in any case, drunk or sober.

They'd been down this road before. When Jennifer Stone had joined the faculty two years prior, Jeremy stopped by her classroom to introduce himself and welcome her on board. For weeks he endured probing questions and suspicious glances.

Their fights grew loud and incessant, and Jeremy survived the occasional slap or two. But when he caught Maggie checking his phone for clandestine phone calls and text messages, he changed his password and gave his friends and family code names. She only stopped bugging him when Jennifer Stone became Jennifer Winters. But then she wanted to know when *her* last name would change to Austin.

Maggie lay her hand on his thigh close to his crotch and squeezed.

He jerked upright and almost slammed his car into a tree. She went on as if unaware of his reaction.

"No, this is what I'm saying," she said, her tone plaintive. "You're not doing anything. So I don't understand. I love you. Why don't you love me?"

He arched a brow but kept his focus on the road. "Do you love me, Maggie? Do you honestly?"

God almighty! Somebody, please shoot me now! He switched hands on the steering wheel, clasped her hand, and with a gentle squeeze, he placed it back into her lap.

Tears streamed from her eyes. "It's almost more insulting." She twisted the rings on her fingers.

"What is?" He glanced at her as he negotiated the turn on her street.

"The fact you're not sleeping with someone else. I would almost prefer if you were. At least I'd understand your withdrawal from me, but you're not, which is worse," she finished as he pulled into her driveway.

Jeremy drew a silent sigh of relief. "C'mon." He put the car in park and cut the engine. "Let's go inside." When he reached to unsnap her seat belt, Maggie slapped his hands away.

"I can do it and you can't answer the question."

Which question? "I didn't realize you wanted me to," he said, his tone flat. *I'm so tired of this bullshit.* He got out of the car.

As he came around to open her car door he slipped on a patch of ice and slammed his elbow on the hood to stop his fall. A muscle in his back jerked and the pain ripped the breath from his lungs, pissing him off more. Straightening, he rocked his shoulders to ease the pain in his back. He'd be in discomfort for some days. Snatching her keys from her purse, he unlocked her front door and let her in, kicking off their footwear at the door.

Together they negotiated the stairs. Jeremy's breath came in short puffs, and he did his best to help her while his back screamed at him to go easy.

At the top of the stairs, Maggie made a gagging noise in her throat and jerked from his grasp.

With a hand over her mouth, she ran for the bathroom. At the first retch, Jeremy steeled his gut and went in after her.

She was on her knees on the gray tile floor, heaving into the bowl. Keeping his gaze focused on the rust-colored wall, he held back her hair while she retched. The odor rose from the commode and squeezed his stomach. He swallowed hard and concentrated on the wall.

When she finished, she leaned her forehead on her elbow and wept.

Jeremy ran a washcloth under warm water then tapped her arm. "Here, Mags, take this," he placed a hand on her back while pushing the warm cloth at her. Unable to take the reek of vomit and liquor any longer, he flushed the toilet.

Without a word, she took the washcloth and covered her face, sniffed, and wiped her eyes.

Jeremy perched on the edge of the tub, shifting his back and shoulders but the pain refused to ease. He rose with slow, stiff movements and opened her medicine cabinet. Taking down the Advil he popped two and swallowed them dry.

Despite the pain in his back, the words telling her he was through with her were on the tip of his tongue, but the timing wasn't right. If she were sober, things would be different.

She rose to her knees, and he grasped her elbow to pull her to her feet. After she brushed her teeth, he guided her into her bedroom where he helped her change into blue silk pajamas and climb into bed.

As he drew the covers, she grabbed his neck and pulled him down with such force, he fell on top of her.

"Oh God!" Pain shot between his shoulder blades, but he ignored it. "Did I hurt you?"

He struggled to rise, but Maggie held him and kissed him with desperate force. He allowed her to kiss him and became aroused, but he had things to do for her. He broke the kiss and pulled her arms from his neck.

"C'mon, Mags, let me up."

"Why do you call me Mags? How come you never call me 'sweetheart' or 'babe' or some other endearment? You always call me Mags."

"Do I?"

"Yes."

He pulled his phone from his back pocket. "I'm sure I call you other things besides Mags." Using his thumb, he began dialing numbers. "Now, stop being ridiculous and let me do these things."

She studied him with bleary, alcohol-hazed eyes. "That's the third time tonight you've called me ridiculous." She turned away. "I must be. For staying with you."

"Huuuhhh," he ground out, releasing some of his exasperation, but he still shouted. "I have phone calls to make on your behalf. I can't do this now."

Hurt shone from her eyes and with effort, he got control of himself. She wanted him to call her something sweet, but she was drunk, and he was pissed.

Shoving down his anger, he readjusted the covers and sat down next to her. Smiling, he tweaked her nose. "Now, do you want me to go to court with you, Jailbird Jane?"

She rolled away. "Don't make fun of me."

"I'm not." He shook her arm. "I'm trying to make you laugh."

She yanked her arm away and wiped her eyes with the sheet.

Jeremy sighed and got up. "Okay," he said. "I'm sorry for making fun of you. I wasn't trying to hurt your feelings."

He waved his phone at her. “I have to call Henry and explain why we won’t be at work tomorrow.”

He walked to the door. “And I’ll come back and spend the night with you. Would you like me to?”

She nodded.

“I’ll be right back.” He left her bedroom.

After twenty minutes he returned to her bedroom, needing a shower from the tirade he endured from their principal, Henry Gibbons. Explaining why he and Maggie would not be at school in the morning, Jeremy reassured Henry he hadn’t been involved but that her friend called him. When the man calmed down, he assured Jeremy, he would find him a substitute.

Next, he took a deep breath and called his friend and department head, Mike Pelletier, and told him what happened.

All Mike said was, “Okay, Jer. Talk to you Thursday,” and hung up.

Mike was pissed and Jeremy would endure an earful. He sighed and went back to Maggie’s bedroom. She was lying on her side, her back to the door, snoring through a stuffy nose. He wanted to go home, but he’d said he would stay, so he lay down beside her on top of the covers, put his arm around Maggie’s waist and went to sleep.

7

There were few diners, so Amy posted herself at the bar to keep an eye on the front window in case Jay arrived. To keep busy, she folded silverware into linen napkins and replayed their phone conversation, regretting the way she'd brought Maggie into their discussion. In her mind she tried out different things she might have said and wished she hadn't said others, all the while fearing she gave him the impression she didn't care.

A glance out the front window showed her an empty Marketplace. As her gaze swept the restaurant, everyone strove to keep busy. Briana cleaned menus, while Jason puttered around disinfecting tables and chairs. Kara called in sick, saying she'd tested positive for COVID.

Amy sighed with boredom at her task but pasted a smile on her face as Frank approached. "What do you say, Amy? Want to call it a night and go play with that little boy of yours?"

She appreciated the offer, but Jay might arrive, and she didn't want him to drive into town for nothing. Since she didn't work tomorrow night, she wouldn't see him until Friday.

"I'm okay, Frankie. Thanks though. Perhaps Bri or Jason would like to go home early."

Frank nodded. "Briana," he called and waved her over.

When she leaned against the bar, he spoke into her ear to avoid the few lingering guests from overhearing them. "Wanna take off?"

"Sure. Unless Amy wants to skip out."

"Amy doesn't," Amy said with a smile.

"Oh, I understand." Briana's eyes crinkled as she offered Amy a conspiratorial grin. “Your honey’s coming tonight, right?”

“No, he’s not. At least, as far as I’m aware.” Amy smiled. “I have a son and I need the money.” A quick shrug and her smile faded. “Besides, he has a girlfriend, and I don’t want to come between them.”

“So why did he come back on Valentine’s Day and again the next night?”

Besides her sister, Lindsay, she had few women friends to talk to. “Because I asked him to.”

The two women studied each other, and Briana cast a meaningful glance at Frank, who gave a heavy sigh and walked away, shaking his head and muttering under his breath. Something about women.

Settling herself on a barstool, Briana tucked her chin into her hand, raised her brows, and waited.

Amy continued to wrap napkins. “Jeremy and I dated in high school for almost two years. We were in love.” It was impossible to hide her quick, shy shrug and soft smile.

“But something horrible happened, and I broke up with him. I never explained why, just”—she waved her hand as if shooing a bug away—“walked away. I hurt him to the core of his being, which I’ve regretted ever since. I asked him to come back because I wanted to tell him how sorry I am about everything.”

Amy stopped wrapping napkins and squeezed her eyes shut. With effort, she pushed down the sudden rush of shame and anger.

“Oh, I’m so sorry.” Briana laid a soft hand upon hers. “Can I ask what happened? How bad was the situation in reality if you think you can mend things now?”

Amy cleared her throat. “I’ve never told anyone this, so you have to promise never to repeat what I tell you.”

“Of course.” Briana’s brows creased as concern filled her brown eyes. Her long blond hair fell over her shoulder in a graceful cascade.

Drawing a deep breath, Amy played with the corner of a napkin. She wouldn’t meet her friend’s eye. After collecting her nerve, she leaned across the bar and whispered in Briana’s ear. “I was raped.”

Briana’s gasp was loud.

“Shhh!” Amy waved a hand while glancing around to make sure no one overheard.

Briana slapped a hand over her mouth as tears filled her shock-widened eyes.

“The guy was a friend of Jeremy’s father, his law partner in fact.

He said if I ever told anyone, I'd be in so much trouble. No one would believe me. I'd be called a slut and a whore. I was an eighteen-year-old, sheltered Catholic girl and I believed him. He said Jeremy would assume I slept around and call me a whore and I was stupid enough—scared enough—to think he was right."

She glanced at Briana. "I was so ashamed. I couldn't be around Jeremy, couldn't let him touch me, couldn't tell him what happened, so I ran."

"Oh, Amy." Briana slid off the stool and trotted around the bar, arms extended.

Amy wrapped her arms around Briana and drew comfort from her embrace. When they broke apart, Briana placed her palms on both sides of Amy's face. "Do you still love him?"

Head down, Amy nodded. She fiddled with the corner of the black linen napkin.

"Then tell Jeremy what happened," she suggested. "If he cares about you, and he must if he came back twice, he won't care about that, only you."

Amy shrugged, not so sure, but she smiled her thanks.

Briana pressed Amy's cheeks and her gaze conveyed her thanks for the trust.

"Frank!" Briana released Amy as she called to the back of the restaurant. "I'll take you up on your offer now."

At ten thirty, Jay entered and sat at the bar. Frank poured him coffee while Amy did last-minute cleanup tasks. Her heart soared when he entered, and when she finished, she approached and slapped her hand on his shoulder.

"Hey there." She grinned. "I'm surprised but pleased you're here. I feared we left things at an ambiguous place."

Crow's feet gathered at the corners of his brown eyes, melting her insides.

"Hey yourself." His soft gaze dropped to her lips and back to her eyes. "We did, but I'm here." He cocked a challenging eyebrow.

"I still have a few minutes to go."

He shrugged. "I have my coffee." He showed her his half-filled cup. "How's business tonight?"

"Dismal."

She indicated the near-empty restaurant. "It's been like this most of the evening."

Jeremy surveyed the dining room. Tonight the room was well lit and contained only a few diners. "Rough." He glanced around. "Must have been a boring night."

"Jeremy." Frank came from the back of the restaurant carrying a clean rack of glasses. "Take her home. Jason and I can finish up here."

"You're sure?" Jeremy put down his cup and gathered his coat.

"I am. All I have left is to turn off the lights and lock the doors."

They slow-walked to the garage and every so often his hand brushed against hers. She had an urge to grasp his fingers and not let go. As teenagers, they went everywhere hand in hand.

"So how was your day?" she asked. Her heart lurched when his knuckles bumped against hers again.

"Interesting."

"How so?"

"Maggie got herself into some trouble last night and I went to court with her as moral support." He shook his head. "Man, I never want to do that again."

"What happened?"

Amy listened in disbelief as he told the story. The way he described her drunken behavior elicited disgust, which she pushed away. After all, who was she to judge? When he got to the part about Maggie's court appearance, Amy pitied her as he described the way she stammered through the session, looking small and frightened by the experience.

He sighed and in a sudden motion, rocked his shoulders as if throwing off a huge weight.

"The poor woman," she said, and Jay peered at her with suspicion. Amy changed the subject. "So you have next week off for winter break. What do you plan to do all week? I, of course, have to work. No rest for the wicked or so they say."

He smiled. "Since you asked, I came to tell you I won't be in town next week."

"Oh?" She lifted a questioning brow. "Where are you going?"

Their knuckles bumped again, and his fingers brushed against hers. Her breath caught.

"Every year at winter break I meet Charlie and his partner at their winter home in Florida. We spend the week hanging around Tampa, going to spring training games, although spring training is starting late this year."

Their knuckles touched again, and this time, his index finger slid down her palm and hooked her pinkie.

Amy clamped her lips to stop a wild chuckle from escaping. "You didn't have to come all the way down here, Jay. A phone call would have done the same thing."

She faced him and didn't bother to hide the amusement in her voice and face.

A sheepish grin tugged at his lips. "True."

"So why are you here? And why are you trying so hard to find out if I want to hold your hand?"

Under the streetlight behind him, a red stain colored his cheeks, and he took a sudden interest in the uneven sidewalk. Road salt sparkled in the light of the streetlight and frozen puddles spread in weird patterns down the concrete.

"My relationship with Maggie is complicated, Amy. I've been with her a long time. Four years, but for the past year I've been reevaluating things." He slid his hands into the front pockets of his jeans.

His brow creased and Amy wanted to stroke his forehead and remove his anguish.

"I thought I'd take her for a romantic dinner to try to jump-start things." He raised a sardonic brow. "But you showed up."

Amy's heart raced. "What did I do?"

"Nothing. My reaction to you caused an argument."

"I don't understand," Amy said. "Your reaction to me would have frozen hell itself, so how could she be jealous?"

His hands popped from his pockets, and he held them up before letting them slap against his thighs. "Maggie has an overdeveloped jealous streak I'll never understand, and I've been prodded and accused of things ever since." He shrugged and started walking again. "Complicated."

Amy followed. "I'm sorry that happened." She entwined her fingers with his. "But Jay, you don't deserve such treatment. If Maggie can't be certain of you after how many years together?"

"Four." His face flushed again.

"After four years," she continued, "she's not the woman for you. She doesn't understand you and she never will, and you'll be unhappy forever if you stay with her."

He lifted their clasped hands. “Does this mean you’re going to make things more complicated?”

She offered a soft smile. “I’m not going to make things easy for you.” She stepped close and squeezed his hand. His body heat warmed her through her unzipped jacket. She thrummed.

Briana’s words came back to her, encouraging her. *If he cares about you, and he must if he came back twice, he won’t care about that, only you.* Three times now.

She gazed deep into his brown eyes. “I’m going to go out on a limb here, Jay, and admit something to you, which may screw things up for me.”

He stretched his neck and straightened his spine as his shoulders drew back. When he met her eyes, his were dark, wary, and devoid of expression.

“When you showed up Sunday night, I realized how much I’ve missed you over the years. I said I wanted to apologize, but more than apologizing, I wanted to find out if we were over forever. Don’t say anything now. Take your week in Florida and add me to the equations you like to make.”

A sudden angry scowl marred his face. “What’s with the equations crack?” His words rang off the buildings. He released her hand and stepped back.

She stepped back as well, staring. “Nothing.” Hurt and anger combined with a defensive distrust in his gaze.

“I journal when I need to think, and I recall, you always did math problems.”

His shoulders slumped and he released a breath that huffed white in the cold night air. “Sorry.” He waved an apology. “My penchant for math problems drives Maggie up a friggin’ wall. What she calls ‘my philosophical mood.’”

“I would suggest she doesn’t understand that part of you either.”

“And what of us,” Jay asked as he grasped her hand again. “Will you give me what I want?”

“Which is what?”

“You know what.” The glint in his brown eyes grew hard and his lips formed a straight line.

If she told him, he’d walk away forever. She tried to disengage her hand, but he squeezed her fingers.

She glared at him to hide the pain of his grip. Arching a brow, she tried to pull her hand away. "I'm telling you, Jay, it is information you do not want." Biting the inside of her lip, she steeled herself against either giving in or crying out in pain.

"Tell me why," he demanded, lowering his face to hers. "Why did you leave me all those years ago?"

His warm breath brushed her cheek.

"Because." She grimaced. "You're hurting me."

He relaxed his grip and had the grace to appear ashamed though he didn't apologize.

Amy yanked her hand free.

His sigh sounded resigned and almost defeated. "Tell me why, Amy. Give me a chance to redeem myself."

"I've told you. You have nothing to redeem."

He sucked in his breath and scowled at her. "God, you're as obstinate as I remember!"

"Yes, I am. Either get used to it or get over it." Instant regret warmed her face. She reached for his hand, and he let her, though his fingers didn't close with hers.

He stared down at their hands as a frown pulled his mouth down. Amy fought the urge to run her fingers along his brow and remove the gnarl above his nose.

"Jay, I'm so sorry. I didn't mean to be harsh."

He raised his gaze, and his eyes were full of sad resignation. "Yes, you did. Some of the old Amy fire I remember. I'd best walk you to your car." He walked away.

Amy's heart lurched. She wanted to throw her arms around him and tell him everything, though she was positive if she did, she'd lose him. But then, she feared she just had.

8

Jeremy stepped off the plane at the Southwest Florida International Airport in Fort Myers, removed his winter jacket, and stuffed the garment into his backpack. Stopping at the carousel, he grabbed his suitcase and headed for the front doors to wait for his brother, who'd arrived from Boston the day before. Except for last year, this visit was a yearly ritual for them, and he was excited.

They'd been close growing up, sharing a bedroom where they often fought for territory, sometimes to the point their father had to restrain them. But they also shared their hopes and dreams for their respective futures.

In their room, Jeremy learned first of Charlie's sexual orientation, which he never divulged until Charlie went public, and where Jeremy confessed his love for Amy while she dated Charlie.

Many nights his brother lay beside him, holding him and letting him weep when Amy deserted him, sometimes crying with him.

Charlie never divulged those episodes to anyone.

Jeremy stepped outside and let the soft warm air touch his face, waking his mind and body. Cars whizzed by, some stopped, spilling family members who squealed their excited hellos amid hugs and kisses. Gas fumes hung in the air.

A quick honk caught his attention as Charlie's car approached. With one hand, he waved to the two men inside as his brother eased his Mercedes to the curb, while with his other, he pulled off the mandatory face mask, which he stuffed into his backpack. He was beginning to gather dark glares from other passengers and citizens anyway.

When the two men emerged from the car, Jeremy first hugged his brother-in-law, Jonathan, then bear-hugged Charlie. They growled with pleasure and slapped backs.

Jeremy clasped his brother's face. "God, I'm so glad to be here." He turned to his brother-in-law and greeted him with his customary teasing. "You're looking tanned, healthy, and wealthy, Jon."

"Real estate, my friend." He tapped Jeremy's chest and leered. "You've got a head for numbers, mate. You're handsome, and with that sexy grin of yours, you could sell a drowning woman a glass of water. Quit the dead-end teaching job and join me in my real estate office."

Jon's cultured British accent was a salve to Jeremy's soul and he laughed. "I'll think about it. Next year."

Grinning, Jon took his suitcase and loaded it into the trunk, shut the top, and returned to stare at Jeremy. He quirked a brow. "Seriously, something's different about you. Lighter. Freer."

"He's right," Charlie said. "Something is different about you."

Still grinning, Jeremy shrugged. He couldn't help himself. "I am so happy to be here. I haven't seen you two in two years. What a pleasure to escape the cold."

"That is the truest thing you've said yet." Charlie slapped him on the back again.

They got into the car, and Jeremy sprawled on the tan leather upholstery. Charlie and Jon had money, which they liked to spend on themselves. "Sweet ride. This new?"

"Well, Jon received a huge bonus from some real estate deals, so we decided to splurge," Charlie said, snapping his seat belt.

Sweeping a hand across the soft leather, Jeremy nodded. Even though he prided himself on investing and had a more-than-healthy nest egg, he recalled an economics professor once saying wealth was not the money one spent, but the money one kept. He never forgot those words, and while he wouldn't consider himself a miser, he was careful about spending.

Of course he could drive a much better car than his Honda, but Vermont winters were hard on a vehicle, and he didn't want to throw his money away on something the road salt would destroy in two or three years.

Charlie glanced at him from the rearview mirror. "So what's going on in your life, Jer? Anything important your older brother should warn you against?" He grinned as he pulled away from the curb and into traffic.

"Not really." Jeremy turned to stare out the window because a grin was about to split his face and make him appear foolish. Palm trees swayed in the soft breeze. Million-dollar homes and well-manicured lawns, with hydrangea bushes and exotic plants he didn't recognize, graced neighborhoods he might only dream of living in.

Jon turned and stared at him. "You're single now."

Jeremy quirked a confused brow. "I beg your pardon?"

"Seeing someone new?" Jon continued.

"What?" He lifted his hands and let them drop back in his lap, but Jeremy couldn't stop the grin.

"I'll figure this out before the week is up. I'll figure out the mystery. You're grinning like a Cheshire cat." Jon wagged a finger at him, narrowing his green eyes before turning back to the front.

Jeremy chuckled, earning a suspicious glance over Jon's shoulder.

After arriving at one of the million-dollar homes, Jeremy grabbed his suitcase and headed into the spare bedroom. He emerged dressed in tan cargo shorts and a Boston Red Sox T-shirt with the name Pedroia curved across the back and a giant number fifteen below the name. He dropped himself on the wicker sofa and crossed his bare feet on the glass coffee table.

Jonathan stiffened and scowled until Jeremy removed his feet and studied his brother and his partner.

"So what's going on with you two? How's the investment banking world treating you, Charles?"

"Charles?" His brother and Jon exchanged bemused glances. "Same old, same old," Charlie answered. "What's gotten into you? Is Jon right? Are you seeing someone new?"

Jeremy's shoulders shook with silent laughter. He was in a carefree mood and couldn't remember the last time he'd experienced such happiness. He wagged his brows at his brother, deepening Charlie's suspicious stare.

"Can we offer you a beer, Jer?" Jon headed into the kitchen.

"Trying to get me drunk at ten a.m., so I'll divulge my secrets? Can't a guy be happy to visit his brother and partner after so long?"

"He can," Jon said from the kitchen. "Such euphoria isn't normal for you." He returned and handed Jeremy a Sam Adams. "But whatever works." He winked.

"So how's Maggie?" Charlie asked.

Jeremy's lip curled as his pleasant mood evaporated. "Fucking Maggie." He swigged his beer.

"Now here's the Jeremy I'm used to," Jon joked. "What did she do this time?"

He told them about her drunken brawl but stopped talking when they couldn't contain their laughter any longer. Instead, he scowled. "What's so funny? She called me a coward in front of her friends. She embarrassed me."

Jon and Charlie shared an amused glance. Charlie saluted him with his beer bottle. "The fact the ice queen would deign to get plastered in the first place cracks me up."

"The ice queen?" Jeremy's gaze shifted between them. "You've never referred to her as the ice queen before."

Charlie reddened and dropped his gaze to his lap. "We've always been careful around you."

Jeremy arched a brow at his brother's apologetic face. He glanced at Jon, then returned his gaze to Charlie.

"I shouldn't have said such a thing. I'm sorry, Jeremy." Charlie lifted his beer bottle and stared at him with the same almond-shaped brown eyes Jeremy possessed. "Forget I said that."

"No, Charlie. Let's not. If we leave your comment alone, we'll have a stinking pile of shit by the end of the week, so tell me what you meant."

Jon sat down next to Jeremy. "You have a lovely turn of phrase, my friend. What Charlie means is while we"—he indicated Charlie and himself— "have never cared for Maggie, we have always recognized you do, so whatever we think of her doesn't matter."

Jon offered Charlie an apologetic glance before turning back to Jeremy. "And in full disclosure, I'm the one who always called her the ice queen. And not because I think she might be frigid in bed…" He raised a hand and closed his eyes. "That's not information I need or want—I always got the impression she was so careful about how people perceive her she comes across as cold and unfeeling. Hence, the ice queen designation." Jon slapped a hand on Jeremy's knee. "I'm sorry, it was unkind of me."

Jeremy nodded in acceptance. He turned to his brother. "How about you, Charlie. Are you of the same opinion?"

Charlie's answer was a shrug and another sip of his beer. "My wish for you, little brother, is to find someone who makes you happy. If Maggie fills the bill…" He shrugged again and swigged. "I can learn to live with disappointment." He licked beer off his upper lip.

Now would be the time to tell Charlie about Amy. Hell, she asked him to remember her to him. As he raised his beer bottle to his mouth, the words, "I'm seeing Amy Taylor again" almost escaped. But what would Charlie say? What if he condemned her and scorned him for falling for her games again?

"Hmm," he murmured and drank his beer.

Jon grilled a beautiful steak for each of them. Jeremy's baked potato steamed with melted butter and sour cream. The green beans on the side added the final touch. He couldn't wait to dig in. Jon was a fantastic cook.

While he ate, Jeremy continued talking about Maggie. "She drinks too much. I mean, I'm not a prude about booze. I'll have a beer or two no problem, but no one needs five or six rye and gingers with dinner." He forked some potato and ate. "I want out of this relationship, but I haven't quite figured out how to extricate myself without hurting her."

"Not possible, my friend." Jon handed him the bowl of green beans. "Want to or not, you're going to hurt her. Best to rip the bandage off and have done."

"When did the drinking start?" Charlie asked.

Jeremy shrugged. "She's always had a relationship with alcohol, but during the quarantine I suspect there was so little for her to do, she started drinking more. She's getting out of hand." He spooned some green beans onto his plate and set the bowl down. "I took her to dinner on Valentine's Day and she had five rye and gingers, her preferred drink."

"What about your sex life, if I may pry?" Charlie broke open his potato and slathered butter and salt on top. "How is sex between you?"

"I thought you didn't want me to tell you such things."

Charlie pointed his fork at Jon. "He doesn't, but you remember what Dad says. 'You can judge a relationship by the quality of the sex.'"

Jeremy's face grew hot, and his shirt stuck to his armpits. He covered his eyes with a hand. "God, I hated that conversation. Couldn't wait for him to stop talking." The brothers laughed over the shared humiliation of Dad's version of the birds and the bees.

When they calmed, Jeremy admitted, "We haven't had sex since this time last year."

He stared at their shocked faces. To cover his embarrassment, he cut into his meat. "Sex became…" He glanced at his brother and partner through his lashes. "Let's say the constant fighting does nothing for my libido."

After a few minutes of silence as they enjoyed their meal, Jeremy put his knife and fork down. He pressed his palms against his thighs and rubbed his shorts. "I have something I should tell you."

They raised their faces. "When I took Maggie to dinner last week, a waitress served us." As he ate, he told them how his evening went. "She's been riding my ass all week because she thinks I flirted with the waitress."

Charlie speared green beans. "Well, if you were, I hope she was an attractive waitress."

"She is."

"Is?" Jonathan tilted his head, brow creased, before a grin lit his face. He pointed at Jeremy. "I knew it!"

Jeremy smirked before turning to his brother. "Amy served us."

Charlie didn't glance up from his plate. "Amy who?"

When Jeremy didn't answer, Charlie raised his gaze.

Lifting his brows, he cast Charlie a significant stare. His brother dropped his fork. "No shit! Our Amy?"

Jeremy squeezed his lips together and nodded.

Charlie stared at him, slack jawed. Finally, he recovered himself. "And were you flirting?"

"I was too fucking shocked to flirt."

Jon's confused gaze shifted between the brothers. "Who is Amy?"

9

The day before Jeremy's flight to Vermont, the stands at JetBlue Park were crowded with fans watching the Red Sox take on the Northeastern Huskies in their first spring training game.

Dressed in a loose T-shirt and shorts, he sipped a beer and relaxed with his brother and Jonathan in the hot Florida sun. In the back of his mind, the warnings about melanoma flashed red, but he'd be back in the cold, gray Vermont winter soon and he wanted to absorb as much vitamin D as possible before then.

Tomorrow the Red Sox were playing the Yankees and Jeremy would have given his left nut to be at the game, but he had to be on a plane.

"Hmmm." A smile played on his lips. "I almost wish I didn't have to go home." He hadn't been this relaxed in years. "They don't call it the sunshine state for nothing, do they?"

"I agree," Charlie replied. "Boston is so cold and dreary. We're thinking of moving here permanently."

"For real?" Jeremy studied his brother.

Charlie nodded, but a Red Sox player hit what might be a home run, stealing Jeremy's attention. He raised his fists to cheer, but the Huskies centerfielder caught the ball.

"Ahh." He waved a hand in disgust. "What do you think of their prospects for this year?"

Jon leaned in. "What are *your* prospects for the coming year?"

Jeremy braced a foot against the bleacher below them. The Red Sox took the field. What was the score? What inning were they in?

"I've been thinking a lot about what you two have said. I think part of the problem is Maggie turned thirty yesterday. Her clock is ticking."

Jon held up a hand. "Hold on. You mean to tell me Maggie's birthday is this week, the same week you always spend with us?"

Jeremy nodded. "So?"

"So why don't you celebrate her birthday with her?"

"She doesn't celebrate her birthday. Never has in the four years we've been together."

Jon's brow creased. "Why not?"

Jeremy shrugged.

"And you've never asked?"

"Nope."

"Why not?" Charlie asked.

Jeremy shrugged again. "Not interested, I guess." He winced and amended his statement. "When we first started going out, I asked her why not and she said in no uncertain terms, 'None of your business so butt out,' so I did. Now, I just don't care."

"You don't care about the reason she doesn't celebrate her birthday, or you don't care about her?"

Jeremy opened his mouth and closed it again. He stared off into the distance as he thought about Charlie's question. He didn't love Maggie. He never had. He wouldn't say he didn't care about her, but she frustrated and angered him more often than not. Belittled him with her cutting humor. They were two people who didn't even come close to speaking the same language.

During the height of the pandemic, when he couldn't spend time with her, he discovered he didn't miss her. After the Governor lifted restrictions, he worked hard to regain the emotional connection only to discover it no longer existed. Now, he wanted to be with Amy.

He turned to Charlie who had been waiting for his answer with concern etched on his features.

"I never loved her, but now I don't want to be with her anymore. She's not right for me." He shook his head with dismay. "God, I wasted four years of my life."

"No, you didn't," Charlie said, letting out a long breath as though he'd been holding it waiting for Jeremy's answer. On his other side, Jonathan faintly uttered, "Thank God."

Charlie nodded but remained silent. He too stared out over the field before turning back to Jeremy. "Did you just now come to this conclusion?"

"No," Jeremy said on a long sigh. "I didn't want to admit this to myself, but I think the pandemic did something to my perspective."

He waved a hand. "Everything was at a literal standstill last year. Because of the strict quarantine starting in March, Maggie and I were apart for a year."

He turned to his brother and brother-in-law. "I was so busy with Zoom school and working on repairs for the house, things I finally had a chance to do, I didn't miss her, which got me thinking. Do I want to be with her? Shouldn't I feel lost and heartbroken to be away from her? How come I'm not devastated?"

"What did you experience in your year alone?" Charlie asked.

Jeremy didn't have to think for long. "Peace." He flapped a hand and let it drop in his lap. "Peace," he said again.

"I'm looking for a woman who will love me without reservation. Without always accusing me of cheating or..." Heat rose in his neck and into his ears and had nothing to do with the warmth of the day. "Calling me her future ex-husband."

Jeremy nodded at Charlie's questioning brown eyes. "Yeah, her favorite expression." His voice rose to mimic a woman's. "'I can't wait for you to become my future ex-husband.'"

"*Are* you cheating?" Jon asked.

Jeremy sipped his beer. The pitcher walked the bases full. He tsked. "Why do they keep that guy?"

The hot sun beat down on Jeremy's head and he wiped the sweat off his brow with his short sleeve. Should he answer the question? He scowled.

Jon gave him the opening he'd waited for, and he almost told them about Amy but beat back the urge to confess. If he were being technical, he wasn't cheating. He'd only walked her to her car a few nights last week, but the fact was, he wanted to cheat.

He met Jon's eye. "No," he snarled. "But she accuses me. All. The. Time."

He glared at them. "Like last Sunday night with...Amy." He hesitated to say her name. "Now all she says is 'Oh, I don't know, Jeremy, I think you're not telling me everything about your waitress.' Or 'When was the last time you went out with her?'" He dropped his head back and stared at the sky. "I can't take the bullshit anymore."

A Huskie smacked a double and brought in two runs winning the game. Shaking his head he pointed at the field. "There it is. A metaphor for my life." Finishing his beer, Jeremy set the cup down beside him.

Though the game was over, the three remained seated to let the crowds disperse.

"I think a lot about Mom and Dad's marriage," he said after some time. "How they communicate and stuff."

Charlie nodded.

"They have something." Jeremy stared into the far distance again, as if the answers he sought were out there somewhere. "Something solid. They love each other. We were never in doubt. They love each other and they trust each other. Do you agree?" He turned to his brother.

"I do," Charlie said.

"I want what they have," Jeremy said in a faraway voice.

Charlie nodded. "You deserve that."

Jon leaned across Charlie. "May I ask a question which, as a married-in is none of my business?"

"Sure."

"Are you in love with someone else? This Amy, perhaps?"

Jeremy's heart seized and he stared wide-eyed at his brother-in-law. How had he homed in on his feelings so fast? He guffawed. "Don't be ridiculous. Charlie can tell you what a huge mistake that would be." He retrieved his empty beer cup and got up. "It's time to go," he said, ending the discussion.

10

So much for the sun and fun. Snow fell hard when Jeremy stepped off the plane, his backpack slung over one shoulder. Once inside Burlington International Airport, he dropped the pack to the floor and pulled on his parka before proceeding to the baggage carousel.

Last night, Dad had texted to say he'd parked Jeremy's car in the lot and attached a picture of the airport lot number.

He'd had a fantastic time with his brother and Jon. He always did, but he surprised himself with how much emotional garbage he'd purged and was grateful for the love and support they gave him minus the judgment.

In the end, he couldn't bring himself to tell Charlie and Jon he was seeing Amy, even when Jon asked him outright, fearing his brother would ridicule him for his foolishness. He didn't want his growing feelings tarnished.

As he drove home, Jeremy ached for the sight of her and if he had any idea where she lived, he'd drive straight over.

The first thing he did after entering the house was turn up the heat. The second was to call her.

She answered on the second ring. "Hi."

The happiness in her voice took his breath away. "Hi, yourself. I'm home, looking tanned and feeling refreshed. How was your week?"

She laughed. "Shithead."

He laughed too. In the background, a child's voice asked a question, and Amy's, "'Just a minute,'" sounded a bit impatient.

He crinkled his brow. "What's going on?"

"Oh," The teasing playfulness disappeared. "COVID is back on the rise, and Lindsay was called in to work, so I'm taking care of her daughter, Jessica."

"Sounds like fun." Cringing, he slapped a hand over his face. "Not for Lindsay, I didn't mean to imply." He stopped talking and sighed.

"I understood what you meant. And yes, she's a sweet kid. I'm getting our lunch together. We're having cat food sandwiches."

"Cat food sandwiches?" He wrinkled his nose, unsure what she meant. "Sounds...yummy."

Amy laughed. "Tuna fish, oh confused one! Jessie loves tuna fish."

"Oh, okay. Well, still not a fan. I'll let you go feed Jessie. I wanted to tell you I'm back in town, I missed you something awful, and if you want me to come tonight, I can." He cradled his phone as he fixed himself some coffee.

"I missed you too, and I'd love for you to come tonight, but you must be exhausted after your trip. Besides, I wouldn't want to stand out like an albino whale next to your tanned maleness."

He laughed. "Never! But okay. Tomorrow night. Make sure Frank or Jason walk you to your car tonight."

"I will and I can't wait to see you. Welcome home, Jay."

"Thanks, glad to be home." He rocked his head. "Okay, perhaps a little lie because it was wicked warm and sunny in Florida, but still."

She laughed and his heart trip-hammered at the sound. They exchanged a few more pleasantries before hanging up.

His second call was to Maggie and went straight to voicemail. Wrinkling his brow, he left a message. "Hey, Mags, I'm home. I had a wonderful time with Charlie and Jon. Restful and fun. They said to say hello." He paused. "Not sure where you are, but um, I do want to connect with you at some point." Another pause. His eyebrows went up and down. "Okay, talk to you later. Bye."

Amy's heart soared at the sound of his voice. She hadn't spoken to him the entire week though he'd told her he would try to call.

He'd bought her story of taking care of Jessica, though Ricky made all the noise complaining he was hungry. She didn't lie, exactly. She was watching her niece today. Lindsay was a nurse who had gotten Amy her job at the hospital.

The pandemic worked her sister ragged, but since the loss of her husband, Lindsay was determined to prevent anyone else from succumbing to the horrific illness. So Amy took Jess often, which worked out for her too by giving Ricky a playmate.

She finished making their lunches and set the plates on the kitchen table. "Cat food sandwiches are up," she called. On their plates were carrot sticks and sliced apples along with half a tuna fish sandwich. Ricky was too small to eat an entire sandwich and Jess would fill up on the fruit and veggies first.

The children came running and scrambled into their seats. As they ate, she made herself a sandwich and sat down with them.

"Aunt Amy, where are your carrots?"

Amy took a bite of her sandwich and got up. "Thanks, Jessie," she spoke around her bite.

She grabbed carrot sticks and cut up an apple for herself. While the children each had a glass of milk, Amy got a bottle of water and sat back down to her meal.

Her heart soared and she had to stuff an urge to jump up and down like a little girl. Jay was back in town. He'd called to tell her he was home, and he was willing to pick her up tonight. She couldn't ask him though. After a long trip, she didn't want to drag him into Burlington so late at night.

Maggie didn't return Jeremy's call, and he grew concerned. She always called as soon as she realized he'd left a message, but now, crickets. He called back one more time on Sunday and again his call went to voice mail. He left another message, this one sounding less confused, more annoyed, and hung up.

"Morning," Jeremy walked into Maggie's office on Monday morning and stopped beside her desk.

Maggie didn't answer. Instead, she made notes on a legal pad, finishing her thought before looking up. "Oh, hi."

Oh, hi. We're back to this game, are we? He sighed. "Welcome back, Jeremy! How was your trip, Jeremy? Did you have fun with your brother and his partner?" He shifted his feet, cocking a hip. "So what have I done this time?"

"Nothing." She flashed a smile as she riffled through papers on her desk as though looking for something important.

He plunked his backpack on the pile on her desk and stared down at her. “Maggie?”

She sighed and after a pause deigned to glance his way. “I think we need to take a break from each other, Jeremy.”

The last few times she made this announcement, he tried to change her mind, but now, she played right into his hand. He should’ve been happy, but instead, suspicion made his heart pound. Looking for the trap, he narrowed his eyes and studied her. “Why?”

She glared. “Because. Since the night of Alyssa’s party, I’ve been doing some thinking.”

“Thinking.”

“Yes. And I’ve been talking with the girls.”

He huffed a small laugh full of disgust. “Of course you have.” In a sudden movement, he yanked his backpack off her desk, scattering papers. “Okay. Catch ya later, Mags.” He started for the door.

“Okay? What do you mean, okay?” Maggie jumped from her chair. “Jeremy!”

He grabbed the door panel and slammed the door so hard the frame shook. He turned on her. “I mean what I said.”

Her brow creased and her lipstick painted mouth parted as she studied him. “Just like that?”

He sighed. “Well, I’m clear on where this is going since we’ve been down this road so many times. ‘We need a break. Our relationship isn’t going anywhere. I love you, but I can’t wait forever.’” He lifted his eyebrows. “Am I getting any of this wrong? Have I missed an essential point? If you called me back yesterday, we could have had this discussion in private.”

Maggie dropped back into her seat. She crossed her legs and let her wrists dangle off the arms of her chair. She positioned herself so he got a clear view down the front of her white silk blouse. He shifted his gaze back to her face, unmoved by the display.

A frown pulled her mouth down. “While you were in Florida, I went out with the girls. I met a guy. I think I’d like to pursue him for a while.”

Even though Jeremy had spent his week working on his own exit strategy, the little green monster made a surprise appearance.

He took a step closer. “You accuse me of all kinds of shenanigans with ‘the waitress.’” He air quoted the two words. “But the minute my back is turned, you go on a manhunt?”

“How dare you!” Maggie shouted, springing to an upright

position. "We're going nowhere, Jeremy. If you wanted to marry me, you would have asked me by now, don't you think?"

He shook his head, unable to believe he was having this conversation. Let alone at school. Typical high school. Makeups and breakups.

"Let's just say, I don't want to be your future ex-husband. Did you ever think of that? Do you have any idea how insulting that is?"

"It was a joke."

"Not. Funny." Jeremy turned to leave again. Her next words stopped him.

"Did you ever wonder why I hate celebrating my birthday? Have I told you the story about how my father walked out on my mother and me when I was fifteen? Guess what day it was?"

Where was she going with this? He didn't have long to wait for the answer. He turned around, his backpack hanging in his slack fingers.

"My fifteenth birthday." After a sharp jerk of her head, she continued, "Yeah, my father's gift was to tell me he was moving out, and not only moving out but marrying his mistress whore, the mother of his three"—she held up three fingers for emphasis— "children. As if *my* mother wasn't the mother of his child." She wiped her eyes and spoke to her desk. "Every time you study Mom's family portrait I cringe. You always remark how much I resemble him. Makes me want to claw your eyes out of your head."

Rage distorted her features and she nodded, no doubt at the astonished stare he couldn't hide. He'd never learned this much about her father.

Her shoulders slumped. "I haven't communicated with him since." She picked up her pen, then threw it back on the desk. "It's not your fault you can't commit to me, Jeremy. You have your issues. Those are mine."

His anger left him, but not his resolve. "Not every man is like him, Maggie. I'd be willing to bet this man you've met is right for you in a way I can never be."

He glanced at the clock. "I have to go to class. The bell is about to ring." He turned and left her office, ignoring the stares and whispers from the women in the front office, grateful he didn't say anything he'd regret later.

Mike came to his classroom in between classes. "Welcome home,

Jer." He extended his hand.

Jeremy was writing quadratic equations on the board in preparation for his next class, but he stopped to shake Mike's hand. "How was your winter break? Did the boys force you to ski all week? Must have been tragic."

Mike chuckled. "Never mind. Congratulations, my friend. Word has spread all over the school."

"What word?" A rushing sound, like the waves of the Gulf of Mexico in full hurricane mode, filled his ears and his body grew hot.

"Your most recent breakup with our illustrious guidance counselor. Janice, in the front office, started a pool over how long this one lasts. I put my money on six weeks."

Jeremy laughed. "Asshole."

"That's me, the department head asshole." Mike grew somber as he squeezed Jeremy's shoulder. "I'm glad you didn't get mixed up in her legal troubles. With the school's zero-tolerance policy, I feared I'd have to let you go and I don't want to."

"Appreciated," Jeremy said, dropping the chalk and sitting at his desk. "Why wasn't Maggie fired?"

Mike shrugged. "Scuttlebutt is Henry put her on probation, which conveniently happened last week. Henry likes her."

"Figures. He'd probably fire my male ass." Jeremy leaned an elbow on his desk. "Can I tell you something?"

Mike perched on the edge. "Shoot."

Mike whistled when he finished telling him about his past weeks with Amy.

Jeremy chuckled. "I'm not technically dating her. I meet her after work and walk her to her car. We haven't had an official date or anything."

"But you want one."

"Like a bear wants honey, but I've needed to deal with Maggie. She doesn't realize what a gift she's given me."

Students began to file into the classroom. Mike pushed himself off the desk and as he left, he waved. "I think I lost twenty bucks. C'est la vie."

"Serves you right," Jeremy hollered at his back.

11

Jeremy sat at the bar, drinking coffee, chatting with another faceless patron, waiting for Amy's shift to end. He put down his cup and stood when she approached with her jacket. They left Lou's after wishing a pleasant night to Frank.

"So, Amy, I was wondering something." As they strolled across the Marketplace, Jeremy grasped her hand, entwining their fingers and slowing their pace to prolong their time together.

"Sure," Amy said through a yawn. "Sorry."

Perhaps he shouldn't ask. Exhaustion left dark circles under her eyes. She yawned again and her eyes watered.

He shook his head. "Never mind," he said and struggled to keep discouragement from coloring his tone.

"No, Jay, don't let's never mind. What did you want to ask me?"

Reluctantly, he pushed forward. "Two weeks from Tuesday night in Johnson, the Peking Acrobats are performing. At the college. They were at the Flynn a few years ago and they're fantastic. I was wondering if you'd like to go. You'd be out of the house another night, I realize, but I think you'll have fun." He hurried to convince her as doubt marched across her face.

Another thought occurred to him. "Unless you don't want to go out with me."

"When have I said that?"

"You haven't, but the expression on your face..." He stopped, fearing he'd say something he might regret.

"Showed surprise at your request, nothing more," she finished his thought for him, smiling reassurance.

He let her reassured him. “So would you like to go?”

“I would.” Amy smiled but another yawn hit her. She apologized again. “Thank you for asking me.” She leaned into his arm. “May I ask a question?”

“Yes.”

She narrowed her eyes. “Since you tried to accuse me of not wanting to go out with you, is this an official first date?”

It took him a second to realize she was teasing. “I guess so.” He chuckled and squeezed her hand.

“Then I accept.” Catching her lower lip in her teeth, she offered a shy smile.

He wanted to kiss her, but instead, he squeezed her hand, and they resumed their walk to the garage.

As the date drew near, Amy gave him her address, making him laugh. She lived in the same neighborhood she’d grown up in.

“I know,” she said. “I’ve gone far in life.”

“You’re telling me,” he teased. She stuck her nose in the air and pretended offense.

On Tuesday night he pulled into her driveway and shut off the engine, but she appeared on the back step and walked to the car.

She got in and buckled up. “Hi.”

“I would have come to the door,” he said, restarting the car.

She giggled. “I’m sorry. I haven’t been on a date in so long, I forgot the protocols. You’ll have to bear with me.”

“I have trouble believing that.” He backed up and drove away from the house.

“Well, I speak true. Trouble is, I work. All. The. Time. So when I have a night off, all I want to do is stay home.”

Her shamefaced, stammered apology made him laugh. “I understand what you meant.” He squeezed her hand to stop her confused and embarrassed apologies. “No offense taken.”

Shaking her head, she turned her face away. After a few minutes she faced front. “Besides,” she continued. “The only two male co-workers I have are gay. Jason at the restaurant and Kevin at the hospital.”

“Frank?”

"Frank doesn't count. He's ten years older than me and extremely happily married." She chuckled. "His wife, Kathy, is a sweet woman."

Jeremy nodded. "I could recommend you to my brother, but he's married to a wonderful man." He laughed as he raised a hand to protect himself from a playful slap on the arm.

"Did you say hello to Charlie for me?"

"I did...not. Sorry, I forgot!"

She shook her head. "Jay, Jay, Jay." She tsked. "You horrible man."

"I am a horrible man." He glanced at her. *Because I still love you but don't dare tell you.* He drove the rest of the way to Johnson telling her about the Peking Acrobats and how much he hoped she would like them.

"Oh, Jay, I can't remember when I've had a better time. They were so much fun. And when that guy did a handstand on top of that stack of chairs balanced on four bottles…!" She pressed her hands over her mouth. "And then did a flip to get down! I was like, Oh my gosh! How does he do that without falling off?"

Grinning at her enthusiasm, he turned right and headed for home.

"I'm so afraid of heights, one chair would have been enough for me," she continued, gushing with enthusiasm. "But he climbed up how many? Ten? Twelve? I can't guess. And those women with those things they were balancing in their mouths?"

"Those things?" A laugh bubbled up. Grabbing her hand, he kissed her knuckles before releasing her fingers. "You're a funny girl."

With a snort, she pretended he hadn't just kissed her hand. "Those lantern-like things. I couldn't tell in the dark what they were, but the women were lovely." She sighed. "I had a wonderful time."

"I'm glad. I thought you'd enjoy them. And I was right. You're lit up like a thousand-watt bulb."

Amy studied him as he drove. Her happiness was so complete that she opened her mouth to tell him about Ricky but reconsidered. What if he didn't ask her out again?

Wanting him to come back and not run for the hills at the idea of her single parenthood, she snapped her jaw shut.

Her happiness chilled with the thought, and he must have sensed her cooling off because he glanced at her out of the corner of his eye.

"Are you okay?"

She tossed him a grin. "Yeah."

A confused grimace creased his brow. His gaze slid to her again as he scratched his cheek. "Okay," he said and fell silent.

When they arrived back at her house, he pulled into her driveway and turned off the engine. He unbuckled his seat belt, but Amy put a hand on his arm.

"Thank you, Jay. I had a wonderful time."

He studied her. "That sounds like a dismissal."

Her lower lip folded over her teeth and with effort, she met his eye. "I'm tired and I think I should go in now." She spoke above a whisper and as kindly as she could. She didn't want to hurt his feelings, but judging from the disappointment in his eyes, she was too late.

He snapped his seat belt again. "Okay," he said. "I'm glad you enjoyed yourself."

"I did. I haven't had so much fun in ages," she said and squeezed his arm. "You were right. They were fantastic." She struggled to think of something to say that would smooth over her curt dismissal, but her mind was stubbornly blank. She couldn't let him come inside and discover she had a babysitter. After a moment of silence, she reached for the door handle.

"Amy?"

She faced him.

"May I kiss you good night?"

She smiled. "I'd like that."

Jeremy slid his palm along her jaw and clasping the back of her neck, he drew her close.

When his lips touched hers, she drew in a breath. Her skin tingled and her heart raced. She breathed in his Old Spice, and the memories of them making out with frantic hunger in the back seat of his Jeep assaulted her. She opened her lips, and he obliged by deepening the kiss. Her heart raced and a moan escaped, but when his tongue touched hers, she jerked away.

Confusion flashed in his eyes.

Pressing her forehead to his, she clasped his wrist. His pulse raced beneath her fingers. "I have to go in now," she whispered and kissed him again before pulling away.

He straightened and dropped his hand. "Good night, Amy," he said but didn't glance at her. He licked his lips and played with the steering wheel.

"Thank you for tonight, Jay," she said and got out. When she got to the back door, she waved, but he was backing down her driveway and she couldn't tell in the dark if he glimpsed her or not.

Lindsay waited in the kitchen. "Well, how was your date?"

"Wonderful." A grin split her face. "I've never seen anything like them. They were…" She broke off, unable to express her awe and wonder.

"Did you tell him?"

The grin disappeared. "No."

"Why not." Lindsay crossed her arms.

"Because the subject didn't come up, Killjoy."

"Oh right," Lindsay scoffed, "because talking about one's children comes so naturally to single people. You have to tell him, Amy."

"Don't nag."

Lindsay made a lower-your-voice gesture. She sighed but dropped the subject. "The kid is asleep. Finally. I'll gather mine and head out."

"Thanks for babysitting, Lin. And for parking at Dad's."

Lindsay stared hard at Amy and sighed again. "Whatever," she said and tiptoed into the living room to gently wake Jessica. She gathered her daughter into her arms and let her fall back to sleep on her shoulder before exiting out the front door.

12

"Come on, buddy, we have to go to Grammy's." Amy tugged Ricky's hand to make him walk a little faster. Jay was coming soon, and she wanted her son at her parents' house before he arrived. But Ricky didn't want to go. Saturdays, he understood in his toddler way, was his day with Mommy, but she was leaving him.

"Nooo, Mommy, Wicky no wants to," he said and tried to disengage his hand. When he couldn't, he used his other hand unsuccessfully to pry her fingers. Instead, she tugged a little harder. "Yes. Now stop this."

He dug his heels in and with his free hand made a claw, grimaced, and started to cry. "Nooo."

Rather than respond in anger, she picked him up and carried him the rest of the way.

"Yes," she said in a firm voice. "For a little while, and if you can behave at Grammy's, Mommy will make you pancakes for supper." She had to work tonight, but at this point, she'd say anything to drop him off at Mom and Dad's before Jay showed up.

Her offer made the boy pause. He loved pancakes, especially for supper. The suggestion saved Amy from admitting she had little food left and couldn't afford to go to the grocery store for another week. About all she had left were a few eggs, some milk, and a container of flour. Enough to make pancakes until payday next week.

As he sniffed in his tears, he studied her. "When you come back?" His voice was tight with sadness.

"This afternoon. I'll only be gone for a little while." She wiped his eyes and kissed his cheek.

Ricky lay his head on her shoulder and Amy kissed him again. She hated to leave him too, but Jay had invited her on a tour of sugar houses in Chittenden County, saving her from having to reveal Ricky to him.

After more tears when she dropped him off, Amy returned to the house with a sigh of relief, and waited in the living room, her jacket still on but unzipped.

Jay pulled into the driveway a few minutes later. She left the house and headed to the car.

Rather than exit the car, he checked to be sure the passenger door was unlocked, and as she approached, he grabbed his backpack and threw it onto the back seat.

"Hi." She got into the car and buckled her seat belt, before leaning in for a kiss. He obliged.

When they broke apart, he smiled. "Hey, beautiful."

Heat flowed up her face and she smiled but turned away.

Jeremy backed down her driveway. "I planned to tour sugar houses, but Saint Albans is hosting their maple festival this weekend, so I thought you might prefer that instead?"

"Sounds like fun."

As they drove north, Jeremy's phone rang. "'Twin'" flashed, and he hit the ignore button on the hands-free dash display.

"You didn't have to ignore your call."

"Emma, we talk weekly. I'll call her back tonight."

"Oh! Tell her I said hello." She cocked her head. "Why twin?"

"A joke." A quick shrug of one shoulder and an embarrassed half smile. "Well, she is my twin."

She nodded. "You guys are still close." She smiled. "Lindsay and I never used to be, but we've changed over the past few years."

He glanced at her. "What changed?"

"Life, I suppose. I'm..." The time had come to open up about her personal life. She glanced at her lap. "I should tell you I'm divorced." Through her lashes, she studied him, waiting. For what, she wasn't sure.

His chin lifted and lowered in one long nod of acknowledgment. "Oh."

His lips pulled down and his brow lowered, creasing his forehead. She'd hurt him with her revelation and struggled with a sudden sense she had betrayed him. She hadn't meant to. "Well, my husband left me, so we divorced a little over four years ago, now. *Same time I found out I was pregnant.* At the beginning of the pandemic, my sister lost her husband to COVID." She shrugged. "His death brought us together."

He glanced at her before focusing on the road. A road sign noting the distance to the exit for Saint Albans flashed past them.

"I'm sorry about your brother-in-law." He switched lanes to prepare for the exit. "How did he get sick? I mean, the governor jumped right on the protocols."

"He did, but Kyle, my brother-in-law, had to go to Jacksonville, Florida for a business conference the January the pandemic started, and at the time, no one understood what was going on with this thing. He was exposed at the conference. Turns out, nine people were positive and asymptomatic. His company sent a letter warning of possible exposure two weeks after he returned, but he was already in the hospital and died a week later. The disease hit him like a runaway train." She shook her head. "Lindsay and Jessica, their daughter, never got sick. This disease is weird." Sucking in her breath, she pushed against a wave of sadness washing over her. "He was a healthy man who didn't smoke or drink much. He exercised every day. Took care of himself, but he still died."

Once in Saint Albans, Jay drove up the street and turned into the parking lot. "For the record"—he cut the engine— "I got vaccinated as soon as it was available to teachers."

"So did I."

They exited the car. Amy chuckled and pointed at the sign displaying the name Taylor Park.

"No relation," she said.

He took her hand, and the move was so natural, he transported her back to high school. Jay had been a hand-holder even then. Some things never changed, and the discovery cheered her.

"What made you decide to vaccinate?" she asked, mostly to have something to say.

"I hated Zoom school. I figured if I wanted to be back in the classroom, and vaccination was the way, fine by me. What about you?"

"Kyle died."

She changed the subject, not wanting to fall into a funk, and she was grateful Jay didn't pursue the discussion any further. She pointed to some booths, and they went over to explore what they had to offer.

They strolled the grounds, stopping at an occasional booth. Amy fingered a quart of maple syrup. Jay bought it, along with some maple candy and two maple frosted doughnuts, and as they strolled, they enjoyed the sweet treat.

He glanced at her and started laughing.

"What's so funny?" Amy drew a finger around her lips. "Do I have frosting on my face or something?"

Still laughing, he faced her, and holding his doughnut in his teeth, he swiped a sticky thumb across the tip of her nose before retrieving his doughnut. "You had a chunk on your nose." He showed her a small gob of frosting. "A maple booger." With a smirk, he sucked the frosting off his thumb.

"Jay, gross!" Amy threw her head back and laughed. "You're disgusting," she said through her laughter as he tugged her hand.

"You've forgotten." He grinned at her. "I was always able to gross you out over any number of things."

"I have not!" she declared with a haughty sniff. "I had hoped you'd grown up some, though."

"Nope."

They laughed together and as she glanced into his face, he locked eyes with her. The sun shone behind him, wrapping his head in a halo, and the wind ruffled his dark hair. His cheeks were red from the cold, but his warm brown teddy bear eyes shone with light and laughter. He was so thoroughly male in the early spring sunshine that he took her breath away. She wanted him to kiss her and must have communicated her want because he started to lower his head towards hers. She licked maple off her lips.

"Hey, coach!" a group of young boys called out amid whistles and catcalls.

Jay jerked back and glanced around before waving his doughnut to a group of boys. Grasping her elbow, he got walking.

Amy raised her brows in question.

"Students."

"Oh." She turned back. The boys grinned and pointed at them. *Let the speculation begin.*

He bit into his doughnut, chewed, and swallowed. "They're gonna give me a raft of shit on Monday." Yet he didn't sound displeased.

After he finished his doughnut, he licked his fingers.

"Serves you right." She leaned in and bumped him with her hip.

Jay staggered and grinned down at her as he leaned in toward her, but instead of pushing her playfully, he put his arm around her. Almost immediately Amy slipped her arm under his open jacket and around his waist.

He stopped walking as a man approached with two boys in tow.

Lifting his arm over her head, Jay held out his hand in greeting. The two shook hands and Amy finished her doughnut as they chatted.

"Amy, this is Mike Pelletier. Mike, Amy Taylor." Jay jerked his head at Mike. "I think I mentioned he's my department head."

She extended her hand. "Oh," Amy drew out the word, as a conspiratorial grin lit her face. "Which means, I shouldn't tell him how back in the day you tried to tutor me in geometry, and it was an epic fail."

Jay snorted a laugh. "Well, I think that ship just sailed."

"What's this?" Mike joined in the banter. "My star math teacher sucks at teaching math?"

Amy held up her hands as if to suggest she was proof.

Mike clapped him on the back. "Which is why I keep him." His speculative gaze returned to her. "A pleasure to meet you, Amy."

He dropped a hand on each of the boys' shoulders. "These two monsters are my sons, Luke and Evan."

"Pleasure to meet you, boys. Are you having fun?" The boys looked to be between eight and ten. They shrugged and kept their gazes locked on the melting snow. Not expecting a coherent answer from either one, Amy raised her eyes to Mike. "Is your wife with you? I'd love to meet her."

Instant silence met her words. Evan gulped. Luke punched him in the arm. Jay scrubbed his nose.

Mike's lips formed a stilted smile. "I'm a widower. Two years now."

Amy gasped. "I'm so sorry. I didn't mean to..." Her face grew hot despite the cold, and she wished the ground would open and swallow her whole.

"No need to apologize." His blue eyes communicated understanding and friendliness as if this wasn't the first time he'd had to explain.

"I'm so embarrassed," she said, horror-struck at her faux pas.

“Please don’t.” Mike’s eyes shone with kindness. “Then I’ll have to be embarrassed, and it will all become a giant mess.”

He kept his kind gaze on Amy until she smiled. “Well, we wouldn’t want that,” she said.

As Mike studied her a little longer, she got the impression he evaluated her worthiness for his friend. When she had the urge to squirm, he shifted his gaze from her to Jay.

“Yep.” He nodded changing the subject. “I’m most definitely out twenty bucks.” He shook his head as though aggrieved.

Jay laughed. “Get out of here!” He pushed at his friend.

Mike shook her hand again. “I’ll leave you two lovebirds alone now. Amy, I’m so pleased to meet you.” He turned to his sons. “C’mon boys, time to go home. See you Monday,” he said to Jay.

The boys called goodbye to Jay and waved at Amy.

After bidding them farewell, she covered her face with her hand. “I’m so embarrassed.”

“Nah, don’t worry.” Jay put his arm around her shoulders and squeezed. He smiled down at her.

Still, Amy crinkled her brow. Such gaffes always made her want to run and hide. She lifted her head. “What did he mean by lovebirds? What did you tell him about us? And what does he mean he’s out twenty bucks?”

“The twenty bucks is an inside joke.” Jeremy shook his head still grinning. “I assure you I haven’t told him anything important. Only I pick you up after work and how we met, but nothing personal.”

Her forehead crinkled over the bridge of her nose. “Nothing personal? What do you mean?”

The grin faded from Jay’s face and the humor left his eyes. “It means I told him...it means what I said. I didn’t give him any details.”

Her scowl deepened. She crossed her arms and shifted her stance, thrusting one hip out. Was he so ashamed of her, he didn’t want to tell his friends about her? “So,” she drew out the word as her eyes narrowed, “you don’t tell your friends about me because...” She swung a hand in a slow circular motion, “Why?”

He did a double take and lowered his brow as if assessing whether she was kidding or not.

“Because.” He opened and closed his mouth as he glanced around at the crowd. Facing her, he planted his hands on his hips. “Have I missed something important here?”

"You're embarrassed to be seen with me, aren't you?" She squinted one eye as the sun slid from behind a cloud to shine on her face.

He flinched and genuine shock rearranged his features. "What? No!" He ran a hand across the back of his neck. "Why would you think such a thing?" After scanning the park as if searching for Mike to return and help him, he dropped his hands from his hips and held them up in supplication. He shifted his feet. "Amy, what have I done?"

"Why didn't you tell him about me?"

"I did tell him about you. I said so."

"No, you said you didn't tell him anything personal. That's not the same as saying you told him about me. What did you say anyway? 'Oh yeah, Mike, some girl I dated in high school was adolescent enough to drop me a note to say she liked me, so I had to humor her?'" She dropped her arms to her sides, her hands clenched in fists. "I'm sure the two of you got a laugh at my expense."

Spinning on her heel, she marched away, realizing she'd projected her fears onto him and couldn't figure out why. She didn't want to fight with him in public. She didn't want to fight with him at all.

A tug on the sleeve of her jacket halted her progress across the park. "Amy, I'm lost. I don't understand where any of this is coming from. What have I done to earn this attack?"

She sighed. "Nothing. You haven't done anything. Forget what I said, Jay. I'm sorry."

He grabbed her arm again, stopping her from walking away. "No, you don't brush me off with a 'Forget what I said.' You started this and now we're going to finish." He stared at her and his eyes, normally soft as a teddy bear, now flashed like a grizzly.

"Start explaining. Why would I call you adolescent? Why would I laugh at you? And for the record, at *NO* time have I been with you to humor you."

She sighed and cursed her insecurities. Grabbing the edges of her jacket she pulled the garment tight around her waist and struggled to draw breath.

Unable to stand his withering glare any longer, she dropped her gaze to the melting snow and drew in a deep breath through her nose and released a long, slow breath. Her shoulders drew down. "I'm sorry." She chewed her bottom lip and chanced a glance at his angry face. "I'm sorry," she said again. "I don't know why I said those things."

Jay didn't answer. Instead, he studied her, brow furrowed, mouth puckered, and Amy would have paid a million dollars to discover what he was thinking. A long silence ensued until his eyebrows flicked up and down and he turned away.

"Okay," he said and waved a hand at her, in disgust.

Though Amy didn't understand what he meant, she didn't dare ask either. "Jay, please. I'm sorry."

His cold gaze moved up and down her body, his jaw crooked to the side. "I don't understand what this is about, Amy Taylor, but I spent the last four years of my life with a woman who did nothing but play emotional games with me. I will not do that again. Do you understand me? I. Will. Not." He stomped away.

Amy despaired as he stalked across the field toward the parking lot. If she hadn't ruined things before, she was certain she had now. She ran to catch up.

By the time she reached the car, she found him leaning with both hands on the hood. He hung his head between his shoulders and his eyes were closed. Not for the first time, she wondered what he was thinking. Amy lay her hand lightly on his shoulder.

His back rose with his deep inhale. Straightening, he slid his hands off the hood. They squeaked as he drew them off. Jay turned a hurt-filled face to her.

She wanted to take him in her arms and kiss away his pain. "I think you'd better take me home," she said instead, above a whisper. "It's getting late, and I have to work tonight."

He closed his eyes and opened them. Without a word, he drew his keys from his coat pocket and moved to the driver's side door. They drove home in silence, their camaraderie chilled, much like the clouds moving in and darkening the day.

When Jay pulled into Amy's driveway, he put the car in park. He hadn't spoken a word the entire way and her heart broke. She'd messed up and on the long drive home, struggled to find a way to break through her self-erected barrier.

On the way home, she'd studied the play of emotions on his face. A few times he turned to her, and she met his frustrated, confused gaze, but each time he turned back to face the road and remained silent.

After what seemed an eternity, they'd arrived home.

"You won't let me into the house," he said, "so I'll pick you up tonight. Usual time." He tapped his fingers on the steering wheel as she unbuckled her seat belt and gathered her purchases.

Why do I do those things? How can I be so dumb? Her heart thudded hard in her chest. Why was she pushing him away when what she wanted most was to draw him so near, he'd never leave?

"Jeremy," she said, hoping the use of his full name would grab his attention. He faced her, an angry hurt little boy shone from his eyes, and she wanted to gather him into her arms and kiss his hair as she would with Ricky.

"I'm an ass," she said. "I screwed up, and if you spend any amount of time with me, you're gonna discover I do so on a regular basis. I'm sorry for the things I said and for starting an argument. I didn't mean to, but sometimes my insecurities get in my way. The last thing I want to do is argue with you and I especially don't want to hurt you."

She tilted her head to peer into his face. "Please don't be angry with me."

He stopped tapping and dropped his hands to his lap, directing his glare to the steering wheel. "I'm not angry. I'm just..." He sighed and turned to her brows furrowed. "You hurt me."

"I did."

Again, the surprise and grief in his voice made her want to take him in her arms and soothe him.

With a scowl, he said, "I can't believe you would suggest I'd be embarrassed to be seen with you..." He broke off and gestured with his hands as if he couldn't think of what to say. Scrubbing his forehead, he stared out the windshield. "I can't figure out where you came up with such an idea."

Amy opened the car door. "I can." When he turned his gaze to her, she ran a knuckle along his jawline. "Despite the way today ended, I had a blast. Thank you for taking me to the festival."

He drew a breath to say more, but fearing he'd start questioning her again, she got out, shut the door, and went inside.

As Jeremy expected, come Monday morning, the boys he'd seen at the maple festival waited for him at the front entrance.

"Coach." Wearing a red athlete's jacket emblazoned with a huge white AHS across the front, one of the boys approached with his companions. A lecherous grin stretched across his face. "Who's the lady friend?"

"Ohhh, lady friend. Way to go, coach!" the other boys teased. "She's prime, Mr. A. Congrats."

Jeremy shook his head but didn't suppress his smile. "None of your business, Patrick," he said to the first boy, then pointed at the group, "and she's *Miss* Lady Friend, to you, fellas."

"Ooh la la," two boys said, laughing while Patrick waggled his fingers at Jeremy who continued walking to the door. His grin told them he didn't take offense at their teasing.

"Hey, coach," one of Patrick's companions jumped in. "Do the dulcet tones of wedding bells peal across the land?"

"Do you even know what dulcet means, Joel?"

Jeremy laughed at the shocked surprise on the boy's face.

Joel recovered and grinned. "Huh huh. Good one, Mr. A."

Pausing at the door, Jeremy grasped the handle. "You boys planning to try out for baseball this year?"

Their chorus of "absolutely" and "sure thing" echoed off the building.

"You hope to make the team?"

"Yes, sir," they said, full of teenage testosterone and confidence.

"Then shut up about my personal life," he said, narrowing his eyes conspiratorially, but still in easy humor, and went inside.

Mike waited for him inside the lobby.

"I saw you coming," he said by way of greeting.

"How was the rest of your weekend?"

"Never mind about me. You said this was new, but you two didn't appear new. How long have you been seeing her?" Mike asked, keeping his voice down in case Maggie showed up.

Jeremy hung his head in resignation. Heat flowed up his neck and warmed his ears and face. He spun Mike around and together they headed toward the Math Department.

"When she gave me my bill, she tucked a note inside telling me when she got off and gave me her phone number," he said, filling Mike in on more of the details.

"I went back to the restaurant later that same night and we've been together since."

Mike nodded. "I knew there was more to the story than you first gave me."

"Oh, come on! I haven't told anyone here anything. Not about

Amy." He glanced around. "I don't want anything getting back." He referred to Maggie overhearing gossip.

"True, you don't say much," Mike said, laying a friendly hand on Jeremy's shoulder. "But you give yourself away, man."

Jeremy stopped in the middle of the hallway as noisy students streamed around them. Lockers clanged and slammed. The bell rang. "How do I do that?"

Mike faced him. "We've been friends a long time, and I've never seen you so…happy…content. The joy on your face Saturday…well, I've never seen that. When you talk about her, your baby browns light up and you don't just smile, you beam like a friggin' lighthouse." He tapped Jeremy on the chest. "Like now."

Jeremy laughed as they started walking again. "Bullshit."

"No bullshit. You, my friend"—Mike tapped his arm— "are a man in love. I'm happy for you. You deserve happiness, which you were never gonna find with our dime-store floozy in the guidance department."

Surprised, Jeremy snorted a laugh. "Maggie's not a dime-store floozy," he said, but his laughter made a mockery of his defense.

"But you're right. I'm in love with Amy. I always have been. She is my soulmate." Jeremy gestured to his classroom. "If I don't go in, I'll be late, and my department head will come down on my ass."

With a shrug, Mike chuckled. "I know the guy. I can help you out."

13

Jeremy absently stared at his dinner twirling in the microwave. He was tired and wanted to go to bed early, but Amy worked tonight. The late nights were killing him, but he couldn't leave her to walk the block and a half to the parking garage, which had a creep factor all its own to set his nerves on edge.

When the buzzer sounded, he removed his Chinese take-out and carried his plate into the living room to have dinner with the Boston Red Sox.

How did Amy keep her grueling schedule? She must have had to rise early for her day job, with no break in between. What motivated her? She was barely hanging on and admitted the other night when she had a night off, she preferred to stay home.

He offered to hang out at home with her, but she wouldn't let him into her house and refused to spend time at his. If he figured out this conundrum, he'd be golden. But the way things stood, he had to take her out if he wanted to spend any time with her.

He settled on the couch to eat when his phone rang. Magpie flashed on his screen and his shoulders dropped. She was the last person he wanted to talk to, but after a short indecisive pause, he muted his TV and answered, putting the phone on speaker.

"Hey, Mags." Though he didn't much care, he asked a polite question. Nothing more. "How're things?" He shoved a forkful of pork fried rice into his mouth.

"Jeremy." The venom with which she said his name raised the hackles on the back of his neck. "Fine. You haven't called in a while.

I thought I'd check up on you."

Thought you'd see if I'm ready to come crawling back?

Giving himself a mental slap for the nasty thought, he tucked a morsel of General Tso Chicken into his cheek. "Well, I've been busy and since you have your new man, I didn't think you'd appreciate my getting in the way."

The comment hung there. J.D. Martinez smacked a home run, prompting a fist pump.

"Busy? With the waitress, you mean?"

He stopped chewing. No doubt she'd learned about Amy from the student grapevine. Since he neither confirmed nor denied his dating life to the boys, the student rumor mill ran full force. Even so, he regretted her having the information and held his breath. What was happening on Maggie's end? He couldn't summon the energy to care anymore. "Did you need something?"

She harrumphed. "So much for, 'Maggie, I assure you nothing's going on with the waitress.' You don't deny it. I bet anything you ran straight into her arms the minute you dropped me home on Valentine's Day, am I correct, Jeremy?"

Eyes wide, he stared at his phone before realizing she couldn't have any idea he'd gone back to talk to Amy, and he wouldn't characterize their first meeting as running into her arms either. He chose to eat.

"Of course." She huffed and rambled on. "Only a matter of time before you scampered off to her. I don't understand your attraction for such a chubby little—"

Jeremy sucked in an audible breath, and she broke off as though not daring to say what she thought.

"Okay." He stretched his neck and shoulders and set his plate on the coffee table. The silverware clanked. "I'm hanging up now. You have your new man. Spew your venom at him." His finger poised over the disconnect button, but her next words ran his blood cold.

"*There was never any man*!" she shouted, sounding pathetic. "You stupid fool. I wanted to make you jealous. I never thought you'd believe me." She sobbed.

He pressed a palm over his mouth and squeezed his nostrils as an infinite number of swear words ran through his brain.

"But now...I was right all along," she continued. "You've been skanking her, the one you denied over and over. So innocent. *You're a filthy piece of shit!*" She drew in a huge sobbing breath. "You had no trouble walking away from me!"

The sound of ice in a glass caught his attention. *Has she been drinking?*

"People talk, Jeremy. You were at the maple festival with her. Hell, you've been all over town with her. You took her to the fucking Peking Acrobats! They were *ours*! And you took *her*. Dave told me."

Fucking Dave! But he wasn't at fault. He told Jeremy he had tickets and discovered he couldn't use them, so Jeremy bought them from him. Dave must have assumed he was taking Maggie.

"The students talk about your new lady friend." She mocked the last two words. "Do you think me so stupid I can't understand people when they talk? You're one of the most popular teachers at school. What you do catches the attention of the students, and they talk."

Enough was enough. "First, Maggie, you're the one who broke things off with me. You told me you met someone new. Remember?"

"Yeah, but I—"

"Second," he raised his voice to talk over her. "Second, the Peking Acrobats don't belong to us. Third, I don't think you're stupid. I did you the courtesy of not seeing Amy until after you said we were over."

Jeremy struggled to remain calm, but a surge of adrenaline shot to his heart, making the muscle pound hard against his ribs. His hands shook and he clenched them into fists. *How dare she? Why can't she go away and keep her dignity intact?*

Even though he told himself to hang up, instead he listened to her weep. "Maggie, may I ask a question?" When she didn't answer, he took her silence for assent. "How much have you had to drink tonight?"

She sighed. "I've had a few."

"How many is a few?"

"None of your business is how many."

"I'm concerned. Since the night I had to pick you up, I've realized you're drinking a lot."

"I said—"

"Okay," he cut her off. "Okay. But, if you're calling in a drunken rage to give me a hard time because I took you at your word, I'm hanging up. Before I go, for the record, I want you to understand you can't call me again like this. Also, I would appreciate you calling Amy by her name, and not 'the waitress.'" He waited for her to respond and when she didn't, he continued.

"And another thing, if you use the word skank or skanking with me one more time, especially about Amy, I will wash your god-damned mouth out with soap." He drew in a deep breath, realizing as he spoke how long he'd kept his feelings bottled up. Letting them go now brought him peace. "Do I make myself clear?"

A long silence met his lecture. "Maggie!"

She sighed. "Yes. You've made yourself clear."

"Wonderful. I'm hanging up now."

"I'm sorry, Jeremy."

"So am I. Goodbye, Maggie." He hung up, blocked her number, and tossed his phone onto the couch cushion. *She lied to me. There was never any man. The bitch lied to me.*

He should be angry but couldn't summon the energy. He picked up his plate and unmuted the TV. He took a bite of his cold food, but his appetite was gone. Rising, he took his plate to the kitchen and tossed his half-eaten dinner in the trash. He had to pick up Amy in a few hours, but he still had a couple of innings before he needed to leave. He stretched out on the sofa as the announcers droned on.

When he woke up, the game was in the eighth inning, and he should have been on the road ten minutes ago. Cursing, he bolted from the house and drove as fast as he dared.

Arriving in Burlington, he parked next to her car and ran toward Lou's. As Jeremy rounded the corner to Church Street, he skidded to a stop as someone called his name.

"Jeremy? I thought I recognized you."

His father's oldest friend, Adam Knox, walked toward him, coming from the direction of lower Church Street.

"Adam? What are you doing here so late?"

"I might ask you the same thing, my friend."

Jeremy clasped his hand and leaned in for a man hug. Adam clapped him on the back.

"I'm headed into Lou's to meet some friends—" Jeremy glanced at his wristwatch. "And I'm late."

"A bit late for drinks with friends, don't you think? And on a school night. Besides, the place appears closed."

Teasing, he tapped Jeremy on his light jacket. "C'mon kid, you can tell me. What are you up to? Soliciting prostitutes?" Leaning in,

Adam nudged him with a conspiratorial wink.

Jeremy's stomach turned and his lip curled. "Adam, you're disgusting."

Adam and his wife Emily were his parents' lifelong friends. Jeremy and his siblings considered them an unofficial aunt and uncle, and their three children as unofficial cousins, but to Jeremy's disgust, Adam's sense of humor always thrived in the gutter.

Maya once confessed she couldn't stand the guy. If their parents had a gathering the Knoxes might attend, she always begged off, and if she couldn't, she kept her distance from Adam.

"Oh, c'mon." Adam squeezed Jeremy's shoulder. "I was joking."

Jeremy stepped away from his hand and huffed his irritation. "You aren't funny. If someone I work with, or a parent, overheard you, they might report me to the school district, who would fire me before you batted an eyelash."

Adam sobered. "I'm sorry, son. I didn't think." He ducked his head as if to hide embarrassment.

"So what are you doing in Burlington so close to midnight?"

"Oh," Adam said with a negligent shrug. "I do legal aid work down at the women's shelter and sometimes the work runs late. I'm on my way home now."

"I wasn't aware of a women's shelter around here." Jeremy's gaze swept the marketplace. "Whereabouts?"

"I'm not at liberty to tell you." Adam shot him an apologetic glance. "I'm not being all mysterious or anything. The policy is for the protection of the women and their children."

"Oh." Jeremy scanned the restaurant's facade. Amy might worry he wasn't coming if he didn't show up. Adam was right. The restaurant was dark because they were closed.

"Well, I'll let you go. I don't want Emily to worry you're soliciting prostitutes," Jeremy couldn't resist throwing Adam's words back at him.

"Oh, as if!" Adam leaned in with a sly laugh. "Those days are long gone, my friend. I'm way too old now."

Shocked, Jeremy faked a laugh as he shook Adam's hand. When they let go, he wiped his palm on his pant leg.

The door to the restaurant opened and Amy emerged. She jerked to a halt, eyes round. An audible gasp escaped her, and she spun on her heel and disappeared back inside before the door shut and locked behind her.

"Was she the friend?"

"One of them," Jeremy admitted. His mouth hung slack, and his brow creased. He stared at the door unable to make sense of her behavior.

"Attractive girl." Adam pointed toward the door as it clicked shut. "Do I know her?"

Jeremy almost admitted he did, but Amy's retreat ran up a red flag. "I don't think so. I'm meeting a bunch of colleagues. I'm sure she came out to see if I'm coming. I'll let you go—." Jeremy walked away. "Say hi to Emily," he called over his shoulder.

"Take care." Adam waved and left.

Jeremy pulled the locked door. He knocked, but when she didn't open up, he knocked again a little harder. With a loud clack of the door handle, she pushed it open.

Ashen-faced, Amy retreated to the corner of the vestibule between the outer and inner doors. Her arms were crossed, almost as if she tried to hide behind them and she struggled for air. She muttered one word over and over: "Okay, okay, okay."

Jeremy frowned. "What's wrong? Are you ill?"

"Who was he?"

A glance back. "Adam Knox. You remember him, don't you? They're friends of my folks."

Nodding, she sank to the floor. "I'd hoped he was dead or something." Her voice, though tight with fear, nonetheless held a note of fury. "After all these years."

Jeremy's mouth dropped open, and he stared at her. Why would she wish such a thing? With a shake of his head, he gathered his wits.

"Did something happen tonight? I'm sorry I'm late. Did you have to deal with an unruly customer?"

A shake of her head indicated the negative. She tucked her knees to her chest and buried her face in them, refusing to meet his eye.

Lightly, carefully, he placed a hand on her kneecap. She didn't jerk away. "Tell me what happened. Why is this happening?"

She shook her head, but tears filled her eyes. The terror on her face before she turned away scared the bejesus out of him.

"Amy. What. Is. Wrong?" His voice shook. "Baby, tell me what's going on." His brow furrowed over his nose, and he kept his eyes on her, ready for any sudden action. "I can't protect you if I don't have any idea what I'm protecting you from."

Lifting her tear-streaked face, she stared at him as if he'd lost his mind, and perhaps he had. For sure, he had no idea what was going on right now.

"Protect me? You can't protect me. It's too late."

"What do you mean?" Jeremy's scalp crawled. "Too late for what?"

Amy didn't answer. She lowered her face again. "Go away, Jay. I never should have...I should have left you alone. I should have let you live your life."

"Yeah, but you didn't." He slid his palm down her head, stroking her hair.

"No," she said with a sigh. "I didn't."

"I'm grateful. And I'm not going anywhere." Jeremy's heart pounded and blood rushed in his ears. "Is this because I was late? I'm sorry. I fell asleep on the sofa."

When she didn't answer, he offered a cajoling smile. "How do you keep this crazy schedule working two jobs and getting so little sleep?"

A negligent shrug. "You do what you have to."

Could she sound any more disinterested? He raised hopeful eyebrows. "Forgive me?"

Amy turned a taut face to him. Her blue eyes shifted back and forth, and his heart pounded harder as he waited for the anxious terror to recede.

She turned away. "Nothing to forgive." Amy's flat, emotionless tone made him want to shake her back to life. She drew in a long hitching breath and waited a few seconds, then slowly exhaled, puffing her cheeks. She didn't glance at him, but she held out her hand.

He took hold and placed a soft kiss on the back.

"I'm sorry, Jay. I acted like a jerk." Tears filled her eyes again. "I didn't mean what I said about going away and leaving me alone." She unfolded her frame and crawled into his embrace.

"Hey," he said softly. "What's this all about.?"

"I need to cry."

Jeremy made himself comfortable on the floor and gathered her in. "Okay," he said, kissing her hair. "You cry all you want for as long as you want. We can talk after."

They sat together for another fifteen minutes before Amy wiped her eyes and sniffled. In the muted light, her puffy eyes and splotchy red face appeared as if she'd been in a brawl. With infinite gentleness, he kissed first one eye, then the other, tasting her salty tears.

He'd sat without speaking for so long, he had to clear his throat. "Are you ready to go home?"

She nodded and slid out of his lap. He was sorry to lose her warm body, but he rose and held out his hands to help her to her feet.

Easing the door open, they stepped into the street. Her gaze swept the area.

"He's gone," he said on a hunch.

Her startled glance surprised him, but she spread her lips into something he thought was meant to resemble a smile but was more of a grimace.

"Why did you say you hoped he was dead?"

"I shouldn't have said such a thing. It isn't right." She wrapped both her arms around his waist.

He held her close and lay his cheek on the top of her head. "No, you shouldn't have, even if you meant what you said, but that wasn't my question. Why did you say it?"

Against his chest, Amy shrugged. "I never liked him." She lifted her gaze. "I'm sorry, Jay. He's a friend of your folks, but I never liked that...asshole."

The venom in her voice quieted him. He squeezed her tight and kissed her head. "Fair enough."

They strolled to the corner before Amy straightened and pulled from his embrace; however, she kept a firm hold on his hand. "How was your day?"

He did a double take. "My day was fine," he said, deciding to take her cue. "What about yours?"

She shrugged and scratched her head. Her gaze swept the marketplace again. "Same as every other—."

Who was she kidding? All evidence to the contrary.

Lightning flickered in the night sky.

Jeremy pulled her hand into the crook of his arm. "I have this one student. Britney Foster," he said. "No matter what, I cannot make her understand algebra."

He ducked his head and amended his statement. "I can tell by the homework she understands how to solve the problems and what steps to take but give her a weekly test and she blows it. Every time. She's failing my class and I worry she's on the verge of giving up. Poor kid.

She works so hard, but her passing or failing depends upon her test grades."

"Did you try talking to her? Offer after-school help?"

A flash of Maggie sitting across from him at Lou's shrugging off his concern and asking the same question made him want to snarl, but he checked the impulse. This was Amy he was talking to. "Several times. I work with her every afternoon, but I'm out of ideas to help her."

They walked along and Jeremy thought of this afternoon. Britney's tearful confession that she hated math and felt like a failure broke his heart. She scoffed when he protested that she did understand more than she realized.

He sighed and continued, "If I give her a problem and let her have the textbook, she understands what steps to take, no sweat, but if I give her a problem and don't allow her to use any kind of help, she's lost again."

Amy's gaze swept the street again. Jeremy ignored the gesture.

She glanced behind them. "You say she can do the homework but fails the tests."

"Yes."

Pursing her lips, her brow knit. "Did you have Mrs. Kelly for algebra?"

"Mr. Myers."

"I had Mrs. Kelly." This time Amy's smile was real. "Hands down the best math teacher ever. I had the same problem. I was able to do the homework because I had the book in front of me, like a security blanket, giving me the steps I needed, but at test time, without my security blanket, I failed my tests too."

As they drew near the alleyway, she stopped, leaned forward, and peered down the lane before crossing.

Jeremy mentally sighed, wishing she didn't feel the need. He was beside her and wouldn't let anything happen to her. Didn't she realize by now?

"But you passed because you took geometry the next year. We were in the same class."

"I remember...Tutor," she goaded him. Her laugh sounded forced and a little manic. Lightning flashed again and this time a growl of thunder accompanied it.

"Careful," he said after a playful nudge. "Your tutor has sensitive feelings." He squeezed her shoulder.

Amy slipped her arm around his waist and Jeremy's heart trip-hammered against his ribs. He breathed a giant sigh of relief. Perhaps she was getting over whatever happened at the restaurant.

Amy continued as they walked along arm in arm. "Mrs. Kelly graded my nightly homework and assigned something like five points for every right answer. When I failed the weekly tests, she added those points to my test scores and soon enough, I started passing the class. She called it 'test anxiety,' where you become so afraid of failing you end up doing exactly that."

Jeremy stopped dead and stared at her. How did he miss such a simple solution?

"I never considered that. Genius!"

Amy's forward momentum carried her out of their embrace, and she turned to face him.

On impulse, he slid his hands over her cheeks and gave her a gentle kiss before pulling away and peering into her blue eyes. "May I ask you something?"

"Of course." She squeezed his wrists.

"Would you come home with me tonight?"

Amy stared into his eyes so long he understood the answer was no. She lay her palm against his cheek and tilted her head to one side. The smile she offered him was full of sad regret. "I can't, Jay."

"Why not?" he pressed. "I'm not with Maggie anymore."

"I know."

"Then why? Does your refusal have something to do with what happened tonight?" He glanced back toward Lou's.

She didn't answer, just pulled her bottom lip over her teeth and bit down. Regret and sorrow filled her eyes.

"Why not?" he asked again with more force. "Spend the night with me, Amy. Please. If you want, I'll come to your house."

"No!" She stepped back. "I'm not ready for...not yet. Besides…" Her chuckle sounded forced. "I'm exhausted. I'd only fall asleep on you."

He was undeterred. "So let me hold you while you sleep. I want to be with you."

"So do I," she said, "but I can't."

The firm rejection tempered with regret dismayed him. Thunder rumbled, echoing in his heart.

He sighed and with effort, kept his frustration in check, which he acknowledged, was getting harder.

"You don't make things easy, do you?" He tried to sound like he was joking, but he heard the hurt in his voice and turned away.

A tug on his sleeve brought him back. She pressed warm palms against his cheeks and stared up into his eyes. "I'm sorry, Jay. I have my reasons. I'm not ready to...I don't think I can..." Sighing, she pulled his head down and kissed him.

He loved kissing her, but he wanted much more and wasn't about to let her distract him this way.

Placing his hands on her shoulders, he gently pulled away.

"I'm sorry," she said when he broke the kiss. "I hurt you with my behavior and I have no excuse. I can only ask for your patience."

Her breath caressed his cheek, and he couldn't resist. He kissed her again. This time, he hoped to persuade her. When she parted her lips, he stepped closer.

Jeremy gathered her into his arms and slanted his lips across hers. His body thrummed and he grew lightheaded, almost forgetting to breathe. He pressed his hips into hers.

With a sudden intake of breath, her hands still on his shoulders, she pushed him away. "No," she squeaked. "I can't. I can't." She turned away and scrubbed her hand across her mouth.

He'd had enough. "Patience my ass! What's gotten into you? What happened tonight?" He pointed toward the restaurant and demanded, "Tell me the truth. Please!"

When Amy sighed, he feared she'd refuse to tell him, but her eyes said he deserved the truth. "What happened was a panic attack." She dropped her gaze to the sidewalk.

The rain started falling, and a bluish flash lit the night sky followed a few minutes later by a growl of thunder.

She cast him a glance before returning her focus to the sidewalk. "You think me weird when I'm walking, always checking my surroundings—."

He started to protest, but she held up her hands.

"Let me finish or I'll never get this out."

Jerking a nod, he crossed his arms and shifted his feet, widening his stance.

"Several years ago, I was..." After a glance in his direction, she too crossed her arms, as though to hide her body from him. "I was raped," she said to the sidewalk and rubbed her arms.

He sucked in a breath and his eyes widened. Pain stabbed his heart as rain pelted his head and dripped down his face. Lightning flashed again followed on its heels by a crack of thunder, but he ignored it as the rain fell harder. This was too important to worry about getting wet.

Amy shrank into herself, small and frightened, and he didn't doubt the truth of her words. Jeremy fought an urge to step close and take her in his arms. Unsure of how she'd react though, he didn't dare.

Studying him with a fearful look, it was as though she was assessing his reaction. Rain dripped from his hair to his face and down his neck, but he didn't wipe away the water.

Her gaze slid away and focused on the streetlight over his left shoulder. "Ever since, I've had panic attacks." She shrugged, met his eyes, and refocused on the streetlight. "Sometimes I have a warning. Most times, like tonight, I don't."

Shivering in the cold rain, hair plastered to her face, Amy appeared fragile, and her vulnerability came at him in waves.

He stepped close and grasped her elbows but made sure his touch remained light. Lightning flashed. Thunder grumbled.

"Is that why when I kiss you, sometimes you let me, and sometimes you don't? Are you afraid of me? Do you think I'm going to hurt you?"

"I don't think you're going to hurt me," she answered his last question. "And I'm not afraid of you. I just..." She broke off with a sigh and glanced down at the sidewalk again. "I can't explain."

Jeremy placed a knuckle under her chin and raised her face, but she let her lids drop. "Look at me, please."

She raised her face. He shook his head to rid his hair of water.

A smile ghosted her lips.

"I'm sorry for what happened to you." He offered a soft smile in response to hers. "I will never do anything you don't want me to do. I will never do anything to make you worry for your safety. Do you believe me?"

She nodded.

"Okay," he said, drawing her close. "I'd like to kiss you if you don't mind, but I won't if you don't want me to."

She stroked his cheek. "I'd like that."

With a light touch, he took her face in his hands and touched his lips to hers, careful not to deepen the kiss unless she wanted him to, but when she didn't indicate a preference, he pulled away. He licked his lips and smiled down at her. "I like kissing you," he said. "I always have."

"I like kissing you, too," she said. "May I have one more?"

His smile deepened. "With pleasure." He lowered his face to hers again and this time, she parted her lips, and he did deepen the kiss. His heart thudded when, for the first time, she kissed him back, giving as well as receiving. His breath left him in a rush when her tongue darted into his mouth, tentative and uncertain. He slid his tongue along her lips and touched the tip of hers before backing off. He had an erection, but fearing another negative reaction, he was careful not to pull her close.

She broke the kiss and leaned her head against his chest like she used to. His heart hammered against his ribs and his knees were like rubber. He closed his arms around her and kissed the top of her wet head.

"Let's get you to your car before you catch your death of cold," he said and turned her toward the parking garage. Wrapped in each other's arms, they started walking.

"Jay?"

"Hmm."

"I was wondering. Tomorrow is Thursday. Would you let me make dinner for you?"

His heart took flight. "What time?"

By the light of the streetlight a few feet away, her smile of relief eased his concerns.

"How about five thirty?"

"Excellent." He studied her. "And thank you for telling me about your experience. You've explained some things I've been wondering about."

"Like what?"

"Like why you never let me into your house. I thought you were a hoarder or something," he teased.

Amy gasped. "Why you—!" Laughing she gave him a playful shove.

Jeremy wrapped his arms around her and kissed her again before growing solemn. He rubbed his knuckles along her jawline. "Seriously," he said. "Now I think I understand. You didn't feel safe having me in your home. I'm sorry if I made you think you couldn't trust me."

She shook her head. "I had different reasons for not letting you into my house, but the time has come for me to fess up."

He arched a brow. "What reasons did you have?"

She grinned up at him. "I'm a hoarder and I need help cleaning my house."

14

Dinner wasn't anything spectacular. Chicken marinated in Amy's favorite homemade secret sauce, potato salad, and asparagus. She hoped Jay liked what she prepared. If not, the meal would be a bust. But perhaps the entire night would be a bust anyway.

She left Ricky in the TV room watching a video while she cooked.

Many times, over the past two months, Amy started to tell Jeremy about her son, but always, at the last minute held back.

On the way to the maple festival, she'd tested the waters by admitting her divorce, but he hadn't acted pleased with the information, so she'd dropped the subject. After the Peking Acrobats, she was so full of enthusiasm and excitement, she almost blurted the truth. But after last night, Amy realized she couldn't keep Ricky hidden any longer. Her secrets were tripping her up.

By admitting her sexual assault, she felt enormous relief and the weight lifted from her. The fact he didn't gawk at her like she'd sprouted a third eye, or placed the blame on her, emboldened her. She only prayed she wasn't about to give him *Amy overload* with her son.

So many times today she kicked herself for her reaction to Adam. Now that she'd told Jay about her rape, would he figure out the rest? The minute he did, she was positive their relationship would be over.

No one will believe you. I have status in this town. You're a kid. The words zinged through her brain, leaving her breathless. She gripped the oven door handle, struggling to stay calm. Her stomach clenched and she fought the urge to vomit. Mustering all her strength of will, she pushed the fear away.

Not tonight. I won't let you take over tonight. Instead, she went back to the moment last night when Jay shook his head to rid himself of the rain soaking his hair. The move was so much like the Jay she remembered she had to work not to smile at the memory. Tonight though, she let her lips rise as her heart palpitated with emotion.

Tires crunched in her driveway, and she glanced at the kitchen clock. Five twenty-five. Punctual, as always.

Amy pulled herself together and smoothed her floral-patterned shirt, checking to make sure she hadn't spilled or dripped anything on it, an embarrassing habit.

Moving to the window, she waited as he turned off his car, unbuckled, and reached into the passenger seat. *Not flowers. Oh Jay, don't screw things up with flowers!*

He got out of the car carrying two bottles of wine and Amy closed her eyes in relief.

She moved away from the window so she wouldn't appear anxious about his arrival and went to the stove to check on the chicken. She'd never live down her mortification if she burned dinner. She pulled open the oven door and peeked in as Jeremy knocked.

"Come on in."

"Hello," he said when he entered. He was dressed in a blue Oxford dress shirt unbuttoned at the throat and tan dress pants with a thin brown belt.

Amy's heart raced at the sight of him. She liked him dressed like a professional.

"Hi." She greeted him with a kiss. "What did you bring me?" she teased, eyeing the bottles.

"Well, I don't recall if you're much of a drinker. In fact, I think we were too young back in the day, but since I didn't ask what you were preparing, I came armed with a red and a white." He held up each bottle.

She took the white. "We're having chicken if you don't mind. I can't afford red meat, which isn't healthy for you anyway, or so they say."

"I like chicken." Jeremy set the bottle of red down on the table set for dinner. He eyed the three plates, and the booster seat, and turned a questioning gaze to her. "Is this some kind of joke?"

She didn't answer the question. Opening her utensil drawer she pretended to rummage until she found the wine angel, handing it, along with the bottle, to him. "I tend to push the cork into the wine."

He took them from her, pulled out a chair, and sat down, placing the wine bottle between his knees. With a few deft movements, he popped the cork and set the bottle on the table, while Amy went to a cupboard and took down two wineglasses.

She washed greasy accumulated dirt from them and set them upside down on the counter. She almost never drank. In her mind, pathetic people drank alone, and she didn't want to be pathetic. She had enough problems.

"You set three plates out?" he tried again.

Amy steeled herself and turned a teasing smile on him. "Wow, Jay, your powers of observation are off the charts."

Cringing at his irritated expression, she apologized for the flippant comment. Last thing she wanted was to get the night off to a bad start.

She turned her back to him. Using the food as an excuse, Amy stirred the asparagus in the pan and turned off the burner. She checked the chicken again and punched the timer on the stove. Five more minutes. She had wanted to ease into this discussion, but she should have realized once he spied the extra place, he wouldn't let her. She sighed and turned to face him.

"Come with me." She headed down the short hallway to the TV room.

At the end of the hallway, she pushed the door open and stepped aside.

Ricky sat on the floor watching an old Sponge Bob SquarePants DVD Amy had found at a yard sale with wide-eyed, unflinching absorption.

She studied Jay's face for what she expected. Rejection. She waved a feeble hand.

"This is my son Ricky."

He studied the boy in silence and the longer Jay stayed quiet, the further her heart sank.

His brows flicked up and down. "Oh."

She couldn't figure out what he meant by his one word, but her heart panged.

Ricky shifted his focus and seeing them, got up and toddled to Amy. "I hongy, Mommy."

She knelt and lay a hand on his belly. "Supper's almost ready." She kissed his forehead. "I want you to meet a new friend. Can you say hello to Jeremy?"

Ricky stared up at Jeremy who also knelt. He held out his hand as if to shake. "Hello, Ricky," he said with a smile.

Ricky neither took Jeremy's hand nor said hello. He stared at him in wide-eyed wonder, sidled closer to his mother, and buried his face in her arm.

Amy stood, lifting him.

Jeremy rose. "Dinner smells wonderful and I'm hungry too." He walked back to the kitchen.

Amy's heart sank. *He doesn't want this and he's too polite to say so.* Well, she would struggle through dinner and wish him well, but for now, she pasted a happy smile on her face and headed back toward the kitchen. She prayed Jeremy might remain a friend. She was desperate for friends.

Amy sat Jay at the head of the table to her right and Ricky in his booster seat on her left to help him with his food.

Ricky bounced in his seat while she took his plate to the counter and cut up his chicken.

"So, Ricky." Jay leaned close his brow furrowed with pretend confusion. "How many are you?"

Ricky held up his thumb and first finger. "I dis many."

"Do you mean you're one with a thumb, or are you two?"

Amy laughed. "He's two. His birthday is at the end of the month, but he's still working on the concept of first and second fingers." She held hers up like a V.

"He's getting a real bed on Saturday," she continued and didn't care she sounded like a proud mama. "My father is bringing my old bed over."

"Does your dad need help?"

"I'm sure he wouldn't refuse a pair of hands that aren't mine."

Jeremy chuckled. "In that case, what time?"

"Around ten."

"I'd like to see your dad again." Jeremy studied the little boy. "What do you say, buddy? Your first bed. That's awesome."

Ricky threw his whole body into nodding his head, making Jay chuckle.

She had forgotten Jay's facility with children. He'd always liked kids and it must have served him well as a teacher. Which reminded her: "Did you speak to your student about her grades?"

"I worked with her today and proposed the idea to her. She agreed with enthusiasm, and I'm sure, a lot of relief. The school year ends in a month and a half, but I'm sure I can drag her over the finish line now, thanks to your suggestion."

She set Ricky's plate down before him, picked up his fork, and held it out to him. He took the utensil with his left hand. She ruffled his blond hair. "Attaboy."

She picked up Jay's dish, intending to place a piece of meat on it.

"I can cut my own food, thank you."

She turned, lifting a dubious brow. "You're sure?"

"Positive. I managed last night if you must know." He held up his hands to show he still had all his digits, keeping the index finger of his left hand bent to appear as if missing.

Amy laughed, giving a thumbs-up. "I'm impressed!"

As she moved close to give him his dish, he slipped his arm around her waist. She bent and kissed him before grabbing her own plate. "Don't wait for me to sit down. Start filling your plate. I run an informal household."

"Okay." He grabbed the potato salad.

Amy dropped a thigh on her plate and sat down. She filled her plate with asparagus and potato salad, remembered the wineglasses, and got up again to retrieve them.

Jay poured the wine.

She lifted her glass in salute. "Thank you for coming tonight."

He touched his glass to hers. "Thank you for inviting me. Is he what's been holding you back?" He gestured toward Ricky with his glass.

She nodded as she set her glass down. "I'm sorry for not being honest with you, but I didn't fall off a turnip truck either."

"Meaning?"

She picked up her fork and speared an asparagus stalk. Peering at him from the corner of her eye she said, "Meaning, I imagine in a day or two you'll kindly explain how much fun I've been, but now your priorities have shifted, and the time has come for you to move on."

He sat back and used his fork to tap at his chicken thigh while his brow knitted itself to the top of his nose. Clenching his left hand he moved it to his lap and shifted to a more upright position.

"Wow, Amy. What a cold thing to say."

She sighed and squelched her exasperation as she kept her gaze on her plate. "I understand how the world works, Jay."

His fork clattered on his plate, and he dropped his fists to either side. He leaned close, and with a glance at Ricky, spoke in a harsh whisper. "What makes you think I'd run because you have a kid?"

Copying him, she also leaned in and matched his irritation. "Because his father did."

Sitting back, Jeremy accepted her verbal slap down. He studied the boy learning to manipulate his fork, but with his mother's attention elsewhere, he grabbed his food and shoved his fist into his mouth, before wiping his fingers on his shirt, smearing chicken, potato, and mayonnaise.

Lowering his gaze to his plate, Jeremy squeezed back an amused grin. "He's cheating," he said, using his fork to point at Ricky in the process of shoving another handful of food in his mouth.

Amy turned. "Hey!" she barked.

Ricky froze, staring wide-eyed, and without taking his eyes from her, he found his fork and scooped his food.

Jeremy didn't dare laugh out loud, but his shoulders shook and when she turned to him, he lifted his wineglass and laughed into it.

Amy sputtered into laughter. "I have to admit he cracks me up."

He cleared his throat and swallowed some wine. "What happened to his father?"

Amy slipped a bite of chicken into her mouth and chewed. She kept her gaze on her plate.

Delighted to find she was an excellent cook, Jeremy continued to eat. He wanted to know what she used on the chicken.

"It's the other reason I invited you over," she spoke to her plate.

"Okay."

She glanced at him, straightened up in her chair, and pushed her food around on her plate, gathering her thoughts.

"I met Peter Cunningham the summer after I graduated from college."

A smile ghosted her lips. "We met through friends, and he kept asking me out and I kept refusing. I didn't want to date at the time, but him, in particular, I didn't want to date." She shrugged at his questioning stare. "I didn't think he was my type."

"But he kept after me and kept after me, so we went on a date. I was hoping he'd go away, but he didn't, and I was too polite to tell him to."

She chuckled without humor. "When you pulled up, I eyed you from the window," she said, switching direction in her narrative.

His gaze went to the window beside the back door and returned to her face.

"You reached into your passenger seat." She smiled at him. "And I thought if you came up with flowers, we were done because Peter always brought me a single red rose before every date and I thought, oh, how chivalrous."

"He's a player," Jeremy said, as a rush of protective anger hit him. How dare the jerk play with Amy's emotions and then leave her with a child to raise by herself. He hoped the day never came he met Peter Cunningham.

"Yeah." She half smiled. "I learned much later that's the mark of a player." Amy sighed and turned to watch Ricky.

When she lay a hand on his blond head, the boy beamed at her. She smiled back, her love for her son shining like a beacon in the room.

Jeremy's heart melted. At least one positive thing came from her marriage.

She turned back to him, and he focused on her face.

"After we married, and he figured he didn't need to impress me anymore, he brought home too many apology bouquets to count, if you get my meaning. Flowers became..." She swiped her lips with her fingers and sipped some wine. When she swallowed, she resumed her story.

"My instincts don't steer me wrong, but I paid no attention. I was twenty-two and wanted to get married. No one else came around banging at my door, so..." A negligent shrug and a sigh followed.

"So he was better than nothing," Jeremy said.

A small smile acknowledged his truth. "Didn't take me long to regret my decision either. The fights started right away, the constant criticism...the cheating. Before the first year was out, I wanted a divorce."

He cleared his throat and sipped more wine.

"Mommy," Ricky cut in.

She turned, looking relieved to focus on him.

"What, babe?"

Jeremy refilled their glasses.

"Wicky done."

"Okay." She got up and after a quick "Be right back," left the room. The bathroom faucet turned on and ran for a bit before shutting off.

Jeremy studied the little boy who sucked on first one hand, then the other. How was he to incorporate a child into his life? If he wanted Amy, he had to find a way. He had to admit Ricky was a cute kid with huge blue eyes and blond hair. He'd be long and lanky when he grew up and had the makings of a baseball player. A lefty too. Jeremy could teach him to pitch.

The boy beamed a smile at him.

Jeremy leaned forward. "What're you grinning at?"

Ricky didn't answer.

Amy returned with a washcloth spread over her right hand. She stopped beside her son. "Gimme."

Ricky removed a hand from his mouth and raised it. She cleaned. "The other."

He presented his other hand and when she finished, she went to the kitchen sink and rinsed the washcloth before returning to the little boy who held his grinning face toward the ceiling, arms out, waiting.

An amused smile quirked Jeremy's lips as they played their game.

"Three...two...one," and together they called, "incoming!" The washcloth closed in on the boy's face and hair.

Ricky laughed beneath the washcloth as Amy scrubbed the food away and left a smacking kiss on his lips.

She threw the washcloth into the sink and lifted him down from his chair. "Go play while Jeremy and I talk some more. Okay?"

"Okay." Ricky stopped at Jeremy's chair and stared up at him.

Jeremy smiled down into his huge blue eyes. "You have your mommy's eyes," he told the toddler. Then his mouth dropped open in shocked surprise when a grimace pulled Ricky's bottom lip tight and instant anger contorted his face. His tiny hands clenched into claws.

"Do not!" Ricky demanded.

He pressed his index finger next to his left eye until Jeremy feared he'd poke his eye out. "My eyes!" he declared and pointed to his mother. "Mommy's!"

Jeremy looked at Amy and the two dissolved into laughter. He picked up his wineglass and saluted the little boy. "Fair...enough," he managed to squeeze out between gales, which left his sides aching.

He turned to Amy, bent double, a hand over her mouth, laughing so hard tears sprang to her eyes.

Ricky eyed them, unsure what was so funny. Then he waved. "Bye, Jamie," he yelled, and took off running down the hall.

"B—bye, Ricky," Jeremy called, wiping his eyes. When the boy disappeared back into the TV room, he shook his head. "Holy crap, he's funny. You have your hands full. He's all boy."

He clenched his fingers into claws imitating Ricky. "What's that all about?"

Amy giggled some more. "He does that when he's mad. I can always tell when a tantrum is coming because"—she imitated him too— "the claws come out." Her blue eyes shone with love and laughter and Jeremy had an urge to take her by the hand and find her bedroom. He thanked heaven he was sitting down.

She sat and covered her eyes. "Oh man, he makes me laugh. I'd be lost without him. He keeps me going."

She sipped her wine. "Well, this family loves to call you anything but your real name. You're either Jay or Jamie."

He shrugged. "I don't mind." Along with a speculative look, he offered her a smile. "I see now why you work two jobs. You do need the money."

Her smile disappeared. "Yes." A nod acknowledged his truth. "But my hands aren't full so much as my parents. I sometimes think the only time I spend with him is when he's sleeping." Unamused tears filled her eyes, and she blinked fast. "I hate giving him to someone else to raise." She sniffed and drank.

Jeremy slipped his hand over hers. Turning sad eyes to him, she shrugged again and squeezed his hand then cleared her throat. "Let's go in the living room to talk, unless you're not finished."

"I'm done," Jeremy said, rising. "The meal was delicious. Thank you."

She grabbed the wine bottle and they moved into the living room.

Jeremy held out his glass. "Are we getting drunk?"

She poured and refilled her own glass. "Do you want to?" she said, setting the bottle down on the floor between them.

He didn't answer, not sure he wanted to enter this quandary. Her vulnerability came at him like a tsunami. He'd pace himself.

She cocked her head as though listening for something. "I should put Ricky to bed. I'll be right back."

"Okay."

Amy went into the back room, came back with a sleepy boy on her shoulder, and as she started upstairs, Ricky waved feeble fingers at Jeremy.

"Good night, Ricky," he said as they disappeared up the stairs. The floor creaked above his head.

From what he'd seen so far, she adored her son, and he understood her reluctance to introduce them too soon. Children complicated relationships. Still, he resented the implication he'd leave as a result.

Jeremy downed the rest of his wine, went into the kitchen to open the second bottle, and returned to the living room.

While he waited, he studied the room. The walls were painted a neutral tan with dark brown shades pulled halfway down the side windows. Houseplants crowded a long table, and beside the table stood a four-shelf bookshelf crammed with books.

A green oriental rug covered a hardwood floor. Paintings and photos hung on the walls. Her high school portrait hung on the stairway wall next to another young girl, Amy's younger sister, Lindsay. Between them, she'd placed Ricky's one-year portrait. Dressed in a blue shirt and white shorts, sitting among toys, his beaming smile shone from the frame.

The room was cozy and welcoming, unlike the man cave he lived in.

He sat down, sipped, and stared out the front picture window to the house across the street.

Footfalls echoed on the stair treads and within seconds, she emerged and sat next to him. Bracing her arm on the back of the couch she leaned her head on her knuckles to study him.

Jeremy caught and held her gaze. He yearned for an inkling of what she was thinking. Instead, he kissed her.

Laying her hand on his cheek, she kissed him back. Her thumb caressed his cheek, a light, feathery touch.

When she opened her lips, he pushed her back against the couch. His tongue slid across hers, tasting the wine. She made a small noise in her throat, and he pulled back, fearing she might not be ready for more, but not before grabbing one more kiss.

"Tell me why Peter left," he said against her lips.

She opened her eyes and gazed into his, searching, questioning.

He sat back. Sipped.

Amy straightened up and coughed once into her fist. "You would need to ask him. Despite what I said earlier, he didn't leave because of Ricky, though I do believe the fact of Ricky wouldn't have stopped him. The truth is, about three weeks after he left, I discovered I was pregnant." She gave him a sardonic glance and rolled her eyes. "Imagine my surprise and delight."

She drank.

"You could have had an abortion," Jeremy said. "Why didn't you?"

Not meeting his eyes, she shrugged. "I almost did. I had the appointment made and everything. One day, I was talking to one of my hospital co-workers, Debbie. I can't think why I told her what I was planning, but I did. Rather than talk me out of it, she told me about her abortion experience."

She glanced at him. "Not the abortion itself, but the emotional impact. The depression, guilt, and shame she experienced, which led to drug use." Shrugging again, she went on. "I figured I had enough problems without adding more, so I canceled the appointment."

She gazed at him, and his heart wrenched at the unspoken question in her eyes asking if Ricky was going to make a difference to him. The truth was, he hadn't yet decided.

She turned away. "Looking back, I'm glad I didn't do it. I can't fathom my life without him." She chuckled. "Sometimes his laughter is the only thing that keeps me going." She sighed.

"As for Peter, I didn't, and still don't, have any idea where to find the bastard. I confess I never put much energy into looking either."

Jeremy grinned at her words as she drained the wine in her glass and picked up the empty bottle of white. She scowled and put the bottle down.

He lifted the red and held the bottle out.

She offered her glass and he poured.

"He did some nasty stuff before he left. Like, drained our bank account. He left for work like always. No indication of his intentions."

She waved the wineglass in a sweeping gesture. "Just reminded me he and his father and brother were hunting that weekend and walked out the door."

Amy took a long swallow. "I went to work as usual and didn't expect him home until Sunday afternoon. Truth be told, I was looking forward to a weekend alone. I'd have two days of peace while he deer hunted." She sipped more wine.

"On Saturday, I stopped at the bank to withdraw cash for the grocery store, which is when I discovered he had wiped me out financially."

She sat forward on the sofa and crossed her arms over her knees, tipping the wineglass at a precarious angle.

Jeremy kept his eye on the glass, waiting for it to fall from her fingers or for the liquid to land on the floor.

She drank and dangled the glass. "Ten thousand dollars, gone from savings, another four thousand in my checking. I stood there with my mouth hanging open like a damned fool and the poor teller, sympathetic and embarrassed, told me Peter had come in the day before and withdrawn everything." Her eyes sheened over, and she blinked and pressed her wrist over her eyes.

She sniffed, and when she spoke, her voice clogged with emotion. "I tried calling him, but his phone kept going to voice mail. You can be sure I left some frantic messages, but he never answered. I called his mother to find out when they were coming back from camp. She said I was crazy because my father-in-law was in the living room watching the football game."

She cleared her throat. "My father-in-law got on the phone and said he didn't have a clue where Peter was, but if I'd been any sort of wife to my husband, perhaps this wouldn't have happened."

She lifted her glass for another swallow, saw it was empty, and lowered it. Jeremy took the glass from her hand and set it down on the floor then set his next to it.

Amy wiped tears away and resumed her story. "I called the landlord, but they'd deposited the check I'd sent. I told them the check would bounce and explained the situation and they were all apologetic and sympathetic on the phone, so I thought I was okay, but when it bounced, they evicted me."

She scrubbed her face. "I called his work but Donna, the secretary, told me he went AWOL three weeks prior, so the company fired him. I drove up to the hunting camp. Empty. His family refused to tell me anything. He's been gone ever since, and I don't care. Debbie, my coworker, her husband is an attorney. He told me under the circumstances I could file for a no-fault divorce. All I had to do was prove six months of separation so on six months and one day I was down in family court signing the papers." She huffed. "I've since learned he's remarried and living in New Hampshire."

Her words were slurred, and her voice shook. "When I started getting sick, I thought my anxiety was kicking in. My mother encouraged me to go to a doctor. Under the circumstances, she thought I might need some medicinal help, so when the doctor said I was pregnant, I wanted to die."

She put her hand over her eyes, puckered her lips, and with effort staved off her tears.

He leaned forward to comfort her, but she held her hand out to him in a stop gesture. He hesitated, then sat back.

She sniffed and wiped her nose on her wrist. "I'm sorry," she said. "Too much wine, I think. I'm not much of a drinker."

"It's all right," he said above a whisper.

He clutched the arm of her couch while she regained control. The urge to hold her and tell her everything would be okay, to say he would stick around, that in his heart he had never deserted her, wanted to burst forth, but he kept the words bottled up and he waited.

Though he made no move and said nothing, his sympathy must have communicated itself to her because she raised her tear-streaked face to him. "Kiss me," she whispered.

Jeremy moved close. Their lips touched. His hand found her jaw. Her lips opened and her tongue slid between his lips. Inhaling, he pulled her tongue further in. His mouth slanted across hers and his hand slid to the back of her neck.

She moaned into his mouth. Jeremy raised his head and gazed into limpid pools of blue, seeking acceptance and encouragement. When she lifted her chin, he found what he was looking for. He claimed her lips again, tasting wine and chicken on her tongue.

"Mommy," Ricky called.

Amy jerked as though a whip slashed across her back. She pulled back, turning her flushed face away.

"Yeah, Ricky." Her voice shook. Using her palm, she swiped her face and cleared her throat. Placing a hand on Jeremy's knee, she rose.

His voice drifted down to them. "I foosty, Mommy."

"Okay." She stopped at the bottom of the stairs. "I'll be right up. Stay in the crib."

Jeremy sat on the sofa, his elbow on the armrest, massaging his forehead as he struggled to bring himself back under control. It would have been so easy to push her down on the sofa, rip her clothes off, and do what he'd been fantasizing about since Valentine's Day.

Amy leaned against the stair rail and offered him an apologetic smile. "I'm sorry, Jay," she said. "But this is what it can be like. He can be an inconvenience, a burden, a pain in the ass, but he comes with the package and if you don't want the complete package then you need to move on."

She advanced. "I'm not asking you to move on. I don't want you to. Stay or go, the choice has to be yours. I'm just explaining the parameters of the bargain."

He studied her, tapping his fingers against the armrest. Coming to a decision, he stood.

"I think I'd better go." He grasped her elbows and smiled down at her. "Thank you for a delicious dinner."

Putting his knuckle under her chin, he lifted her face. "Thank you for sharing your story with me. I appreciate it." He spread his fingers, took her chin in a gentle grasp, and placed a soft kiss on her lips, offering promise but making no demands. He kissed her eyelids, tasting salty tears.

She wrapped her arms around his neck and held him tight.

Her soft floral perfume swirled around him making him tipsier than the wine. He tightened his embrace, allowing his emotions the freedom to express what words never could.

Her breasts pressed into his chest. He slid a hand around and squeezed.

Amy gasped and arched her back, pressing against his hand. She pulled his face down and claimed his lips.

"Mommy!" Ricky called again, insistent.

Jeremy snapped his head up, eyes closed, fighting to regain control.

When he opened his eyes again, they stared at each other, as if unsure how they got to this place. He released his breath and unclasped her arms from his neck, and with a light kiss on her lips, he gently pushed her away.

"Good night, Amy," he choked out and left.

15

Shaking like a leaf in a windstorm, Amy stood at the window watching as Jay strolled across her greening front lawn to his car. A deep ache gnawed at the pit of her belly and her heart pounded in her ears.

When he backed out of her driveway, she turned away, struggling to hold back overwhelming sadness.

"Moooommmy!"

"I'm coming," she called to Ricky and tried to squelch her irritation, but heat prickled her eyelids. He wouldn't want anything to do with her now. Not a drunken fool with a child in the picture. Fine. She didn't have to explain about Adam.

He walked out. He doesn't want you. Not like you want him. Not with Ricky. Let him go.

She resolved to do that, but her breast tingled where he'd touched and squeezed. Desire, like a physical ache, pulsed through her body and she groaned.

In the kitchen, she got down a sippy cup, which she filled halfway with water and brought upstairs.

After Ricky drank his fill, she left the cup next to his crib, laid him back down, and went downstairs to clean up, making a mental note to check his Pull-Ups before she went to bed.

Instead, she sat at the table and poured herself more of the red. No sense in wasting the wine. She'd clean up later.

As she drank, Amy stared in sullen despair at the messy kitchen. "This was a huge mistake. I never should have told him."

She sighed and drank some more. "He pretended to accept Ricky."

Another swallow. “Well, why not? A free meal is a free meal, right? He couldn’t leave fast enough.” *Asshole.* Amy deliberately beat herself up so that when he either rejected her outright or simply ghosted her, she’d be prepared. Expectation management.

“Why did I tell him? Now he hates me.” She sniffed and wiped her face.

“Ugh!” The sound of her hands slapping the table was loud in her ears as she pulled herself to her weary feet. “Well, no more. I tell you no more, Jeremy Austin. If you’re going to run, I’m done.” She hollered to her back door before dropping into her seat again. “Fuck. Now I’m drunk enough to start talking to myself. I’m so pathetic.”

She rose again, gathered up the remnants of her meal, and scraped the plates into the trash before rinsing and stacking them in the dishwasher. With a full day of work tomorrow and Lou’s right after, she couldn’t leave a messy kitchen. Sometimes though, she wished she had someone to help carry the load.

With the kitchen cleaned, she picked up the half-empty bottle of wine, intending to pour more, but changed her mind. Her stomach was growing sour. She took the bottle to the sink and dumped the red liquid, along with the remainder of her glass, before jamming the glass in the dishwasher and hitting start.

A glance at the kitchen clock showed a little past nine. She locked the kitchen door, drew the blinds, turned off the light, and headed to bed. Perhaps the wine would help her sleep.

Jeremy schooled himself to drive with care. The wine buzzed his head and his blood still flowed hot from denied passion. It had been more than a year since he’d had sex and the drought deepened.

But what kind of man walks away from his family? From her? Jeremy couldn’t.

A conversation he’d had with Charlie while in Florida popped into his head as they drove home from the ballgame.

“Jeremy was quite the stud in college,” Charlie teased him while telling Jonathan.

“I was not,” Jeremy said.

Since Jon was driving, Charlie turned in the passenger seat and faced him. “Yes, you were. You had a new girlfriend every month for a while. Maya used to call them the flavor of the month, but what always struck me, was how much they all resembled Amy. All blue-eyed, all with straight brown hair, same height, same weight give or take."

From the back seat, Jeremy stared at him flabbergasted.

Charlie nodded. "With the exception of Maggie." He'd gone on to say he hoped with Maggie's long frame, auburn hair, and hazel eyes, Jeremy had finally gotten Amy out of his system, but Charlie had been wrong. In his heart, Jeremy never left Amy.

He had no doubts about staying with her, but would she think he stayed because he wanted to or because he was trying to prove her wrong? Amy was obstinate when she wanted to be, and he remembered how hard he had to work to convince her of something once she set her mind on a different interpretation of the facts.

And Amy was convinced he'd leave her now. But the truth was, her son was adorable. His beaming smile made Jeremy go weak at the knees if such a thing was possible from an almost three-year-old. When he grinned at him, he saw Amy's school girl grin, innocent and unfettered by life. A stab of unexpected jealousy hit him square in the chest. She'd let someone else father her child. Ricky should be his. With effort, he stuffed down his irritation. Wasn't her fault he was nowhere in the picture.

His phone rang and "Twin" flashed on his dash display screen. He punched the accept call button. "Emma! How the hell are you, sis?"

A pause. "What's gotten into you?" Her voice, full of suspicion, came through the radio speakers.

"Nothing," he said too fast. "I had some wine tonight."

"You sound funny. Where are you?"

"In my car. I'm on my way home from a date." With his tongue, he snapped the T in date.

Emma sighed. "Drinking and driving, Jeremy? Are you out of your mind?"

"Oh, don't go all lawyerish on me," he said. "If I want that shit, I'll talk to Dad."

"Are you back with Maggie?" she asked. "I had a sense I needed to call you tonight."

He glanced at his dash. "To answer your question, no, but if I was, why so...nasty?"

"I have nothing against Maggie," she said. "I just never liked the way she strings you along. She's the kind of woman who, if I'd met her alone, I might have liked her enough to call her a friend, but I didn't. So I don't."

"Wow." He braked for a light. "I had no idea."

"Sorry, but it's the truth."

"Why is this all coming out now?" His brows furrowed over his nose. "I mean, first Charlie, now you. Why are you telling me things now?"

"Charlie said something?" she asked. "What did he say?"

Jeremy drew in a deep breath through his nose and exhaled. "He called her the ice queen and Jon said it was something he started, but Charlie basically said the same thing. He didn't think Maggie made me happy and if I was done with her, he was relieved."

He negotiated a turn in the road. "So I ask again, why now?"

"I don't know," Emma said. "Sounds as if you're now in a place where we can tell you these things and you'll listen."

Perhaps. He shrugged as if Emma sat in the passenger seat and could see him. He didn't want to talk about Maggie. "You don't like anyone you think might do me wrong," he said. "Hey, Em, can I tell you something? In confidence?"

"Sure."

He hesitated. "Um, I've been seeing someone, since, well, Valentine's Day—"

"Jeremy! How wonderful! Why didn't you tell me this before, you jerk?"

He chuckled. "Well, because I wasn't sure how you'd react. I haven't told anyone in the family because I was worried about...condemnation."

"Oh, dear God, Jer, who is she?" Emma sounded disgusted, as if she needed to protect him from another Maggie. "A hooker off the streets?"

"Emma! Come on!" Surprise made him shout. "Have you been talking to Adam?"

"What?"

"I don't *do* hookers."

She paused. "I was being sarcastic, but now I'm confused. What has Adam to do with anything and why would we condemn either one of you?"

"Because" he paused before plunging in. "I'm seeing Amy Taylor again. I had dinner at her house tonight."

She stayed silent so long he thought he'd dropped the call, but the phone didn't make the distinctive *ploop* of a lost connection.

"Emma?"

"I'm here," she snarled. "So you're back with her."

Emma's attitude was why he didn't tell Charlie. No way he'd say anything to Maya either. She'd kill him then go after Amy.

"Yes."

"Honestly, Jeremy! Your taste in women! After what she did to you, why?"

Sighing, he turned his car onto US 7, and headed north, staring straight ahead.

"I still love her, Emma." He swallowed hard with the admission and his hands gripped the steering wheel. "I love her. I always have. Till my dying day." He flexed his fingers willing his hands to relax.

"After all these years?" Her voice sounded tight. "After all she did to you," she said again. "To us?"

He gripped the wheel again and glanced at his dashboard as if his sister's face floated in the display lights. "Please don't make me regret telling you."

"Oh, Jeremy," she said, and her disappointment almost dripped from his speakers. "She put you in the hospital. They had to operate on your leg because she knocked you down. For a while, Mom and Dad thought you were going to..." She didn't finish the thought.

"Take my own life, I know." His chest grew tight with the admission and heat radiated from every pore of his body, flaming his face. He had never been suicidal, just enraged and too young to understand what to do with his rage. But the idea his parents thought he might kill himself shamed him.

Jeremy drove through the gathering darkness, casting deep shadows on the protected wetlands outside Colchester. Mating birds swooped and swirled in the gathering May dusk. Leaves budded in trees, greening the landscape after the long cold winter. In the west, the last glow of the sun reflected pink and orange on the gathering clouds above the silver ribbon of Lake Champlain.

His headlights picked up a turn in the road and he braked to slow down as their conversation came to a standstill.

When she didn't speak again, he picked up his end. "Hey, Em, what do you remember about that day?"

Emma's sigh sounded as if she wished he'd never asked. "Uh...I remember us coming in the house after school. We were all laughing and joking with each other, and Amy sat on the kitchen stool. She kept her back to us. I don't remember much more. Impressions more than anything. What I do remember most, Maya said something about Dad and Adam going golfing, you said "'Hi,'" and dropped your hand on her shoulder, and she went off like a Katyusha rocket, screaming and crying—and knocking you to the floor—before running from the house."

Jeremy nodded in places, confirming Emma's memories matched his own. Remembered pain shot down his right thigh at the memory of her pushing him off balance, his crutches flying over his head, the unyielding cast twisting his torso as he landed on the kitchen tiles. The instant it happened he realized he'd rebroken his femur, and once he'd regained his breath, he screamed bloody murder.

"I remember the same thing," he said. "But I never figured out why." He shifted in his seat and the pain evaporated.

"Me either," Emma said. "That still doesn't justify her actions."

Jeremy sighed. "I handled things badly in those days too, Em. I chased her down, tried to force her to tell me what happened, which only drove her further away." A light turned red. He braked. "I'm trying a new tactic now."

"Oh yeah—?" Emma chuckled. "What?"

"Well, as Mom would say, "'You attract more flies with honey—"

"Than you do with vinegar," Emma finished. "What's the honey?"

Jeremy chuckled. "Why, my charm of course."

Emma scoffed, but they laughed.

Another pause and Jeremy opened his mouth to say something when Emma spoke again. "I suppose I made mistakes too. I tried to find out what happened, but she wouldn't tell me. So I tried to make her listen to reason. I tried to guilt her for your leg, and I did make her cry, but she didn't apologize or come visit you."

Emma paused, then went on. "Finally I cornered her on the tennis court at school and called her every filthy name I could think of because I was so mad at her. She let me ream her ass, Jer. She took my ranting in silence, which, looking back was so unlike her. She didn't try to defend herself. She acted like she agreed with me when I called her things like a cheap bitch." Emma hitched a breath. "I was trying to make her mad, but I couldn't. And when I finished, she just said she was sorry and walked away."

A heavy sigh. "Are you sure you want to date her again, Jer? I don't mean to be negative, but I also don't want her to hurt you again. Amy was my best friend, but I will never forgive her for the way she treated you. Not explaining, cutting you off, shredding your heart like a plaything she no longer wanted." A pause. "She ditched the entire family. She ditched me too."

His heart lurched at the thought. Emma had tried to get through to her, believing their friendship would overcome everything, but she'd been wrong. Amy abandoned her and he recalled how much the rejection hurt. Emma cried for weeks at the loss of her best friend.

What his poor parents must have gone through between the two of them.

"Does she still call you Jay?"

He chuckled. "Yes." He licked his lips. "Em, I would appreciate keeping this conversation between us for now."

"Fine." Emma sighed. "I hope you understand what you're doing, little brother."

Jeremy smiled. "I'm only your little brother by eight minutes, elder sister."

"Still makes you the baby in the family."

Jeremy pulled into his driveway and said good night to Emma before disconnecting.

He unlocked his door and hung his coat on the tree inside. He called this room the entrance room because he had no other name or purpose for it. At some point, the room had been a back deck until someone enclosed the space and added a small bathroom on the right, then built another back deck off the door.

Tan utility carpet covered the floor, which he often thought of replacing, but in the four years he'd lived here, he'd never bothered. The walls were wood panel, and the room was empty.

Moving into the kitchen, Jeremy stepped around the bar that jutted into the room and cut it in two. He went to the fridge to grab a beer but thought better of drinking any more. He'd had enough alcohol. He let the fridge door swing shut and moved into the living room.

Eyeing his surroundings, he compared them to Amy's warm and welcoming home. In this room, the walls were a medium blue and his leather sofa and recliner chair, the only pieces of furniture besides a small coffee table, were black. He had no pictures on the walls, just his sixty-four-inch TV attached to the far wall. Blinds on the windows instead of curtains blocked the casual viewer from peering in, but they were only there because his mother had put them up when he moved in.

To his right, a staircase with a landing led to the upper floor and his bedroom, also sparsely furnished with a bed, dresser, and a nightstand.

He moved down a short hall to a small bedroom he'd converted into a computer room. His laptop lay unopened on a desk in the middle of the room.

Returning to the living room, Jeremy dropped himself onto his sofa and turned on the TV to catch a few minutes of the ballgame.

Over and over, his mind played his interlude with Amy in her living room. If not for the wine and the exquisite timing of a certain toddler, his year-long drought of celibacy might have ended tonight.

His body responded to his wanderings, and he got up and readjusted himself before sitting back and concentrating on the ballgame.

His conversation with Emma stirred afresh those things he thought long buried. Anger, hurt, confusion, and heartache stabbed him like a sword to the heart, as if Amy's desertion had happened that morning.

Once he got home from the hospital, he tried for weeks to make her talk to him, but every time he confronted her, she'd duck into a girl's bathroom or change direction. Still hobbled by a full leg cast and crutches, he did his best to chase her down.

He'd made Charlie drive him to her house one afternoon and refused to leave, demanding answers, insisting she admit to his face she didn't love him anymore. She retreated indoors and refused to come out of her house, and Jeremy only left when Mr. Taylor threatened to call the police and Charlie dragged him, screaming epithets, back into the car, crutches and all.

He shifted on his sofa again, face burning at the stupidity of his eighteen-year-old self and tried to push away his memories by concentrating on the game, though he had no idea what inning they were in, which team they were playing, or who was up.

An image of Ricky beaming at him as he waited for Amy to come from the bathroom, a washcloth draped over her hand was...adorable. No doubt. He was smitten.

His phone dinged. Leaning forward, he dug it out of his back pocket. "Twin" flashed on a text message Jeremy thumbed open, and his eyes widened. “I also remember a lot of blood. In the bathroom.”

Blood? In the bathroom? What did she mean? Why would there have been blood in the bathroom?

Before he was able to process this strange information, his back door rattled as though someone tried to unlock his door. He closed the text, and as he moved to the entrance room, he dropped his phone on the charger on the kitchen counter.

The evening had been full of revelations and surprises and Jeremy didn’t want any more tonight. He pulled the door open, blinked, and scowled. Maggie stood on his back deck dressed in a pair of tight designer jeans and a green silk blouse. Gold chains around her neck touched her cleavage, which she left on display. She held her set of keys.

I have nothing against Maggie. I just never liked the way she strings you along. She’s the kind of woman who, if I’d met her alone, I might have liked her enough to call her a friend, but I didn’t. So I don’t.

“Hi,” she said and moved to step inside.

He was going to be polite and let her in, but his tired, wine-soaked brain shot words out of his mouth like a cannon.

“You lied to me,” he said. “How many times over the years have you done that?”

He stepped back and slammed the door in her astonished face, locked it, turned off the light, and went to bed.

16

Amy lay in bed staring into the darkness. A glance at her alarm clock showed eleven. She stared at the ceiling and wished to die. What was Jay doing now? Why did she make such a stupid move? In what universe was inviting him over to introduce him to Ricky a smart idea? What made her think he was ready for the news?

Because of the wine. And once I started drinking...And throwing myself at him like a cheap whore...God!

She slapped her hands over her face and groaned. She'd been so stupid! Slamming her hands down to her sides, Amy grabbed the blankets and yanked them over her head, rolled over, and faced the wall.

Hot tears slid down the side of her face. Jay didn't want her. Because of the rape or Ricky? He'd acted so gentle and kind when she told him what happened, but what if he was like Peter, always presenting one side until the ugly parts couldn't stay hidden any longer?

Not Jay. He had never been that kind of operator, but people could change. And he did want her. No. Lusted for her. Nothing more. Not the same thing.

It was spring. Mating season.

Trying to conjure up every negative nasty argument, she tormented herself with doubt, but in the back of her mind, she understood. Jay being Jay, he'd stopped because of the wine—and Ricky.

Amy got up and by the light of the night light studied her son's innocent, sleeping face. An intense wave of love washed over her. What would she do without this little boy in her life? Her difficulties weren't his fault but facing them without him was impossible.

He sprawled across the crib, which he'd outgrown more than a year before, so she settled him closer to the middle and pulled up the blankets. Pressing her fingers to her lips she lay them on his forehead and went downstairs. Ricky needed a new bed, but she couldn't afford one and when she finally confessed to her parents about her problem, her father made a disgusted noise.

"Well, why didn't you say so sooner, Amy?" he'd growled. "I have your bed in the basement. I was just waiting for you to tell me when you needed it."

Her life was full of miscommunication.

She picked up her phone and called Jay, but he didn't answer. "Hi, this is Jeremy. If you're a student, Mr. A. Leave a message," sounded in her ear. She smiled at the Mr. A designation, hesitated, then left a message. "Hey, Jay, this is Amy. Um, we both had a bit too much to drink tonight, so I'm checking to make sure you got home okay." She stopped and waited. "When you get this message, call or text, so I know you're okay." Another pause. "Well, okay. Bye."

She disconnected and held the phone in her hand, thinking. After a moment, she made another call.

"Hi," Lindsay said in a sleepy voice. "What's up?"

"Too late to talk?"

"Never."

"Good." Amy burst into tears.

While Jeremy sipped his morning coffee and got ready for work, he checked his phone and found two messages, both from Amy. He dropped two slices of bread into the toaster before searching for the Advil. His head ached and his mouth was fuzzy as if he'd chewed cotton all night long.

He found the bottle and dumped two into his hand to down with his coffee. While he waited for his toast, he dialed in for his messages.

In her first message, she asked if he'd gotten home all right since they'd had so much to drink. She was sweet to worry. At the prompt, he hit save. He saved all her messages. When he missed her, which was every minute they spent apart, he listened to them for the sound of her voice.

The second message popped up. “Call from...” the mechanical voice said, “Amy Taylor...time...twelve...forty-five...a.m.... Friday...May...tenth....” Beep.

“Hi, Jay, this is Amy again.” A pause. “Um. I wanted to say you don’t have to come to pick me up tomorrow night. Well no, I guess that would be tonight. Friday. At Lou’s. You don’t have to come tonight.”

Jeremy stopped buttering his toast and scowled at the phone. What game was she playing now?

“I’ll understand if you don’t want to come around anymore. I can’t imagine how difficult things might be dating a woman encumbered with a child.” She sniffed.

“And you don’t have to come help with Ricky’s bed. I appreciate the offer, but um if you have other things to do, I’ll understand.”

Was she still bombed? Delusional?

“Anyway, um. I hope we can remain friends, but um, I think I would prefer not to pursue a relationship with you...with anyone...for now.” Another sniff. “I’m sorry, Jay.” The phone went dead.

He stared and his mouth hung open. Emma was right.

Raising his coffee cup to his lips he sipped and stared at the phone. What happened after he left? He punched his messages and listened to them again hoping to ascertain where she went from making sure he arrived home safely to I don’t want to see you again.

He chewed his toast, sipped coffee, and listened. After the third time through, he dumped the remains of his cup in the sink and stormed to the bathroom to brush his teeth. When he was done, he punched the messages again. When they played through one more time, he slipped his phone into his back pocket.

Tough luck, Amy. He had promised to help set up Ricky’s bed and he kept his promises. She wasn’t getting off so easy. Not this time. He grabbed his backpack and his keys and stormed out of the house.

When Amy answered the door, he didn’t smile at her surprised expression.

“I told you I’d come to help. Here I am,” he challenged with a glare. “If I’m allowed in.”

“Of course you are.” She sounded breathy, and her fingers played with her shirt collar. She stepped back, pulling the door open.

Extending a hand, she said, “You remember my dad, don’t you?

Dad, this is Jeremy Austin."

Mr. Taylor extended his hand. "Welcome back, son."

"Thank you, Mr. Taylor." Jeremy shook the older man's hand. Amy's father had changed quite a bit. His dark hair was now gray and deep lines furrowed his face, but his blue eyes, so much like Amy's, still sparkled with the gentle humor his daughter had inherited.

Nevertheless, his heart pounded. The last time Jeremy had seen Mr. Taylor, he'd threatened to call the police for harassing Amy, but her father appeared not to remember the incident. Instead, he chuckled. "You're an adult now, call me John."

Jeremy nodded. "John."

"Well, I must say"— John picked Ricky up and sat him on his lap— "this explains who Jamie is." He chucked Ricky under the chin. "All day yesterday and this morning, all this boy talked about was Jamie this and Jamie that."

Jeremy smiled and shook Ricky's sneakered foot. "I didn't think I made much of an impression, but I like this little bag of energy." He glanced at Amy. She eyed him with suspicion and turned away.

"He is a bundle for certain. Keeps his Grammy and Poppy busy."

John set Ricky on his feet. The boy stared up at Jeremy, who smiled back at him.

Jeremy held out his hand. "Happy to make your acquaintance again, Rick."

Not sure what to do, Ricky sucked his two middle fingers, then removing his hand from his mouth, he slapped Jeremy's palm with a high five and put his fingers back in his mouth.

Jeremy and John exchanged amused glances, and wrinkling his nose, Jeremy wiped his palm on his jeans, before clapping his hands together. "Well, John, what do you say? I saw the makings of a bed in the back of your truck when I came in. Are you ready to wrestle the bed, box spring, and mattress?"

"Let's do this," John agreed, and together they headed outdoors.

The stairway was narrow and both men struggled to bring the mattress and box spring up them. By the time they did, Jeremy had worked up a sweat. He pulled his T-shirt from his chest and sweat dripped down his back.

"How you doing, John? Need a break?"

John shot him an amused glance. "I may be old, son, but I ain't dead yet."

Jeremy chuckled.

Following behind them with her vacuum, Amy snickered.

He ignored her.

"No, sir, you're not."

In the other room, she set up and plugged in the vacuum and moved in and out of his vision while the vacuum hummed. He planned to have it out with her as soon as they were alone. Until then, he would pay as little attention to her as possible. Make her sweat for a change. Figuratively anyway. He pulled at his shirt again.

Once the men took the crib apart, Amy vacuumed the area before carrying the pieces down to the basement.

While they worked, the two men used few verbal cues to put the bed together. They grunted at each other or used one- or two-word sentences such as "right there" or "hang on" while they set up Ricky's bed.

It was impossible for him to ignore Amy standing inside the bedroom door, arms crossed, watching and waiting for them to finish.

When the mattress was on, she opened a package of bedsheets with tiny red, blue, and green dinosaurs and began to make the bed.

"I have one more request for you two strong men." She tilted her head to one side.

Suspicious, Jeremy narrowed his eyes. "Your wish is our command, my lady," he teased with a slight bow because her father was in the room, but he shot her a dark glare.

"Oh, be careful what you ask for, dear sir"—. She smiled.

He dropped his hands to his hips, cocked a foot forward, and scowled. A what-do-you-want eyebrow rose until her smile disappeared.

He smirked.

"Um, I wondered if you'd be willing to move my bed into the room across the hall. If Ricky's old enough to have a bed, he's old enough to have his own room."

Jeremy and John glanced at each other.

John shrugged. "Sounds reasonable to me. What do you think, Jeremy?"

He waved a hand. "Let's go." Within minutes the two men had Amy's bed deconstructed and moved while she made up her son's bed. When she finished, despite her protestations, Ricky jumped up and down on the mattress and called to "Jamie" to come and see.

"Hang on, bud," Jeremy called back as he and John put Amy's bed back together.

While they worked, Amy's voice drifted to them. "Oh, gross. Dust bunnies galore." The vacuum hummed to life again.

When she finished, she unplugged the vacuum and took it downstairs. A shriek rent the air, and as he and John rushed from her new bedroom, Amy bolted up the stairs and pushed Jeremy out of the way to stand in front of him.

He stared in disbelief as the boy threw himself on the floor, weeping and screaming, his fingers contracted into little claws.

Amy gawked at her father as if seeking his help. John knelt in front of Ricky. "Now, now, what is this?" He wrapped the boy in his arms. "Tell Poppy what's got you all kerfuffled?"

Red-faced, and shaking like a leaf, Ricky hiccupped and pointed at the place where Amy's bed used to be. "Mooooommmmmyyyyy!" He hiccupped more sobs.

Amy went to her son and took him from her father's arms. She crooned and kissed him and gently rocked while he calmed down. Over the boy's head, she met Jeremy's eye and her gaze said, *This is what I tried to tell you.*

He became aware he still held a screwdriver and returned to her new room. Ricky wasn't his son and she had things under control. Best he stayed out of the way. From across the hall, he listened while she shushed and crooned, and Ricky hiccupped and wept.

Amy patiently explained she wasn't leaving him and walked him to her new room where Jeremy and Poppy silently worked on her bed.

When he understood she would be sleeping here from now on, she led him back to his room and redirected him with questions about what kind of play area he wanted where her bed used to be.

Jeremy glanced at John who grinned at him. "You'll grow used to such outbursts, son. If you don't, you won't last long." He accompanied his words with a sideways assessing gaze.

Jeremy caught the warning in the man's voice. He gestured with the screwdriver. "What was that all about?"

"Thought his mother was leaving him."

Jeremy jerked his head back. "Seriously?" He peered into the other bedroom where Amy stayed on her knees, pointing and talking to him. She kept her arm around his little waist while she dried his tears and kissed his hair.

Ricky was calmer now and was soon clapping his hands. He gave a small jump while she talked. He turned back to John. “How did you figure that out so fast?”

John smiled. “I raised two of my own. As I said, you grow used to it.” With a conspiratorial wink, he returned to work.

When they finished, Jeremy stopped inside Ricky’s bedroom door. Mother and son lay prone on the floor creating a dinosaur park and a racetrack area. If it was possible, he fell more in love with both of them.

After Amy made her bed, she herded them downstairs to pay the men back with a couple of hot dogs and a beer.

Ricky tried to jump on Jeremy’s back while hollering, “Play with me, Jamie,” despite Amy telling him to stop.

Willing to entertain the boy, Jeremy dropped to his knees and grabbed Ricky. Growling, he pretended to throw him on the floor before tickling his belly. Ricky screamed with laughter and squirmed trying to hide his stomach under his small hands. Jeremy laughed with him before releasing him. He rose up to his knees.

The boy rolled to his belly before jumping to his feet. Running around behind Jeremy, he leaped on his back, knocking him flat to the floor.

“Jay!” Amy threw her hands over her mouth. Above her fingers, her blue eyes were round with concern. “Are you alright?”

Jeremy chuckled. “I’m fine. I did it on purpose. I’m not hurt.” He raised himself to his knees again and reached over his head to drag Ricky over his shoulder and into his arms. He blew a raspberry on the boy’s stomach. Ricky shrieked with laughter and wriggled out of his arms.

John raised a brow. “You sure you know what you’re doing, Jeremy?”

He laughed. “I have three nephews.” He made his fingers into claws and growled at Ricky. Ricky copied him and growled back.

“Well, I’m outta here before he takes my old knees out from under me.” John kissed Amy’s cheek as she thanked him. He said goodbye to his grandson.

“Bye-bye Poppy.” Ricky raised his arms and Poppy lifted him, planted a kiss on the boy’s cheek, then set him back on his feet.

“Welcome back, Jeremy.”

“Take care, sir,” Jeremy said and his breath whoofed out in a pained gasp as Ricky barreled headfirst into his abdomen. He wrapped one arm around his midsection and braced his other hand on the floor thanking God Ricky's head didn't land lower. He did want children someday. He blinked away tears of pain.

"Five'll get ya ten *that* wasn't on purpose." John's cackling laugh followed him out the door.

"Enough!" Amy grabbed her son and smacked him on the butt. "You don't hurt people."

Ricky's lower lip puckered, and Jeremy pitied him a little. "He's okay." He got to his feet. "He landed high enough to avoid doing any serious damage."

Amy stared at him with skepticism. "Yeah, well...he needs to learn."

She made Ricky apologize before turning him loose to play in the TV room. He wasted no time doing as told.

When he was gone, Jeremy stared at her, struggling for something to say. He'd wanted to have it out with her but wasn't sure how to start.

Amy eyed him up and down. "I said you didn't have to come today."

"I told you I would."

She nodded and squeezed her lips together. She opened her mouth to say something, but instead, pressed her lips again. Her gaze swept him and landed on the floor between them.

"What happened?" he asked.

She shook her head.

"Tell me what happened," he pressed, unsure if he was asking about the other night or ten years ago.

"Nothing. I... I just..." She broke off and eyed him. "Why do you want me? I'm a wreck, I suck at relationships. A soiled loser. I can't even keep a creep like my ex-husband in my life, so why would you want someone like me? You can have any woman in the world! Why me? A single mother with nothing to show for her life but an almost three-year-old boy and two lousy jobs."

Amy threw her hands over her face and stormed into the kitchen.

Jeremy found her standing in front of the sink, staring out the window. He slid his palms across her shoulders and leaned his forehead into the back of her head.

"I don't want any woman in the world. I want you, Amy Taylor," he said into her hair. He grasped her shoulders and turned her around.

"I love you. I always have. I always will. No matter how much of a wreck and a loser you think you are, you are beautiful and valuable to me."

Jeremy gathered her into his arms. "You're a wonderful mother. Ricky's lucky to have you. I'm lucky to have you. We can't live without you."

Amy wrapped her arms around him and wept.

17

Amy cried while Jay held her and crooned to her. Tucking her into his arms, he stroked her hair with one hand and rubbed her back with the other, while rocking back and forth as if she were a child.

In his arms, she felt a safety she hadn't known since she was a teenager and he held her then, too. He was as he had always been. Her rock, her security. Jay was back and he loved her, so her tears poured out and she was helpless to stop them.

She'd called Lindsay after he left the other night and cried to her about how she'd introduced Jay to Ricky and described how he'd left. She knew she'd garbled her story and couldn't remember if she told Lindsay that he stayed for dinner or not, stayed to talk afterward or if she just told her she introduced the two and Jay left. That part still remained in the fog of her inebriation. She admitted the wine drinking because she couldn't hide it. Amy seldom drank and between her tears and her slurred speech, she didn't make a good impression on her sister, who told her to dump Jeremy if he wasn't willing to accept Ricky.

So she'd called him back and left a message telling him she didn't want to see him anymore, her heart in her throat all the while as she wondered whether he'd accept her decision this time.

When he showed up that morning, her heart almost stopped beating and relief flooded her soul and made her face redden, which she knew by the heat that flowed from her heart to her hairline.

At last, she stopped crying, mostly because Jay was kissing her hair, her eyes, and her lips, and she couldn't cry and return his kisses at the same time.

He pulled back, and smiling, wiped her eyes and face with his hands. “Feel better?”

Nodding, she turned her face away, but he gently turned her back.

“Mind telling me what that was all about?”

A shrug. “I’m not sure. I’m so glad you came this morning.”

“I said I would.”

“I know. You’re a man of your word and I love that about you, but I feel like I make your life a living hell and you could do so much better than me.”

Jay chuckled and placed a soft kiss on her temple. “You just don’t get it, do you?” he softly whispered in her ear. “You pulled me from a living hell, and I don’t want anyone else, better or otherwise. I want you.”

He pulled away and gazed into her eyes. His soft, brown, almond-shaped eyes crinkled at the edges as he smiled down at her. “I love you. I always have. I always will.” His eyebrows rose and he licked his lips. “Like it or not, Amy Taylor, I’m not going anywhere this time.”

Drawing him back to her, she once again melted into his embrace. She lay her head on his shoulder and reveled in the feel of his strong arms encircling her, giving her his comfort and his love, and she soaked him in like a sponge absorbs water.

“Maybe we should go see what he’s up to,” Amy suggested when she realized she hadn’t heard any noise from the TV room.

They found Ricky sprawled on the floor, thumb tucked in his mouth, surrounded by dinosaurs, brontosaurus beneath sleeping fingers. Jeremy lifted him into his arms and carried him upstairs with Amy on his heels.

She tucked him in, and Ricky rolled over, thumb still in his mouth, and sighed in his sleep.

They exchanged a smile. Jay grasped Amy’s hand and led her into her new bedroom.

Shutting the door, he took her into his arms and kissed her. The pit of her stomach jolted and twisted as a shot of hot desire pierced her.

“I was thinking.” Jay smiled down at her. “I’d hate for you to climb into bed tonight and have the damned bed collapse on you.” He brushed his lips against hers. “I think we’d better test your bed to make sure."

"You do, do you?" She smiled as his lips found her cheeks and eyelids.

"Mm-hmm."

His hands slid up her sides and cupped her breasts. Her heart pounded and her breath stuttered in her throat. Rocking her head back, Amy closed her eyes as his lips slid down her neck and he pushed up her shirt. When her hands found the sides of his face, she didn't guide him so much as follow his lead.

He lifted his head, brows quirked in a question. "How long does he nap for?"

Amy stared, uncomprehending, then sputtered into laughter.

Jay looked affronted, which only made her laugh more. She tried to pull his head down to kiss him, but he resisted.

"I'm not kidding. How much time do we have here?"

She continued to laugh, pressing her face into his chest, she shook in his arms.

The absurdity must have struck him because he too laughed. "I've never had to ask such a question before," he said, chuckling. "You'll have to forgive me."

Amy covered her mouth while she pulled herself together. "On average, he sleeps about two hours. Will that give you enough time?" she asked through more giggles.

At his smile and nod, she pulled his T-shirt over his head and dropped it to the floor. Her palms moved across his hard chest, and she lifted her eyes to his. "You have more hair than I remember."

His deep brown eyes turned to melted chocolate as he stared at her. "I've grown up."

She kissed his chest, moving her lips over his firm muscles, through the hair on his chest. The scent of his Old Spice filled her nostrils transporting her back to those days in the back of his Jeep. "You sure have," she whispered.

With her shirt up around her chin, she pulled away enough for Jay to remove it, and drop it next to his. His fingers slid around her rib cage, tickling. Her bra came loose, and Amy shrugged it off.

Raising her arms, she wrapped them around his neck, pressing her naked breasts against his chest, while his warm hands slid up and down from her jeaned hips to her rib cage. His smooth palms left goosebumps in their wake.

Amy ran her hands down his back feeling the way his muscles contracted with her touch. Her fingers traced his spinal column, feeling him, remembering him, and she sighed.

Jay kissed her shoulders and neck before sliding his lips down and taking first one breast and then the other into his mouth. As his tongue circled her nipple, Amy moaned and arched her back. She wanted him so bad. So many times when they were kids, she almost gave herself to him and it took all the strength she had not to give in to the desire. She felt no such compunction now. She wanted him to make love to her. Now. She couldn't wait any longer.

Her hands found the sides of his face and she lifted his head to claim his mouth with a wet, sloppy, tongue-filled kiss. Her hands moved to his waist, and she fumbled with his belt but couldn't find what she was looking for without stopping the kiss—and she wasn't about to do so. He brushed her hands away and undid the buckle, then unbuttoned his jeans for her.

She kissed his clavicles and chest as she pushed his hands away. Drawing his zipper down, she reached inside the waistband of his underwear.

His hands roamed her body. "Oh God, Amy," he moaned. "Hurry. Touch me."

Lifting her head, she stared at him. A small smile played on her lips as she slid her hands under his jeans and pushed them off his hips.

Jeremy unbuttoned her jeans and tugged them down. She stepped out of them. He gazed at her, his face soft and brown eyes drunk with desire.

When he reached for her, she returned to his embrace. Her panties dropped to her feet, and he pressed himself against her. His hands on her buttocks pushed her against him and she cried out and pressed her face to his shoulder, not wanting to make too much noise in case Ricky woke.

Jay jerked away, holding her at arm's length. His brow wrinkled and fear and doubt warred for domination in his gaze. "Do you want me to stop?" His eyes shifted back and forth, as though he searched for a sign.

Amy stared up at him. Why was he pushing her away? "What?"

"I told you I won't do anything you don't want me to."

His grip on her arms almost hurt.

"Do you want me to stop?"

It took a minute for Amy to grasp what he was saying. Finally, she whispered, "Make love to me, Jay."

His mouth swooped down on hers, hard and insistent.

He bent and she felt herself being lifted off the floor, then Jay's weight pressed down on her, and she couldn't remember how she got to the mattress.

Groaning, Amy raised her hips in invitation. His fingers moved along her crevice, and she cried out and clasped his neck, kissing him with feverish need.

"Hurry, Jay. Please."

He pushed her legs apart and entered her. Sweet release swept her. It had been years since she'd had sex, but this was so much more. She pressed her face into his shoulder and shuddered.

His arms tightened around her, and he began to move, driving into her each stroke harder than the next, his breath harsh in her ear.

She grasped him with her arms and legs as he pulled back and drove into her again. Crying out, she matched him as another orgasm built. He stroked her and she could do nothing now but hang on to him for dear life. When her climax came again, she cried out and clung to him as her body shuddered again, harder than the first time.

She'd wanted this for so long, waited ten years for him, and she thanked heaven he came back to her. She was never going to let him go if she had anything to do with it. Amy lifted her head off the pillow, mouth open, asking for a kiss, which he gave with savage desire.

"Amy," he moaned against her lips. "I can't wait anymore." He pushed in again with such force she banged her head on the headboard. His hand moved to the crown of her head as a long, shuddering groan escaped his clenched teeth. Beneath her hands, his buttocks clenched as spasms rocked his body. He pushed in one more time and with a shudder, collapsed on her.

Spent, Amy slowly, reluctantly unwrapped her legs from his waist. His breath, still hard, brushed her cheek. When Jay kissed her, he managed to convey his thanks and gratitude, something her ex-husband would never have done.

With Peter, sex was for his gratification. She was merely the tool. When he was through, he simply withdrew, turned his back on her, and went to sleep. Many times she thought of tapping him on the shoulder and telling him he owed her money.

She gasped when Jay pulled out.

"Did I hurt you?"

"No." She smiled and kissed his upper arm. "I wasn't ready for that."

He smiled as he made himself comfortable beside her, brushing his fingers over her cheek, touching her short hair. "I like your hair. Short is sexy on you. It was the first thing I noticed at the restaurant."

She smiled. "A few years ago, I saw a picture of the actress Jennifer Lawrence. She wore her hair in a shoulder-length bob, which was so flattering on her, I grew mine out to match. After about a year I got sick of my hair being too short for long hairstyles and too long for short hair control. It constantly fell in my face, driving me crazy, so I went to the hairdresser, showed her a picture of Michelle Williams with uber short hair and said, 'Do this' and she did."

As she talked, Jay rose up on an elbow, bracing his face on his palm to gaze into her face, while his other hand explored her body.

"Later that evening," she went on, "I had dinner with some friends. My friend, Leslie, was like, 'I love your haircut,' but it was her husband who sealed the deal for me." She smiled as she remembered that conversation. "He smiled at me and simply said, 'Better.'"

She chuckled. "Ever since, I've kept my hair short."

A smile played on Jay's lips as he leaned to nibble her earlobe. "Mm. Makes it easier to do this," he said against her neck.

Giggling, she laid a palm against his cheek and kissed him as the first stirrings of new desire began to take hold. Yet before making love to him again, she had to set the record straight. She pulled away and gazed into his eyes, alight again with desire.

"I'm sorry about my phone message, Jay." She traced her fingers up and down his arm, sending goose pimples over him. "I don't know what I was thinking. The way you left...I was drunk…I thought...I understand now why you did, but I wasn't right in my head and..."

He kissed her, cutting off her words.

"Don't apologize," he said. "I understand." He ran an index finger along the pucker of stretch marks marring her abdomen. Amy slapped her hands over them, blocking him. "Don't."

Jay hesitated for a second. He looked into her eyes his own soft brown orbs filled with love. A soft smile played on his lips and with gentle care he pushed her hands away.

"Don't cover them. I think they're beautiful." He lowered his head and pressed his lips to her abdomen. "As beautiful as you are."

His kisses moved lower and opened herself to him. "Oh God," she gasped and lost control.

He raised up and she mewled with his absence, but then he entered her and covered her mouth with his so she wouldn't wake Ricky.

Because Jay declared he couldn't get enough of her, they made love again, before Amy suggested Ricky would wake from his nap soon.

"I'm famished," he said, throwing back the tangle of sheets and rolling on top of her. "Got any leftover potato salad?"

Downstairs Amy made him a ham-and-cheese sandwich with potato salad. As she served him, Ricky appeared at the kitchen door, bleary-eyed and yawning, hitting the two-hour mark with exquisite precision.

Amy chuckled. "He has full mobility now." She shook her head as though sorry for the development.

To the surprise of both adults, Ricky stumbled to Jay and tried to climb into his lap. Jay gave a questioning glance at Amy.

"He likes to cuddle when he first wakes up," Amy told him. "If you don't want him, I'll take him."

He lifted Ricky onto his lap and settled him in. "No," he said. "I'm honored." Wrapping the little boy in his arms, he held him close. Ricky tucked his thumb into his mouth and snuggled his cheek against Jay's chest. When he wrapped his arms around her little boy, she realized if he'd had any doubts before, they'd disappeared.

Turning away, she swallowed a ball of emotion and busied herself making a sandwich. She brought her plate to the table and watched Jay eat with one hand and cuddle Ricky with the other.

By the time Jay finished eating, Ricky was ready to be set free.

Jay let him go and glanced at the clock. Three forty-five.

"I need to let you go," he said, getting up. "You have to get ready for work."

"Yeah," she said, also standing.

He took her in his arms and kissed her, a long slow kiss conveying his love and desire, and Amy melted in his arms. Just like old times. After a few minutes, Jay broke away.

"Thank you for making sure my bed is safe," she said in his ear. "Maybe you can come back tonight and test it for safety in the darkness?" She raised a teasing eyebrow.

Jay chuckled. “Count on it,” he said then took her chin in his fingers as a teasing smile twisted his lips. “But if I don’t leave now, you’ll be late for work. I promise to return for another test tonight and into tomorrow morning.” He widened his eyes in a lecherous leer.

They didn’t move. He pressed his forehead to hers and chuckled. “Why do I feel as if I’m back in high school? Reluctant to leave, yet knowing your father is in the other room listening and waiting.”

She laughed and cupped his face. “He’s not and we’re not kids anymore.”

“Amen to that,” he said, opening the door. “I’ll see you tonight.” He kissed her again before stepping outside.

“Jay.”

On the back step, he turned. She leaned against the doorjamb, the doorknob in one hand.

“I love you,” she said.

“I love you too, babe.”

Jeremy pulled into his driveway, REO Speedwagon blaring on the radio. He cut them off mid blare as he shut off the car. Strolling across his yard, he whistled the last tune playing on the radio. He approached the high lattice privacy wall of his back deck, heart soaring. He’d experienced an afternoon filled with the best sex he’d had in an extraordinarily long time. Not only did Amy tell him she loved him, but when Ricky climbed into his lap, he thought his heart would burst. The best decision he’d made was to ignore her messages, grateful to know she regretted making them. He couldn’t wait to pick her up tonight and had no intention of coming home. Now that they were on a new level of their relationship, could he convince her to move in with him? Maybe not, but one thing was for sure. Ricky needed a bed, and a room of his own for those nights he could convince her to stay with him. Did Ikea make dinosaur-shaped beds? He’d have to go online to find out.

He hopped up the steps and rounded the side of the privacy wall. His whistle died when he spotted Maggie sitting on the wicker sofa, legs crossed, one sandal-clad foot swinging, her toenails painted bright red.

“You’re in a carefree mood,” she teased, standing and tugging at her brown capri pants. Her olive green tank top hugged her breasts and accentuated her long, slim waist. “I can’t remember the last time I’ve heard you whistle."

He stood at the top step scowling. Why was she here? What did she want?

Perplexed, Maggie held up a brass key. "I was going to let myself in, but my key doesn't work."

Stepping toward her, he snatched the piece from her fingers. "I changed the locks. What are you doing here?" He slipped the key into his pocket.

"Hardly a friendly reception." She eyed him up and down. "Where've you been, Jer?"

He moved across the deck and unlocked his door. "That's my business."

She lifted a brow and made a show of sniffing him. "You've been with her," she accused.

"So what if I have?"

"You smell like sex," she persisted.

He ignored the remark as he entered the house. Maggie followed him.

Jeremy sighed. *Why now? Why did she have to show up now?*

"You didn't answer my question," he said, as she moved around him and went to the refrigerator where she retrieved two beers.

She handed him one, which he took reflexively, then slammed the bottle down on the bar. He moved into the living room. "Why are you here?"

She opened her bottle and drank, then shrugged. "I didn't have anything pressing to do and I thought, on a hunch, you might like some company."

"What, no one to skank tonight?" Jeremy snarled, then flinched at his harsh tone and the vulgar word.

Her gasp of surprise gave him some small satisfaction.

"I'm sorry, Jeremy. I never should have said those things about..."

He glared a furious warning.

"About Amy." She dropped her gaze, turned, and brought him the bottle of beer he'd left in the kitchen.

"Please," she said. "Truce?"

Reluctantly he took the beer and sipped.

He plopped himself into the corner of the sofa.

She perched next to him and tapped her bottleneck against his. "Cheers," she drank.

Jeremy didn't. What was she doing at his house after so much time? Hadn't he made it clear they were over? He hadn't spoken with Maggie since the night he slammed the door in her face. At school, she acted like he didn't exist, which made his life so much easier.

"You blocked my number," she said, studying him.

"I did."

She drank and wiped her upper lip on the back of her hand. Her hazel eyes were shading more to brown, a sign she was growing nervous.

"To what do I owe such a silent, angry reception?" She held the bottle in both hands, rolling it between her palms.

Jeremy didn't answer. He pressed his knuckles into the side of his head and continued to study her, the beer bottle tilted on his thigh.

Her gaze slid around the room and returned to his stony face. "What, no math problems?" Maggie's laugh sounded forced and nervous. She stopped.

A labored sigh left him as he rubbed his fingers across his forehead. "Why do my math problems bother you so much?"

Her brow creased. "They don't. I was joking."

"Yes, they do," he growled, shutting her down. He swigged, holding the neck of the bottle in a loose grasp.

She studied him with a wary eye and peeled at the label on the neck. After a sip, she resumed peeling, letting the pieces drop from her fingers.

"Stop dropping shit on my floor!" he demanded, startled by the intensity of the anger coursing through him. He wanted her gone.

"I'm sorry," she said and put the bottle down.

Slouched against the arm of the sofa he contemplated her until she began to squirm. Fearful concern rearranged her features and she cast him another wary glance.

"Your car isn't outside," he said. "Where did you park?"

Maggie swallowed hard. "I had a friend drop me off." She pasted on a smile and slid a well-manicured hand across his jeans to squeeze his knee.

He raised his eyebrows.

"I thought you might drive me home later."

Jeremy pushed her hand away. "Who's your friend?"

"I beg your pardon?"

He curled his lip. "Your friend. The one who dropped you off.

You're going to need to call him or her to come pick you up. Now."

Her brows creased and she stared at him as though he were a creature from another planet. "Jeremy," she said as though he were slow-witted. "We can't be over. I love you."

Thus ends the discussion.

"Yes, we can, Maggie. We are."

Anger boiled his blood and for the first time in his life, he feared doing physical harm to a woman. As angry and hurt as he'd been when Amy ran out on him as a teenager, he'd never entertained any thought or desire to cause her physical pain. Maggie, though, was a different story and he needed to gain space from her. "Why did you come here?" He got up and took his beer to the kitchen, dumping the contents into the sink.

"I've missed you," Maggie said, voice quavering. She covered her eyes, but Jeremy noted the lack of tears.

Tossing the bottle into the recycle bin, he strolled back to the living room.

When he didn't speak, Maggie rose and came to him. "I love you."

"No," he said, moving away again, narrowly avoiding her grasp. "You don't love me. You love control, and you thought you'd given me more than enough time to stew and perhaps come to my senses. When I didn't come back on my own, you figured I needed reeling in, like a fish on a hook." He shook his head and turned away. "God, how dumb I've been all these years."

"You're not dumb," she cried and tried to close the distance again, but again, he backed away. She tried again. "I just...I just...want us to be like we used to be."

Incredulous, he stared at her. "Like we used to be? What did we used to be?"

She sniffed and wiped pretend tears away.

"We used to be easy around each other. We used to be friends and lovers, but you haven't touched me in more than a year, and I don't understand what happened." She drew in a ragged breath. "I've struggled all that time to understand what happened to you."

"I'm sorry, Mags. I'm not that man anymore. I want more. I want to marry and have a family."

"You don't think you can have those things with me? I love you, Jeremy. I've loved you for years. I can be those things for you. I can be whatever you want me to be." She rushed to him, and this time, he grasped her upper arms to hold her off.

"Don't leave me for her!" Maggie screamed at him.

He pushed her to the sofa and made her sit. Perching on the coffee table, he rubbed his face to gather his thoughts and calm himself.

As he dropped his hands between his knees, he looked at her. "I don't want you to be whatever you think I want you to be, Maggie. You wouldn't love me long if I made you live like that." He sighed. "The fact is, I realized when the pandemic separated us that I don't love you. Long before Amy."

He grasped her hands and gazed into her eyes. "I owe you a major apology because I strung you along for another year without being honest with you. It was wrong of me and I'm sorry."

"I don't believe you," she snarled, hazel eyes snapping green fire. "You're leaving me for her. You're no different from any other man. Run away when something better comes along. You're just like—" She broke off, but he understood.

"I'm just like your father."

Her answer was a hate-filled glare.

Jeremy tried again. "And…" He turned her hand over and lightly stroked her palm with his fingertips, keeping his voice calm. "I don't believe you love me. I think you love the idea of being in love with me, but that isn't the same thing. There's something else, too." He raised his gaze and met her eyes. "You don't trust me."

He dropped his gaze back to her hands. Her many rings sparkled and winked in the light from the window. Releasing her hands, he straightened up. "You never will," he said. "You don't trust any man and distrust is not the foundation on which to build a strong marriage. Sooner or later, you or I would leave. Please. Let's end things now as friends."

She grimaced. "For God's sake, Jeremy," she snarled. "Can't you talk straight with me for once? What do I have to do? Tell me what I have to do?"

"Maggie!" he snapped, out of patience with her.

Standing, he pulled her to her feet. "You need to go home. You'll regret this tomorrow."

Maggie tried to throw her arms around his neck. "Jeremy, you don't mean what you're saying. Please, you don't. I know you don't."

"Maggie, stop!" He pushed her arms down. "I'm sorry, but I can't be with you anymore. We're over." He raised his hands and let them drop at his sides. His heart pounded and his body shook from frustration because he wasn't getting through to her. It took every fiber of his being not to throw her bodily out of his house. His hands found his hips and he squeezed to be sure he kept them to himself.

He sighed. "I'm in love with Amy," he said with force. "I intend to—"

A million stars exploded in his left eye and a white-hot pain seared his cheekbone. He pitched backward, arms flailing as the backs of his knees caught the edge of the coffee table and he crashed onto the wooden surface. The table splintered beneath him.

A piece of wood hit him in the forehead. Seconds later his head slammed the oak floor. More stars exploded, and darkness shrouded the edges of his vision, but he struggled to remain present and regain his feet.

With effort, he braced his palms on the floor and got to his knees. More blows rained down on him and he sank to the floor, covering his head with his arms. She pounded his back and arms, the backs of his hands taking a brutal beating as she tried to find his head. She kicked his thighs and connected once with his tailbone, sending him sprawling on his face. Flaming pain shot up his spine and he cried out.

With each blow, she screamed invectives. He stayed on the floor, waiting for the pounding to stop, making no effort to defend himself, fearing what he'd do to her if he tried.

When the hitting finally stopped, Jeremy got to his unsteady feet, but his throbbing tailbone wouldn't allow him to straighten to his full height.

His back was to her, so he turned around. If she was going to hit him again, he wanted to be ready for the blow, though he'd missed the first one. And how could he see it coming with his eye swelling shut? The thought triggered a surge of hysterical laughter that blew out of his mouth along with bloody spittle. He wiped the blood from his lips and chin.

Maggie panted and the expression of shocked surprise on her face made him laugh harder and for a split second, Jeremy feared he was losing his mind. He blinked back tears of pain and fought the urge to vomit on her as blood continued to fill his mouth. He didn't want to swallow and wasn't quite sure he could walk to the bathroom to spit. The thought sent a wave of pain up his spine, so he stayed put.

"You lying, cheating bastard," she screamed and with one last stinging back-handed fist, she hit him again. His head rocked to the side, shot the blood from his mouth, and splattered against the wall. One of the rings on her hand opened a new cut on his cheek as the sting and instant wet made clear.

Seconds later the back door slammed.

He weaved on his feet, staggered to the bathroom, and threw up.

The song he'd been whistling when he arrived home started playing in his head. A song by REO Speedwagon, a band his father had loved as a teenager. They had it partially right. Though it didn't hurt him emotionally to say good bye, the physical pain was certainly something else. And no doubt in Jeremy's mind. It was time for him to fly. From Maggie, anyway. He started to laugh again, the sound echoing around the toilet bowl. Talk about irony.

18

I should call a doctor. His left eye was swollen closed and black and blue. He pulled his eyelid open, and the bloody sclera scared him. Jeremy studied his other injuries in the bathroom mirror. The blood in his hair also concerned him. With shaking fingers, he touched a massive knot on his scalp. By far, the most worrisome injury was the blow to his spine. He feared she cracked a vertebra or two. He drew in a pained breath.

Grabbing his phone, he called his doctor's office to make an emergency appointment, telling them he'd had an accident. After reassuring them he didn't need 9-1-1, they referred him to urgent care.

His stomach made an unpleasant gurgle, so he returned to the bathroom, and when he finished vomiting, went upstairs to take a shower. The hot water might settle things down. He considered calling his mother, but he didn't want her to see him. Not like this.

The water stung his cheek, but he kept his face in the spray, letting the warmth soothe his cuts. He touched the cushy swelling around his eye and cheekbone. His fingers found a knot on his forehead, and he remembered a piece of the coffee table hitting him in the face.

He turned and let the water stream down his neck and back while he washed. After shampooing his hair, he faced the stream again and bent his head forward, letting the steamy water spray the top of his head and the back of his neck. He stood with his eyes closed, one hand on the tiled wall, swaying until the water began to cool. He shut the shower off, dried himself, and naked, walked back to his room for clean clothes.

Near nine o'clock Jeremy left the emergency room at UVM Medical Center. He'd gone to urgent care, but because of the nature of his injuries, and the possibility of spinal damage, they'd transported him by ambulance to the hospital in Burlington, leaving him without a car.

The ER doctor had wanted to call the police. She told him she was a mandated reporter, and she'd seen enough domestic violence to assess Jeremy's injuries were a result, but he refused. As angry as he was at Maggie, he couldn't report her. She'd lose her job.

With a disapproving shake of her head, the doctor treated him for his injuries, stitched and bandaged his forehead, and sent him on his way. He had a goose egg on his head, but concussion protocols were negative.

He thought of heading to Lou's, but the restaurant was two miles away and he didn't have the strength to walk that far. He was tired and achy and wanted to go home. But Amy would worry.

He pulled out his phone to leave a message. Frank didn't allow his employees to have their phones on them.

As expected, her phone went to voice mail. "Hi, this is Amy. Please leave a message and tell me what time you called so I can call you back. Thanks."

"Hey babe. Listen, I'm not gonna be able to come tonight. I'm not well. I've been vomiting. I stopped at an Italian place for dinner, and I think I ate something wonky. I'm so sorry, honey. Can you ask Frank or Jason to walk you to your car?" He sighed. "I love you, Amy. Bye."

He disconnected. His next call was going to be worse. He thumbed through until he found "Perry Mason" and hit the call button. The phone rang twice.

"Hello?"

"Hi, Dad, this is Jeremy. I need a ride home. Can you pick me up?"

19

Jeremy eased himself into the passenger seat and buckled up. When the seat belt snapped, he raised his eyes and waited for whatever his father would say.

Dad's concerned brown-eyed gaze roamed over his face. "What. Happened?"

Jeremy sighed and tried to tease. "I got into a bar fight. You're not gonna tell Mom, are you?"

Dad tsked. "Jeremy," he snapped as he pulled away.

Jeremy covered his eyes with a hand, which stung his cheek, so he dropped his hand. "I broke up with Maggie in February."

"Really?" Dad said, raising an eyebrow. "And the injuries are just now showing up?"

Despite his strong desire to cry, Jeremy chuckled. "Yeah. This will be easier if you don't interrupt with your sick jokes, Counselor." He sucked in a sobbing breath and forced himself to calm down, but he was in pain and deeply embarrassed. Tears leaked from his eyes, and he sniffed.

Dad pulled over and awkwardly embraced him. "I'm sorry, son."

Jeremy waved a hand as if to say, *Ignore me.* He cleared his throat. "So I broke up with Maggie in February. She came to the house today, I guess thinking she'd left me alone for far too long because I didn't come crawling back on my own and she needed to put me back on her leash. I told her to leave, and she beat the shit out of me. And no, I'm not pressing charges," he said when his father started to speak.

Dad closed his mouth again and gave a disapproving nod. "All right," was all he said.

"She punched me in the eye, and I fell backward and crashed into the coffee table you and Mom bought me as a housewarming gift, which, I'm afraid is nothing but kindling wood now. A piece flew up and caught me here." He pointed to his bandaged forehead. "Four stitches," he reported when Dad's wary gaze assessed the gauze covering.

"Slammed my head on the floor, but no concussion thank God, a black eye and a fat lip. Not to mention a kick in the ass, literally, that I thought broke my spine. My tailbone hurts worse than anything else. The price I had to pay for freedom, I guess."

"An interesting way to put it."

Jeremy sighed. "Don't mind me. I'm..." He ducked his head. "I'm angry but I'm not so much as I'm embarrassed, humiliated...which I guess was the purpose. Please don't tell Mom. I don't want her to...please, Dad." Tears filled his eyes, and he blinked them back.

"Not possible, I'm afraid. I had you on speaker and she was in the room when you called. Can I tell her you're not with Maggie anymore?"

"Will she be pleased?"

Dad tilted his head. "I wouldn't say pleased. Relieved perhaps. Especially after this," he said with a vague wave at Jeremy's face.

Jeremy studied his father. "I didn't realize everyone hated her!"

Dad smiled. "Hate is a strong word. It was obvious she sapped the happiness from your soul. I confess we all conspired to keep mum. We even threatened to sit on Holly to keep her quiet."

"Holly!"

Dad laughed. "She never liked her. I swear for a seven-year-old, that girl can see through people like they're panes of glass. She'll make an excellent attorney one day."

Despite his fat lip, Jeremy chuckled. "Holly. Sonofabitch," he said. "Who knew a seven-year-old could be that astute?"

Once at the house, telling Mom or not was a moot point because her car was in his driveway. Dad took an arm and helped him despite Jeremy's protestations. On the deck, they found his mother sitting on a deck chair in the cool night air waiting for them.

When Jeremy laboriously climbed the back steps, leaning on Dad despite his protests that he could manage, she rose and went to him.

He hugged her while Dad unlocked the back door. "I'm okay,

Mom."

She pulled back and studied his injuries in the light of the back porch. "What happened?" she demanded.

"Alicia let's talk inside," Dad said as he pushed open the door.

Mom nodded and taking Jeremy by the arm, she walked him inside and sat him gingerly on the sofa. Her eyes widened at the sight of the coffee table pieces and when she saw the blood on the wall, her face went white.

Dad whistled. "I guess so," was all he said.

"Let me fix you something to eat," Mom said, staring at the wall. She jerked herself into motion and went to the kitchen. "Are you hungry?"

He was nauseous. "Not really. I don't think I can keep food down right now."

She switched gears. "Where's your bread? I'll make you some toast and tea."

He pointed to a cupboard and Mom made him food while Dad began cleaning up the mess.

Jeremy moved to help, but Dad pushed him back on the sofa and told him to relax.

Mom placed a plate of toast in his lap and handed him a cup of tea, then went to the cupboard under the sink and got cleaner and some paper towels to wash the wall.

Jeremy was sure he heard her sniff a time or two as she sprayed the wall and wiped up the mess.

Between sips of tea and small bites of toast, Jeremy told his parents what happened. The toast made him realize at some point in the attack he'd bitten his tongue and he found it hard to eat.

For an hour Mom hovered while Dad asked anxious questions. He loved his parents, but Jeremy wanted them to go home so he could lick his wounded pride alone. As they pulled away, he turned off the outside light and locked the door. He was tired and sore, so he went to bed. The time was close to eleven and he prayed Amy got his message. He undressed down to his underwear before climbing into bed. So much for making love to Amy tonight.

Clicking off the light, he rolled over. Usually he kept his phone downstairs at night so text and email dings wouldn't disturb his sleep, but tonight, he brought it with him in case he needed to make an emergency call.

His phone buzzed and he picked it up. *Catnap* flashed on the screen. He considered answering, then put the phone back down. He'd talk to her tomorrow. It buzzed three or four times before shutting off. Rolling back over, he went to sleep.

Jeremy entered Lou's around nine thirty and sat down at what he'd come to consider his corner of the bar. Frank served drinks at the other end but acknowledged him with a nod and a small wave. Jeremy lifted a hand and settled in.

As soon as Frank finished, he grabbed a coffee cup and the pot and walked over to Jeremy. He set the cup down and poured.

"What about them Red Sox, eh? Mid-May and they're in first place. For now," Frank said, grinning, but when he raised his gaze, the grin disappeared. "Holy shit, Jeremy." He extended a hand toward his face and Jeremy pulled away.

"What happened to the other guy? That why you didn't come in last night? I walked Amy to her car."

"Thanks." Jeremy nodded. "I couldn't see well enough to drive in the dark."

"Have you seen a doc? Your eye is gross, and your face is wicked swollen," Frank said. "Man." He shook his head and walked away.

Jeremy gingerly sipped his coffee because of his still swollen lip. He searched the restaurant but couldn't find Amy.

"She's on break," Frank told him when he returned. He dropped a bag of ice wrapped in a towel in front of Jeremy. "Hold this to your face."

"Thanks." Jeremy lifted the towel to his cheek and eye. The cold soothed his still burning eye. He offered a chagrined smile. "You're dying to ask, I can tell."

Frank lifted his hands. "Hey man, none of my business. Besides, in this line of work, I've seen everything."

Amy appeared from the back. A smile of greeting lit her face.

Jeremy's heart pounded. How would she react? He put the towel down and faced her, readying himself for whatever she might have to say.

Concern replaced her smile. "Oh my God." Her brows furrowed, as she reached to touch his face.

He grimaced and pulled away. "Don't," he said. "It still hurts."

She dropped her hand. "What happened? Did you have an

accident?"

"No." He sighed and puffed out his cheeks. "I'll tell you, but not here."

"Is this why you didn't come last night?"

He nodded.

She cocked her head and studied his bruise. "Your eye is ugly. And bleeding."

He shook his head. "No. The doctor says the redness is normal for an eye injury and not to worry."

"I'm glad you went to a doctor." Amy grasped his chin and turned his head. "So what happened to the other guy?" She traced light fingers over the swollen bruise under his eye.

He raised his coffee cup to hide the smile twisting his lips at the way she echoed Frank. *She beat the crap out of me before storming out of my house.*

Amy placed a gentle kiss on his cheek under the bruise. Without a word, she went back to work.

Jeremy sipped and studied Amy until Frank wandered back his way.

"Frank, can I ask a question?"

"What's up?"

"Wednesday night I showed up late." Jeremy flipped a hand. "I dozed off and when I woke up, I was late. The restaurant was closed by the time I arrived."

Frank nodded, as though he explained something.

"When I got here, Amy was in the vestibule, upset and angry. I apologized, but she acted as if I'd abandoned her and left her in extreme danger."

Frank leaned on the bar. His gaze went to Amy smiling and speaking with a couple while she wrote on her pad.

He returned his gaze to Jeremy. "Had a panic attack, did she?"

"That's what she said, but I have no idea what I did. Besides being late, I mean." He shrugged. "The only other thing I can think of is when she came outside, I was talking to an old family friend, but I can't imagine why he should upset her."

Jeremy shook his head at the memory. "Amy spun herself around and marched right back inside. When she finally let me in, I found her muttering under her breath. Then she sat down on the floor and just started crying. I have no idea what I did. Can you help me out?"

The memory of her sitting on a barstool in his father's kitchen flashed in Jeremy's mind but disappeared so fast he couldn't latch onto it. His brow creased and smoothed out almost as fast.

Frank shrugged and offered up a possible explanation. "I've seen men play grab fanny and send her into oblivion. Others she handles with professional ease. I've never figured out which is going to happen when, though."

"I asked her if she had any jerks for customers, but she said no."

"Mm," Frank said, thinking the matter over. Finally, he raised a brow and gave a quick shake of his head. "Yeah, I don't recall any problems either. Another possibility, sometimes she comes in here already cooking from her day job, which she hates. Don't be so quick to think you did anything wrong."

Frank faced him and met Jeremy's eye. "My best advice is to stay calm, don't try to grab her, keep your voice modulated, and talk her off the ledge. And don't take offense at anything she says. She's usually not in her head."

Jeremy sipped his coffee. So perhaps Adam's presence wasn't the problem after all. Most likely, she'd had a bad day, or in his tardiness, Adam became an excuse. He held out his cup and Frank poured.

He decided he'd handled the situation well enough for the first time encountering one of her panic attacks. Still, for some reason he couldn't put his finger on, he had a suspicion Adam was somehow responsible. *I'd hoped he was dead or something. After all these years,* she'd said. But why?

20

“Can we sit for a minute?” Jay asked. “What I have to say will take longer than our walk to the car.”

“Okay.” Amy perched on the edge of the bench facing him. His sad serious tone made her heart pound with fear he was going to end their relationship.

The corner of his mouth quirked, and he studied the brick walkway of the Church Street Marketplace. Couldn’t he even meet her eye?

“When I got home yesterday, Maggie was waiting on my back deck.”

“Oh,” she said. *He’s going back to her after she convinced him he doesn’t want a woman with a son.* He told her that was the dynamic of their relationship. Best to hear him out and get this over with.

She offered a sad smile. “Why do I have the impression I’m not going to like what you have to say?”

Jay’s fingers played with a bruise before he straightened to face her. “Please,” he said, “before *you* beat the crap out of me, just listen.”

Amy’s eyebrows shot up at the emphasis he put on the word *you*.

Raising a hand, she touched the bandage on his forehead. Her own brow furrowed with anger at the thought of someone doing violence to him. “She beat the crap out of you?” Amy demanded. “Why?”

He sighed and looked away, but with gentle fingers on his chin, she forced his face back to her.

Sad, angry, hurt brown eyes met hers. “Because she tried to seduce me back, and when I told her no, she started hitting me.” The muscles on his face grew taut. "I swear, I never raised a hand to her."

That he would raise a hand to Maggie never occurred to her because Jay wasn't such a man. Rather than answer, she studied his cuts and bruises under the light of the restaurant. The dark stain of humiliation spreading on his cheeks made her take him in her arms. "I'm so sorry, Jay," she spoke above a whisper.

"She hit me hard...punched me..." A vague gesture toward his eye. "I wasn't ready. I fell, which is where most of my injuries came from, but she went ballistic. Kicking and hitting any place she found an opening."

Amy touched the scabbed-over cut on his cheek and studied his black eye and the bandage on his forehead, as if she could make his injuries go away as if by the magic of a loving touch. As she would with Ricky, she kissed the worst of his cuts.

"I mean, she's lost her temper in the past and cracked me a sound one once or twice, but she's never done something like this before," he said.

"She did you some real damage." Amy's fingers traced his cuts and her lips followed. "You should report her. Domestic violence isn't only men who beat women. Women do beat up on men."

Searching his face, Amy tried to make her point. "Listen to me, Jay, I know what I'm talking about."

Meeting her gaze he offered her a small smile of thanks and lifted her hand to gingerly kiss her fingers.

"I'm sorry you do." He dropped his gaze. "I'm not going to report her. For one thing, I'm embarrassed enough and for another, I don't want to compromise her job. The school board has a no-tolerance policy."

Amy jerked her hand back. "So you'll protect her." If she had her way, Maggie would pay for what she did to him.

"Yes, I will," he said, sounding annoyed and defensive.

"Then you're a fool, Jeremy Austin. What if she reports you for sexual assault just for revenge?"

"She won't."

Amy scoffed. "How can you be sure?"

His shrug looked so much like Ricky her heart broke for him.

Raising his voice, he snapped at Amy. "I have to trust Maggie has a little integrity. That our four years together meant something to her."

Amy raised her hands, fingers like claws, and grimaced with

frustration. He grinned, which only angered her more. “What’s so funny!” she demanded.

Jay shook his head and chuckled. “You,” he said and mimicked her clawed hands. “Now I see where Ricky gets it from.”

Amy didn’t go down that rabbit hole. She studied him, wanted to make his hurts go away. “Look at what she did to you,” she whispered as her fingers traced cuts on his lip. Then she smiled.

“As I said, you’re a fool.” Laying her warm palm against his cheek, she leaned close, peering deep into his eyes, to emphasize her point. “But—what if—she tries to humiliate you more and accuses you of sexual assault. Her word against yours. You’ll be—” Breaking off, she had a sudden vision of Adam staring down at her, warning, accusing…*It’ll be your word against mine and who do you think they’ll believe?*

“Amy? Are you okay?”

Jay grasped her arm, jerking her back to reality. She waved her fingers. “Sorry.”

Amy clamped her lips between her teeth. She’d said her piece. She wouldn’t argue with him or try to anger him. Reaching up, she stroked his hair back from his temple.

Jay closed his eyes, and she knew she soothed and comforted him.

“Domestic violence isn’t funny, Jay. What makes you think she won’t do something like this again?”

“Nothing,” he said, opening his eyes. “But I can take care of myself.”

“Huh!” Amy snarled and nodded at his face. “Clearly.”

“Why are you so angry?” he asked, brow furrowed.

“Because. Violence makes me angry. Because she hurt you, and she doesn’t have a right to hurt you!”

A smile tugged at his lips. “Are you concerned about me?” He cajoled, leaning close, pressing her into the bench as he kissed her.

Hmm?” Jay continued, kissing her. “Are you worried about me, Amy Taylor? You’re so sweet to worry about little ole me.”

With gentle care, she claimed his lips and let her anger dissipate.

Pulling away, Jay teased her some more. “Are you afraid I can’t take care of myself?”

As he leaned in to nibble an earlobe, Amy started giggling and playfully tried to fend him off.

“Stop it! You’re like kissing the Stay-Puft Marshmallow Man.”

Jeremy laughed into her neck and the vibrations sent shivers of delight down her spine. She gasped when he nipped her throat, and shaking with laughter, slid her arms around his neck.

"Sss-st-stop, you lech!"

He was laughing with her, and she reveled in the joy of being with him. Her eyes closed when he cupped a breast and she arched into him.

"Jay." Opening her eyes, Amy lurched as a strangled scream caught in her throat.

Adam Knox leered at her, and for a second, she was in Mr. Austin's office, this man staring her down, intimidating her into silence.

Her fingers dug into his shoulders as she fought to escape his embrace.

Jay pulled away. "What's wrong?"

She didn't answer. Couldn't answer. Her gaze locked behind him.

When Jay's weight disappeared, she scrambled upright.

"Adam!" Jay jumped off the bench, and stood in front of her, blocking Adam's view of her.

"Oh my God!" She breathed. Terror choked off her breath and made her heart skip beats.

Ten years. Ten years went by with her never having laid eyes on this bastard and now twice in the space of months. Was it Jay's proximity to her or just bad luck? She didn't know and didn't care. *Flee!* Her brain screamed. *Run now!*

"What are you doing here?" Jay's question came to her as though she were underwater.

Rather than answer, Adam leaned around him to peer at her, a sly grin pulled up one side of his mouth.

"Oh my God, oh my God," Amy whispered as though the words were a charm to make Adam go away.

"I might ask the same thing, my friend." Again, Adam craned his neck peering past Jay. "Although that appears obvious." He looked at Jay for the first time and his eyes widened. "What happened to your face?"

He pointed, not waiting for an answer. "Is she the young lady you were with before? Drinks with friends, Jer, or one friend in particular? A particular friend," he said, leering at her. An eyebrow went up and down and he licked his lips. "Quite the drink," he said, his gaze roaming Amy's body. He shifted his briefcase to his left hand before extending his right hand to Amy. "Introduce me."

Amy fled.

"Hey!" Jeremy called as she rounded the corner on Cherry Street. In his shock at seeing her run, his brain couldn't grab hold of her name before she disappeared around the corner.

"Strange girl." Adam sounded amused.

Jeremy turned on him, but whatever happened was not his fault. Without a word, Jeremy ran after Amy. Adam could think anything he wanted. Could go to hell for all he cared.

At the corner of Bank Street, Jeremy caught up with her, bent double, hands on her knees, gasping for breath.

Grabbing her abdomen, Amy slowly straightened. When she turned to him, tears streaked down her face.

"Wh…what was…that…about?" Grasping her shoulder, he squeezed. "Why…did you…run?"

Pressing her forearm against her eyes, Amy bit her lip before inhaling with a gulping sob.

"He was there standing behind you like some kind of…" Another sobbing breath. "Scared the shit out of me."

"Okay." Jeremy took her in his arms. "You're okay now, and I won't let anything happen to you."

With a nod of acceptance, Amy folded herself into his embrace. His arms encircled her, and she clung to him, fingers digging into his back, twisting his shirt in her fists, and her legs shook so hard against his he dared not let go.

"Why does Adam freak you out? You know he does. Don't deny it."

Instead of answering, she shook her head and wept.

"Sweetheart, I'm sorry to upset you, but you've had this reaction twice now. Please, baby." He pushed her away and wiped her eyes with his hands. "Tell me why he scares you. How can I protect you without the whole story."

With effort, Amy stopped crying, but she clung to him and didn't answer his question.

When her shaking slowed, he kissed her forehead. "Are you all right now?"

"Yes," she said, nodding and huffing a breath. "I'm sorry. We were giggling and laughing and when I opened my eyes, he was…there." She flapped a hand "Grinning down at us like a…a…freaked me out." She sniffed and fell silent.

"Yeah," he nodded. "That would have scared me too."

He tightened his arm around her shoulders. "C'mon," he said, turning her toward the garage. "Let me take you home."

When they entered the garage, she spoke again. Her voice was still shaky.

"Jay?" Amy cleared her throat.

"What."

"Did you love her?"

"Maggie?" *Once upon a time. Perhaps way back in the beginning, but probably not even then.* Jeremy shifted his feet and puckered his lips. "Depends on what you mean by love."

"Jay!" Her nostrils flared as her brows crowded the top of her nose. "Don't play semantics with me. This is too important." Fresh tears sprang and she blinked them back.

Hands out, he tried to reassure her. "There are different kinds of love and I want to be clear about what you're asking. Do I love her like a friend? I did. For a long time. Not anymore. Do I love her like a lover? Yes, I did, but not for more than a year. Do I love her like someone I would spend the rest of my life with? No. Never."

By the shift in her features, he saw she accepted the truth of his words. "You made me realize what a rut I was living in."

His gaze slid away as the heat rose in his face. "Things hadn't been right between us for a long time. Since before the pandemic." Returning his gaze to Amy, he forced the truth from his mouth.

"But I stayed with her for the simple reason I was too lazy to end things." His gaze found his shoes, and he shrugged one defensive shoulder. "I'm not proud of myself either. My inaction caused us both a lot of pain."

Brushing his fingers through her short hair he pushed a strand off her forehead. "Being with you made me aware of the many stupid things I did in the past several years, but you also gave me a second chance to fix or change and perhaps make amends for those things."

Running his fingers along her jaw, she turned her head to kiss his palm, sending a jolt of desire up his arm straight to his heart.

With her face in his hands, he drew her close. He touched his lips to hers and melted, unable to resist her and not wanting to.

Drunk with desire, Jeremy pulled away but kept his lips close to hers. "Amy, I love you," he murmured. "I've always loved you."

Sliding his arms around her waist, he crushed her against her car. His lips traced her throat to the base of her neck, and she moaned when his hands found her breasts. Her nipples hardened under his palms, and he pressed himself against her. Her hips lifted, pressing against the hard length of him.

Amy broke the kiss. "Jay!"

"What." He left hot molten kisses against her neck, which goose-pimpled at his touch.

He kissed her, his hands on her hips, holding her tight to him while she moaned into his mouth. They were hands and lips now and if he let this continue, he would take her right here. In the parking garage.

As if she'd read his thoughts, Amy broke the kiss again and sucked in air. "Jay," she said again.

"What?"

"I need…I need…oh God…I need to go home."

His hands squeezed her breasts and pinched her nipples. "Oh God!" she said again, arching her back.

"So do I." He nipped at her earlobe. "So go home with me."

"I need…to pick up…Ricky," she gasped between his kisses.

"Okay. I'll go home with you."

Her tongue darted into his mouth and with a sharp inhale he claimed her lips. He'd long since learned to control himself, but with her crushed between his body and the car, he would lose it if he continued one more moment. Still, he was powerless in her arms. With supreme effort, he released her but pressed his forehead against hers, his breath leaving him in huge gasps.

"Come home with me, Jay."

Jeremy lifted his head and made no effort to hide his little boy, Santa's-on-his-way delight, making her laugh.

With a swift kiss, he headed for his car. "Race you to the house!"

21

Amy was halfway home before the familiar doubts assailed her. What was she thinking? She couldn't have Jay. Not if Adam continued to pop in and out. She should have ended things the first time she encountered the bastard. He was always going to come between them, would always snatch away her happiness.

Jeremy won't want you. He'll think you a whore. She glanced into her rearview mirror. He was behind her. She sped up to gain some distance. When a light turned yellow, she went through. Jay stopped.

She breathed a sigh of relief. Hopefully, she'd beat him back to the house. She had to end this craziness. Adam's presence meant Jay would never forgive her.

Her phone dinged and a text popped up on her dash display. "Hey, speed demon. I have to make a stop. I'll be a few minutes."

At her parents' house, Amy forced a false smile and donned her pretend happiness like a coat of armor while Dad brought Ricky.

After evading questions about Jeremy, she said she was exhausted and wanted to go home. When she pulled into the driveway, Jay still hadn't appeared.

She unlocked the door and brought Ricky upstairs to put him to bed, careful not to wake him. Hot tears spilled on his Spiderman pajamas as she drew the covers over him.

Through the open window, the sound of Jay's tires crunching in her driveway reached her as the beam of his headlights slid across the wall. His car door closed and within seconds he was knocking.

Amy froze trying to decide what to do.

"Amy!" Jay called, trying not to wake the neighbors. Amusement laced his words. "Babe, open the door, let me in."

Amy covered her face in her hands. She couldn't leave him standing on her step.

"Amy!" He didn't sound so amused now.

She rushed to the window. "Hush, you'll wake my neighbors. I'm coming down."

Ricky stirred and she prayed he didn't wake.

She pushed the window closed and ran downstairs. Turning on the kitchen light, she opened the door.

He started to enter but she put a hand on his chest and stopped him. "I'm sorry, Jay, I changed my mind."

"What?" His brow creased and he glared at her through his uninjured eye. "What are you talking about?"

His bewilderment broke her heart.

He held up a brown bag. "I am cognizant of the risk we took the other day, so I stopped at the pharmacy for condoms. It took some time to find an open store."

Tears spilled. "I can't." She gestured toward her ceiling. "Not with Ricky. How would I explain to him in the morning?"

Jay blinked and stared. "What question do you imagine he's gonna ask? Did you have sex with my mother last night?" He huffed. "The answer will be, yes, son and Saturday afternoon as well. Not to mention all the nights to come."

He tried again to enter and again she stopped him as she tsked and narrowed her eyes at his crudity. "You're not funny."

Anger flashed in his eyes. "No, Amy, you're not funny." His voice rose. "This isn't funny." Jay lifted his hands and let them drop to his sides. The bag snapped against his leg. "Why are you doing this?"

She shook her head. "I'm sorry," she spoke with more force as she pressed her shoulder against the doorframe and held the door to her side, blocking him.

"Why? Tell me." His confused gaze ranged up and down her body. The furrow in his brow deepened and his jaw grew tight. "Seriously, Amy. Are you gonna let me in or what?" Anger darkened his eyes and drew stark lines in his face.

Fear stabbed at her, and she almost gave in, but drawing a deep breath, she held on to her resolve with both hands.

She shook her head. "No. And I can't be with you anymore

either."

His jaw dropped.

Her heart seized at the don't-do-this-to-me-again fear on his face.

She shut the door, twisted the lock, and turned off the kitchen light, then ran upstairs and threw herself on her bed.

Jay pounded on the door and shouted her name, neighbors be damned, for another ten minutes. When he kicked at the door, she almost changed her mind, but the way Adam leered at them helped her maintain her resolve.

She did nothing to stop Jay from beating on her door. After all, he was right. She was a selfish fucking bitch, a whore, and a cock tease, but she had her reasons.

At last, the pounding stopped. His car roared to life and, tires squealing, he drove out of her life. Forever, she feared and hoped.

As Jeremy approached the front doors of the school, he let loose with a heavy sigh. The day hadn't started and already two thirty couldn't come fast enough. His boys called to him and tried to tease and joke, but he ignored them as he entered the front doors.

After a week, his bruises and eye healed and the scabs were almost gone. He'd replaced the bandage on his forehead for a Band Aid. He'd told anyone who'd asked at school he'd been in a car accident, unable to bring any more humiliation on himself.

Perhaps the time had come to call Amy. He'd been wrong to let things go so long. His parents always worked things out, not letting the sun go down on their anger. They would spend the entire night without sleeping if necessary to work out their issues. When the school day was over, he'd call her. Back off, back up, start over. The idea boosted his spirits, and he began to whistle a tune as he walked to his classroom.

Jeremy had forgotten a department meeting this afternoon. He had his work session with Britney until three thirty and the meeting at four. By the time it ended, he knew there would be no chance to call Amy before she arrived at Lou's.

He sat at his desk waiting for Britney to arrive, his chin braced on the heel of his hand as he stared without seeing the back of his classroom, his mind replaying last Monday night. A week. A week without her was like a year. A long, torturous year. He had to work this out, but how?

"Mr. Austin?"

He snapped his head around.

Britney Foster stood at the corner of his desk, clutching her math book against her chest. Her long blond hair flowed over one shoulder.

"Britney." Jeremy faked a smile and cleared his throat. "I'm sorry. I didn't hear you come in." He fiddled with papers on his desk.

"Are you okay?"

He smiled and nodded. "I'm fine." He extended a hand to the worktable at the back of the room. "If you're ready, let's go to work."

Britney didn't move. "We don't need to meet, Mr. A, if you don't want to. You don't look well. Are you sure?"

"Positive. I received some troubling news. Nothing to worry about."

"I'm sorry." She moved to the table and opened her textbook. "About your accident?"

He nodded. "How'd you do on your extra credit?" Jeremy sat down next to her and accepted the sheets of lined paper she handed him and struggled to keep his mind focused on his task. "Why did you take so many steps with these?" He cringed at the harsh demand in his voice and closed his eyes. "I'm sorry, I didn't mean to sound so gruff."

"That's okay." She cast him an uncertain glance and shrugged.

"You got the right answers," he reassured her, "but you can solve these in five steps. You took eight on this one, and... ten here. I mean, you drove around the block a few times to arrive at the correct answers, so I'm curious."

Embarrassment and frustration fought for control of her features.

He pressed his fingers on her forearm and removed them, always mindful of touching his students, especially the females. "I'm not criticizing. I'm trying to figure out how your mind works."

A wistful sigh escaped. "I wish I knew," she lamented, eliciting the first chuckle Jeremy had had in a week.

He grabbed a sheet of paper and turned to a new problem in the textbook. "Like this." He wrote the problem out and as he solved the equation he explained the shortcuts. When he finished, he studied her furrowed brow.

"How did you do that?"

"Easy." He meant to explain the procedure again, but she jumped in.

Irritation wrinkled her brow. "No, Mr. Austin." She tapped her finger on the algebra equation. "If it were easy, I wouldn't *be* here every afternoon. I mean, how do you solve the equation without all the steps? How come *I* don't see those shortcuts?" Britney pressed her knuckles into her forehead. "I have to take all those steps, or I can't figure them out."

"Fair enough," Jeremy conceded. "Take as many steps as you need. As I said, you're arriving at the correct answers, so I suppose the how doesn't matter."

Britney sniffed and offered a smile. "My dad says," she deepened her tone to mimic a male voice, "the way to solve a problem is to reduce it to the lowest common denominator and build from there."

"He's right," Jeremy said. A scowl pulled at his brow as a sudden thought came to him. Had Amy had an affair with Adam at some point? Were they still?

Britney gulped. "Did I say something wrong?"

He jerked himself back to the moment and forced a smile at his student.

"You did not. In fact, I think the teacher has met his match. Thank you, Brit."

"You're welcome. Can I go home now?" She lifted her eyebrows as hope filled her blue eyes.

Jeremy laughed. "Nice try. You get an A for effort. Explain your reasoning on some of these problems and I might let you leave early."

Britney gave an exaggerated sigh. "Fine," she drawled and got to work.

At 3:10 p.m. he wrapped up their session. She understood step-by-step how to solve the math problems, though the concept, he concluded, would always elude her.

"Mr. Austin, did I pass my last math quiz?" She closed her textbook and slipped the book and her notebook into her backpack.

"You did. You earned twenty-five points on your accumulated homework assignments, which brought your quiz score to seventy-eight. More than enough for passing."

He shook the homework sheets she handed him. "You keep this up and you'll find yourself a junior next year."

She grinned. "I want to thank you. Sometimes I think most of my teachers don't care if I pass or not, but you're different. My mom says you're a godsend."

"Well, I can tell you for a fact all your teachers want you to succeed and if they don't, they shouldn't be teaching." He smiled. "And tell your mom, I said, 'You're welcome.'"

They strolled to the front of the room.

"I'm glad you came up with the idea." She offered a small smile. "I'm surprised but the tests don't stress me out so much, now that I have a backup."

As if realizing how her words sounded, she shot him a nervous glance. "I don't mean to say I don't try on the tests. I do. But knowing you're gonna add my homework points helps me think better."

"I'm glad." He started picking up papers on his desk. "I wish I could take credit for the idea, but a friend of mine told me her math teacher did the same thing. It worked in her case, so I decided to try with you."

Britney stopped at his classroom door and studied Jeremy. "Is she the reason you're so sad and angry?"

God! Am I so obvious? Grabbing his phone off the desk, he slipped it into his back pocket and forced a friendly smile. "Have a wonderful evening, Brit. Keep up the excellent work."

Britney didn't move. He glimpsed her from the corner of his eye and faced her.

"I was with my dad in Home Depot a couple of weekends ago," she said. "You were holding hands with a woman and a little boy was on your shoulders. You were looking at paint."

He remembered. He and Amy had gone to Home Depot because she wanted to find a paint color for her bedrooms. Ricky had been a hyper two-year-old, frustrating Amy, so he settled him on his shoulders. The new vantage point kept him quiet as he surveyed his surroundings from up high. He didn't recall seeing Britney though.

"I'm sorry I didn't say hello. I must not have seen you."

"You wouldn't have. We were at a cash register. We were so far away I would have had to shout to say hi. Then you guys walked to the back of the store."

Britney smiled. "I told my dad I thought she was your girlfriend. He said he was pleased. If you're having trouble, Mr. A, just tell her you love her, and everything will be all right."

He smiled at her innocent assessment of the situation. Britney had a lot to learn. "Thanks, Brit."

She smiled a bright, happy smile. "'Kay." She flipped a hand. "Bye, Mr. A." She pivoted and left.

"Bye, Brit," he called after her.

As she walked away, Mike stepped out of her path. "Hey, Jer." He leaned on the classroom doorframe. "Meeting in thirty. Are you seeing Amy tonight?"

"Why?"

"Dave's putting together a poker game and the boys are with Erin's parents for the week so I'm up for going."

Jeremy shrugged. He wasn't interested in poker games and being sociable.

"So what happened?" Mike crossed his arms.

"What makes you think something happened?"

"C'mon, Jer. We've been friends a long time. I can read you like a well-worn book, as Erin used to say," he said, referring to his late wife.

Jeremy gave him a dubious glance.

"Okay." Mike chuckled. "The kids are talking in the hallway. Mr. A has turned into a flaming a-hole and a rat bastard. And those are the kinder comments. So I ask again. What happened?"

The strength left Jeremy's legs and he dropped into his chair. He slammed his elbows on his desk and buried his face in his hands.

Mike shut the door, walked over, and sat next to him.

Jeremy arrived at Dave's apartment at six forty-five armed with one hundred dollars, a six-pack of Sam Adams, and take-out chicken wings, his contribution to the poker game. After a quick knock, he let himself in and went to the kitchen to deposit the beer and wings.

"Hey, Dave," he called, and hearing voices down the hall, he walked toward the back room where Dave, Mike, and Eric, who taught science, were seating themselves around a card table.

"Wings and beer in the kitchen," Jeremy said, taking a seat.

Dave jumped up. "Well, they are of no use to us in the kitchen, my friend." He left, returning a short time later with Jeremy's wings. Eric had brought Chinese take-out, and Mike brought more beer.

Eric dealt the cards while Jeremy gathered his chips.

Mike smoked a cigar and Jeremy coughed with mock politeness, prompting Mike to blow the smoke straight into his face.

"Asshole," Jeremy said through a laugh, waving away the foul smoke. "How can you smoke those nasty-ass things?"

Mike grinned. "A gift from a friend," he said with airy disregard.

"Erin hated them too. Poker needs cigars. Don't know why."

"Jeremy." Dave resumed his seat and picked up his cards. "The grapevine says you and Maggie have parted ways permanently this time."

"Yep." Jeremy arranged the suits in his hand. "I thought word was all over campus before the first hour was out. How did you not learn about it until now?"

"A rumor," Dave declared, "as other rumors before, so I ignored it."

Jeremy glanced at Mike who raised a conspiratorial eyebrow and smoked.

"No offense, pal," Eric put in, "but you've said this before." He dropped a card and picked up one from the pack. "So when did this happen?"

"You guys didn't join the pool?" Jeremy threw down two cards, picking up two. "Mike threw in twenty bucks. We split up three months ago today."

"Wow, specific," Mike said then pulled on his cigar.

Jeremy glanced at him from under his lashes. After admitting he'd told the administration he'd had a car accident, he'd revealed the truth to Mike. He also shared how Amy had shut him out.

Mike finally convinced him to come to the game and let off some steam with the guys.

"Well, yeah," Dave said, throwing down three and picking up three from the pack. "I put in fifty bucks. I figured I won last time and third times the charm, right?"

Eric picked up a card and threw one down. "I put in twenty-five bucks, but I never win."

Mike drew on his cigar and as he released the smoke, his lips drew up in an I-got-your-back grin.

"So when do you pay out?" Jeremy asked. "I might want a cut of the winnings since you're all gambling on my life."

"End of the school year," Mike said. "If you can stay away from Maggie, you win the goods. Kitty's up to eight hundred dollars." He grinned and did a Groucho Marx move wagging his brows and twitching his cigar.

"If you do stay away, you don't mind if I have a go at her, do you?" Eric said. "I've always had a bit of a hankering for Maggie."

Jeremy laughed as he arranged his cards. Chubby Eric, all five foot seven inches with the beginnings of a beer belly, unruly brown hair, and horn-rimmed glasses. Like a true scientist, he wore a pocket protector. The idea of Eric taking on the likes of Maggie, who towered over him by at least three inches, cracked him up.

"Well, Eric, she's not a racehorse, but if you think you can handle her, be my guest." Jeremy said throwing down three cards and accepting three from Eric. He curled his lip at what he received and slipped them into his hand.

"Excellent," Eric said, throwing down a card.

"You'll have to do better than your place, though," Jeremy said. "Maggie has champagne tastes, and you live on a water budget."

"You mean she's expensive," Eric said, wariness filling his blue eyes.

"I mean, you're gonna have to raise your standards. For one thing, you'll have to move your mother out."

They burst into laughter and for a while, Jeremy relaxed as they played, but as the night wore on, he started glancing at his wristwatch.

"Are we keeping you from something?" Dave asked, laying down his hand.

"There are a million ways in which you are not," Jeremy said, again glancing at Mike who dealt the round. He offered Jeremy a sympathetic glance.

"So what's up with the constant checking the time? Would you rather be someplace else?"

Yes.

He snatched up his cards and began sorting them. "Sorry, Dave," he said, eyes narrowed. "I wasn't aware I was annoying you. I'll stop checking the time."

Mike laid a steadying hand on his forearm.

"Hey, guys," Eric piped up. "This is a friendly game. C'mon."

Dave and Jeremy glared at each other before Jeremy dropped his gaze to his cards. He moved suits and rearranged his hand, looking for patterns to play.

"Jer." Mike knocked on the table. "You awake? Your turn."

Jeremy jerked his head up, drew in a breath through his nose. "I'm thinking."

"If you have to think so hard, man, pass."

"Pass."

During the fourth round, the front door opened and closed but

Jeremy paid no attention.

Dave grinned. "Call."

They went around the table showing their cards. Rather than show his cards, Jeremy folded his hand and threw them in, face down, conceding. He grabbed his beer and drank, using the motion to glance at the time.

"Hello, everyone." Maggie entered. "Got room for one more? Sorry I'm late, babe," she said to Eric, sliding into his lap. With a sideways glance at Jeremy, she leaned in and planted a seductive kiss on Eric's lips.

Shit! Jeremy shook his head. "You might have said something." He sounded nonchalant, but his blood boiled.

"She asked what I was doing later, and I told her I was playing cards with the boys."

Eric attempted to grab another kiss, but Maggie adroitly avoided him.

Already. Poor Eric.

Jeremy shook his head. He might have taken the time to explain the rules of her game to him, but why not let him learn for himself? Turning to Mike, he rolled his eyes before glancing at his wristwatch again. It was ten o'clock. He shoved his chips at Mike. "Cash me out. I have to go. I need to take care of some things."

"What?" Dave put his cards down. "Why? It's still early."

"Not for me."

Mike exchanged Jeremy's chips. "Go easy, buddy. Rest up. You look like shit."

"Thanks." Jeremy smiled without humor. He rose to go. "I love you, too, mom."

"Running to the waitress?" Maggie sat in Eric's lap an arm curled around his neck.

"What?" Eric stared at Jeremy. "Who's the waitress?"

Jeremy ignored him, freezing Maggie with an icy glare. With his knuckles on the table, he leaned in close and glared at her, and when he spoke his voice was deadly calm. "Where I go, what I do, is none of your damned business."

He turned to Eric. "If you want her, you can have her. Be careful what you wish for."

"How about Thursday, May twenty-seventh, at two p.m.?" Amy

forced a smile and glanced up at the elderly woman in front of her. "Dr. Theriault has an opening."

Mrs. Marconi harrumphed. "I play bridge on Thursday afternoons."

Amy stared at her. *You can't skip one lousy bridge game for your health?* She raised a brow and returned her attention to the monitor, moving the mouse and searching for another day within the designated week to reschedule the old bat.

"Um, can you do Thursday at ten?"

Mrs. Marconi harrumphed again, and Amy suspected she started all of her sentences with a disgruntled snort.

"Young woman! I said Thursdays will not work for me."

Amy narrowed her eyes at her. "No. You said Thursday at *two* wouldn't work for you. I'm asking about ten o'clock in the morning." Frustration laced her words, earning a sidelong glance from Kevin. Too bad Amy couldn't foist her off on him, but he checked patients in. She checked them out and scheduled their next appointments.

Mrs. Marconi didn't answer. Instead, she raised her chin and stared down her nose at Amy with glacial blue eyes.

With a sigh Amy searched for a new day and time, but the doctor wanted her back in two weeks and he had few slots left open. She searched and forced herself to remain calm.

"Would Friday morning work for you?"

"I have breakfast with my friends on Friday mornings," Mrs. Marconi announced.

"Eleven thirty?" Amy glared.

"Monday will work for me," Mrs. Marconi announced.

"Dr. Theriault doesn't have an opening on Monday."

"Make one."

Teeth clenched, she stared at the imperious biddy and quietly informed her, "I can't make one. He either has an opening or he doesn't, and Monday is already full. I have Thursday morning, Thursday afternoon, or Friday at eleven-thirty. Pick one."

"I can't pick one. None of them work for me. You'll have to find a more suitable time for me."

Mrs. Marconi put her through this dance every time she came in, so why did she let her irritate her?

Because Jay kept his word. He'd left five nights ago and remained silent ever since.

She'd called once to apologize, but the phone stopped ringing mid-ring, telling her he declined her call. She hadn't tried since.

Ever since Monday night, Amy lived on the knife edge of emotion and was barely civil to her co-workers, customers, and patients.

She sighed, her irritation flowing like lava.

Grabbing an appointment card, she wrote Thursday and circled the a.m. and wrote ten on the card. She slammed her hand down on the counter and pushed the card at the old woman.

"If you don't want to drop dead from a heart attack, you'll come at this time."

"Well," Mrs. Marconi snarled as she snatched up the card. "I've never been treated with such rudeness in my entire life."

"I have a hard time believing that" Amy snapped.

Kevin, sitting next to her, pressed his knuckles against her forearm as a warning. She ignored him.

Mrs. Marconi gasped, retrieved her card, and stormed away all while muttering "Well, I never."

You should. Bitch.

"What is *wrong* with you, girl?" Kevin snarled in a whisper.

Amy turned her head, so she talked to the back wall. "I can't stand her," she snarled back.

"Clearly, but you need to be careful. If Miranda gets wind of your attitude, you'll be out of a job." He gestured toward the elevator where Mrs. Marconi departed. "And the bitch won't hesitate to complain, you know."

Amy shrugged as if she didn't care, but the fact was, she needed this job like she needed air, and he was right. She couldn't afford to annoy Miranda.

"How're things with Mr. Wonderful?" Kevin asked.

"Not so wonderful," she said and struggled not to burst into tears. "We had a colossal fight last week and now he's ghosting me." She couldn't bring herself to tell him she forced him into the decision, and honestly, what did she expect? She'd teased Jay with the promise of sex. Led him on and let him down.

"I'm sorry," Kevin said, ending the conversation when the next patient stepped up to check in.

Glancing around for signs of Miranda, her boss did not allow cell phones at the work stations, Amy slipped her phone from her back pocket, which she concealed under the counter as she checked for messages. Nothing. What did she expect? The phone would have vibrated in her pocket. She sighed and put the device back. She should call him. And say what, exactly? I'm sorry? I fucked up? How many times might she draw from that well?

At last, the day ended, and Amy raced to the bathroom to change into her waitress uniform before heading to Lou's. She didn't want to work another job after a long and difficult day, but she had no choice. She had a son to raise. Alone.

Walking to the shuttle station she mentally kicked herself.

Fourth of July, the summer of their junior year, popped into her head. She and Jay had gone to the fireworks in Burlington.

On the way home, he stopped at their favorite secluded place, where they made out in the back seat of his Jeep. Coming dangerously close to giving him her virginity, she put a stop to the action. He was furious with her and called her a tease.

She tearfully confessed her fear of becoming pregnant, and as a minor and a Catholic, she didn't have the nerve to ask her parents to go on birth control.

Jay finally came around to her point of view, but he took some strong convincing and a reminder no means no. He drove her home sulky and silent the entire ride.

To break his still-angry silence, she proposed a deal to him.

"Have you slept with any girls, Jay?" she asked him, her heart in her throat.

"You know I haven't," he'd growled.

"Not even Melanie?"

He scoffed. "No."

She nodded. "I have an idea," she said, more for something to break his sullen silence. "How about if we remain virgins until we get married. We'll have our wedding night to look forward to and if I get pregnant, no problem."

He blinked but didn't say anything. He hadn't needed to. His blink told her he was considering her idea.

Pulling up in front of her house, he'd turned to her and taken her hand. "Deal," he'd said, kissing her knuckles. "Virgins until marriage. And Amy"—his brown-eyed gaze had penetrated hers— "I *will* marry you."

Amy smiled. He'd been so confident. Too bad so much had changed, and she couldn't entertain the possibility of marriage to Jay, the thing she wanted more than anything else except Ricky.

But Adam made the terms of their deal null and void. Her fear was groundless now, and the rational part of her brain tried to get through to her, but she'd carried her emotional baggage for so long, that she had difficulty parting with her insecurities.

No, she'd done the right thing on Monday night, no matter how much she hurt. Love and happiness were not in the cards for her. The hardest part of all was Ricky's constant refrain, "Where Jamie go?" to which she had no answer.

Staring at the ground, she replayed the scene Monday night with Jay. A familiar deep ache in the pit of her belly left her breathless. She knew what she had to do.

She took out her phone. After each argument, Jay always extended the olive branch first. Now was her turn. She hated to admit the time had come to tell him everything and let the chips fall where they might. He said he loved her, and they weren't kids anymore.

He had taken her other revelations well. On the other hand, this might be the straw that broke the camel's back. She had to take the chance.

She dialed his number. The phone went to voice mail. Amy sighed and disconnected.

"Hey," the bus driver hollered.

She jumped.

"Are you riding or what?"

Amy climbed on and sat down. She had to find a way to talk to Jay. To fix the problem of her making. As the shuttle pulled away, she stared out the window and began rehearsing in her head what she would say.

22

The green and brown of the baseball diamond stood out in stark colors on this chill gray Saturday morning. Jeremy tossed a baseball in the air with one hand and swung the bat while his boys fielded their positions. They had a game on Tuesday against Essex, one of their toughest rivals, so he called an unusual Saturday morning practice. At least, that's what he told the boys. He needed something to do to occupy his mind and time. Since he cut off all communication with Amy last week, he felt lost and incredibly lonely.

When he'd left the poker game last night he intended to drive to Burlington, but halfway home, from Dave's he changed his mind. He was tired in mind and body. No, not tired, exhausted. So he went home and went to bed, but he kept waking up from dreams of Amy. Dreams of the type he hadn't had since puberty, and they frustrated and annoyed him.

Irritation shot through him as he sent the ball spinning to his second baseman who fielded the ball and tossed it to Patrick, his first baseman.

"C'mon, Joel keep your glove on the ground!" Jeremy shouted, earning a confused stare as Patrick rolled the ball back to the catcher.

Joel and Patrick glanced at each other before resuming the ready position, knees bent, upper body in a slight crouch, glove on the ground.

Jeremy smacked another ball harder at Joel who kept his glove firmly on the ground, but the ball took a funny bounce and rolled up his arm, popping him in the mouth.

“Ow!”

Jeremy dropped the bat and ran to him as Joel slammed his glove into the dirt, his hand clapped to his mouth. He turned his back on Jeremy.

“Are you alright?” Grabbing his student by the shoulder, Jeremy tried to turn him to assess his injuries.

“Fuck you, Coach,” Joel snarled and spit blood. He yanked his shoulder from Jeremy’s grasp.

“Here, let me see,” Jeremy encouraged, not taking offense. He considered foul language a teenage rite of passage into manhood. Besides, Joel had a right to be pissed. Jeremy was taking his anger with Amy out on the boys and had done so all week. He deserved a ‘*fuck you*’ or two. Or three.

With gentle fingers, he pulled at Joel’s lip. A half smile quirked his own. “You’ll have a fat lip. Join the club. You might want to go to the school nurse just in case though.”

Joel shrugged him off. “I don’t need no fucking school nurse. I fielded the first ball clean.”

“You did. I apologize.”

Joel glared at Jeremy then offered one angry, gruff nod. Bending at the waist, he swept his glove off the dirt. “Let’s get back to business.”

Jeremy clapped him on the shoulder and returned to home plate. As he strolled back, he wrangled his anger under control. Amy’s indecision and fear weren’t their faults.

By the time he reached home plate, retrieved the bat, and resumed fungoes, now aiming the ball to Andy, his third baseman, he resolved not to take his personal feelings out on his boys, though he still buzzed over how she denied him.

After returning home from practice and taking a hot shower, Jeremy made himself a PB&J sandwich and gulped down a bottle of water.

He sat at the bar with his sandwich and water, and as he ate, he returned to Monday night when Amy ran away. They were making out on the bench, teasing, and laughing. And then she ran. Without warning. Without reason. Like before.

No, not true. Adam had appeared out of nowhere, scaring the crap out of her. He couldn’t blame her for her reaction, but it didn’t justify turning Jeremy out of her life.

Unless...

He took another bite of his sandwich and swallowed a gulp of water. When the bottle was empty, he went to the fridge and got another. As he twisted off the top and tossed it in the trash, he finally took hold of the question tumbling around in his head since talking with Britney. Had Amy and Adam had an affair? Did they still?

She said she opened her eyes, and he was leering at them. Jeremy had to admit Adam would have scared the bejesus out of him too. But why tell him she couldn't be with him anymore? Unless Adam had come to meet her, and Jeremy was in the way.

Adam was his father's friend. They'd been law school roommates and the best man at each other's weddings. He couldn't square the Adam he knew with a sexual offender. Lewd and disgusting at times, with a penchant for dirty jokes, Adam was not a rapist. *He's a lawyer for God's sake. He knows better.* So, the only other explanation was worse. They were fooling around. Better to find out now. But poor Emily.

And the lecherous gleam in his eye when he caught them together—he might have been embarrassed, amused, or both. He might have been pissed and hiding the fact. The first time they'd run into each other, Adam suggested he recognized her. Was he covering? Was her reaction, her panic attacks born of fear they might reveal themselves to him? Her wish he was dead might have been for his benefit. *Sonofabitch!*

How long had this gone on? Was Ricky really Peter's son or was he Adam's?

He shook his head. Ricky's features were nothing like Adam's, whose dark hair and more compact frame didn't fit with Ricky's almost white blond hair and more slender build. He dismissed the idea and prayed he was right.

Sonofabitch! Damn her! He pushed the thought away and continued to search for a better alternative.

After popping the last bite of his sandwich into his mouth, he reached for the phone. He opened the text Emma sent him the night he'd had dinner with Amy and met Ricky.

"I remember blood. In the bathroom. A lot." What did she mean?

When they got home from school, Amy was alone in their house. Had she gotten her period and was embarrassed? Many things those days embarrassed her.

They'd had a regular day at school as far as he remembered. He didn't recall her behaving any differently, but the particular day was lost to his memory, so he might be making this up.

He relaxed on his barstool and let the entire scene play out, but this time, he took himself out of the equation.

His siblings walked into the house. Still on crutches, in a cast from his thigh to his ankle, Jeremy brought up the rear. Amy sat motionless on a stool in the kitchen staring off into space, tears tracking her face.

Emma was right. She didn't turn around. Even when Charlie said, "Hey, Aims, 'sup?"

She sat rigid, as though she didn't hear, staring straight ahead, picking at the skin around her fingers. The four of them exchanged confused glances.

Jeremy placed his hand on her shoulder to ask what was wrong. She jerked, and he pulled his hand away as though he'd touched a hot stove.

While he and his siblings exchanged bemused glances, she continued to stare unseeing out the kitchen window, picking the skin around her fingers while her hands shook.

Maya found Dad's note on the counter and read aloud, "Be back in a couple of hours. Golfing with Adam."

Amy lurched at Adam's name and came out of her trance.

Jeremy balanced on his crutch and grasped her shoulder again, and she went off as Emma had described, like a rocket.

Her attack was so violent, that his crutch flew out from under him, and he fell, landing on his cast. The searing pain in his leg elicited a bloodcurdling scream. The next thing he remembered Amy was gone. Emma was crying into the phone, while Charlie and Maya bent over him trying to hold down his writhing body and screaming anxious questions.

Jeremy blinked. He was losing a connection and needed to refocus.

His mind kept repeating a refrain he often said to his students: find the value of X. Find the value of X? X being what? A sharp intake of breath brought him back to reality. He grabbed his water bottle and phone and headed into his office.

Yanking open a drawer, he grabbed a notebook and pen and wrote a mathematic equation where Amy was a set number, and her attacker was X. He tried multiple possibilities but came up with nothing. A small voice in his head whispered Adam was X, but he couldn't bring himself to write the equation. Throwing his pen down, he grabbed his phone and called Emma.

"Hey, Jer." She sounded impatient. "Is this important? I have a meeting in a few minutes."

"You're working on a Saturday?"

"We have a huge case coming up and yes, I work on Saturdays if necessary. What's up?"

"I wanted to talk to you about the text you sent me. About blood in the bathroom."

"Oh."

"What did you mean?"

He listened to her breathe, then off the phone she told someone to inform "them" she would be along in a moment.

"Em?"

"All I can say for now is talk to Maya. She might have the information you need."

"Maya?"

"Yes."

"What does Maya have to do with this?"

When Emma didn't answer, he prodded. "Em?"

She sighed. "It's not my story to tell, Jer." Again she spoke off the phone to someone else. "I gotta go, sweetie. Talk to Maya." Emma clicked off.

Jeremy held his phone. Talk to Maya. Why? The mystery was deepening. He scrolled through his contacts and when he stopped on "Hanover", he called his oldest sister and put the phone on speaker.

While her phone rang, he studied his equation again and was becoming so absorbed, he jumped when she said, "Hi, Jer."

"Hey, Maya," he said. "How're things in the Jackson household?"

"Ducky. How're things with you?"

In the background, her kids yelled, "Hi, Uncle Jeremy."

He chuckled. "Hi, Holly, hi, Chris!" he shouted into the phone.

"He says hi. Now scram, both of you. I understand you flushed Maggie from your life. Emma told me."

His defenses shot up. "What else did she tell you?" Emma had never betrayed a trust before, and he didn't believe she would do so now, but his hackles rose.

Rustling sounds came through the phone along with Maya's voice away from the phone. "Christopher, leave your sister alone before I grab the strap."

"Ugh." She returned to the conversation. "He's such a five-year-old."

Jeremy laughed. "Leave him alone, he's an awesome kid."

"You say that about all kids."

He chuckled. "Well, yours in particular, as well as Emma's boys, I suppose, so yeah. I admit, I love my one niece and three nephews." *Damn, how does one broach the subject?*

She sighed. "I was sure you'd call before too long." She sounded resigned.

He grew concerned. "What do you mean?"

"Emma said you're asking questions about Adam."

"Did she say why I'm asking?" He furrowed his brow, prepared to call Emma back and launch into a furious diatribe, meeting or no meeting.

"No, only that you asked interesting questions."

He breathed a sigh of relief. "I just spoke with her, and she said I need to talk to you."

"Yeah," Maya said. "She told me you might call."

"Maya." Jeremy glanced at his phone. "I realize we haven't been close. I don't talk to you or visit like I do Charlie or Emma, but I do love you. You're my sister."

"Wow, Jeremy." She chuckled. "How unexpected. Sweet, but unexpected."

"I mean it."

"I'm glad, and the fault is as much mine. The phone works both ways as do the roads we travel." She sighed. "Ask me your questions."

When he ended his call with Maya, Jeremy pushed his phone aside. She could put a mafia boss to shame with her vague generalities. After a few minutes of his grilling her, she said she had to hang up, remembering she had to talk to Dad about Memorial Day weekend and opening the summer house. Before Jeremy said another word, Maya disconnected.

He was staring at the phone in disbelief when "Perry Mason" appeared. Okay, she couldn't have talked to Dad already, so his father must have been calling about something else. Answering, Jeremy put the phone on speaker.

"Hey, Dad."

"Hey, Jeremy. I'm on a mission for your mother."

Jeremy smiled. "What mission?"

"She wants you to come to dinner tomorrow night. I think she wants to go all Nurse Nancy on you. Besides, she hasn't seen you since..." He broke off.

"And she's having withdrawal symptoms?"

Dad chuckled. "You are the only one left who can let her act like a mama again."

He chuckled. "Tell Mom I'd love to come to dinner."

"Okay," Dad said. Dead air on the line caused Jeremy to raise his head from his equation.

"Anything else?"

"Well, yes...something...of a delicate nature...I'd like to ask you, son."

Son? Jeremy stared at the phone. What had he done wrong?

"Such as?"

Dad sighed and Jeremy pictured him staring at the ground, scuffing a toe. He sat up straight and waited.

"I had an uncomfortable conversation with Adam a couple of days ago and I need to talk to you about what he told me," Dad said.

Jeremy's attention perked. "What did you talk about?"

A long exhale.

"Dad, spill. What did Adam say to you?"

"Are you soliciting prostitutes, Jeremy?"

Jeremy sputtered into laughter. "Whaaat?" The question was so far from what he thought Dad was going to say, the visual struck him funny.

"No!"

"Would you tell me if you were?" Dad said.

"No!" He let go and laughed. The idea was too ludicrous. "Where did you get such an idea?"

"Adam," Dad said, sounding relieved. "He also suggested you were in some kind of brawl, but I told him you explained what happened."

Jeremy sobered as he recalled the night in late March when he'd run into Adam in front of Lou's. The night of Amy's first panic attack. Adam had asked the same question. "Are you soliciting prostitutes, son?"

Adam sounded amused and hopeful. Dad was concerned.

"Why would Adam think I'm soliciting prostitutes?"

Was he wrong on the affair angle? Was Adam leering because he thought Jeremy was in the arms of a prostitute?

"Well, he says he encountered you the other night...uh...shall we say...quite engaged...with a young lady. He says he's seen you many nights very late, walking in downtown Burlington with women. He wasn't sure this was the same woman he's seen you with before and if not, he wanted to inform me he thought you might be engaging in risky behaviors, which doesn't sound like you, but sometimes men need to do what they need to do."

What the f— "Men need to do what men need to do? Seriously?" Jeremy gaped at his phone. "Are you suggesting, you've on occasion 'done what you need to do'?"

"Don't be impertinent, Jeremy. I've never cheated on your mother."

"Thank God."

"Are you seeing someone, son?"

Rather than answer the question, Jeremy said, "Dad, can I ask a question?"

"Of course," he said.

"Do you remember the day Amy ran out of the house?"

"Amy? What does she have to do with this conversation?"

"I don't know, but do you remember that day?"

"Of course, I remember, Jer. You scared your mother and me to no end."

He ignored the reference. "Was Adam at the house at any time Amy was?"

His father was quiet for so long he imagined Dad reeling back in his memory banks. "Yes," he said. "We were going golfing, and he was waiting for me in the kitchen when Amy rang the doorbell. I let her into the house, and we left."

"And you left together?"

"Yes. Although…"

"Although what?"

"I'm sure it's nothing," Dad said.

"Tell me anyway."

"Well, I seem to remember Adam saying he had to use the john before we left and went back inside. He was gone so long I almost went back inside to see what took him so long. What's this about?"

"I'm not sure yet," Jeremy said. "But as soon as I am, I'll tell you."

He told his father to expect a call from Maya, and after he ended the call, Jeremy studied his equation again. This time, he wrote Adam in as the value of X and with his heart in his mouth, began again to solve the equation.

Forty-five minutes passed and he decided he'd had enough. He didn't like the conclusion he was coming to and pushed his notebook away with a glance at his wristwatch.

Four o'clock and he was restless. Since today was Saturday, Amy would have left for work by now. If he went to her parents' house, would they let him take Ricky to the park? He didn't have a number to call, but what did he have to lose? He wanted to see Ricky. He grabbed his keys and left the house.

Jeremy pulled up to the Taylors' front yard, and unbidden came the embarrassing memory of screaming vile insults at Amy as she ran to avoid him. John storming out of the garage threatening to call the police and waving at Jeremy like a wild man, fists clenched as if to do battle. Charlie's arms, one around his neck and shoulders, the other around his waist, dragging him backward despite his crutches and cast and forcing him back into his Jeep.

He reached to start the car and drive away, but John stepped out of the garage and stood on the driveway, watching.

He cut the engine. "Hey, John." He walked across the lawn and extended a hand.

John shook it. "What can I do for you, son?"

"I know Amy's at work, and you and Carol usually take care of Ricky, but I wondered if you'd like a break. I thought I'd take him to the park, with your permission of course."

John smiled. "Come with me," he said and headed back into the garage.

Jeremy followed him out to the back porch. In the backyard, Jessica and Ricky played together, kicking a ball back and forth. His face fell. Ricky didn't need him.

John clapped him on the back. "What are your plans for dinner, Jeremy?"

He raised his brows in question.

"I'm grilling chops. Since you drove down here, why don't you stay and eat?"

Jeremy smiled. "Thank you." He was reminded of something and narrowed his eyes. "You don't still cook your chops until they are ashes, do you?"

John cackled a laugh. "You're ninety-eight percent carbon anyway. What's a little more?" he teased. "But no, the girls finally convinced me they don't like eating ashes, so I leave some flavor and a little meat behind."

Jeremy laughed. "In that case, I'll stay."

"Jaaaamieeee," Ricky's delighted shout rent the air as he ran across the backyard toward the back porch.

Jeremy went outside and scooped him into his arms. "How you been, Sport?"

"Good." Ricky wriggled and squirmed, and Jeremy put him on his feet.

With both hands, Ricky grabbed his index finger and tugged. "Play with me, Jamie."

That was all Jeremy needed. They kicked the ball around the backyard. Next time he'd bring a baseball and teach Ricky and Jessica how to play catch.

After a while, Jessica declared she was tired and wanted to play with her dolls. Jeremy, holding Ricky by the waistband of his pants, flew him around the backyard like an airplane, while making zooming noises. Ricky screamed with laughter and whenever Jeremy put him down, he yelled, "Do it again, do it again!"

By the time Carol served dinner, Jeremy was exhausted, but he'd had fun. How long had it been since he just let go and played? He couldn't remember.

After dinner, they sat at the table drinking beers and talking.

"John, I want to apologize to you for my behavior when Amy and I broke up in high school. Her rejection came from out of the blue and I admit I behaved like a total asshole."

John's blank stare told Jeremy he had indeed forgotten the incident. The man shrugged and waved away his apology. "We all do stupid things when we're kids," he said and took a swallow of his beer. He set the bottle down. "What I want to know now, Jeremy, is what your intentions are toward my daughter?"

Jeremy didn't hesitate. "I love her, sir. If I can convince her, I'd like to ask her to marry me." *If she isn't screwing Adam that is.*

"What do you mean if you can convince her?" Carol asked. He studied Ricky sleeping on her lap. Jessica slept on the couch on the other side of the porch.

Amy's words at dinner twanged his heart. *It seems the only time I spend with him is when he's sleeping.*

Jeremy took a swallow of his beer, using the time to form his thoughts. He swallowed. "I have trouble convincing her whatever happened between us ten years ago doesn't matter to me now. But she thinks it does or should."

Carol nodded as her body swayed back and forth, rocking her grandson in her arms. "Something happened," she said. "Her demeanor changed completely afterward."

Jeremy waited for her to say more, but she remained silent. He opened his mouth to ask what she meant when Carol spoke again.

"She used to be a happy-go-lucky girl, but then without warning, she shut down, turned angry, sullen, resentful. She refused to eat for weeks, remember John?"

He nodded.

Carol studied Jeremy. "I always assumed whatever happened was because of you." She tilted her head in apology. "I'm sorry, but I thought since you two were graduating and probably off to different schools, you'd broken up with her and she was angry, though she refused to talk to me."

Jeremy waved away her apology. "If I did something to her, I'm completely in the dark about what and was then too. To be honest, I don't know what happened. She keeps telling me it wasn't me, but she refuses to answer my questions."

He raised his beer bottle again and caught sight of his wristwatch. Eight-thirty. How was it he'd been here for four and a half hours already? He finished his beer and leaned forward to set the bottle down. He was just about to say he had to be getting home when John stopped him with a question.

"Are you going to pick up Amy tonight?"

For a heartbeat, Jeremy almost said no, but instead he nodded, not wanting to anger her parents.

"Good," John said. "Don't give up on her, son."

Jeremy peered her father. "What did she tell you about us?"

John pushed his chin out and gave a quick shake of his head.

"Nothing I couldn't see with my own two eyes when we put the beds together."

23

Frank was waiting for Amy when she got to the restaurant.

"Hey, Frankie," she said as she moved past him to stop at her locker.

"Come to my office, Amy. We need to talk."

The smile left her face, and she studied him. Was she in trouble?

"Is something wrong?"

He inclined his head to his office door and disappeared inside.

Amy dumped her belongings in her locker and shut the door with a clang. With a heavy tread she stepped inside his office door. Was he going to fire her? Why? She needed this job. As fast as possible, her brain skimmed past the last week trying to find something she'd done to justify Frank's austere demeanor.

He pointed to a chair, and she perched on the edge as he took a seat behind his desk.

"Okay," he said without preamble. "Tell me what's going on."

She peeked at him from beneath her lashes. "What do you mean?"

He sighed and rubbed his eyes. "I mean, you've been unusually quiet and uncommunicative and border-line rude to the customers."

His displeasure made her heart pound. "I've had complaints about your scatterbrained service, your unfriendly demeanor, and borderline rudeness, which isn't like you at all. Coupled with," he held up a finger "I haven't seen Jeremy all week, so I ask again. What's going on?"

Shamefaced, she stammered an apology for Frank's no-nonsense evaluation of her job performance. How could she tell him what happened?

"You do understand anything you say is safe with me, right?"

She sniffed and nodded. "I've been keeping something from him, but a situation came up the other night."

She pressed her lips together, unable to say the words. "So I told him I can't be with him anymore."

When Frank didn't speak, she raised her gaze and found him gaping at her. "Why?"

"Because."

"Because is a child's answer, Amy."

She picked at her thumb until the cuticle bled. "I had to. He can't find out." She sucked at her thumb.

"Find out what?"

Sniffing again, she wiped her eyes with the back of a hand. "When we first started dating again, I told him I had been..." She broke off and stared at Frank. She'd never told him either. With a hard swallow and her gaze firmly fixed on her hands nervously moving in her lap, she started talking. "When I was eighteen, I was raped." She peeked at him to see his response.

His eyebrows went up, but he said nothing.

She raised her head. "By a friend of his father's. I never told him. But something happened a month ago, and I had to tell him why I reacted the way I did. I told him what happened without giving any details and thankfully, he didn't ask."

Frank's Adam's apple bobbed.

Amy fell silent.

"What happened to compel you to tell him when you did?"

"I left the restaurant and found Jeremy talking to the guy, and I freaked."

Frank lifted and lowered his chin in a slow, deliberate motion. "Is this the night you had a panic attack?"

Her mouth dropped open.

He waved a hand. "Jeremy feared he hadn't handled the situation well, so he told me what happened and asked for advice." He studied her. "You haven't asked for advice, but I'm giving it anyway. Tell him everything."

"If I tell him, he'll dump me."

"You said you dumped him, so how can he?"

Amy shook her head. "The guy is like an uncle to him. Who do you think they'd believe? Him or me? He's a partner in Jay's father's law firm for God's sake. He'd chew me up and spit me out and Jay will have nothing to do with me ever again."

"Is this what the perp told you?" Frank stared hard at her his steely blue gaze tried to penetrate her defenses. "Jeremy won't desert you," Frank said. "He loves you. And you're selling him way short."

Amy shook her head, finding his words hard to believe. She dropped her gaze to her lap.

"Amy." He leaned close. "Do you love him?"

"With all my heart."

"Trust him with the truth. He deserves that. Give him the information and let Jeremy decide what comes next."

"I don't think I can."

"Why not?"

"We ran into the guy again last week and I cut Jay off the same night. He's pissed at me, and I can't blame him. I don't think he'll take a call from me."

"Again," Frank said, "give him the benefit of the doubt. Go see him if you must and tell him you need to speak with him." He tilted his head. "Hell, this type of information deserves a face-to-face."

Wanting to end the conversation, she nodded. "Okay," she said. "Can I have a few minutes? I'll call to set up a time to meet."

Frank rose. "Take as much time as you need." He walked to the door and turned back. "Trust him, Amy. Trust the fact the man loves you."

She smiled. "Why are you so certain he loves me? Has he told you?"

Frank shook his head and smiled. "He doesn't have to. Plain as the nose on your face."

He stared at her for a while and Amy thought he was going to say something else. She raised her brows.

"Call him," Frank said, "and let's go to work." He left.

Amy sat with the device in her hand, thinking about their conversation. Despite what he said, she wasn't sure if Jay did love her enough to overcome the revulsion that she was sure would follow if she told him the truth. Still, she did as instructed and called him, unsurprised when she got his voice mail. With a heavy sigh, she disconnected, slipped the phone into her back pocket, and went to work.

"Hey, Dad, how many nights a week does Adam work at the women's shelter?"

He sat in the living room at his parents' house. The delicious aroma of Sunday dinner made his stomach growl.

Dad shrugged. "Three or four. I told him one night a week would be fine, but he says with so much need, one night would be an injustice."

"So, Jeremy, how's school going?" Mom, a retired history teacher, never tired of talking education. When he got his teaching degree, she told anyone who would listen, she was thrilled to have another educator in the family and feared the gene had skipped a generation.

He shrugged and swigged some beer. "Almost over for the summer, thank God. At this point in the year, I'm either sick of my students or I'm sorry the year is ending. This year was tougher than most, but better than last year's 'Zoom school.'"

"Why is this year tougher?" Mom glanced at him. Though she worked in the kitchen fixing dinner, the open concept of their kitchen and living room allowed her to be present for the conversation.

Again he shrugged. "Just a lot of changes going on."

"Academically?" Dad sipped his beer.

"More like...personal."

"Oh?"

Jeremy drank and shrugged, wishing the subject hadn't come up. He held the beer in his mouth before swallowing to gather his thoughts.

"Is everything okay, Jer?" Mom walked into the living room. "You're not happy. From the minute you walked into this house, I sensed something's troubling you. What's wrong?"

Through his lashes, he offered her a teasing glance, but he couldn't hide his sadness in the smile he gave her. "Your JerBear is fine, Mommy."

"I don't think you are," she challenged, ignoring his teasing use of her nickname and crossing her arms. "You're my son. I can tell. I love you."

At least someone does. He half shrugged, sighed, and rubbed his fingers against his forehead.

"Are you still grieving over Maggie?" Mom tilted her head.

He stopped rubbing and gaped at her. "No," he said. "At least, I wouldn't call it grieving."

"I have to say I'm relieved. I don't like what she did to you." Anger laced her words and he thought of Amy, angry on his behalf, urging him to report her.

Mom perched on the arm of Dad's chair and waved a hand between them. "In any case, we never thought her right for you."

Dad slid his arm around her waist as if in support of what she had to say.

He studied them. "Why didn't you?"

She frowned, thinking. "In her own way, I think Maggie loves you, but she always struck me as Lucy with the football and you're her Charlie Brown. Besides, you don't love her. You never have. All these years, I've worried you had the past stuck in your heart, but since February I've seen a massive change in you, Jeremy, and I've begun to hope you've finally found the woman who could dislodge Amy Taylor from your heart."

He jerked his head up and stared, dumbfounded.

"Oh, yes," she nodded. "I may not say much, but I pay attention. Don't misunderstand. I loved Amy and hoped one day she'd be my daughter-in-law, but after ten years, Jeremy, the time is long past to put that painful chapter away."

Jeremy propped his elbow on the arm of his chair. His fist pressed against his lips, pressing them against his teeth as he tried to swallow a surge of emotion. If she only knew how deadly accurate her aim was, she'd be shocked. Tears filled his eyes, and he didn't know if he should laugh or cry. He blinked and knuckled an eye.

"Jeremy!" Mom slid off the arm of Dad's chair and knelt in front of him. "Where is this coming from?"

He half chuckled, half sobbed and drew in a ragged breath. "What's wrong with me? Why can't I keep a relationship?" He squeezed the words out of his constricted throat and slid his arms around his mother's neck.

Mom's arms tightened around him, and she crooned as if he were three years old with a skinned knee.

"You're all right, honey," she assured him. "You're safe here."

Jeremy wept. Wordless sobs from deep within his soul. His fingers grasped at her shirt as he pulled himself deeper into his mother's embrace, soaking up the comfort he didn't realize he needed until now.

Dad joined Mom on the floor in front of him. His hand squeezed Jeremy's knee in spasmodic concern.

When his sobs slowed, Mom patted Jeremy's shoulder, kissed his cheek, and got to her feet. She went to the bathroom and returned with a box of tissues, which she placed on the arm of his chair.

He smiled his thanks and took several to blow his nose.

"Now, if this isn't about Maggie, then who? This new girl? Dad says you told him you're seeing someone. You could have brought her with you. We would have loved to meet her."

Jeremy blew his nose again. "We ended our relationship the other night."

"Why?"

"She isn't being honest with me, and I can't take anymore."

Mom patted his arm. "Well, as with Maggie, you did the right thing." She studied him and her brow rose. "You love this girl."

He covered his eyes before dropping his hand to grasp hers. "I have no luck with love."

"You'll find someone, my boy. Trust me. You're too kind and sweet to go much longer before the right woman comes along."

Jeremy hugged his mother again. When he pulled away, he kissed her cheek. "You have to say that. You're my mother." He sniffled and smiled.

"I speak the truth."

She gave him a quick squeeze and went to check on dinner. He smiled through his tears. As always with Mom, food made everything all better.

The food and conversation relaxed Jeremy. Mom cooked more than necessary so she could send him home with leftovers.

He explained why Adam thought he was soliciting prostitutes.

"She's a waitress at Lou's Restaurant in downtown Burlington. I met her in February and each night after her shift I walk her to her car, which is two and a half blocks away and in a parking garage which creeps even me out." He sighed. "I had no idea Adam had seen us walking around town, but it's the gospel truth."

Dad's eyebrows shot up and down. "Well, that explains everything."

"Honest to heaven, Paul," Mom said. "Adam has a filthy mind I've ignored for years, but when he starts making accusations against my children, well! I'm unwilling to put up with it."

Jeremy's eyes widened when she slammed her fist on the table for emphasis, jarring silverware and glasses. He had no idea Mom felt this way about Adam. She'd never given herself away as far as he could remember.

Dad's response was a heavy sigh. He placed a gentle hand over hers, but said nothing, making clear to Jeremy they'd been over this territory many times in the past.

Suspecting an argument in the making, Jeremy tried to calm the situation. "Don't worry, Mom. You're right, Adam is a disgusting man who never graduated from puberty, but overall, I think he's harmless."

When Jeremy sat down, he'd placed his phone on the table beside his plate. The device vibrated and Catnap appeared on the screen. He glanced down before flipping the phone over.

"Who's Catnap?" Dad said, eyebrow raised.

"She's no one." Jeremy's face grew hot, and his ears burned.

"No one, eh?" Dad smiled. "I haven't seen 'no one' make you blush so hard since high school."

Jeremy shrugged and stabbed his broccoli.

"Honey." Mom took a sip of her water. "Don't you want to answer? She might be calling to apologize."

He glared at his plate. "I have nothing to say to her."

24

The sounds of the ballpark hadn't changed since Amy was in school. As she and Ricky approached the baseball field, parents called encouragement to their kids, and the boys in the field and dugout called encouragement to each other.

The metallic clank of the ball hitting the bat conjured images of watching Jay play. In those days, he was the star second baseman for Essex until he broke his leg sliding into home base during the state championship.

She remembered hearing his scream of pain as the catcher's knee came down on his femur; the sound of the bone snapping still sent an icky quiver down her spine. Back then, her mother, a nurse, sitting in the stands was down on the field beside him before Amy could count to ten.

The game was already in progress when she arrived.

As soon as she came home from work, she changed, grabbed Ricky, and here they were. She'd tried calling him Sunday night, but he wouldn't answer. She left a message telling him she wanted to talk but he didn't respond. *Well, if Muhammad won't come to the mountain....*

The Essex team was up, and she checked out the visiting dugout. Jay was there, pacing back and forth, calling instructions to his team, giving signs and clapping his hands. His red baseball cap, with AHS across the top and an arrowhead poking through the H, left a shadow across his nose and mouth and hid his eyes.

He called something to his first baseman and did a double take as he obviously spotted her watching him.

The first baseman punched his fist into his glove and assumed the ready position.

Amy lifted Ricky into her lap. “Behave now, okay?”

He nodded and paid attention to the game with fascination—for about thirty seconds before he wanted to get down.

Amy was reluctant. He might try to run onto the field, and she feared she might not stop him before he got hurt. She should have brought some of his toys. She dropped him to his feet but held him between her knees, even though he struggled to gain his freedom.

“Ricky, if you can’t behave, we’ll go home without seeing Jamie.” He settled.

She turned to the man sitting beside her. “Hi,” she said. “What’s the score and inning?”

The man leaned close. “Five-two Milton, but we’re in the third inning. Still time to turn this thing around.” He smiled as he eyed her. “You’re too young to have a kid on the team,” he said by way of asking.

She laughed. “I have a friend who is, in fact, the coach for the Milton team, but I’m a former Hornet and I would prefer to sit on the home side.”

The man chuckled. “Go Hornets,” he said and resumed watching the game.

When the inning ended and the Arrowheads were up, Jeremy trotted out to the first base line to stand in the coaches’ box. He glanced at Amy but didn’t acknowledge her.

“Jamie!” Ricky called and bolted to him.

Jeremy smiled and waved his fingers at him before consternation widened his eyes.

“Ricky, no!” Jeremy held out both hands in a stop gesture. Behind home plate, the ump called time.

Amy jumped up, and before he got to the edge of the field, she grabbed him by the back of the shirt, dragging him to her seat. Parents around her chuckled as he cried for Jamie and held out his arms to him. As quietly as possible, Amy tried to calm him down and explain why Jamie couldn’t come over just now.

Shamefaced, Jeremy swung his arms, slapping the side of one fist into the palm of his other. Between signs to his batters, he glanced at them, and when the inning ended, he trotted over to Ricky and gave him a hug. "Stay here, bud," he said. "I can't play right now. I'm working."

"But why?" Ricky whined.

"I'm working," Jeremy said again. "But I'll come see you as soon as I'm done. Okay?"

"Hey Coach," the umpire called. "Let's go."

Jeremy dropped a quick kiss on Ricky's head and with a cold glance at Amy he rose and ran back to the dugout.

Amy sighed.

His boys won seven to five. Jeremy should have been ecstatic. The boys were. Shouting, whooping, and high fiving each other, they congratulated themselves on their win. Usually, they fell to Essex so to win was huge. He knew from his days playing for the blue-and-gold Hornets they were the best in the league. He high fived and congratulated his boys and dreaded going out to talk to Amy.

"Okay, guys, let's gather our gear," he said, clapping his hands. "Be at the bus in ten."

"Hey Coach," Joel said as he gathered up the bag of bats. They clinked together when he lifted them. "Who is the lady with the kid sitting on the bleachers? Is she Miss Lady Friend?" Joel batted his eyes, teasing.

"Ooohhh!" the other boys chimed in.

"Enough!" Jeremy barked. "I don't mind a little good-natured teasing once in a while, but my personal life is off-limits!"

The boys fell silent in the face of his rare wrath.

"Yeah, sure thing, Coach. Sorry," Joel said, hoisting the bag to his shoulder. "Sure thing."

Joel walked away, but Jeremy was sure he heard him mutter, "Fucking asshole" as he passed.

Chastened, the others gathered up the remaining equipment and sauntered off the field toward the front of the school and the bus waiting to take them home.

The shadows lengthened across the baseball diamond and Jeremy couldn't put her off any longer. He wandered over. Ricky ran to him, and he scooped him up, threw him in the air, and walked him back to Amy as the boy implored him to "do it again."

She rose as he approached and when he stopped in front of her, he put Ricky down, but the boy clambered to play.

"Ricky," Amy said, "why don't you run on the field like you wanted to. You can now."

He needed no further urging and took off, running across the diamond as he'd seen the older boys do.

Smiling, Jeremy watched him play. He'd have to teach him the game. His smile disappeared. He would never have the chance to teach him the game.

He turned his glare on her. "Why are you here?"

She drew in a deep breath and exhaled. "You have a right to your anger," she said.

"Oh, thank you very much," he snarled.

Her gaze glanced off him shifting to where Ricky was and returned to him.

"I talked to Frank the other day," she said, obviously ignoring his sarcasm.

"And what did he say?" His hands found his hips.

Amy sighed. "He said I should tell you everything, so here I am. I'll tell you what you want to know. Everything."

"Frank said." He shifted his stance. "You needed your boss's permission to tell me the truth?"

"What? No! I meant—"

"I don't care what you meant," he said as hurt pulsated through his body. He started walking. She told Frank, a friend at best, rather than him. Just like Maggie, she didn't trust him. What did women find about him they couldn't trust?

"And what makes you think I care anymore?" he said over his shoulder.

"What? Jay, stop. Talk to me!"

He halted. Then turned to find Ricky partly to make sure he was safe, but mostly to give himself time to gather his emotions.

The boy was in a squat picking up fistfuls of dirt and flinging them in the air. Oh to be three years old again and without a care in the world.

He turned back to her. "I told you at the maple festival I'm done being emotionally blackmailed." He slashed a hand through the air in emphasis and turned to leave. "Done."

A new thought came to him, and he turned back. Pointing at Ricky, he narrowed his eyes at her. "You brought the perfect weapon with you, which makes you the lowest kind of..." He broke off, unwilling to insult her so cruelly. Even as furious as he was, he couldn't bring himself to say hurtful things to her.

"Have a wonderful life, Amy Taylor," he said and started walking.

"Jay!" Her voice sailed across the field, hurt and impatient. "Please, let me explain." She ran to him and grabbed his arm. Though she tried to turn him, he slipped his arm through her grasp and kept walking.

She jumped in front of him, and he stopped. "You told me on one of our first nights together you were going to hound me until you got the truth. Now you're about to get what you want, and what? You're gonna run away?" Her blue eyes snapped fire, always a sign he should go lightly, but he didn't care.

Jeremy leaned close until he was almost nose to nose with her, but she didn't back off.

"Oh how sweet, coming from you, the queen of running away!" By the time he finished his sentence, he was shouting in her face. He backed off, hands on his hips, his gaze boring craters into the earth.

He pushed the bill of his hat back on his head. "I figured out why you don't want to be associated with me."

She blinked and stared at him with startled surprise. "You figured what out?" Her words came out in a strangled whisper. She cleared her throat. "Then let's talk. Let's work this out. Come home and have dinner with us."

"Hey Coach, hurry up. I need to get the kids back!"

Jeremy turned to the bus driver standing at the loading zone, holding up his arm and tapping a pretend watch.

Jeremy waved and turned back to Amy. "We have nothing to work out," he said again and conjured all the venom he could. "You are, or perhaps did have an affair with Adam." He shot his index finger out at her and knew he was dead-on when her mouth dropped open and she stared at him as though he'd turned green and started speaking Martian. "That's what you've been so afraid of my finding out."

"Are you kidding right now?" she shouted. "Because if you are"—she jabbed her index finger into his shoulder— "you're a bigger ass than I could have ever given you credit for!"

"Hey, Coach, c'mon!"

"I have to go," Jeremy said, swatting her hand away. He gave her a dismissive wave and walked away.

Jeremy steeled himself not to not turn back when Ricky asked where he was going. It was all bullshit anyway. More emotional blackmail. How dare she use her son to manipulate him. At the bus, he muttered an apology and boarded.

As the driver settled into his seat, he waved his boys down and congratulated them on their win, pretending to care. He talked about the next game, and his gaze slid out the windows.

The vehicle lurched into motion. Amy walked to her car with her son's hand tucked into hers.

Jeremy found Mike in the teacher's lounge, sitting at a table reading through the obituaries.

"Morbid," Jeremy said.

Grinning, Mike pushed the paper away. "My mother used to say if her name wasn't in the obituaries she'd go to work."

Jeremy smiled. "Got a minute?" He sat down.

Mike glanced around the busy room. "Do you want to go to my office?"

Jeremy nodded and they headed down the hall, discussing school topics on the way.

When they got to his office, Mike closed the door. "What's up?"

Jeremy told him his theory of why Amy dumped him at her kitchen door. When he finished, he waited for Mike to congratulate him or at least give him a thumbs-up. Instead, Mike stared at him as though Jeremy had completely lost his marbles and was unsure if he should tell him so.

Mike opened his mouth and closed it again. He stared and Jeremy could feel the heat building up in his torso and rising to his ears.

"What?" he finally said.

Mike continued to stare at him. Finally, he glanced away and returned his gaze to Jeremy. "That's about the...dumbest...thing I think I *ever* heard you say."

"What?"

"You said the man scares her. He gives her panic attacks. How does that translate into an affair? Besides, you said she works two jobs and you've had a hard enough time finding an hour or two you can spend with her, so when would she have the time? Or the means?"

It was Jeremy's turn to flounder like a landed fish. "Well, I...I... thought..."

Mike scowled. "Stop thinking man. You're gonna blow yourself up."

"Well, Mr. Smartass," Jeremy said, annoyed he didn't have his friend's support, "what's your theory?"

"My theory? Perhaps this guy is the rapist running about town. I mean, it's possible, right?"

Jeremy dismissed the possibility. "I gotta say, I have a hard time believing Adam is the Queen City Rapist. I would think a rapist has to be in excellent physical shape to...perform..." He shook his head to rid himself of the visual of Adam attacking women.

"Adam is in his fifties. He's got a pot belly, graying hair. His being a rapist doesn't square with the man my siblings and I consider an uncle. Yes, he's crass and crude with a gutter brain, but he never struck me as a rapist."

Mike crossed his arms. "How many rapists have you met in your life and how many of them struck you as rapists?"

Jeremy's mouth fell open. He'd never considered that.

Mike sat forward and stared hard at him. "Something about him scares the shit out of Amy. You said so yourself. Right?"

"Yes."

"Since she won't tell you what, have you tried talking to Adam?"

"No." Jeremy lifted a brow. "I never thought of speaking to Adam."

"Call him. Ask him to meet."

The pocket of Jeremy's Dickies vibrated. He dug out his phone. *Catnap* flashed. He showed the screen to Mike, hit decline.

Mike's brow creased. "Catnap?"

"The first time I called her, I woke her up from a catnap. Now I suspect she had gotten Ricky to bed and fell asleep out of sheer exhaustion."

"Call her back. Tell her you're ready to listen to anything she has to say, no judgment, but talk to Adam first. Listen to his side of the story." He rose, indicating the talk was over but jerked his chin at Jeremy's phone.

A grin tilted one corner of Mike's mouth. "So who am I?"

Grinning, Jeremy scrolled until he came to *Yoda*. He showed it to Mike, who laughed out loud. "Jackass," he said. "Go to class before I fire you."

25

“Jeremy, I don’t remember the girl,” Adam said, insistent.

The small diner outside Milton buzzed with patrons. Considered a greasy spoon, Jeremy usually bypassed the dive, but Eric told him the sandwiches were delicious, so he invited Adam to meet him for lunch there.

“But you do remember Amy Taylor, the girl I dated in high school, my senior year.”

Adam lifted his hands and shook his head in a helpless gesture. A lock of white hair fell over Adam’s face, ruining his Ted Danson looks. “I... you had several girlfriends in high school, as I recall. Quite the stud in those days.” He swept the hair off his face, restoring his Dansonesque appearance.

Jeremy scowled, ignoring the rabbit hole. “Yeah, but this one, short, petite, brown hair, blue eyes.”

Again, Adam shook his head. “What is this about, Jer? Why am I getting the third degree about a teenage girl I do not recall?”

Jeremy tried again as Adam bit into his sandwich, the lettuce crunching loud across the table.

“Do you remember the night you ran into me in front of Lou’s? I said I was going in for drinks with friends?”

Mouth full, Adam nodded and chewed.

“When a woman came out and went back inside, you asked me who she was. You said she seemed familiar. Do you remember?”

“Mm-hmm,” Adam said and sipped his soda.

“Well, that was her. And since you thought her familiar, I

wondered if you remembered her from ten years ago."

Adam creased his brow. "If I recall anything, I'd say just the face, but not her in particular." He drank. Put his glass down. "Why?"

Though Jeremy didn't have permission to share her story, he took a chance. "She told me she was sexually assaulted years ago."

Adam, chewing his sandwich, began to cough and splutter.

Holding a hand to his chest, he struggled to regain control. "I beg your pardon?" he said, gasping.

"Did she come to you for help?" Jeremy asked, ignoring Adam's distress.

Adam picked up his drink and sipped before putting the glass down. "I can't give you an answer, Jer." His voice was still tight from his coughing fit.

Jeremy sighed, letting his frustration show. "Dammit, Adam, why can't you answer a simple question?"

"Because, for one thing, your question isn't simple. For another, even if I wanted to, I couldn't answer your question. I can't violate a confidence. You should understand, with two attorneys in your family."

Jeremy sat back defeated. He rubbed a hand over his face. "Yeah. I do. Sorry." He sighed. "Forget I asked." He picked up a fry and chewed, thinking.

"Well, no. Let's not forget you asked. You must have a reason for inviting me here and asking all these strange questions."

"Because I think you're linked somehow. Why does she run or have a panic attack every time you show up?"

Adam lifted a brow. "What do you mean?" His gaze slid around the diner as though assessing. Was he worried someone might overhear their conversation?

"The night we talked in front of Lou's, Amy came out, spotted you, did a one-eighty and went back inside. Remember?"

After Adam nodded, he went on. "When I went in to get her, she was in a full-blown panic attack."

Wisely, he chose not to tell Adam that she had wished him dead. He picked up his Coke, drank. "Not normal behavior if you're unafraid of someone." Jeremy shifted in his chair. "The night you caught us making out on the bench..."

Adam leered. "Oh, was that her? I only caught a glimpse." He waggled his brows as if to congratulate him and ate one potato chip.

Jeremy studied him. "Yes, and when she recognized you..." He broke off and furrowed his brow. She'd been laughing and playing with him, before she ran, much as she did ten years ago. But he had to admit what Adam did would have terrified him too.

He stared hard at Adam. "She tried to break up with me the same night, so I'm trying to figure out why you cause such extreme reactions in her. I mean, you have to admit making out with someone doesn't justify a breakup a half hour later, do you agree?"

Jeremy studied Adam's face for the telltale signs of lying. He'd been teaching long enough to realize when someone wasn't truthful. Adam's pupils dilated. Dismay crushed Jeremy's chest and left a sour flavor in his mouth.

Adam's gaze bounced around the room and returned to Jeremy shadowed by anxiety.

Jeremy picked up another fry, which he dangled in his fingers. "You're in Burlington most nights. Are you two having an affair?"

"What?" Adam exploded. People several tables away glanced in their direction.

Jeremy shrugged and tried to hang on to his self-control. "C'mon, Adam. You're not a very convincing liar. Makes me wonder how you win court cases. You can't possibly think I'm not aware of your many indiscretions. Why Emily stays with you is beyond my comprehension." He dropped the fry back onto his plate and rubbed his fingers to remove the salt.

Shifting in his seat, Adam took a bite of his chicken salad sandwich and chewed. When he swallowed, he put his sandwich down, wiped his mouth, and placed his hands on his napkin. He glared at Jeremy with steel-blue eyes.

"My marriage is none of your business. Hell, you've never been married. Therefore, you can't understand what goes on in anyone's marriage. And if you ever do get married, you probably won't understand what goes on then either." Adam glared.

He picked up his sandwich again but threw it back on his plate. The top bread flew off and lettuce dropped on his plate. "How dare you question my allegiance to my wife. I have never conducted affairs. I love Emily!"

Methinks the man doth protest too much. Jeremy said nothing, but he held Adam's gaze, peering deep into the older man's blue eyes. Anger lurked but also fear. Did he fear discovery? Did he fear Jeremy would run to Emily?

"Answer me one question. Honestly, if you can," Jeremy said. "Are you banging my girlfriend? Is she the reason I kept running into you in front of Lou's? Is working at the women's shelter some elaborate ruse you concocted for a reason to be in Burlington so late at night? Have I been in competition with you all spring?" The questions poured from his heart and Jeremy was powerless to stop them. With each question, his heart thudded in his ears, his fists clenched on either side of his plate. Perspiration formed on his upper lip. He grabbed his napkin and swiped at his mouth.

Adam jutted his chin and didn't answer. In a sudden move, he slammed his fists on the tabletop, rattling dishes. He stuck his finger out and jabbed the space between them. Eyes narrowed to mere slits and Adam growled in his throat. "How dare you, you little fucker. If you were ten years old again, I'd take you over my knee, you little shit!" Spittle flew from his lips. "Until I saw you downtown, I had no idea the little bitch existed."

Jeremy's eyes widened at the insult, but he kept quiet and let Adam speak. Perhaps he'd say something incriminating.

Adam rose and leaned across the table so close, he forced Jeremy back against the booth seat. "I don't remember her from your high school days. I have no idea who she is period. End of statement." With that, he straightened up.

Wiping his cheek, Jeremy ignored the outburst. Students who lied to him often responded in anger when confronted with the truth. "Did you enjoy telling my father I was out soliciting prostitutes?"

"Of course not! But what was I supposed to think? You wander the streets of Burlington so late at night, always with some woman I now realize is this Amy, but I didn't at the time."

Jeremy rose, facing him, and squared up, as if looking for a fight.

"Amy is so scared of you she tried to break up with me. Twice. So, I gotta ask, why? Why is she so afraid of you?"

"I have no idea." Adam stared back at Jeremy, holding his gaze.

"I don't think she's afraid of *you*," he said. "She's hiding something about you from me and you can protest all you want about what a fantastic marriage you have." Jeremy leaned close and spoke in quiet tones, so his words reached only Adam.

"But your many...shall we say...indiscretions...are common knowledge in our house." He stepped back. "I pity Emily. She's too classy a woman for you."

Staring at Adam's astounded face, Jeremy drew in a long breath through his nose and exhaled. He reached back, pulled out his wallet, and dropped a twenty-dollar bill on the table. "Thanks for meeting me."

He left the restaurant.

All Jeremy accomplished with his meeting was to piss Adam off. He'd insisted he didn't remember her, and Jeremy had to accept what he said. That didn't mean he had to believe Adam though.

Amy had called him again the other night and he finally broke down and answered. Partly because he took Mike's advice and set a time to listen to her, without judgment, and partly because he missed her too much to remain silent.

Now, he drove to her house to hear her side of the story. He was early, he knew, but he couldn't wait.

When he knocked on the door, a young woman he didn't recognize answered.

"Can I help you?" she asked.

His brow creased. She resembled Amy and recognition hit them both at the same moment.

She pointed to him. "Are you Jeremy?"

He chuckled. "You must be Lindsay." He peered past her. "Is Amy home? I need to talk to her."

"She's gone to the grocery store and wanted to shop in peace. Come on in," she said, stepping aside. "It's about time one of you came to your senses."

Smiling, Jeremy stepped inside. Children's voices came from the TV room. "Amy told me about your husband. I'm so sorry."

Lindsay nodded. "Thanks," she said. "Can I offer you some coffee or something?"

"Uh, how about some iced tea or water? I drink too much coffee."

Lindsay opened the fridge. "Amy has some seltzer water if you'd like."

"Sure." He pointed down the hall. "Do you mind if I say hi to Ricky?"

"You know about him?"

"I do."

"Thank God." She inclined her head toward the TV room.

Jeremy went down the hall and pushed open the door.

Ricky sat on his knees with a brontosaurus, threatening the life of a Barbie doll in Jessica's grip. She lay on her stomach, uttering high-pitched, pretend pleas for help.

"Hey, Sport." He got to his knees. Arrayed around the children were dinosaurs, Barbie dolls, and cars, and he couldn't imagine the world they'd conjured for themselves. "Hello, Jessica." He smiled at the girl.

Ricky stared at him as if assessing the change in his reality. He drew in a deep breath. "Jamie!"

The boy got to his feet and flung himself at Jeremy who scooped him into his arms. Holding him, Jeremy's heart panged with the realization of how much he missed him.

He squeezed Ricky tight, kissed his cheek, and buried his face in the boy's neck, breathing in his scent. "How you been, Sport? Being a good boy for Mommy?"

Ricky nodded but began to squirm, and Jeremy let him go. He cleared his throat and swiped a hand down his face.

"Hi," Jessica said tentatively.

"You can call me either Jeremy or Jamie, whichever you prefer."

She studied him. "Which one is right?"

"Jeremy."

"Why does Ricky call you Jamie?"

"Because he's working on Jeremy."

"Oh," Jessica said. She rolled onto her back and raised her jeans-clad knees. "Hi, Jeremy," she finally said.

He smiled.

"We go to the park, Jamie?" Ricky got to his feet, ready to bolt out the front door the minute Jeremy acquiesced.

"Not today, Sport. Sorry."

Ricky's face fell. "Why?"

"Tell me about your game."

After Ricky and Jessica related the details, he declined Ricky's invitation to play and returned to Lindsay waiting for him at the kitchen table.

He sat down and popped open the can of water. "Your daughter is a pretty girl."

"Thanks." Lindsay smiled. "She's great."

Jeremy sipped. Played with the can. "What did you mean it was time one of us came to our senses?"

Lindsay studied him and he could see in her blue eyes, so much like Amy's, she was trying to figure out what, if anything, she should say.

After sipping her water she shrugged. "Amy has shared much of your relationship with me."

He studied her. "Can I ask a question?"

She raised her eyebrows.

"When Amy and I broke up in high school, did she ever tell you why?"

Lindsay shook her head and stared at him in disbelief. "You mean to tell me you don't have a clue?"

"No," Jeremy admitted. "One day we were doing fantastic and the next, she wouldn't have anything to do with me. Have you ever seen her have a panic attack?"

Lindsay drew in a sharp breath. "Oh, yeah. They scare me, and I'm a nurse."

Jeremy nodded. "Me too. That day she had one I suspect. And afterward, she refused to speak to me again. We graduated soon after and parted ways, as people do, but I've never been able to figure out what I did." He stared out the kitchen window, thinking, seeing those days in his mind.

"I don't think you did anything."

He raised a brow.

"I once asked Amy what you did or said, but she said you had nothing to do with it. She said she couldn't tell anyone what happened because no one would ever believe her. I pressed her to tell me, but she told me to mind my own business."

"She tells me it wasn't my fault too. Why don't I believe her?"

Lindsay shrugged. "The thing with Amy, if she doesn't want you to find out, your chances are slim to none, so you've gotta ask yourself one thing." She placed her hand, cool from her refrigerated can of water, on his forearm. "Which do you want most? The truth or Amy?"

She sat back, sliding her hand off his arm. "Don't answer." She lifted her can of water and glanced out the window. "She's back."

Lindsay got up and propped open the kitchen door while Amy struggled up the driveway, arms loaded with grocery bags.

Jeremy went outside and took the bags from her.

"Let me help you," he said and carried them into the house. He went back out and grabbed two more bags from the car, carried them inside, went back out and got the last two, shut the hatch, and brought them in.

Lindsay shut the door while Amy unpacked groceries.

"Well," Lindsay said, clapping her hands and rubbing them. "Since you're home, I'm going to gather my own package and leave." She turned to Jeremy and held out her hand. "It was a pleasure to see you again."

Taking her hand he leaned in and kissed her cheek. "Thanks. Same to you."

Once Lindsay and Jessica were gone, Jeremy leaned against the counter, arms crossed while Amy unpacked her groceries and pretended that he wasn't in the room.

"I know I said on the ballfield we were done, but I wanted to give you one more chance. You said that day you were ready to tell me everything and I didn't listen."

She continued to put food away.

"I had lunch with Adam today."

Amy's body halted in mid motion. Then, she grabbed lettuce, thunked the head in the fridge, and slammed the door.

"I asked him questions." Jeremy studied her. Her jaw tightened and when she grabbed a loaf of bread from the bag, her hands shook.

"He was evasive in his answers. Like when I asked if he remembered you from when we were kids. He said no, but there was something in his eyes, something that told me he was lying, so I'm thinking he does remember you. The question is, why? What's going on, Amy? Are you fooling around with him? Are you two having an affair?"

The words barely left his mouth when the loaf of bread whizzed past his head and smacked into the wall behind him.

He stared at her, astonished.

Her hands shook, and she gripped an orange until her fingers left dents in the rind. Was she going to throw that at him too? She spiked the orange into the fruit bowl on her table. The fruit rolled and came to a stop at the bottom of the bowl. Juice leaked from its misshaped rind.

"You bastard!" she snarled. "If that's what you think what's the point of talking? You've already made up your mind."

When she grabbed a cantaloupe, he wrenched it from her hands.

“Stop this. Let’s talk.” He held the melon to his chest.

Amy grabbed a package of meat from the grocery bag, opened her freezer, threw the hamburger inside, and slammed the freezer door. She leaned against the table and bowed her head.

When she raised her gaze, tears sheened her eyes. “Why?” she growled eyes narrowed with fury. “Nothing I could say will make a difference.”

This time Jeremy recognized the furious sarcasm and forced himself to remain calm. He set the cantaloupe on the counter behind him.

“You keep saying the truth will kill me. The only conclusion I can draw is you’re having an affair with my father’s best friend. Which is why I keep running into him in front of Lou’s. The first time, in April, you panicked because we were talking together. The second time you didn’t run because he scared you, you ran so I wouldn’t find out.”

He held out his hands when she opened her mouth to speak. “No, let me finish,” he said, “let me finish.” He drew in a breath and collected his thoughts. “For the longest time, I didn’t understand why you can’t or won’t tell me the truth. But now I do. Now I understand why you kept saying if I knew the truth, I’d hate you.”

Tears streamed down her face and dripped off her chin and Jeremy fought the urge to take her in his arms, but he couldn’t countenance her infidelity. They had been apart for ten years and yes, for four of those years he’d been with Maggie, but he didn’t love Maggie. Never had. Amy always lived in his heart. He’d never married. He’d never had children who weren’t hers. But Amy had done those things. She had moved on from him. Yes, she came back, but she’d gone away from him first. Adam had to be the reason.

He held up a hand, fingers outstretched, before closing his hand into a fist. “I don’t hate you. I’ve loved you too long to hate you.”

She placed a palm over her mouth and squeezed her nostrils together. Silent tears flowed over the back of her hand.

Finally, she removed her hand. “Is this your way of listening judgment free? Because if so, you suck at it.”

He pressed his body into the corner, between the sink and the stove, praying she’d deny the truth of his claims, but she didn’t, and his world careened. Staring out the window he struggled to breathe. A cardinal hopped along the top of a swing set. Another hop and amid a flutter of wings, it flew off. His brows lowered and he blinked fast.

He stared at her, giving her one last chance to deny everything, but she crooked her jaw, stared at the table, and remained silent. Tears left small puddles on the table.

"We're getting nowhere," he said. "I'm wasting my time."

He pushed off from the counter and headed toward the living room. "I'll leave you alone now."

"Jamie?" Ricky stood in the hallway. His brontosaurus hung slack in his fingers, looking every bit like the small boy he was. He peered up at Jeremy with sad blue eyes. "Where you go?"

The boy's plaintive question was too much for him and Jeremy stormed out the front door.

Putting the car in gear, he roared away from her house vowing never to speak to her again.

26

Amy let him leave. He thought her a slut, as Adam had said he would. Jay had lunch with Adam. What did that dirty rat bastard say to him? What stories did he concoct? If not for the fact that she'd lose her son and spend the rest of her life in jail, she'd do serious bodily harm to that shit bird.

Ricky sobbed. She sighed and carried him into the TV room to comfort him while he wailed and screamed for Jamie.

I feel your pain, kid. As she held him, she thought about their Saturdays at the park, Jay pushing Ricky on the swings or chasing him around or teaching him how to play catch. She thought of the day during spring break when they went to Home Depot to buy paint. Ricky had been hyper because Dad had given him chocolate earlier and Amy couldn't control his impulses, but Jay didn't lose his cool like she did. He simply hoisted him up on his shoulders and continued to shop as though nothing had happened.

She rocked him until he fell asleep, exhausted from his tears, and for the millionth time, she wished Ricky was Jay's child.

The boy twitched in her arms, and lifted his head. "Where Jamie?"

"Jamie's gone home."

"Why?"

"Because. C'mon sweetie. Let's take a nap." She carried him upstairs and into her room. Amy lay him on her bed and stretched out beside him. While he slept, she wept.

"Blow out your candles, Baby." Amy's pretend happiness drove her crazy, but she was determined to put a positive face on for Ricky. Jay had left her house a week ago, and Ricky constantly whined, demanding Jamie come back, as though the fault was hers. Perhaps he was right. Either way, she was running out of excuses.

Amy had received no word from him since last Saturday either. He didn't call, didn't text, and though she cried herself to sleep each night, she told herself Lindsay was right. She got what she deserved.

Adam would always claim any happiness she might find with Jay because once his family found out about them— they and he—would never forgive her.

Lindsay sat on the wicker couch on Dad's back porch watching the birthday celebration but not taking part in the festivities.

Ricky tried to blow out his three candles but only managed to spit on them. Poppy helped him before Grammy whisked the cake away for cutting.

Jessica sat at the table, swinging her feet, and waiting for her slice of cake while Ricky ripped open his gifts.

Amy had saved money all month for these few gifts, no small feat even with both jobs.

Like in the days right after Peter left, panic nibbled around the edges of her brain, which she beat back like a lion tamer. How would she live without Jay? Would she ever be happy again?

A tall narrow gift wrapped in balloon wrapping paper sat on the table. Amy turned the gift over in her hands. No card or other identifier as to the gift giver.

Amy turned a questioning gaze to Lindsay. "Is this from you?"

Lindsay pointed to a small box. "That one is Jessica's, and the larger box is mine."

"Who is this from?" Amy turned the package over in her hand.

"Jeremy brought it by this morning," Mom announced. "I invited him to stay, but he said he couldn't. He was busy today, but he wanted to give Ricky a birthday gift."

Dad chewed a toothpick, made a squishing sound as he sucked food from his teeth. "Yeah," he said, sliding his gaze sidelong to Amy. "Can't think why he didn't go over to your house, but he didn't."

Amy and Lindsay shared a glance.

Lindsay raised an eyebrow. "Jeremy Austin strikes again."

Mom smiled. "I'm glad you're seeing him again, honey. Of course, you've done worse than him"

"Thanks, Mom." Irritated, Amy wished the conversation would move on to a new topic.

"Well, she's not seeing him again," Lindsay said. "She has a knack for screwing things up with Jeremy."

"Lindsay, shut your mouth."

Dad got up and took the kids to the backyard to play.

"No, Amy," Lindsay said, disgust in her voice and anger in her eyes. "I don't think I will shut up. You had a sweet, wonderful guy eating out of the palm of your hand and you threw him away!"

Lindsay's eyes filled with tears. "You...bitch." She got up from the wicker sofa to go into the house.

"Now, girls," Mom whined, as Lindsay moved past her.

Mom grabbed Lindsay's arm, halting her. "Today is Ricky's birthday. Let's not argue." She waggled Lindsay's arm. "C'mon, Lin, sit down."

Lindsay jerked her arm free and went back to the sofa. She drew her knees up and curled herself into the corner, crossing her arms and scowling.

Amy sighed. She couldn't be mad at Lindsay. She was right. She threw Jay away with both hands, but her sister didn't understand she had reasons for doing so.

Mom called Dad and the kids back onto the porch as she cut Ricky's dinosaur-decorated cake.

"Well, too bad he couldn't be here today. Ricky is always talking about Jamie this and Jamie that," Dad said as he resumed chewing on his toothpick.

"Yeah, well, he has a hard time with 'Jeremy,'" Amy caressed the name.

She handed the package to Ricky, who clutched the gift with both hands and searched each face as the realization that Jeremy was missing finally dawned.

His confused gaze landed on Amy. "Where Jamie?" His brow puckered and a pout formed on his lips.

Amy pulled her lips into a small, sad smile. "Jamie couldn't be here today, buddy."

"Who's fault is that?" Lindsay sneered.

Amy shot her an irritated glare. "Shut up."

Lindsay mocked her.

"Why?" Ricky's wail stopped the argument.

"Because he couldn't," Amy said, with a fake smile. "Open your gift. See what Jamie got you!"

She urged to distract him. *How do I thank him? Would he take a call or should I text? Damn him!*

Tearing the multicolored balloon wrapping paper, he squealed with delight over the Jurassic Park-style T-Rex snarling behind the cellophane on the front of the box. He tried to pry the box open.

"Here." Amy reached out. "Let me, but you have other presents to open."

Jessica pushed her gift at him. "Open mine, Ricky."

Distracted from the T-Rex, Ricky opened Jessica's Matchbox cars and the new pants and shirt from Aunt Lindsay.

Amy sat in the chair next to the wicker sofa, still holding the box. She blinked at the pressure building behind her eyes and tried to laugh at something Dad said, but she couldn't concentrate. Why did Jay have to buy him a birthday gift? Why couldn't he leave them alone?

"What are you gonna do?" Lindsay said, getting up for another can of water. "Are you gonna call him? Text him? What? He'll tell you to fuck off, which is nothing less than you deserve."

"Girls! Lindsay Anne!" Mom exclaimed, shocked and angry. "Such language." She pressed a hand to her heart. "You should apologize to your sister."

Lindsay sneered at Amy. "No, Mom. I don't think I will." She grabbed a can of seltzer water and sat back down, popping the top with a loud snap and hiss. She leaned close and spoke in quiet tones to Amy.

"I'd sell my god-damned soul for ten more minutes with Kyle and you threw Jeremy away like so much trash. How dare you?" Wiping her eyes, she sat back and sipped her water, having said her piece.

Chastened to the core, Amy picked at a piece of wicker poking from the arm of her chair while Ricky opened his gifts. She offered a feeble smile every time he showed her what he'd received.

When Ricky finished opening his presents and had frosting smeared all over his face, he went back to Amy to claim his dinosaur. Before she let him have the toy, she made him thank everyone for their presents.

After he went around and kissed Grammy, Poppy, and Aunt Lindsay and hugged Jessica, she handed him the plastic monster. All his other gifts went untouched.

Once the party ended, Amy carried a sleeping Ricky down the

street and around the corner. His T-Rex dangled from his hand, so she retrieved it from his slackening fingers. After a bath, she put them to bed.

She went downstairs and grabbed her phone. Most likely he wouldn't answer, but she needed to try. She thumbed the green phone icon.

The phone rang three times. "Hi, this is Jeremy, or if you're a student, Mr. A. Leave a message."

She almost hung up, but with a tired sigh, she left a short message. "Hi, Jay. I wanted to say thank you for the dinosaur. He was a hit. Ricky wouldn't play with anything else. You didn't have to buy him a gift, but I appreciate your thinking of him. I wanted to tell you."

Should she say I love you? What was the point? "Thanks again. Bye."

She flipped over to text and wrote. "Thank you," and hit send. She dropped her phone on the charger, went upstairs, and cried herself to sleep.

27

By mid-June with no word from Jeremy, Amy finally gave up hope he'd come back. He didn't even acknowledge her call thanking him for Ricky's dinosaur.

He went nowhere without the toy and played with no others but his dinosaurs, now with the added benefit of T-Rex's ability to eat the smaller ones, rather than Brontosaurus. In fact, now poor Bronto was in danger of becoming a meal.

School had let out for the summer the day before and Amy wondered, not for the first time, what Jeremy was doing with his time. Probably relaxing, unlike her.

On such a beautiful summer evening, diners flocked to the restaurant and Frank opened their outside café area.

Like a chicken with her head cut off, Amy bounced from table to table in the packed restaurant.

Every time Briana seated someone new, she apologized, annoying Amy, and even Jason, who never appeared troubled by any circumstance, had no sense of humor as he buzzed from table to table.

Because Kara quit without warning, Amy had to deal with outside customers as well, adding to her confusion. Her normal station was indoors while Jason and Kara handled the outside tables, so Amy kept forgetting she had guests outside.

As she finished with a couple at table seven, Briana told her she seated a couple outside. Amy headed out but stopped short when she spied Adam and his wife perusing the menu.

Her heart raced and bile shot up the back of her throat. To avoid going over, she turned to a pair seated next to her elbow.

"How is everything?" she said and tried to keep her voice from shaking. "Would you like anything else?" They indicated they were fine, so Amy moved away and with heavy steps, started toward the Knoxes.

Adam glanced up and Amy lost her nerve. She spun on her heel and headed back inside.

"Frank."

"What." He made a drink with swift sharp movements.

"The couple outside. I don't want to serve them."

Frank did a double take. "What are you talking about?"

She sighed. "A couple. On the terrace. I don't want to serve them. Please, can I have Jason take them?"

"Jason has enough tables without adding any of yours. I realize Kara quitting has put extra strain on us, but don't add to the problem, Amy, please."

Amy closed her eyes. She wasn't handling this well. "Frank, you don't understand. He's the guy—" She got no further before he cut her off.

Frank braced an arm on the bar and frowned down at her. "What I don't understand is your behavior. I've never seen this from you before, so here's what I'm gonna do. You've always been one of my best employees, so I'm going to pretend this conversation never took place." He lowered his head and gave her a stern grimace. "Go back to work, Amy."

She stuffed down her panic and went back outside. Drawing in a deep breath, she gathered her strength and courage and stepped up to the table.

"Good evening," she used her most cheery professional voice. "A pleasure to see you this evening. My name is Amy and I'll be your server tonight."

Mrs. Knox's warm friendly green eyes smiled up at Amy. She seemed happy to be out with her dirtbag of a husband.

"Hello, Amy," Mrs. Knox said, without a hint of recognition, which angered her, considering the number of years she'd hung out with the Austin's. Amy had practically been part of the family.

"We're celebrating our anniversary tonight." Mrs. Knox looked incredibly pleased.

"Emily, the girl doesn't care about our anniversary." He leered at

Amy and the small hairs at the back of her neck rose.

"Of course, I do." Amy turned to Mrs. Knox and smiled back. "Congratulations. How many years?"

"Thirty," the woman dropped her hand on the table as if she'd said one hundred and thirty.

Amy smiled. "Wow, that's a long time. Congrats again."

She turned to Adam who eyed her up and down. She held her ground.

"Hello, Amy." He placed his napkin in his lap before smiling up at her. "Do I know you? You have a familiar face."

With a quick shrug as though shucking his gooey charm she answered, "Well, I work here most nights of the week, so I'm sure you've seen me if you spend any time downtown." *You've seen me before, Jackass! Making out with Jay, right over there.* She glanced at the bench almost directly in front of them and regretted doing so when he smirked.

"Ah, yes," he said with a nasty chuckle. "Now I recall."

She flipped a page of her notepad. "Are you ready to order? Can I start you off with drinks or an appetizer?"

Mrs. Knox ordered a Vodka Collins and Adam asked for a Sam Adams Boston Lager. Amy walked away with the drink order, promising to return soon.

Jason served their drinks and Amy returned. "Have you decided what you want?"

Mrs. Knox chuckled, shamefaced. "I simply can't decide. What do you suggest?"

"Well, I'm not going to say anything bad about the food here." Amy forced a small laugh. "But since today is your anniversary, and the special tonight is my favorite, I suggest the prime rib au jus with garlic mashed potatoes and maple-glazed carrots."

Adam snapped his menu closed. "Sounds delicious."

Mrs. Knox handed hers up. "Sure does."

"Wonderful," Amy said, taking the menus. She started to walk away.

"Amy."

She turned.

Adam held up his fork. "My fork is a bit dirty. Can you please bring me a new one?"

She walked back and tried to pluck the fork from his hand, but he wouldn't let go. He leered at her as she tried again, but again he refused to give in. She dropped her hand and glared at him while biting back a snarl of frustration.

Raising a brow in challenge, he extended his arm a fraction and she tried again.

Mrs. Knox placed a gentle hand on his arm. "Really, dear, stop teasing the poor girl. She's far too busy for your shenanigans."

Adam released the clean fork.

Amy shot an appreciative glance at Mrs. Knox and slipped the utensil into her apron pocket. "I'll bring a new fork out right away."

She walked away. *So we're going to do this are we?*

She returned a few minutes later with a new silverware package, which she placed at Adam's elbow before scooping up his old knife and spoon.

"So," he said, "I understand you're the young lady who's been seeing our Jeremy."

Amy's heart lurched in her chest.

"Oh." Mrs. Knox smiled. "I didn't realize Jeremy was dating anyone new." She assessed Amy. "And why not? You're a lovely girl."

Amy couldn't help smiling at her compliment. "Thank you," she said before turning to Adam. "But you must be mistaken."

"Oh," Mrs. Knox said, drawing out the syllable in disappointment. She cast a confused glance at her husband. "Too bad."

Adam's nostrils flared. "Why not," he sat forward, sounding like a concerned friend. "A sweet thing like yourself." Below the table, his fingers crawled up the side of her leg.

Amy's pulse raced and her hands went icy. She chose to walk away rather than stab him in the eye with the steak knife in her hand. Inside the restaurant, she leaned against the bar and drew in a deep breath.

"Hey," Jason growled. "Table seven is ready to go. Do your job!"

She gaped at him. No matter how busy or crazy things were, Jason never lost his cool. His sense of humor left customers laughing no matter how difficult they tried to be. Oh, why couldn't she give him Adam's table?

"Sorry," she called back and went to table seven. She gave them their bill and walked away to check on the prime ribs. When she returned, the man stopped her.

"Yes, sir," Amy smiled. "Are you ready for me to take your card?"

"No." He did not appear happy. "We didn't order the sea scallops. I had the ribeye, and my wife had the balsamic chicken."

"Oh, shit," Amy said and slapped her hand over her mouth. "I apologize, for the mess-up and for my language."

"I should hope so," the wife said.

Amy shuffled through the bills and found the correct one. They made the exchange among her profuse apologies.

The man handed her his card, which she took with a feeble smile. He didn't leave a tip. *Jerk.* She processed his payment and returned with the card.

She worked a few more tables and when the Knoxes food was ready, she returned with the tray.

She placed Mrs. Knox's plate before Adam's. After asking if they needed anything more, she turned to walk away.

"Amy," he called out.

She stopped. Drew in a breath. Turned. "Yes." She returned.

Adam tapped his meat with his fork. "I believe I have a hair in my food." He leered at her. "I can't eat this."

She studied his plate, found no hair, but with a shaking hand, retrieved his dish. With a watery smile, she said, "I apologize. Let me bring you a new meal." Her throat constricted.

She turned away on rubber legs, but not before she caught the questioning glance his wife gave him.

He shrugged. "I found a hair in my food," he insisted as Amy departed.

He's a jerk. What's the worst he can do? He's in public. He can't do anything. I wish Jay were here. Why isn't Jay here? Adam can't hurt me. Adam can't hurt me.

She returned a short time later with a new plate which she plunked down in front of him harder than she intended. Out of sight of his wife, his hand slid across her buttocks.

Amy gasped and jerked her body forward, slamming into the table.

Mrs. Knox shot a startled glance her way, but Amy held up her hands. "I'm so sorry. I lost my balance."

Concern shone in Adam's eyes. He stood and slid his hand up her back in a solicitous manner. "Are you unwell? Would you like to sit down?"

I'd like for you to go away!

"I'm fine." Amy backed up. She pivoted and walked away, using every ounce of strength she possessed not to run.

Inside, she placed dishes on a tray to bring to another table. Her shoulders tingled and her hips throbbed, followed in swift measure by a searing hot pain in her insides. She grasped her abdomen and doubled over, groaning.

"Are you okay?" Briana lay a hand on Amy's back.

"Cramp," Amy ground out. "Must be my monthly. I wasn't paying attention."

"Oh," Briana said. "Do you need to go to the bathroom? I can cover for you." Her gaze swept the room to be sure no one overheard them. "I have tampons if you need one."

"Thanks." Amy blinked back tears. "I'm okay. I'll serve this and hit the john."

"Sure." Briana went to greet a new couple.

Amy picked up the tray and got halfway across the room when a red-hot poker seared her abdomen a second time. She stopped short and clamped her eyes closed. Jason, serving a tray of drinks, collided with her. Plates, food, silverware, glasses, and drinks went everywhere.

The crash of smashing glass silenced the restaurant. Someone started clapping. Other patrons joined in with whistles and jeers.

Jason swore so loud Amy was sure Adam heard him outside. In tears, she dropped to her hands and knees to gather broken dishes. Now, if someone would come along and put a bullet in her head, she'd be grateful.

Frank appeared and sent Jason to the back for a mop bucket and cleaning supplies. He got on his knees beside Amy.

"What's going on?" Frank snapped as he swept up broken glass with his cloth.

"I'm sorry, Frank. I'm so sorry."

"Is your customer giving you a hard time?"

"Nothing I can't handle. Wouldn't want to be unprofessional, right?" She couldn't keep the anger and bitterness from her voice or the tears from dripping off her face.

He gaped. "I went out and checked them out when you brought his plate back. You don't have something going on with him, do you?"

"Frank! God no!" She stared at him, horrified by the idea. "He's the guy I told you about. He's the Austin's friend."

Frank stared at her in utter shock, but Jason returned with the mop and bucket, effectively keeping him quiet.

Amy offered to clean up, but Jason, red-faced with anger, shooed her away with the dripping mop he slapped against the terracotta tiles. He swiped with a vengeance.

"Go back out to work," Frank told her. "I'll be right here if you need me." He placed a hand on her shoulder and tried to tease.

"You're a mess."

But Amy wasn't having it. "I just had four meals dumped on my head. Of course, I'm a mess." Her voice carried across the restaurant, but she didn't care. She raised her hands, spun on her heel, and headed for the bathroom.

Jeremy sat in the dark, drinking, and staring at the TV, where the Red Sox moved about. He picked up his phone and went to the voice mail, letting the phone play her last message. He'd kept them all and played them occasionally for the sound of her voice. Her tearful thank you for the dinosaur—a dagger straight to his heart. He should have called her back, listened to what she wanted to tell him. She had said at the ballpark she was ready to tell him the truth, so why didn't he listen?

Because you're a jackass. You're no better than her ex-husband. He also walked out on her for no reason, Douchebag!

Lifting his beer bottle to his mouth, he drank and propped his feet on the new coffee table his parents bought him. Why they thought he needed one he had no clue, but the thing was useful for putting his feet up.

He drank and glared at his backpack sitting in the corner of the living room, waiting for the next school year to start.

Standing, Jeremy grabbed the bag, which he tossed on the sofa next to him, and dropped back down onto the couch. He put the beer bottle down and unzipped a small pocket. Reaching in, he removed a small black velour box and opened the top.

On a blue satin cushion, a diamond solitaire ring sparkled back at him. He'd bought the ring shortly after her confession of her sexual assault. The problem had been finding the right moment to ask her. Every time he thought the time had come, something happened to drive them apart. Was it a sign?

He loved Amy. For his entire life. And when she invited him back into her life, he bought the ring in hopes she'd never leave again. What a fool he'd been. He still had the receipt upstairs in his sock drawer.

He snapped the box closed and dropped it back into the pocket, zipping it before throwing the bag across the room where it landed with a splat and slid across the floor. One of these days, he'd have to return the ring. His face burned with the idea, and he pictured the jeweler laughing at him once he left the store.

School had ended for the summer the day before and in despair over the prospect of a long and lonely summer, he'd gotten drunk and called Emma last night. He'd wept and said things he never should have. Poured his soul out to her. Today, he hadn't even bothered to dress and spent the day slouched in pajama pants and a Red Sox T-shirt, swigging beer, and throwing himself a pity party.

His back door rattled but he ignored the sound, hoping his unwanted guest would go away but they pounded harder on the door.

"Fuck off!" he shouted toward the open window.

"Jeremy," Emma called.

He jerked upright.

"Open up."

Swearing, he rose and stumbled to the door. He'd had more to drink than he realized and hadn't eaten much that day either.

He unlocked and opened the door before stumbling away.

Emma entered and put down a suitcase inside the door. She walked into the kitchen and wrinkled her nose. "God almighty," she said as her gaze swept the mess.

Jeremy opened the refrigerator and pulled out two beers while struggling through a weird déjà vu. Same scenario, different person. He cleared his throat. "What brings you here, Em."

"You do." Emma leaned a hand on the bar and grimaced at the sticky mess on her palm. "After our chat last night, my twin instinct kicked in and I had a sense I should be here. I was right."

"I don't need your sanctimonious crap, so if you're here to lecture me, go the hell back to Philly. I didn't ask you here."

He slammed a beer bottle on the counter in front of her and took the other one to the living room where he dropped himself onto the sofa.

"We're twins, Jer. When you hurt, I hurt." She studied him. "So..." She left the beer on the counter and walked into the living room. With arms crossed, she stared at him. "Amy Taylor strikes again, eh?"

"Leave me alone."

"No." She picked up the remote and turned off the TV. "How many of those have you had?"

"Hey!" he hollered, ignoring her question and waving a feeble bottle at the screen. "I was watching that!"

"Oh yeah?" She tossed the remote back on the coffee table. "What was the score? Who was ahead? Who was playing?"

He didn't answer.

She wrinkled her brow. "Is this the coffee table Mom and Dad bought you? Why anyone thinks you need a coffee table anymore is beyond me."

"One of 'em," he muttered.

"What?"

"Nothing," he said.

Emma shuffled through the junk on the small table, sorting through his mess. "You've got three weeks' worth of unopened mail here. Don't you want to pay your bills?"

He shrugged, held the bottle to his mouth but didn't drink. "Screw the bills." Tilting the bottle back he drank.

Emma glanced out the window and went back to cleaning up. She got the living room in some semblance of order and began on the kitchen, stopping every so often to peer out the window.

"What the fuck is so interesting outside?" he snarled.

"Nothing. I'm waiting for reinforcements." She threw a glare his way. "And keep a civil tongue in your mouth."

"What?"

"I called for backup. I'm waiting for them to arrive."

He stared at her in utter drunken confusion.

"Charlie and Maya."

"Why?" He jumped to his feet and staggered. "Did you tell them? I told you not to. Dammit, Emma!"

"No. I didn't tell them. I told them something happened, and we need an emergency family— well, sibling—intervention."

She returned to the living room, pushed him back onto the couch, and sat beside him. "Time some truths came out, which might help clarify things with Amy."

"Why would you care? You didn't want me back with her anyway."

When he raised his beer, Emma grasped his wrist. “I never said I don’t want you back with her, I just...I don’t want you hurt again.” Disgusted, she waved a hand at his appearance. “Which, apparently, I’m powerless to stop.”

He leaned his elbows on his knees and covered his face. “I hate my fucking life.”

Emma slid an arm around his back and pulled him into an embrace, cradling his head on her shoulder.

“Cry, Jer. Then tell me what she did.”

He didn’t cry, but he let his sister comfort him. “Turns out she’s fooling around. With a married man. Adam.” He sat up and wiped his nose on his hand. He started to raise the beer bottle to drink but made a face as his stomach rebelled.

“I think you’ve had enough,” Emma said, taking the bottle from his hand. She went to the kitchen and as she poured the contents down the sink, she peered out the window again. Grabbing a roll of paper towels she returned to the living room. Holding out the towels she ordered, “Blow your nose.”

Chastised, he ripped off a sheet, wiped his eyes, and blew his nose. He ripped off another and wiped his nose again before dropping the wadded sheets on the coffee table. Emma tossed his phone into his lap.

“Order some food.” Her gaze swept him from head to toe and back up, distaste curling her lip. “When was the last time you ate anything? Or showered?”

He shrugged.

“I’m hungry for Chinese,” she said.

When the back door rattled, Emma sighed. “They’re here.”

Jeremy found the local Chinese joint and opened the app but didn’t call. Instead, he moved to the back door.

Maya’s expression changed from bright welcome to concern. Her fearful gaze swept him.

Charlie’s smile of greeting froze and died away. He opened the door, letting himself and Maya into the house. “Jesus, Jeremy. Has a freight train hit you?”

“Love you too, brother,” Jeremy said. He leaned in to kiss Maya on the cheek, but she slapped her hand on his chest.

“Shit, Jeremy,” she said, waving a hand in front of her nose. “Go take a shower And for the love of God, brush your teeth.”

He backed up. “Why don’t you all get the hell out of my house. I didn't invite you."

From behind, Emma snatched the phone from his hand. She tapped the app and placed the call. "We're having Chinese," she said to her siblings while the phone rang. She turned to Jeremy. "Maya's right. Go take a shower."

Adam and Mrs. Knox were in no hurry to leave, and he ran Amy ragged. A hair in the food, the meat was cold, the vegetables undercooked, he wanted dessert. The coffee was too strong, or not strong enough. She was about ready to take a tray and smash him in the back of the head. She summoned anger to hedge against her heart-pounding, nauseating anxiety. He signaled and she approached with a fresh pot of coffee.

"Can I refresh your cups?"

Adam pushed his coffee cup close, and Amy poured. "Ma'am?"

Mrs. Knox shook her head. "I'm fine for now. In fact," she said, "I have to use the ladies' room." She ended her statement on a questioning note.

Amy gave instructions and when Mrs. Knox walked away, she turned to leave, but Adam grabbed her wrist.

She tried to pull away, but his grip was tight, and she couldn't break free. Amy's chest constricted. "Let go of me." She pulled but couldn't gain her freedom.

He stood up and with his iron grip on her wrist, he forced her arm down. "You and I had a deal," he said, towering over her. "You promised."

"I haven't said a word," she balked, hoping if she leaned away, she'd force him to let go. "I swear, I haven't said a word."

He pulled her close. "You're lying," he said. "You told Jeremy our little secret."

"I did not!"

"Yes, you did. He told me you did."

Amy blanched. Did Jay betray her trust? Terror rode hard on her heels. What was Adam going to do to her? He released her wrist. She stumbled back and would have fallen, but she bumped into the greeter's stand instead. Pain shot up her spinal column. Hot coffee sloshed but stayed in the pot.

Amy squared her shoulders and pulled herself together. Turning, she headed back inside on rubber legs.

A patron enjoying dinner with his wife eyed her, raising a brow in question. She shook her head and kept on going.

He returned to his meal but fixed his gaze on Adam.

Once inside, Amy pressed a hand against her chest and struggled to draw breath. The coffee pot clattered onto the warmer.

"Miss."

Amy jumped.

The man who eyed her stood next to the bar. He was burly, with pecs and shoulders for days. "The man giving you a hard time, did he threaten you in any way?"

She shook her head.

"Ma'am," he tried again, and sliding his wallet out of his pocket, he showed her a badge. "I'm an off-duty police officer, former Army Ranger, and if he's harming or threatening you, please tell me."

"I'm fine," she choked out, slapped a hand to her mouth and ran for the employees' bathroom.

Shutting shut the door, she dropped to her knees before the toilet and threw up, gagging and gasping for breath as another wave of nausea hit her. She let go, eyes watering. When she finished, she leaned her forehead on her arms until she was sure she had nothing left. Amy rinsed her mouth, then sat on the floor, bracing her feet on the toilet with her back against the door. She pressed her knuckles into her mouth and struggled not to make a sound, but ragged, panicked sobs escaped her as she banged her head against the wood.

Jeremy had to admit the shower made such a difference in his outlook he decided to shave. Something he hadn't done in several days. Amy would never let him grow a beard. He smiled thinking how many times she reminded him to shave the moment his face prickled hers. He squirted foam into his hand and slathered his face.

Once the stubble was off, his clear face and smooth skin improved his outlook more. He slapped on some Old Spice and went to his bedroom to pull on a clean pair of jeans and a T-shirt. When he went downstairs, Maya was serving the food.

His brother and sisters cheered his appearance, prompting him to give them all a good-natured finger.

General Tso, his favorite, filled Jeremy's empty stomach.

During the meal, the siblings chatted, catching up with each other.

Jeremy listened but didn't share details of his life.

"How about you, Jer?" Charlie said, taking a bite of his beef and broccoli. "You haven't told us what's up with you."

"He never does," Maya said. "Have you ever noticed"—she pointed her fork at him— "he's a master at getting everyone else talking so he doesn't have to say anything? Before long, everyone's going on about what a fantastic conversationalist he is, and days later, you realize you did all the talking and he never said a word."

Jeremy waggled his eyebrows. "You found me out." He grinned and stuffed his mouth with food.

"So." Maya swallowed soda. "Why are we here?" She turned to Emma. "What's your SOS other than Jeremy hasn't learned proper hygiene."

Amid the laughter, Emma said, "We need to talk about Adam."

The room went silent, and Jeremy inhaled so hard, he choked on his food.

Charlie pounded him on the back while Maya and Emma knelt on either side of him. His face grew hot, and he grasped at his throat. A strong gag brought the gob of chicken back into his mouth. He raised a hand for Charlie to stop beating him and went to the kitchen to spit the half-masticated food into the trash. He coughed a few times and came back to sit down.

After wiping his mouth on his napkin, he studied Emma. "What do you mean, 'We need to talk about Adam'?" His voice was tight. He cleared his throat.

Maya returned to her seat. She picked up her lo mein and pushed the food around before putting the container back on the coffee table.

"Maya," Emma said, placing a hand on her sister's knee. "You have to tell him."

"Tell me what?"

Maya sat forward covering her knees with her arms, pushing Emma's hand away. She brought her arms in close and twisted her wedding rings.

Frowning, Charlie put his food down. "What's going on?"

"A week before I graduated from high school," Maya said, "Adam tried to attack me."

"Tried?" Charlie said, sitting forward.

"What do you mean, tried?" Jeremy squeezed his can of soda, making the aluminum pop. "What do you mean, Adam tried to attack you," he repeated, glaring at Maya.

Maya sighed and covered her face with her hands. "I never thought this day would come," she said through her fingers. Dropping her hands, she turned a worried, brown-eyed gaze to Emma who smiled encouragement.

"I wouldn't ask," Emma said, "but this is important. I don't think Jeremy will go off the deep end like he did last time, but his mental health is at stake."

"How?" Charlie asked.

Emma gestured to Jeremy. "We talk every week. Jeremy's been asking questions about Adam. Asking if I remember what happened to Amy."

"Amy? Amy Taylor?" Charlie stared at Jeremy, confusion in his brown eyes. "You mentioned her in Florida. What does Adam have to do with Amy Taylor?"

Emma turned to Jeremy. "Time you told them the truth."

"You've gone into lawyer mode," Jeremy tried to tease. "You sound like Dad."

Emma sighed. "Now's not the time to deflect, Jeremy. Tell them you've been dating Amy Taylor."

"Emma!"

"What?!" Maya and Charlie exclaimed.

"Well, I'm back to not dating Amy Taylor again, aren't I?"

Charlie put his hands up. "Wait. Stop. Would someone please start at the beginning?"

So Jeremy took a deep breath and started talking. Once, during the recounting of his time since Valentine's Day, his phone buzzed. Catnap flashed.

Jeremy froze at the sight of the name. His eyes widened, but rather than answer, he pushed the phone away with his foot.

"Is Catnap Amy?" Charlie asked.

"Yes."

"Catnap?" Maya asked.

"Long story. She catnaps because she works two jobs and doesn't sleep much."

He told them about the night of Amy's first panic attack. Jeremy was talking to Adam when she came outside. Leaving off the part of them making out on the bench, he relayed the circumstances of their second meeting and how she'd run away.

"I invited Adam to lunch and asked him if he remembered her. He got so nervous and shifty I sensed he was lying to me when he denied remembering who she was. The only conclusion I could come to is she's having an affair with Adam. They were supposed to be meeting those nights and I got in the way. I put two and two together."

"And came up with ten," Maya said. She pointed her fork at him. "God knows, I've had my issues with Amy, but she'd never do such a stupid thing."

Emma huffed a laugh. She chewed her egg roll and nodded in agreement then swallowed. "Boy, Jeremy, I gotta say. For a smart guy, you're such a dumbass."

The room fell silent.

Jeremy's jaw went slack, and he stared, wide-eyed at his sisters. "Thanks a lot." He scowled and pushed the rest of his food away, his appetite gone.

"Well, think for one second. Do you honestly believe Amy would have an affair with Adam? He's gotta be...Dad's age." Maya added.

"Well," he said. "You tell me why young women have affairs with older men." He held up his hand and rubbed his thumb across his fingers. "Money."

Charlie lightly smacked him in the back of the head.

"Hey!" Jeremy shouted pressing a hand to his head.

"Are you calling our Amy a gold digger? If you are, you don't understand her very well."

Jeremy's brows shot up. "Our Amy?"

"Yes, our Amy. You forget I dated her too. And the thing I remember most is her loyalty. If she was seeing you, she would *never* cheat. We didn't go out together long before she asked me what we were doing," Charlie said.

"I confessed and asked her to stay with me for a while longer until I found the courage to come out, but she was free to date other guys if she wanted to. She never did. Not until you two had something simmering and she asked my permission to end things." Charlie narrowed his eyes and leaned forward as if to emphasize his point. "She asked my permission," he said, glaring at Jeremy. "Does that sound like a cheater to you?"

Jeremy bowed his head. Heat rolled up his neck and warmed his ears and face. He rubbed his forehead. "God," he groaned. "I am a dumbass."

"Yes," Maya said, smiling. "Yes, you are. But you're our dumbass and we love you. Why else would we drop our lives for you?"

Jeremy smiled for the first time in three weeks. He air-kissed her and she returned the gesture.

"Out of curiosity," Emma said, "what did she say when you accused her of chicanery with Adam?"

His smile disappeared and he dropped his hand to his lap. "Nothing." He picked up his soda can. "She just...cried."

When Charlie raised his hand again, he jerked away, pointing at him. "Don't you hit me again!"

But Charlie only reached for his dinner. "You've inflicted enough pain on yourself. I don't have to lift a finger."

Emma turned to their sister. "Okay, Maya. Your turn."

Maya sighed and the expression on her face made Jeremy think she wished this moment never came. As she shifted into a more comfortable position, Jeremy readjusted himself on his sofa so he could see her better as she talked.

She rubbed her forehead with her fingers. "A week before my graduation, Adam called the house. I answered and he said I was just the person he was looking for. He and Emily had a graduation gift for me, but they also had a private, personal gift, something they hadn't done for Charlie. He asked me to come over to the house, so they wouldn't hurt Charlie's feelings."

She twisted her wedding rings. "When I got to their house, Adam was the only one home. He said the gift was in his office, so I went with him. He closed the door, grabbed me, pushed me up against the door, and tried to kiss and fondle me." She cast a wary gaze around at them.

Jeremy's heart froze and he couldn't breathe. Is this what Amy didn't want him to find out?

"Did he...did he...?" Jeremy couldn't say the word.

"You mean"—Maya swept him with a contemptuous glare—"Did he rape me?"

Unable to speak, he nodded.

Sighing, she cast her gaze to her lap and continued twisting her rings. "No. But only because when he forced me to the floor I got scared enough to fight back." She raised her gaze. "He tried to straddle me, and as I fought, I kicked out and got him between the legs."

Charlie and Jeremy groaned.

Back straight, she glared at them. "It was accidental but allowed me to escape."

Jeremy rose to his feet and pulled her up. He hugged her. "I'm sorry, Maya."

She hugged him back. "I'm sorry too, Jer."

Jeremy turned to Emma. "How about you? Did he ever try?"

"No. Maya warned me never to be caught alone with him and if he called on such a pretext to ignore him."

"Did he try a pretext?" Charlie asked.

"He did. I told him no thanks, and he didn't go any further."

"Did neither of you tell Dad? Or Mom?" Charlie asked.

"No!" they said together.

Jeremy's shoulders dropped. He and Charlie stared at each other.

"It's complicated, Charlie." Maya moved from Jeremy's embrace and sat down. "How do you tell Dad? Adam is his best friend. Since law school. You've listened to the stories ad nauseum like the rest of us."

She picked up her soda can. "What do you say to Mom? She'd be upset, but would she do anything? She might talk to Dad, but he'd tell her we exaggerated, or misunderstood the situation, and she would go along."

Jeremy's phone buzzed again. Catnap flashed, and again, he ignored her.

Seconds later, the phone dinged, and a message flashed up. He didn't catch all the words, but the name, Frank got his attention.

He grabbed his phone and opened the text, which he read aloud. "Jeremy. Frank. Emergency!"

He held the phone in both hands and stared at the screen. A ploy perhaps?

"Who's Frank?" Emma asked, her tone laced with suspicion. "Why would he be calling on Amy's phone?"

"Her boss," Jeremy said. He continued to stare at the screen, brow furrowed, unable to decide what to do.

"Call him back," Charlie said. "We're here for whatever happens."

Jeremy swiped his phone, placed the call, and hit the speaker.

Frank answered on the first ring. "Jeremy," he managed to invoke terror into his name.

"What's going on?"

"No clue, man. She's locked herself in the employees' bathroom.

She's in hysterics saying he's gonna attack her and she never should have done...something. I can't understand her, but Jeremy, I've never seen her this bad. She's banging her head against the door, and I can't make her stop."

Jeremy's gaze swept his siblings, all with expressions of concern. "What touched her off?"

"Some couple came in. Gave her a hard time. The fork was dirty, the food uncooked, a hair on my plate." Frank sighed into the phone. "She did something she's never done before. When they came in, she asked me to give them to Jason and I told her no. I should have let her, but I said no. We're shorthanded tonight, and crazy busy and, I confess, we're all short-tempered and impatient."

"Who came in?" Jeremy's gaze met each of his siblings as they leaned forward, riveted to the call.

"Some guy and his wife. Listen, man, can you come down? We can't coax her out of the bathroom, but I thought you could do something. I realize you haven't been around in a while but please, Jeremy, come down. I'm begging you. I couldn't think of anyone else to call."

Jeremy stared at his siblings. They nodded.

"I'm on my way, Frank."

"Hurry up, man."

Jeremy disconnected. "Can someone drive me? I've had a lot to drink today. I don't trust myself."

Maya got up and tapped Emma's elbow. "Charlie, you take Jeremy. Emma and I will clean this place in case you need to bring her back here."

28

The drive to Burlington was long, tense, and silent. Anger rolled off Charlie like a wave. Jeremy couldn't think of anything to say, so he studied his older brother. Charlie focused on the road and drove the speed limit, but the hard lines of his face gave away his ire.

"You're mad at me."

Charlie's frown deepened. The lines around his nose grew stark "Geez, Jeremy, what gave you that idea."

"C'mon, Charlie."

Charlie glanced at him, and if looks killed, Jeremy would be six feet under now. "All this time," he mused. He had his left elbow propped against the open window and his fingers curled around the frame.

"What?"

"All this time," Charlie said again, scowling. "All this time and the only person you told was Emma and you swore her to secrecy."

"What's your point?"

"You're a dickhead, is my point," Charlie shouted.

"I beg your pardon?"

"I said you're a dickhead, Jeremy. What part of dickhead did you not understand? You bitch because Amy wouldn't tell you the truth, but you're no better."

Jeremy gaped, caught off guard by the intensity of Charlie's anger. "I'm not keeping secrets. Not like her."

"Oh really?" Charlie shifted his arm down. "You spent a week at my house. Jon and I entertained you and you were dating her, but you told us half-truths and obfuscations. Jon specifically asked if you were seeing someone, and you denied it." He glared at Jeremy who now understood Ricky's reaction when Amy chastised him. "You were a guest in my house, you ate my food, and lied to my spouse."

"You're right. I'm sorry, Charlie. Please forgive me. When all this is over, I'll call Jon and apologize to him as well."

Charlie drew in a loud breath through his nose and exhaled. "Have you told Mom and Dad?"

Jeremy turned away. "I told them I was seeing someone, but we ended things. Been over for at least a month."

"But did you tell them she was Amy?" Charlie persisted but softened his tone.

"No," Jeremy admitted.

"See? Dickhead."

"Stop calling me names!"

"Why? You bitch about her keeping secrets, but why did you keep her a secret from us? She's your soulmate. Always has been. We would have rejoiced with you, but you denied us the opportunity. Asshole."

Charlie made a noise in his throat and fell silent. He scrubbed his forehead with the side of his hand then glanced at Jeremy from the corner of his eye and sighed. "What have you been afraid of, little brother?"

Jeremy dropped his gaze to his lap. "I don't know," he said and made a disgusted face. "Yes, I do. I was afraid she'd leave me again and you would all mock me for being stupid. A part of me didn't believe I deserved love. And if I didn't say anything, no one would find out I'd made a fool of myself a second time."

"Hmm." Charlie glanced at him. "I don't think so."

"What do you mean?"

"I may have some of my facts wrong, but based on what you've told us so far, I'd say you set her up so *you* could be the one to leave *her* this time."

Jeremy scoffed. "That's the dumbest thing you've ever said."

"You think so? Well, let's consider the facts. Dickhead. You were so afraid she'd leave you a second time, you insisted she give you something she said she couldn't. And when she maintained her position, you turned your back on her." He glanced over. "Then," he continued, relentless. "When she finally says she's ready to spill the beans to you, you refuse to listen and accuse her of having an affair with Adam."

"Hey," he barked, jabbing his brother in the arm. "She cut me off two weeks before, so you don't have any idea what you're talking about." Jeremy chose to ignore the truth of Charlie's words.

"Yeah?" Charlie's voice dripped with sarcasm. In a baby's voice, he went on with burning sarcasm. "Did widdle Amy hoot Jewemy's feewings?" In his normal voice, he continued, "What happened? She wouldn't let you into her bed?"

Jeremy gawked. His mouth dropped open, and he struggled to think.

Charlie burst out laughing. "Whohuhho! Whodathunkit? Our sweet little Amy has a backbone."

He glanced at Jeremy's burning face. "You dumped her because she wouldn't let you get laid." Laughter shook Charlie's body. "Atta girl, Amy." Shooting Jeremy a contemptuous glance, he said, "You don't deserve her."

"You're right. I don't. But that isn't why," Jeremy insisted, coming close to confessing to having bedded Amy the day before.

"No, that wasn't why," Charlie agreed. "You needed the excuse to walk away and take revenge on her for what she did to you."

Jeremy turned away and knuckled an eye. He didn't argue because, well, how did one argue with the truth?

He sighed. "So what do you suggest I do?"

"Take her back, man. Tell her, first, you're sorry. Second, you don't care, and third, you're not taking no for an answer. You love her, she loves you. End of story."

"I did. She told me no."

"Which served you right, but something's changed. If she wants to tell her story, listen without judgment, and especially without comment. Let her talk. She might be ready to purge. If so, all the better for you. If not…" Charlie shrugged, as if to suggest they'd find another way later if necessary.

Jeremy stared out the car window noting the landmarks of the approaching city. Charlie was right. He didn't deserve her, but he had to find a way to win her.

Once in the city, Jeremy directed him to the parking garage. He had Charlie park next to Amy's car and they ran to the restaurant.

Jason and Briana worked the room. When the brothers entered,

Briana pointed toward the back while Jason glared with displeasure. Jeremy smacked the door separating the employee area and flew through.

Frank stood with his forehead pressed against a white door, his hand grasping the doorknob. He turned when the door opened, and Jeremy met a wild-eyed, scared Frank.

He jerked his thumb at his brother. "This is my brother Charlie."

He pushed past Frank and knocked on the door. "Amy? It's me, Jay." He turned the doorknob, which moved in his hand, but he couldn't budge the door.

Charlie chuckled. "Jay," he muttered, but when Jeremy glanced at him, Charlie smiled and shrugged.

"Amy, can you say something or knock on the door if you can understand me?"

The only response was a slow thud, thud, thud.

"There she goes again. I think she's banging her head against the door," Frank spoke fast.

"Amy, honey, can you open the door? I came back," Jeremy called, encouraging her. "Please?"

He waited. Turned the handle and pushed. The door wouldn't budge. Brow knotted in confusion, he turned to Frank. "How come I can turn the doorknob, but I can't open the door?"

"The bathroom is a small space. She might be sitting with her back to the door and her feet braced on the toilet, which means you're never getting in if she doesn't want you to."

Jeremy pressed his forehead to the door. "Baby, open the door. This isn't the time to be stubborn. Please, I'm sorry for everything." He sighed. Tried again. "Charlie's here. He wants to say hi."

Charlie stepped up to the door and tapped. "Hey, Aims." He glanced at Jeremy. "Hey, is this any way to greet your former boyfriend? Can you let us in, sweetie?"

Jeremy twisted the knob again, gave a gentle push. Nothing. He sighed. Placed a hand on the portal. "Amy, honey, I think I understand what happened with Adam. What happened is his fault, not yours. I'm not mad, I don't hate you, I could never hate you."

A pause.

"Baby, I love you. Will you please let me in? You don't have to say anything if you don't want to. I want to be sure you're okay."

He turned to Charlie for help.

"Yo, Aim," Charlie called. He grasped Jeremy's shoulder and gave a reassuring squeeze.

The door thudded again, a rhythmic thud, thud, thud.

"Amy," Charlie's tone grew sharp with concern. "If you're banging your head on the door, stop before you give yourself a concussion. Listen." He pressed his fingers against the wood. "Jeremy's right. We should make sure you're okay, but first, you need to let us open the door. If you don't want to, fine, but I'm warning you, we'll sit out here all night if you insist, so I suggest you let us in."

Charlie gritted his teeth and creased his brow, looking nervous.

Jeremy hoped his brother said the right thing. The thudding stopped and drawing in a hopeful breath, he tried the door again. No-go.

He turned to Frank. "What happened? What set her off?"

"A customer." Frank gestured with his hands as if to say, what can you expect? "Some men are jerks. Come here with their wives and still try to manhandle my staff. Pisses me off, but it happens."

"Someone tried to grab her?" Charlie's brow creased and anger darkened his brown eyes.

"I have the entire exchange on a security camera, which points up Church Street. Their table is in plain view. I can show you."

"Go." Jeremy jerked his head toward Frank. "Check if it was Adam."

"I think we have the answer, but since we've no place to go, Frank, lead the way." Charlie held out an arm.

Frank led him back to his office where he closed the door.

Jeremy turned back to the white portal. He knocked. "Amy, honey, please open the door. I'm so sorry for everything. I swear I won't let Adam scare or bother you again. Can you please let me in so we can talk?"

Weeping on the other side was his only answer.

"Baby don't cry. We can fix this. I promise we can fix this."

Minutes later, Frank and Charlie reemerged from the office. Charlie gestured to Jeremy who moved away from the door to huddle.

Anger sparked in Charlie's brown eyes. He planted his hands on his hips and jutted his chin. "He didn't only complain about food and stuff, camera shows him grabbing her ass and at one point, he had a grip on her wrist and was saying something to her, scaring the bejesus out of her. From what I can gather, I think he threatened her somehow.

So bad, when she got away, another patron followed her into the restaurant. My guess is he was checking to make sure she was okay. Frank promises to keep the security footage."

Jeremy closed his eyes. "Next time I see him I'm gonna beat the shit out of him."

"I'll hold him down."

He returned to the door and drew in a deep breath. "Amy? Adam was here tonight. He grabbed you, didn't he?"

As slow as possible, so as not to make a sound, Jeremy turned the doorknob. He pushed and the door opened a crack. With a quick, hopeful glance at Charlie, he opened the door to his body width and slipped inside.

Charlie followed him. Closing the door, he leaned against the wood, as though protecting them from intrusion. She'd forced herself into a small gap between the commode and the sink, wrapped her arms around her knees, and shook like a leaf in a windstorm. Her eyes were wild and unfocused.

Jeremy squatted in front of Amy, unsure what to do. She was a mess. Her face was splotchy from crying, her eyes red and swollen and her nose dripped. Her hair as matted with food as her uniform.

"Did you have an accident?"

She ignored the question.

He reached for her knee, but she moaned and covered her head with her arms. He froze.

"You're all right, Amy. I'm not gonna hurt you. Charlie's here. We're here to protect you."

Amy wiped her face with her sleeve, smearing tears and snot across a cheek. She shook as her wild gaze darted between them, uncomprehending.

"Good God," Charlie whispered. "What happened?"

"Charlie," Jeremy spoke with quiet authority and without taking his eyes from Amy, "ask Frank to call 9-1-1."

Charlie stuck his head out the door. He gave the instruction and shut the door again.

"Look at me, Amy." Jeremy didn't take his gaze from her face. "Amy. Focus on me," he said when she didn't immediately respond.

She tried and he smiled and nodded. "Atta girl, babe. Focus on my voice."

He tilted his head and studied her. "Can you hear me?"

She nodded.

"Okay. Now, breathe in deep through your nose if you can." He smiled.

She tried. Her mouth opened and she drew in a long breath.

"Close enough," Jeremy said with a chuckle. "You're a snot machine. Worse than Ricky. And what's all over your uniform?"

"Who's Ricky?" Charlie asked, but Jeremy held up a hand and he fell silent.

"Let your breath out slowly." He stretched the word, sounding like verbal slow motion.

She exhaled, blowing her lips a little.

"Good girl. Again. Deep breath in," he encouraged her.

She inhaled and exhaled.

He shook his head. "Slow down, Amy. Bring your breathing back under control. Deep long breath in."

She inhaled, lifting her shoulders. He inhaled too, copying her.

"Hold for three seconds. Okay, now long breath out to release."

Again she puffed her cheeks as she exhaled.

"Atta girl. Keep your eyes on me," he urged when her gaze strayed.

Jeremy felt a tap on his shoulder and from the corner of his eye, Charlie held a wad of paper towels. He took them and extended them to Amy. "Want to dry your eyes?"

Her hand shook as she snatched the towels from him and drew back to fold her arms as if afraid that he might try to touch her. She wiped her nose.

In a sudden burst of movement, Amy scrambled to her knees and hung over the commode before a massive heave left her gagging into the bowl.

Jeremy jumped when she made the sudden move, but he grasped her shoulders while she vomited.

Hard spasms rocked her body. Yellow bile left lacy patterns in the bowl. He turned his face away with a nervous grimace. Charlie turned green.

She drew in a gasping breath as though a strangler released his grip on her throat. Before she drew in another breath, a second spasm hit, and she retched again. She collapsed against the porcelain.

"That hurts," she wailed.

"I'm sure." Jeremy rubbed her back. "I hope you didn't crack a rib."

He slid his hands to her shoulders and drew her off the side of the toilet. He sat on the tile floor and settled her between his knees, the same way he did the first time he helped her through a panic attack. He put his arms around her and held her head against his shoulder. "If you need to cry, go ahead and cry."

She shook her head but settled in closer to him. She placed a hand on his elbow and her fingers unsteadily moved over his arm.

"Tell us what happened," he said, and fearing she'd go off on him again, he amended. "Tonight. Tell us what happened tonight."

Amy's body shook, though, from the retching or her fright, he couldn't tell.

She covered her face with her hands and Jeremy held her tighter.

"What happened, babe? You're safe now."

She drew in another long, ragged breath and started to cry. "He raped me," she wailed.

Jeremy and Charlie exchanged glances.

Jeremy dropped his head against the tiled wall and closed his eyes, vowing Adam would pay.

Another ragged breath. "In your house."

Another gulp of air. "I was a kid...but he...raped me and warned me...never to tell. He said I would be in trouble if I told anyone. He said no one would believe me. He said you would call me a slut and a whore, and you'd leave me." She huffed air. "Please believe me." She wept and clutched at his shirt.

Jeremy lay his cheek on the top of her head. "I do believe you."

"So—" Charlie cleared his throat. "So do I."

"I couldn't tell you. I didn't want you to hate me," she went on.

"I wouldn't hate you."

"Yes, you would," Amy insisted and moved to sit up. He released her, fearing he might trigger more terror.

Bracing a hand on the floor she turned her tear-streaked, splotchy face to him. Clear mucus ran from her nose. "You would. We made a deal. We would be each other's firsts. I couldn't keep the deal. You would have thought I'd slept around when I didn't. He took you away from me. The other day when you said...when you..." She shook her head as if unable to say the words. "I realized you'd never believe me."

Jeremy cringed. "I'm sorry I said such a thing. I can't believe I entertained the idea, but I was grasping at straws, hoping to shock you into telling me the truth."

He had forgotten their deal. Confident they would marry, they promised to come to their wedding night each a virgin for the other. Amy had come up with the plan because they were moving dangerously close to a sexual relationship and her Catholic upbringing would neither permit her to go so far nor use birth control.

"When you came to the restaurant on Valentine's Day, my heart ached. All these years, I thought I was over you, but I was wrong. The minute I laid eyes on you, I knew. I still love you." Fresh tears overwhelmed her.

Jeremy closed his eyes and squeezed her tight.

"You weren't happy with her," she said against his shirt, and he wondered if she was talking about his relationship with Maggie or that night in general. "The furious glare you gave me when you left hurt more than I wanted to admit, but I figured nothing ventured, nothing gained. I deserved it though."

She wiped her nose. "But you came back."

"I did."

"Why?"

He sighed and dropped his head back against the cold tile wall. "Because when you said, 'Hello Jay,' my heart exploded."

She stayed silent so long Jeremy thought she'd gone to sleep, but then she spoke.

"I thought we were going to be okay, but you were talking to him, and I panicked. Which scared me. I hadn't had one in a long time. I thought he was telling you to stay away from me, I was soiled goods, and you could do better than me."

She covered her face with her hands and swiped. "I tried to end things with you because sooner or later you'd find out and be so disgusted with me. But you pursued me anyway and when I started to think we'd be okay again, he found us on the bench. He scared me so bad, I realized he would always be watching and waiting to snatch away my happiness. He wasn't going to let me have this...you."

"That wasn't his decision." Jeremy squeezed her. "It was mine. And yours."

"He would have told you."

"No, he wouldn't," Charlie said, sinking to his knees to be eye level with her. "He would have taken your secret to the grave. If the world found out what he'd done, he'd have so much shit come down on his head. That's why it was in his best interests to keep you so scared you'd stay quiet."

She lifted her head and eyed him.

"Which is why he threatened you," Charlie added. "He doesn't want to lose his law license and his reputation. He especially doesn't want to go to jail."

"Charlie's right," Jeremy said. He took a chance and kissed her temple.

"Your father will hate me. If he finds out, he'll come after me for ruining his friend's life."

"Amy," Charlie said, "what if I told you you're not the only one in the family he tried this on?"

Amy froze in Jeremy's arms. She lifted her head and peered at Charlie, then turned to Jeremy as if to assess if they told her the truth.

"He's right," Jeremy said. "Maya told us earlier this evening, he attacked her too, but in a twist of fate, she managed to escape him."

Charlie lifted a brow and nodded. "He used some ploy to get her to his house and tried to attack her." He held her gaze. "She never told a soul until tonight either."

Amy stared at Charlie as if seeing him for the first time. She sat up and quirked her brow. "What are you doing here?"

Jeremy and Charlie chuckled. "I think," Charlie said, "you're going to be okay."

A knock on the door startled them. "Paramedics."

Charlie rose and opened the door. "There isn't enough room in here for everyone. I'll leave."

He stepped out and a blue-uniformed EMT knelt in front of Amy and began assessing her.

In the hallway outside Amy's hospital room, Jeremy sat in a hard, uncomfortable chair, Charlie beside him.

The brothers waited for the doctors to emerge and tell them something. While they waited, Jeremy called John and Carol. When he finished explaining and calming them, he decided he wanted his friend with him too, so he called Mike who said he'd be down first thing in the morning.

Jeremy put his phone away, closed his eyes, and leaned his head against the wall, giving in to sudden overwhelming fatigue.

Beside him, Charlie bounced a knee.

"Cut it out," Jeremy said, eyes still closed. "Please."

Charlie set his foot flat on the floor, but his nervous energy found its way into a toe-tap instead.

Jeremy sighed. "In the car when you bitched me out for being so secretive…."

"Yeah?"

"Well, you've been quite secretive yourself. I mean, how long did you date Amy to hide the fact you're gay?"

"That was different."

"No, it wasn't."

"Yes," Charlie insisted. "I wasn't hiding something that might hurt someone's feelings. Being gay wasn't as accepted as it is today. Many of my friends turned on me. Dad judges me."

"No, he doesn't," Jeremy said, but doubt assailed him. Did their father judge him? He turned his head toward his brother but didn't open his eyes. "How does Dad judge you?"

Rather than answer the question, Charlie said, "I didn't hide from Amy. I mean, I did, but I didn't." he smiled. "She was kind about everything and encouraged me to tell Mom and Dad. Even offered to sit beside me holding my hand when I did."

"Sounds like her."

They didn't speak again for a while and Jeremy started to drift off.

"Still."

Jeremy opened his eyes.

"Sometimes I think Dad wishes I wasn't a gay man. Like if I were married to a woman, he'd be able to hold his head up. Because of my insecurity Jonathan, and I fight all the time before we come to visit, which is why we don't come often."

"Did you fight this time?"

"Nope." Charlie chuckled. "When I said you were in trouble, he had my bag out and packed before I finished the sentence. I think he feared Marguerite got her hands on you somehow."

Jeremy laughed.

The brothers fell silent again.

"Dad doesn't wish you were straight, Charlie," Jeremy said, coming out of his torpor to resume their earlier conversation. "He loves you like he loves the rest of us and wants you to be happy."

Charlie shrugged. "Sometimes I think he wants me to choose between his family and mine."

Jeremy studied him. Charlie fiddled with a gold wedding ring on his finger. Jeremy clasped his hand. "I hope you'd choose yours."

"Hands down," Charlie assured him. "But I'd lose you guys."

Eyes closed Jeremy smiled. "No you wouldn't. We're all adults. We can make our own choices." He eyed his brother from beneath his half-closed lids. "Besides, if I lost you, who would call me dickhead?"

Charlie sputtered a laugh. "You're still a dickhead."

Jeremy slid his arm around his brother's neck and drew him into an embrace.

When they broke apart, he sighed. "We're a family of secret keepers," Jeremy said. "Maya kept quiet, I don't say much, you keep your relationship with Jonathan close to the vest."

The doctor stopped in front of Jeremy. The brothers rose.

"Amy is doing fine. She's suffering from exhaustion. We've stabilized her and she's sleeping, which is the best thing for her. You might as well all go home. She'll sleep for several hours yet. You don't have to remain here."

Jeremy shook his head. "I'm staying. You can go home if you want." He turned to the doctor. "Can I go in? I won't wake her, but can I go in?"

After a moment's consideration, the doctor nodded.

Jeremy handed his keys to Charlie and told him to go home.

Charlie gave Jeremy a hug and promised to return first thing in the morning. Once his brother was gone, Jeremy entered Amy's room and pulled a chair beside her bed. He took her hand and kissed her knuckles. Then, he lowered the side rail and scooted close, lay his head on her shoulder, and fell asleep.

Jeremy's shoulder shook and he jerked his head up, confused and disoriented. He rubbed his aching neck muscles, stretched, and yawned. Another light touch on his shoulder made him jump and he gazed, bleary-eyed at the morning nurse.

Sitting up, he studied Amy's sleeping face. She had color in her cheeks again, no doubt from the oxygen flowing through the tube lying under her nose.

"I must check my patient, sir, if I can ask you to step outside for a few minutes," she suggested, smiling with quiet authority.

Jeremy nodded and rubbed his face again, expelling the last

sleepiness from his brain.

"Sure." He got to his feet, his body stiff from sleeping slumped in the chair. Moving his legs, he eased the ache from his hips and thighs. At the bathroom door, he asked permission and when the nurse nodded, he went in and shut the door.

When he finished, he splashed water on his face and washed his hands. He emerged from the bathroom, wiping his hands on paper towels, and entered the hallway.

Charlie and his parents milled outside. Dad grabbed him and drew him into a bear hug. "God almighty, boy. What did you think we would do? We love you. We only want your happiness, son."

Jeremy spoke against his father's shirt. "I'm sorry for lying to you." He pulled away but couldn't meet his father's eyes.

Dad squeezed the back of Jeremy's neck. He winced at the pain but said nothing.

When Dad released his grip, Jeremy sighed with relief.

Mom hugged and kissed him. "I know what I said about Amy, honey, but I'm happy to be wrong."

Jeremy squeezed her before kissing her cheek. "I'm glad. You have no idea how close I came to confessing that night."

"I wish you had," she admonished.

"Me too."

Dad and Mom found a love seat across the room while Jeremy and Charlie took the seats by the hospital room door.

"I left the girls at your house and drove over to Mom and Dad's. I spent the night with them and told them everything." He glanced at Jeremy. "Sorry, but it was the most expedient thing to do."

Jeremy nodded and sighed. "Were they judgy?"

"No," Charlie said, sounding pleased. "Mom didn't appear surprised," he smiled. "Dad kept asking why you didn't want to tell them the truth." He gestured. "Not in an angry way. More bewildered, I guess would be the word." Charlie eyed him, his brows creased. A pained and angry expression chased across his features. "They told me what Maggie did to you."

In a quick move, Charlie took Jeremy's face in his hands and placed a gentle kiss on his forehead. "I'm so sorry, little brother."

"Mm, thanks," Jeremy mumbled. He hadn't been fair to his parents or his siblings, or to Amy if he were to put a fine point on things. In the car, Charlie had asked him what he was afraid of. He was afraid of spending the rest of his life alone, like Maggie, angry and resentful over old hurts. Never moving past them. *And where has that gotten you, Jeremy Paul Austin?*

He shifted and dropped his head on his brother's shoulder. Charlie's arm snaked around the back of his neck and with his other hand, he patted Jeremy's cheek. "Just like old times," he murmured, and leaning his cheek on Jeremy's head, they fell silent.

Maya and Emma showed up with Emma carrying a box of doughnuts while Maya carried a box holding four cups of coffee.

"We didn't think they'd let us bring a big box of coffee in here, but they have a cafeteria downstairs if you all want some." Maya handed one to Jeremy. "I assumed you wouldn't want to be any farther than two feet from this door, so here."

"Ah." He took the cup, his eyes lighting up. "I always thought you were useful for something, sister of mine." He sipped as she air-kissed him. He swallowed and returned the gesture before taking a doughnut from Emma's box.

"I'm so hungry," he spoke around his maple frosted doughnut. He chewed, swallowed, and took another bite. A smile tugged his lips recalling the maple festival and how she'd laughed, blue eyes shining while he swiped maple frosting off her nose.

"What are you smiling about?" Emma eyed him with suspicion.

He shook his head and chewed.

"So what's going on now?" She passed the box around.

Jeremy motioned with the last bite of his doughnut. "The nurse threw me out so they can do whatever they're doing. She's still sleeping. I don't think she woke up during the night. If she did, I slept through it."

"What did they say is the diagnosis?" Mom perched herself on the edge of a chair.

"Exhaustion," Jeremy told her, "but it's a lot more than exhaustion. She has panic attacks."

Jeremy turned to Charlie. "Last night was"—he slashed a hand through the air— "worse by far than anything I've ever experienced. Most of the time I'm confused, but last night, she scared me shitless."

Charlie raised his eyebrows. "Me too."

"What did you see?" Mom's gaze bounced between the two, but a shrill child's voice split the quiet in the corridor.

"Jamie!"

Everyone turned.

"Who's Jamie?" Emma said.

Ricky flew down the hallway, sneakered feet slapping the tile floor, his T-Rex in one hand, a bright smile on his face.

Jeremy shoved his coffee cup at Charlie, jumped from his chair, and ran to the boy, scooping him into his arms and squeezing him to his chest while Ricky wrapped his little arms around Jeremy's neck and held on.

From behind, he heard his father's, "Well I'll be."

Carol approached and took the T-Rex from the boy's hand.

"Jeremy." John clasped his shoulder. "What happened? Is she all right?"

"Uh, I'm not sure. The nurse is with her right now, but you can go in as soon as they're done." Still holding Ricky, he walked them back to his family.

Lindsay came around the corner and headed down the hall dressed in hospital scrubs. She called out and he turned, shifting Ricky to hold out an arm to her.

Lindsay hugged them and kissed her nephew.

"I forgot you worked here." He took note of her blue scrubs and name tag hanging from her waist.

"I do," she said. "I'm a nurse."

He glanced around the hallway. "Uh, everyone, this is Lindsay, Amy's sister, and her parents, John and Carol."

Emma was already in Carol's embrace when he introduced them. The rest of his family gathered around renewing their acquaintance.

Jeremy smiled at Ricky. He shifted him again, so he stared straight into the little boy's face.

"How have you been, Sport? I missed you."

Ricky's blue eyes stared hard into Jeremy's. A scowl wrinkled the little brow and his lips pulled down. He placed his small hands against Jeremy's cheeks. A drop of saliva lay on the tip of Ricky's lower lip. "Where you go?" he demanded.

Mom gasped and lay her hand against her heart.

Jeremy's heart lurched. He understood what the boy was asking but decided to make light of the situation in front of everyone. "I'm right here."

But Ricky wasn't satisfied. He knew what he was asking and tried again. “No, Jamie.” He pounded his little hands against Jeremy’s shoulders in time to his words and stared hard into his eyes again. This time, his small lip formed into a pout and his brow furrowed as anger darkened his face.

“Where you go?”

Jeremy’s throat tightened and he gathered him into his embrace. “I’m right here, Ricky, and I’m not going anywhere ever again. Would you like that?”

Against his ear, Ricky nodded. “Yeah,” he said in a toddler’s plaintive way.

Jeremy sat and cuddled the boy. Charlie sat next to him. “Would you care to introduce us?”

Jeremy smiled and tapped Ricky’s shoulder. “Hey.” He pointed to Charlie. “This is my brother, Charlie. Charlie, this is Ricky Taylor.”

Charlie held out his hand. Ricky peered at Jeremy who encouraged him with a nod. Ricky held out his left hand and rather than correct him, Charlie shook.

“Pleasure to meet you, Ricky,” he said with a smile. “I’m a friend of your mommy’s.”

Ricky stared.

“True.” Jeremy turned to the room. “Everyone here is a friend of mommy’s.”

Ricky studied Jeremy as if assessing him. Then his eye fell on the doughnut box. “I want one,” he said, pointing.

Rather than say yes, he asked a question. “Did Grammy feed you breakfast this morning?” He didn’t want to give him any sweets. This wasn’t the place for a hyperactive kid high on sugar.

Ricky nodded. “I want one,” he insisted, waving his finger at the doughnut box again.

Beside him, Charlie chuckled. “Oh dear, let’s see how you handle this.”

Jeremy flipped open the box and broke a plain doughnut in half and in half again before holding it out to Ricky, who shook his head, pushing Jeremy’s hand away.

“No, that one,” Ricky said, eyeing a chocolate frosted one.”

“Absolutely not,” Jeremy said. “You can eat this one.”

Ricky’s hands curled into claws and his brows drew down, but Jeremy was undeterred. “This one or none at all. Which would you prefer?”

After a moment's thought, he took the doughnut from Jeremy's fingers.

Dad chuckled. "You'll make a fine father, Jer."

The nurse appeared from Amy's room, and everyone stopped talking.

"You can visit, one at a time, but keep in mind, she's still asleep, so please be as quiet as you can."

"We're her parents." Carol stepped forward, pointing to her husband. "Can we go in together?"

"Of course," the nurse nodded, "but after, one at a time." She walked off.

Carol took Ricky from Jeremy and entered Amy's room. Lindsay sat down next to Jeremy. "Tell me what happened."

Jeremy thought for a second. "Remember when you said sometimes her panic attacks scare you?"

"Yes," Lindsay said squeezing her fingers.

"Well, take one of those and multiply that about one hundred times," he told her.

"She cried, was in hysterics, vomiting, banging her head against the door, her eyes were unfocused, and she was incoherent," Jeremy recalled the images, grateful Carol took Ricky. He didn't want either of them to overhear.

Her fingers found her lips. "Oh my God, Jay," she said, sounding so much like Amy, it hurt.

"She crammed herself into a tiny space," Charlie added, "between the sink and toilet. How she wedged herself in there, I'll never know."

Lindsay shook her head. "Something happened. I'm a trauma nurse. Lindsay shook her head. "With Amy, they don't occur out of nowhere." Her blue-eyed gaze shifted between the brothers.

"We think something did," Jeremy told her, "but we need more specifics and I need to talk to Amy to be sure we're right."

Lindsay studied them. "Okay."

"Jeremy," Mike called from the end of the hallway.

Jeremy excused himself and went to greet him. They embraced and Mike slapped him on the shoulder. Jeremy introduced him around, and Mike shook hands one by one.

"And this is Lindsay Buckman, Amy's sister."

Mike held out his hand and Lindsay stood.

"Hello," she said, and a corner of her mouth slid upward.

“How do you do.” Mike grasped her hand as his eyes lit and lingered on her longer than necessary.

A flush stained her cheeks. Lindsay excused herself and entered Amy’s room.

Mike kept his gaze on her until she disappeared behind the privacy curtain. He double glanced at Jeremy, who grinned at him like a Cheshire cat and lifted a sardonic brow.

“Shut up,” Mike said, as a chuckle escaped.

Jeremy held up his hands. “I didn’t say a word.”

Mike narrowed his eyes, but a sheepish grin pulled at his mouth, and a red stain flushed his face. “Yes, you did. In your head. Loud and clear, so shut up.”

For the first time in weeks, laughter bubbled from the core of Jeremy’s being. His exhausted body shook, and he couldn’t breathe. Reaching his emotional limit, the uncontrolled laughter took control of him. He pressed his fist to his mouth, but another surge overtook him, and he leaned against Mike who wrapped a good-natured arm around him, holding him up.

“Buddy,” Mike said, laughing with him, “you need a drink.”

He clapped Jeremy on the back.

Charlie, drawn into Jeremy’s hysterics, leaned in. “No, he doesn’t,” he said, so only the two heard. “He needs to get laid.”

Amid the questioning eyes of the others, all three collapsed in hysterics.

29

When Amy woke, Emma, Charlie, and Maya, as well as Mr. and Mrs. Austin stood around her bed, along with Mom and Dad, Lindsay, and Ricky in Jay's arms. She didn't understand why and didn't care the moment she spied her baby. Bursting into tears, she reached out her arms and Jay gave him over to her for cuddles and kisses.

When Ricky got antsy and began crawling on her, Poppy picked him up and cuddled him. "What do you all say we give these two a minute alone together, eh?" With a wink at Amy, he turned and walked to the door. Without a word, everyone followed his lead.

Jay sat in the chair next to her, held her hand, and kissed her knuckles. He was so happy to see her, yet she couldn't comprehend the change. The last she knew he didn't want anything to do with her anymore.

She crooked her finger at him, and he leaned close. "Am I in trouble?" she whispered. "Why am I in the hospital?"

He shook his head. "You're not in trouble," he said a note of surprise in his voice. "You had—"

"I had a panic attack."

"Yes." He studied her, concern and love in his beautiful teddy bear brown eyes. "According to the doctors, brought on by severe exhaustion."

Her gaze roamed the sparse hospital room. A machine behind and to her right beeped a steady rhythm. "Must have been a doozy."

Jay's lips slipped upward. "Talk about putting things mildly." Lifting her hand he kissed her knuckles again. "Babe, can you forgive me?" he spoke behind her hand.

She blinked. "Forgive you for what?"

He jerked backward. "For everything I said. Everything I accused you of. I was being stupid. Charlie suggested I set you up so I could be the one to break up with you. At first, I thought the idea ridiculous, but the more I consider his point of view, the more I think he's right."

Her brow quirked. Perhaps she was still overtired because he didn't make sense to her, so she remained quiet.

"Remember when I told you I had been unhappy with Maggie but too lazy to end things?"

She nodded.

"I don't think I was being lazy. Ever since February, when you came back into my life, I realized I was waiting for you."

"Oh, Jay," she choked out through tears. Lifting her arms, she invited him into her embrace. Snapping down the bar on the side of the bed, he leaned into her. She lifted her back and he slid his hands behind her. Amy hugged him and kissed his cheek.

"I'm so sorry, for everything," she said into his ear. "I love you so, so much. You're my soulmate."

Tears dripped onto her hospital gown, and he laughed and sobbed into her ear. Amy's arms tightened around him, and she stroked the back of his head. He lifted his face and kissed her, not a passionate, sex-laden kiss, but one filled with love and longing. When he pulled away, he smiled down at her.

She slipped her hands to his face and pulled him close for another kiss. When his lips met hers, she slipped her tongue in and found his, tasting the sweetness of his doughnut and coffee. His sharp intake of breath sounded loud in her ear. Jay deepened the kiss and fed her more until she thought she might pass out.

Disappointment shot through her when he pulled away, but he grinned down at her, a mischievous gleam in his eye.

"Control yourself, Miss Taylor," he teased.

Amy laughed. "Two words I *never* thought I'd hear you utter, *ever.*"

Resuming his seat in the chair, he laughed with her.

"Jay?"

"Hmm." With his left arm propped on the open window, he drove, leaning his head on his knuckles. He looked so lost in thought, Amy was sure he was ruminating about something hurtful she'd done or said to him in the midst of her attack.

"Did I do or say something I need to apologize for?"

He lifted his head and glanced at her, questioning.

She shrugged. "When those things happen, sometimes I say or do things and I don't remember, so if I need to apologize would you please be honest and tell me now so I can say I'm sorry?"

He smiled. "You didn't say or do anything to me or Charlie you need to apologize for."

"Charlie," she whispered, heart pounding. Her brow knit. "Yeah, he was there too."

She couldn't let her doubts go. Perhaps he was being polite. "You're certain? You're not saying that?"

"I'm certain. I'm not saying that."

She studied him.

He laid his head back on his knuckles and continued to drive.

"Okay." She cast him a quick glance. "But I'm sorry, anyway."

He gazed at her from the corner of his eye and his lips slid into an amused smile.

She stared out the window as Colchester slid away and they passed the exit for the Champlain Islands.

"Jay?"

He turned to her.

"Are we okay?" She studied him. "I mean, do we have things we need to talk about?" Despite their kisses and words of love in the hospital earlier in the morning, she worried.

Lifting his head up from his knuckles, he lowered his arm and drew in a breath through his nose.

He stared straight ahead. "Do you love me, Amy?"

"Yes," she said without hesitation.

"Enough to let me back into your life permanently?"

"Yes."

He nodded and glanced at her. "I love you too. With all my heart and soul. Do you believe me?"

"Yes." A nod. "I do."

"We have nothing to talk about. I want to get you home so you can take a nap if you wish."

"You're driving me to your home where we'll be alone, and you expect me to nap?"

His answer was a salacious grin.

They pulled into Jay's yard and Amy glanced around her. She'd never been to his house, and she was impressed. His house, an L-shaped early-twentieth-century farmhouse stood on the main drag in Milton, but the backyard was deceivingly large. He cut the engine and she stepped out of the car. As he came around the front, he reached out and she took his hand.

They walked across the yard and up the steps to his back deck.

"This is nice." She took stock of the high privacy walls and the wicker furniture placed around the deck in cozy nooks.

He smiled. "I like it here."

"I didn't have you pegged for a wicker furniture man," she teased.

He chuckled. "The previous owners didn't want it, so I had them include it in the sale price."

"Mm," she said, wrapping her arms around his waist and leaning in to kiss his throat and nibble his earlobe. Blocking his view of the door and making him fumble with the key.

"You seem to have some trouble with the key," she said, and lightly bit his jaw.

He laughed. "Cut it out, woman, or you'll find yourself ravaged right here on my back deck."

"Really?" Amy giggled in his ear and nibbled some more.

Grabbing her hip, he pulled her to him. "I warned you," he teased and kissed her with a hot, impassioned kiss that sucked the air from her lungs. He pressed himself into her and Amy was instantly aflame.

Her hands found his belt loops and she pulled him to her until his erection pressed hard on her. He pushed and rubbed himself against her.

She lifted her leg to his hip and Jeremy grasped her thigh, holding her in place with his hips and his hand. His hot wet kisses inflamed her, and she demanded more of them.

Unable to breathe and she broke the kiss as the first spasm hit her.

"Ahhh!" She wrapped her arms around his neck and hung on as spasms racked her body.

He tightened his grip on her thigh while he pushed against her again and again.

"Jay," she gasped before pressing her face into his cotton T-shirt and screaming into the fabric.

She heard a vague "hunh" in her ear as he pushed hard one more time and rocked himself against her pelvis.

His body relaxed while he panted for breath. He released her leg before turning for a kiss.

"Oh my God," he said against her lips. "You're remarkable."

"So are you," she said, stroking his cheek. She kissed him again, this time a soft, slow kiss of thanks and love.

They broke apart and Jay returned his attention to unlocking the door.

Grinning, Amy slid her hand down to the wet spot at his crotch. "Oh, dear, Jay, what happened here?"

He grinned and gave her a sidelong glance. "If you don't know, I can't help you," he said and pushed the door open. Without warning, he picked her up.

Amy shrieked with laughter as he carried her over the threshold, through the entrance room, and toward the stairs. His keys dangled, forgotten, in the lock.

Amy sat up with a gasp and spun her upper body around, eyes straining in the meager light shining in from the streetlight below the window. Her bed and room placement were wrong, but darkness shrouded her ability to see, and a surge of panic made her heart pound.

Jay sat up and grasped her shoulder.

She jerked away, slumped, and dropped her face into her hand. "Jay." She reached for his arm. "That's right."

"Are you okay?"

"Yes. I didn't know where I was for a second." She lay back down, and he snuggled his chest against her back. His fingers caressed the side of her breast and teased her nipple. Desire tightened her abdomen.

He kissed her shoulder and nuzzled her neck.

"You're held captive in my home," he teased as he kissed and nibbled her earlobe.

Shivers raced down her spine and she stretched her neck while tracing her fingers up and down his arm. As he loomed above her to kiss her, she wrapped her arms around his neck and drew him close. "Well, thank God," she whispered and opened herself to him.

When she woke again, Jay slept beside her. She had to use the bathroom and hoped she could find her way in the dark. The numbers on the clock read two fifteen. His arm lay draped over her middle. Careful not to disturb him, she slid out of bed. Her stomach growled, making her realize her only meal the day before was a hospital breakfast before they discharged her.

Moving in the dark, she groped her way to the bedroom door. In the hallway, a nightlight beckoned in a room across the hall. When she approached, she leaned in the doorway and breathed a sigh at the sight of the toilet. She stepped in and closed the door.

The flushing toilet almost drowned out the soft knock on the door.

"I'll be out in a sec," Amy called as she washed her hands in warm water.

"No problem," Jay spoke through the portal. "I didn't want to scare you when you opened the door and found me standing here."

Amy opened the door. "Thank you." They did a small dance as they tried to move around each other, and chuckling, Jay grabbed her shoulders and moved her aside.

Her stomach growled again, and his teeth flashed in the muted light. "I'm hungry too." He entered the bathroom but didn't close the door.

Amy turned her back and cringed at the sound of his stream hitting the water. "Do you have food? Bacon and eggs or something? I can make breakfast."

Jay flushed and washed his hands. "No." He glanced at her. "But if you want, the grocery store up the street is twenty-four hours. I can run and get some. About the only food item I keep well stocked is coffee."

Amy grinned. "Not a food item, but...thank God."

In each other's arms, they headed back to the bedroom but were too hungry to go back to bed.

Jay pulled on his jeans and a T-shirt and Amy pulled on her clothes from the day before. She wanted to shower before changing into clean clothes, but she mentally thanked Lindsay for having the forethought to pack her some clothes and her toothbrush.

Though the idea was to go and get breakfast food, Amy went into full grocery shopping mode once they entered the store.

As she filled their cart, they talked about what to do to thank his brother and sisters for coming quickly and began to shop with purpose. They bought chicken breasts, ground beef, and hot dogs, and Jay sweet-talked Amy into another potato salad. She also suggested calling their mothers and asking them to bring a dish as well.

"Would you object if I invited Mike?" Jay placed a dozen eggs into the cart. "I thought there was an attraction between him and Lindsay."

"Don't force him on her, Jay. I don't think she's ready for a new relationship. She's still mourning Kyle."

"I realize that." He added bacon and sausage to the cart. "But Mike is a widower. He can help her navigate her grief."

The day of the maple festival loomed in her mind and how she had stupidly asked if she could meet his wife.

Jay explained, "His wife, Erin, died three years ago. Breast cancer. She was a beautiful woman inside and out and he loved her with all his heart, but he's lonely and I want him happy again."

Amy lay her hand on his cheek and rubbed her thumb against his stubble. "You're a sweet guy. Has anyone ever told you so?"

He shook his head as a horse shakes his mane, and closing his eyes, lifted his chin in mock pride. "All the time," he announced with a haughty sniff and sauntered away as she laughed.

While they moved around the store, Amy considered what he'd said about Mike. She remembered him from the maple festival and liked him right off. It took a few days before she realized his lovebird comment was innocent and he meant nothing untoward. He had seen them laughing about something and assumed what was obvious for all to witness.

She caught up with him. "Mike is your best friend, right?"

"He's my closest friend. You're my best friend." He plopped a light kiss on her lips before walking to the dairy aisle for milk and half-and-half.

"Invite him," she agreed yet pointed a finger to emphasize her point. "But don't push."

The aroma of bacon, eggs, sausage, coffee, and toast wafted through the house. Jeremy sipped coffee and waited, salivating, for Amy to finish cooking breakfast. The clock on the kitchen wall read four o'clock. Dawn approached. Birds chirped for all they were worth.

"How are you doing?" He eyed her as she flipped an egg.

She glanced at him and turned another egg. "I'm fine, why?"

"Just wondered if you're getting tired again."

Amy smiled at him. "I love how you worry about me, but I'm not so delicate as you might want to think."

She slipped the spatula under the first egg, which she dropped onto a plate, and retrieved the second egg. "I'm a single mother, after all." She dropped two sausages on a plate she handed to Jeremy before cracking two more eggs into the pan. "I don't have the luxury of being delicate."

He buttered toast for himself and put two more down while she continued to cook.

When the slices popped from the toaster, he retrieved them, careful not to burn his fingers, and buttered them.

She laid the fried eggs on a plate. She glanced over.

"Eat! Don't wait for me," she said.

He picked up his fork but still, he studied her face in profile. She grabbed two slices of bacon and dropped them on her plate next to the eggs and brought her breakfast to the bar.

After she settled on the barstool across from him, he handed her the buttered toast and began to eat.

He raised his head to thank her for the excellent food but stopped short.

Amy wiped tears from her face.

"What's wrong." He rose, but she waved him back down.

She reached for his hand. "I'm sorry, Jay," she said through a half sob, half laugh. "I've been such a stupid fool. Since February. And you paid the price over and over. I don't understand why you took so much from me."

His heart wanted to burst. Lifting her hand, he kissed her knuckles. "Because I love you."

He cocked his head as his brows creased.

"What's wrong, baby? Why are you unhappy?"

She sniffed and wiped her face. "I'm not unhappy. Quite the opposite. I love you so much, I almost fear what might happen to ruin us again."

Jeremy got up and came around the bar to pull her off the stool. "Nothing will come between us ever again." He peered into her tear-filled blue eyes. "Do you believe me?"

She nodded and sniffed.

"Good," he said and gently kissed her lips. "Now eat your breakfast. You'll improve after your stomach is full."

She nodded but reached for another kiss. He obliged before moving back to his seat.

More tears coursed down her cheeks, and she waved away his

obvious concern.

"Don't mind me," she said as her voice hitched. "I think I'm coming down off my drug high." She chuckled, then started to eat.

They ate in silence, satisfying their hunger. Eggs and sausage, but Jeremy reveled in the food. Amy was an excellent cook.

"May I ask you a question?" He put his fork down and wiped his mouth on a piece of paper towel.

"You just did." She offered an impish grin.

"Wiseass."

"What's your question?" She tore a slice of toast in half.

"Do you remember in the bathroom the other night talking about the deal we made when we were kids? About being each other's firsts?"

Amy's eyes went blank, and she stared off into the distance. His heart sank. She meant what she said when she told him in the heat of a panic attack, she seldom remembered afterward what she might have said or done. Her brows furrowed, and she tilted her head.

"Yeah," she answered, drawing out the word. "I think I do. I remember sitting on the floor and you had me between your knees." She glanced at him. "Charlie was against the door, right?"

"Right." He waited for her to piece the scene together in her mind.

She dipped her toast into the yolk and ate while she thought back. "It's coming back to me and more will fill in as time goes on."

"Well, do you remember reminding me about the deal we made about being each other's firsts?" he asked again, needing her to remember, though he didn't understand why.

"I...I remember the deal. I'm not sure I remember saying anything the other night, but if you say I did, I believe you."

He shrugged, deciding as long as she remembered making the deal years ago, it was good enough. "I wondered if that was why you ran out on me." He finished in a hesitant voice. "Because of the deal."

"I ran from terror, shock, pain—physical and otherwise—and not being in my right head." When she glanced up at him, regret and sadness flashed in her blue eyes.

Lowering gaze, she spoke to her plate. "Adam took you from me. We made the deal in an effort to remain chaste for each other, silly as it sounds now. But I feared when you discovered I was no longer a virgin you would think I cheated on you and wouldn't believe me if I told the truth."

She raised her gaze. “Because of my extreme shame, I had no intention of telling you what did happen, so there was no way you could come to any other conclusion.”

She stared at him for so long he thought he should say something, but words eluded him. He cleared his throat, but she continued.

“I decided the best thing was to tell you I didn’t love you anymore and to go away.” A small smile tugged at her lips. “I didn’t count on your tenacity, but when you finally got the message, I was both relieved and broken-hearted.” She squeezed his fingers. “I’m glad to find your tenacity hasn’t changed.”

After breakfast, they pushed their dishes to the side, and over another cup of coffee, they talked, sharing their experiences in honesty and in an unspoken judgment-free zone, clearing their past and preparing for their future.

“My parents have a rule,” he said, raising his cup to his mouth, but the coffee was cold, so he put the cup down. “Never go to bed angry with each other, never go to bed even out of sorts with each other. So I propose we adopt the same rule. If we need to work something out, we leave the lights on until we resolve everything.” He studied her. “What do you say?”

She nodded. “Rule adopted. My parents also have a rule: never air your dirty laundry in public. Any dispute we have we will conduct behind closed doors.”

He nodded. “Adopted.”

She gazed into his eyes with a mischievous grin. “Is it time to turn out the lights or do we need to leave them on a little longer?”

Jeremy smiled. “We can turn them out now.” He studied her, narrowing his eyes. “Why do you ask?”

“Because.” She gave him an impish grin that never failed to melt his heart. “I don’t know about you…” She came around the breakfast bar and slid her arms around his neck. His hands found her waist and he pulled her close. The essence of sex, bacon, and Amy turned him on.

“But I think we need to go back to bed,” she whispered.

Grinning, he nuzzled her neck, and his lips found the sweet spot at the base of her throat.

Her soft exhale made him rock hard in an instant. He pressed himself against her, and with hands under her buttocks, lifted her. She wrapped her legs around his waist and her arms around his neck.

"I couldn't agree with you more," he said and slid his tongue along her lower lip, tasting their breakfast. He grabbed her lip in his teeth, let go, and carried her upstairs.

30

Jeremy awoke and studied Amy while she slept. She lay on her side, her buttocks firm against his hips. Long soft lashes lay on cheeks pink and healthy-looking again. She was warm and soft, and he thought of waking her with soft kisses, but she needed rest, and he needed the bathroom. Careful not to wake her, he slid out of bed.

When he returned, he couldn't help himself and kissed her awake.

Her eyelids fluttered open.

"Good morning, my love," he said, kissing her cheek and sliding his lips to her neck.

Amy groaned as he rolled on top of her, capturing her beneath him. "Morning sex," he said in her ear. "I love morning sex."

"So do I," she said, "but you need to let me up first."

In mock frustration, he rolled off her with an exaggerated groan. "Fine," he drew out the word much like Britney when he pushed her for her homework. "But hurry up. I must have you."

"You had me at least a dozen times last night," she said as she headed to the door.

"What's your point," he said, and her laughter drifted back from the hallway. He loved the sound of her laughter.

When she returned, he tried to take her in his arms, but she shook her head.

"Mm-mm," she said and pushed his hands away, moving out of his grasp to kneel beside him.

As she braced her hands on the pillow on either side of his head, her blue-eyed gaze, saturated with desire, took his breath away. Her breasts dangled tantalizingly close and when he raised his face to kiss one, she pulled away. Confusion knit his brow and he gave her a questioning glance, but she raised a teasing brow and shook her head. Instead, he reached to touch a nipple hardened with her lust, but again, she pushed his hand away and slowly shook her head.

Lowering her face, Amy kissed him with a wet, tongue-filled kiss that made him groan with pleasure. She grasped his wrists and held his hands down so he couldn't touch her. Her lips slid off his mouth, to his jaw, to the base of his throat where he could turn her on with one kiss. To his surprise, as her wet tongue touched the sweet spot, a shiver ran down his spine and his breath caught in his throat.

She straddled him but didn't lower her body to his. Instead, her lips inched their way down to his chest, and her tongue circled his nipples as he had done to hers. Her thumb brushed the other. He was hard and impatient for her.

She released his hands, and he gripped her hips, attempting to pull her down, but again she brushed them away. "Mm-mm," she said again and with a lust-filled grin, she slowly shook her head.

A grin lit his face as he understood she wanted to please him, not the other way around. He settled in and allowed himself to enjoy the experience, which turned him on even more.

Her lips found his shaft and her wet tongue circled the head of him before she slid her mouth over him. With a groan he lifted his hips and reflexively grabbed the back of her head. He curled his fingers into her short hair and held on.

"Amy." He gasped as her mouth drove him to the edge. "Don't make me come. I want you," he croaked out.

Releasing him, she lifted her hips. He pulled her up to kiss her as he guided himself into her. She groaned against his mouth.

His breath left him in a rush and he grabbed her hips, moving her.

Bracing her hands on his shoulders, she rode him hard. Within minutes, her muscles contracted around him as she arched her back and cried out.

Her breasts bounced and he rubbed his palms against her hard nipples. Pulling her down, his mouth found first one, then the other as his hips ground into hers faster and harder. Jeremy pushed her down on him, their bodies coming together with a slap.

Again, Amy cried out then exploded. Ecstasy tightened her face muscles. Her head was back, her mouth open in a silent scream, her hands at her sides, fisted as her body rocked with her orgasm. He too cried out. His head came off the pillow as he emptied himself inside her.

Amy collapsed on him, breathing hard. Pulling her down, Jeremy wrapped his arms around her and held her tight. He withdrew, and Amy slid off him to lie at his side. She kissed his cheek until he turned his head and kissed her lips, tasting her tongue. "Thank you," he said. "I think you gave me the best sex ever."

She huffed a chuckle. "Funny, I was thinking the same thing."

They drifted off again and when they awoke, the clock showed nine thirty. Time to greet the day.

Amy peeled potatoes while the water heated in a pot. Eggs bubbled in another pot on the stove.

Behind her, footsteps sounded on the stairs and she turned. Jay came around the corner of the landing, his hair still wet from their shower.

He trotted down the last few stairs dressed in a pair of shorts and a T-shirt. She smiled as he approached. He was so thoroughly male he took her breath away and she still couldn't believe he was back in her life. For good this time, she prayed.

"Want coffee?" she said by way of greeting.

"Yes, please," he said, crooking a finger at her.

Amy walked over and kissed him. "Good morning," she said, kissing him a second time and sliding her arms around his neck.

Jay slid his hands down inside her shorts and over her butt while he nuzzled her neck. "Good morning to you."

She offered him a teasing *Oh, please* glance and tried to push herself away. "You're incorrigible."

His unrepentant shrug made her laugh. "What can I say, you make me hot!"

She laughed. "I do not. You've been sex-starved. Too much feast after so much famine."

He laughed and when she tried to wriggle free, he released her. After she fixed him some coffee, she returned to peeling potatoes.

"Do you think this is the smart thing to do, Jay?" A hard knot tightened her stomach. Part of their reason for having his family over for dinner, besides as a thank-you to his brother and sisters, was to tell his father what Adam had done. But despite how much Jay assured and reassured her, she feared his father's reaction when she told him.

On the drive back from the hospital, Jay had expressed a belief now that he knew Adam had raped her all those years ago: his father's friend might be the Queen City Rapist.

Amy objected at first. She didn't think him so brazen, but Jay pointed out all the times they encountered him, or he had seen them, and an attack occurred the same night. When she asked why he didn't go to the police with his suspicions, he shrugged. "Suspicion isn't proof," he said, leaving no room for argument.

"Amy, he has to know."

"Why?" She put down the peeled potato and picked up another. "Why can't we just let this go? We know. Isn't that enough?"

"Don't you ever fear he might do the same thing to some other young girl?"

"All the time."

"Speak out. Save some other teenage girl from rape." He sipped his coffee. "Do you remember I told you I worked with my female student, Britney, every afternoon?"

She nodded.

"Well, I'm as careful as I can be in my behavior toward my female students. I'm careful about touching them or saying anything that could be misconstrued. I worry about their safety. So many of them are naive. Some, like Britney, are downright innocent. Those are the girls I fear for the most."

Amy licked her lips and bowed her head. "You're right. I didn't think of that. I'm being selfish."

"No," he said, but she cut him off.

"Yes!" She faced him. "My fear is borne out of a selfish desire not to be seen as ruined, or stupid for falling for his tricks, or I asked for it in some way."

Picking up another potato she got back to work.

They had a few hours before everyone was due to arrive, so while the potatoes cooked, Jeremy brought Amy into his computer room and showed her his work trying to figure out if Adam was, indeed, the Queen City Rapist.

While she sat on his lap, he opened an Excel spreadsheet showing all the dates they had seen Adam and the corresponding attack dates, where the attacks occurred, when, and how many. On some nights, more than one attack was reported.

Amy pointed out some discrepancies in attacks reported, like when Adam was in their presence. The night on the bench for instance, but Jeremy pointed out the victim also noted she was unclear on the exact time, so he couldn't rule it out.

She didn't think he'd proved his case and they almost got into an argument, but Jeremy dropped the subject.

As she put the finishing touches on her potato salad and made the marinade for the chicken, she yawned and stretched.

"Are you okay?" he said.

She glanced at him. "I'm getting tired. Do you mind if I lie down on the couch?"

"Nope."

"I think I still have some of the hospital drugs running through my system." She shook her head. "I'm okay for a few hours and then I want to stop and go to sleep."

"Do you want to go upstairs to bed?" Jeremy asked, concerned. "Should I call tonight off?"

"No," she said, sounding amused. She came to him and slipped her arms around his neck.

Jeremy pulled her close. "I worry."

"I know." Drawing him into an embrace Amy kissed his cheek. Jeremy nuzzled his face into her neck and sniffed his shampoo.

"Mm, I like the scent of your shampoo," he said, nibbling her earlobe.

He tried not to respond to the memory of their shower that morning. Amy giggled and pulled away.

"You're incorrigible," she teased him again, stepping out of his arms. "The chicken is in the fridge along with the potato salad. Watch TV if you want. I can nap through it." She walked to the couch and lay down.

By the time Jeremy stepped to the side of the couch, she was asleep. He didn't turn on the TV. Instead, he went to his computer room and got back to work on tracking Adam Knox's movements. One thing was sure. One way or another, he was going to make the man pay for what he did to Amy.

31

Poppy got Ricky out of the car and set him on his feet. When he saw his mother, he ran to her. Amy was waiting for him in the backyard. She scooped him up and hugged him tightly and carried him to the deck where Jay embraced them both. He kissed Ricky and ruffled the boy's hair but didn't try to take him from his mama.

When Ricky wriggled to be set free, Amy let him go. He ran to the yard, entertaining himself.

Charlie, Emma, and Maya sat in one corner of the deck talking quietly but Amy sensed they were watching her and Jay's interactions with each other. She tried not to feel judged while at the same time acknowledging she'd earned their distrust. There was only one way to fix that. She walked over.

"Mind if I join you?"

"Not at all," Charlie smiled up at her and Amy took a seat. She stared straight at Emma. "Ask me anything you want to know. I'll tell you the truth, but first, Emma, for what it's worth, I still love you as my dearest friend. That never stopped."

Emma's eyes filled with tears and she offered Amy a pleased, pained smile. "Thank you." She sat forward. "I do want to know some things," she said and Amy sat back prepared to clear the air.

The four of them talked for a quarter of an hour without Jay, as though he sensed he didn't belong in that conversation, so he played with Ricky in the backyard

"Amy!" Mom called from the kitchen.

"Yeah." She headed inside.

Alicia and Mom rummaged through cupboards. "Where are the salt and pepper?"

Amy shrugged and went back outside. "Jay, our moms need the salt and pepper."

He followed her into the house.

When they came back outside, the seasoning crisis averted, she glanced around and smiled.

Before everyone arrived, Jay had asked her to move in with him. While disappointed he didn't propose, at this point, she would take what he offered and agreed. Standing at the top step, she eyed her son playing in the yard, imagining their children at play, truly making Jay's house their home.

On the concrete pad at the bottom of the step, her father and Paul were busy at the grills, preparing them for the meat later. Dad was to cook the hamburgers and hot dogs for any who wanted them, and Paul, the chicken. As they worked their stations, each with a beer in one hand, they talked, getting better acquainted.

Jay's hands brushed the tops of her shoulders. "What are you thinking?"

She leaned against his chest and his arms went around her. Unsure how to put into words how happy and content she felt at that moment, she didn't answer.

He kissed her and she turned in his arms, holding him much the same as he held her in her living room the night he'd come for dinner. She let her emotions say what words failed to accomplish.

Jay's arms tightened around her. He understood. As they broke apart and smiled at each other, Charlie's voice broke in.

"God almighty, you two. Get a fucking room."

Everyone laughed.

Jay leered at his brother, sliding his arm around Amy's waist. "Get a fucking room or get a *fucking* room?"

Amy smacked him in the abdomen. Her face grew hot, but she laughed with the others.

A car pulled into the yard and they turned as another car pulled in beside the first.

Mike emerged with his two boys and a cooler of drinks. The boys ran off to play with Ricky. Mike waited for Lindsay and introduced himself to Jessica who struggled to hold the cake they'd brought.

After walking with Lindsay to the deck he kissed Amy on the

cheek and shook Jay's hand.

When Jessie safely delivered the cake, she ran off to play with the boys.

"Amy, do you play cornhole?" Mike asked.

"I love cornhole." She nodded.

He grinned and took her elbow. "Well come on. You and me against Jeremy and your sister."

For more than an hour, they played. The thump of seed-filled sacks hitting wood, accompanied by laughter and teasing comments filled the afternoon. When Mike put all four of their sacks into the hole, he and Amy did a double high five, and he gave her a quick congratulatory hug.

Following two more rounds Mike and Amy easily creamed Lindsay and Jeremy. They won two games out of three, thanks to Mike's more accurate throws, even with a beer bottle in one hand, and she conceded it was hard to throw accurately when laughing so hard.

As the heat of the June afternoon built, cicadas buzzed and crickets chirped their songs.

Mike wrapped a friendly arm around her shoulders. "Oh, man," he said. "I can't remember when I've had so much fun. Thank you for inviting us."

She slipped her arm around his waist and gave him a friendly squeeze. "You're certainly welcome. I'm glad you came and brought your boys." She turned to him. "I wanted to apologize again for my gaffe at the festival."

But Mike shook his head. "You couldn't have known. I don't consider it a gaffe so much as an honest mistake, and it says a lot about you if your natural instinct was to want to meet my wife." A soft smile pulled at his lips. "She was a wonderful woman," he said without a hint of sadness.

Jay strolled up. "Hey," he said, teasing. "Hands off my woman."

Mike laughed. "I'll fight you for her." He held up his fists.

"Now, now, boys, none of that," Amy said coming between them. "Let's have fun."

"Okay," Emma called out. "The food is almost ready. C'mon in, kids, and wash up."

As she made the announcement, Mom and Alicia came out of the house, hands filled with bowls of food, while Maya set up a paper plate and utensil area in preparation for the meal.

While their guests lined up at the buffet table, Amy glanced back. Mike and Lindsay stood together, gathering plastic forks, knives, and paper plates all the while talking with each other.

Turning, she eyed Jay with suspicion.

“I thought I told you not to push,” she murmured.

“I didn’t.” He too glanced back. “They met at the hospital. He’s had his eye on her ever since.”

Amy narrowed her eyes at him.

He shrugged. “I’m not doing anything to curb this, and neither will you.” He kissed her nose.

Once the children were eating, the adults served themselves and the deck grew quiet as everyone ate and engaged in general conversation and complimented the various chefs.

Mom’s deviled eggs were a hit as was Amy’s potato salad.

After everyone ate their fill, the children ran off to play some more, but when they grew quiet, Amy did a check.

In the lengthening shadows of late afternoon, Jessica played catch with Luke while Ricky and Evan lay on their stomachs in the grass pushing cars through the lawn.

Dinner was a huge success. There was more than enough food, laughter, connection, reconnection, and love to go around.

They wrapped up the evening with coffee and a slice of Lindsay’s Jell-O angel food cake, which was delicious and also received high compliments. Mike asked for a second slice, which made Amy eye Jay with more suspicion.

He shrugged and continued to eat, but he gave her a lecherous smile.

As the early summer sun slid toward the western horizon, the women rose to clean up the paper plates and Solo cups, while Dad cleaned Jay’s grill. Mr. Austin collected the soda cans and beer bottles and placed them in a recycle bin.

Amy reclined on the wicker sofa, exhausted but happy. Ricky dozed in Mom’s lap, thumb tucked in his mouth. The sun had set and darkness edged the eastern sky. She should get him to bed. She didn’t move.

Jay stopped beside her. “You okay?”

She sat up. “I’m fine. Full belly, heavy eyelids.”

"Maybe we should go home," Lindsay stood.

Mike rose with her.

"You look tired, Amy," Lindsay said and knelt in front of her, taking her wrist in her first and second fingers and gazing at her watch.

Amy sighed. "I'm fine, Nurse Nancy," for which she earned an *Oh, please* glare from her sister.

"Don't go yet," Jay said. "I have something I need to say, but first, I'll be right back." He trotted into the house and returned a few moments later, his right hand tucked behind his back.

Lindsay rose and stood beside Mike.

Jay took Amy's hand and pulled her to her feet. "I've been carrying this around since the end of April, trying to find the opportune moment, which, let's face it, with you, is never easy." He laughed, and the others joined in as he produced a small black box.

His hand shook as he opened the top. Inside, tucked within a blue satin cushion was a diamond solitaire ring.

Gasps and murmurs made the rounds. Holding his hands out, he acknowledged the presence of their families. "This isn't how I envisioned proposing to you, Amy Taylor, but if I've learned anything being around you, I've learned nothing ever goes the way I think it will, so I'm asking with all humility, and I'll get on one knee if you require, but will you marry me?"

Amid the murmured laughs, she stared wide-eyed, mouth open, unable to speak.

He uttered a nervous laugh. "You look like a codfish."

She snapped her jaws closed, clicking her teeth. Reaching a tentative hand toward the box, she stared at him with questioning eyes. "You want to marry me? After everything?"

"Yes, I want to marry you." His voice shook, and his face turned scarlet. The uncertainty in his eyes said, *Dear God, don't say no!* "Call me a glutton for punishment."

Holding out the box, Jay waited for her to say or do something. Her mind whirled as she continued to stare in awe at the ring in the box.

He tried again. "Earth to Amy Taylor."

With effort, she raised her eyes from the ring and met his eyes filled with love and longing and trepidation.

"I've wanted to marry you since I was eighteen years old," he said. "I've waited ten years for this moment. So I'm going to ask you again." He started to lower himself to one knee, but she grabbed his shoulders, stopping him.

"You don't have to," she spoke fast, "unless you want to. But yes, Jay, I'll marry you. I've waited ten years for you to ask me."

Amid gasps and cries of delight, they kissed and hugged, his arms tight around her waist.

"God, you scared the crap out of me right there," he whispered in her ear.

"I'm sorry," she said and kissed him again. As he removed the ring from the box, she held up her hand and he slipped the diamond on her finger.

They broke apart as everyone gathered around to offer congratulations and view the ring.

Mike grabbed Jay, hugged him, and slapped his back before reaching for Amy.

"I'm happy for you, Amy," he said kissing her cheek. "You two are made for each other. Anyone can see that."

"Thank you," she mouthed.

Soon Amy found herself wrapped in Mrs. Austin's embrace and her second mother welcomed her to the family. Amy's emotional control broke. The two women cried and held each other.

When they pulled away, Lindsay grabbed her shoulder.

They embraced and Lindsay kissed Amy's cheek. "I'm glad you came to your senses at last, stupid sister!"

Amy laughed again. "I love you baby sis." She squeezed her tight. "Thanks for being willing to tell me what a jerk I can be."

"Well, young man," Dad's voice cut through the exclamations as he held his hand out to Jeremy. "I guess this means I have a house to sell."

"Yes, sir," Jay said. He shook Dad's hand.

"Hmm," he said, regarding Jay with narrow eyes. "I'll be keeping my eye on you. I won't see my daughter mistreated again."

"You don't have to, Dad," Amy stepped close. "He's not that kind of man." She slipped her arm around Jay's waist as if defending him. His arm went around her shoulders.

"I am not." Jay stared him in the eye. "You don't have to worry, John. I'll take excellent care of Amy and Ricky. I already think of him as my own son."

Dad studied Jay and appeared to come to a decision. "You give me your word?"

"I do."

He held his hand out again. Again, Jay shook it. "Welcome to the family, son."

The party broke up amid general congratulations, and Amy's family began to leave. Mike and Lindsay spoke a few words before he rounded up his sons, thanked Jay and Amy for the afternoon, and they departed. Lindsay left soon after and Mom and Dad followed a few minutes after.

The Austins would stay for a family meeting after everyone else was gone.

Amy turned to Jay. "I need to put the monster to bed. Then I'll come back."

"Okay." He settled on the sofa. "Take your time."

After Ricky said good night to everyone, Amy took him inside, bathed him, and got him into pajamas before brushing his teeth.

"Do you like it here, buddy?"

He nodded.

"Do you like Jamie?"

Again he nodded, yawned, and rubbed an eye.

"Would you want to live with Jamie forever?"

She caught the boy's attention. "Where?"

"Right here, in this house."

He thought about it. "What about my toys?"

"We'll go to our house and bring them here. If we do will you want to live here with Jamie?"

He nodded.

Amy smiled. "I'm glad. Because I want to live here with Jamie too."

She walked him to the bedroom Jay had set up for Ricky, excited for his reaction to the sports car bed Jay bought for him.

Ricky's face lit up. "Mommy!" He pointed. "A car!"

"Wow!"

He drew in a breath and stared in wide-eyed wonder, before running across the room and throwing himself onto the mattress.

Amy laughed. "Do you like your bed?"

"Looks like he does," Jay spoke from behind her. "They don't make dinosaur-shaped beds. I had to come and see what he thought." Jay sat down beside Ricky. "Hey, Sport." He pulled back the covers.

Ricky climbed in and lay down.

"I have a question I need to ask you."

"Okay." Ricky snuggled into bed and reached out toward the dresser.

Amy glanced over to see what he wanted. On top of the dresser was his T-Rex, which she brought to him.

When he tucked the toy into his arms, Ricky gazed up at Jay.

"I'm glad you like your T-Rex."

Ricky nodded.

"So, Ricky, the question I wanted to ask. I want to marry your mommy. Do you mind? I love her very much. I love you very much and I want you two to come live with me. Would you like to?"

Ricky fingered the dinosaur and said, "Yeah." He didn't meet Jay's eyes. "But Jamie?"

"Yeah."

Amy walked to his side and placed a hand on his shoulder.

Ricky didn't speak, just continued to fiddle with his toy.

"What's on your mind, buddy?"

Ricky fingered the toy, glanced into Jay's eyes, and back to his dinosaur. "Will you still be Jamie?"

"If you want," he said carefully. "If you want..." Jay hesitated, a questioning glance at Amy. She nodded her encouragement.

"If you want," Jay said again, returning his attention to the little boy, "you can call me Dad or Daddy, but if you would rather stick with Jamie, you can."

"Daddy," Ricky whispered, testing the word. "Daddy," he whispered again. He sat up and put his arms around Jay's neck. "Daddy," he said out loud.

Amy's throat ached and she blinked back tears as Jay held the boy tight and wiped an eye with his thumb. He kissed Ricky's temple and laid him back down.

"I like the sound of Daddy," his voice choked with emotion. He reached for Amy's hand. "Good night, son."

Amy leaned close and kissed Ricky. "I love you, baby," she said. "Sleep tight."

"Night-night, Mommy." Ricky rolled over, tucked his thumb in his mouth, and went to sleep.

Amy and Jay walked out arm in arm. In the hallway, she stopped and embraced him.

Jay kissed her. "I love you, Amy. I never thought for a second how much I would come to love that little boy, but he has lodged himself into my heart as much as you have."

She chuckled. "I told you. It doesn't take long." She drew in a deep breath and exhaled. "Not to be a Debbie Downer, but I think the time has come we do this thing and not keep your family waiting any longer."

He nodded. "Let's go."

They returned to the back deck. Amy offered coffee, and once all had their fill, she sat in the corner of the sofa, her knees tucked tight to her body and her arms around her knees.

Jay sat down beside her and placed a hand on her knee. He rubbed her leg offering her support.

Amy fidgeted, sipped coffee, adjusted her seat, and leaned in close to Jay who put his arm around her shoulders and held her.

Placing her coffee on the table in front of the sofa, she stood and readjusted her seat again. She surveyed her audience and her gaze landed on her future father-in-law.

Why am I doing this? How many bridges am I going to set aflame?

When she didn't speak right away, Jay squeezed her shoulder.

"You got this," he said with quiet assurance. "And I'm right here. I won't let anything happen to you."

"None of us will," Charlie said.

Maya nodded. Emma threw Amy a kiss. Amy pursed her lips and tried not to dissolve into tears. Besides Jay coming back into her life, she didn't realize how much she'd missed her best friend until she, too, returned.

"Okay," she said, and gestured as if to say, *I'm ready*. Her heart slammed against her ribs. Her hands went cold and clammy, and she squeezed them together, rubbing them as if she were washing her hands. She grimaced at Jay.

He smiled back and squeezed her shoulder again.

Paul and Alicia appeared so happy for them and she hated what she was about to do.

"So you're Catnap?" Paul said, surprising her. He sat on a bench across from her, a beer bottle held in one hand.

She laughed and crinkled her brow. "What? Am I whom?"

Jeremy laughed. "Yes, Dad, she's Catnap."

Paul chuckled. "Thank God," he said, making the rest of the family laugh.

Not getting the joke and fearing they laughed at her, Amy gave Jay a confused glance.

He gestured for her to move and retrieved his wallet from his back pocket, then grabbed his phone and scrolled through his contacts. When he got to her designation, he stopped and showed her the screen.

"Catnap?" She wrinkled her brow.

He opened his wallet and removed the crumpled note she'd given him at the restaurant.

"You still have my note? Geez, Jay, throw it away."

"Look," he said.

She read aloud. "I get off at eleven," and beneath her phone number, in different color ink and in Jay's handwriting, was the word *catnap*.

She studied him again, still perplexed, until she remembered and threw her head back and laughed.

"The first time you called, you woke me. When you apologized, I said I was grabbing a catnap."

Everyone laughed.

She shook her head. "I had just gotten Ricky to lay quietly beside me and drifted off, when you called."

"And I blew your rest by calling. I thought I heard you whispering, too." He slipped the note back into his wallet which he returned to his pocket.

She giggled. "I was. Trying to keep him quiet so you wouldn't hear him." With an apologetic glance, she squeezed his hand. "I'm glad you called." Then with a gesture toward his wallet, she shook her head, teasing again. "But I gotta say, you're one weird guy, Jay Austin."

"Yeah," he said, drawing out the word, "but you love me."

"I do," she said.

Paul cleared his throat, bringing them back.

"Jeremy shared you've been divorced," he said. "I hope you don't mind his telling us."

She shook her head. Her left hand was resting on Jay's knee, and she clenched her fingers, studying her ring. He covered her hand with his own. She shifted her fingers to intertwine with his.

"He also said your former husband abandoned you before you

discovered you were pregnant."

"Right."

"And you have no interest in trying to find him?"

She cocked her head. "Are you interrogating me?"

To her surprise, Paul chuckled. "Occupational hazard of an attorney. I'm sorry. I'm not trying to interrogate you."

"Well, to answer your question, no. I have no desire to find him."

"But you're missing out on child support. They could garner his wages since he proved to be a deadbeat dad."

"Peter doesn't know about Ricky, and I don't want him finding out. He'd try to take him from me. Not because he'd want to parent Ricky, but because he couldn't think of any better way to hurt me than to take my son away." She said, her voice strong with her conviction. "And if you garnered his wages, he'd refuse to work. No, Paul. The only thing I want from Ricky's dad is what I already have: my son, my peace, and his absence."

"Fair enough," he said and fell silent.

"Dad, Amy has something she needs to tell you and Mom, which I'm afraid isn't pleasant." He gestured toward his siblings. "Emma realized something was wrong and she rallied the troops."

"I sensed Jeremy was in some emotional trouble and called Maya and Charlie, and without giving them specifics, I asked them to come here. We showed up Friday night, when Amy had her breakdown."

She eyed Jay, questioning, but came to a decision.

"Jeremy was also on the verge of emotional collapse as well and would not have been in a position to help her if we hadn't been here."

Paul and Alicia glanced at each other.

"Thanks, Em. That helps," Jay said in a sardonic tone.

Alicia sat upright in her chair. "Oh, dear," she said. "Are you ill, Amy? Jeremy, what happened to you?"

"I'm fine, Mom, but I wasn't in a healthy place Friday night. I didn't call and ask them to come— Emma did and I'm grateful. But we've done some note comparing and realized we all have parts of a story to tell. You won't like what Amy has to say, but we need you to listen without judgment."

Amy scrubbed her hands again as her fingers grew cold. When she became aware, she dropped her hands to her lap.

"All right," Alicia said, reaching for her husband's hand, clear she expected the worst. "What do you need to tell us?"

Sipping her coffee as she gathered her thoughts, Amy prayed his parents took what she had to say well.

She drew in a deep breath through her nose, leaned forward, and set her coffee cup down on the table. When she peered at Paul, she stuffed down the urge to run.

Jay grasped her hand and squeezed. She covered his hand with her own and held on tight hoping to still their shaking.

After she cleared her throat, she swallowed hard. "That day." She glanced at Jay. "When we were kids. The reason I did what I did was because..."

Jay let go of her hand to rub her back.

Paul waited, expressionless. He went into lawyer mode the minute Jay asked him to listen without judgment.

"I was raped." She faced Paul. "In your office."

Paul recoiled and sucked in his breath through his nose but didn't speak.

Alicia started to speak, but he raised his hand in an abrupt gesture and cut her off. Amy flinched.

He studied Amy until she began to fear he didn't, wouldn't believe her. She'd been right.

Paul spoke two words. "By whom?"

She licked her lips and watched him through tears. She thought she saw fear in his eyes, as though he knew the answer already but needed her to say the words and didn't want her to.

"Adam," she said, but so softly Paul leaned forward. She dropped her head and covered her face. Her hands shook.

"I'm sorry, Amy. I didn't hear you," Paul said.

After a deep inhale, she dropped her hands then raised her gaze to meet his eyes. Hers were wet and she said louder, "Adam."

Alicia gasped.

Paul half rose from the bench and Jeremy made a move as if to protect her.

Charlie also rose as if he too needed to come to Amy's defense.

Paul sat back and the boys relaxed but stayed alert.

"You let me in," she said as if nothing happened.

"I remember."

Amy turned to Alicia. "You weren't around for some reason, but I don't recall why."

Paul turned to Alicia. "You had a church convention at Jay Peak."

Amy stared at him. "How do you remember such things?"

He half smiled. "It was an unusual day. One not easy to forget," he said, and his gaze went to Jeremy. "Please continue your story."

She swallowed hard. "You and Adam were going somewhere, but you said to come in and sit at the bar." She gestured, needing to talk with her hands. "You teased me about knowing where all the food was kept and to help myself."

Paul nodded, and again a smile ghosted his lips.

"I remember saying hi to Adam. He was putzing around the kitchen, waiting for you, and then you two left through the garage, but a few seconds later, he came back in." She glanced at Jay again seeking his reassurance.

He squeezed her shoulder, nodded.

"I didn't think anything of it," she continued. "I thought he forgot something. He..."She made a flowing gesture with her hand. "He walked up to me, took hold of my elbow, and ever so gently, pulled me off the stool. Never said a word. I was confused I guess, but I'm not sure confused is the word. More like, 'What are you doing?' than anything else. You know what I mean?"

Paul nodded. His eyes never left her face.

"He walked me into your office and shut the door and I still wasn't scared. I remember looking at him, like 'What do you want?' He took me by the shoulders, spun me around and pushed me over the arm of your sofa. One hand he kept pressed into my back between my shoulder blades and with the other he pushed my skirt up."

A quick glance to Jay revealed his reddened face. Anger tightened his features. He was hearing the details for the first time as well and she prepared herself to give back his ring and to tell Dad not to sell the house.

Squeezing her lips together, she faced Paul to gauge his reaction, and though he was stone-faced, anger rolled off him in the same way it rolled off Jay. She sighed. She was done in this family.

Amy glanced around at the others. The women had tears in their eyes. Charlie appeared distraught more than angry, but anger shone from his brown eyes too.

She drew in a deep breath and continued, "He pushed my knees apart, pressed my hips onto the sofa so I couldn't move, and I got scared. I tried to fight but he had me pinned in place. He pushed my panties aside and shoved himself into me. He was fast, and brutal, and

I couldn't even scream because of the searing pain. Afterward, he put himself back together and spoke." She focused on the small table in front of the sofa she and Jay sat on, unable to meet anyone's eyes.

"What—" Jay cleared his throat. "What did he say?"

Amy sniffed and glanced at him. Her brow puckered at the sadness in his brown eyes. She scratched her ear.

"Uh, he said he was sorry to do that to *you*," she emphasized the word. "Not me. You. Because he liked you." She turned away. "He said I could tell you what happened if I wished, but he would deny everything, and you would believe him, not me, and in your eyes, I would be a slut and a whore."

He drew a palm over his eyes. "This explains so many things," he ground out. Tears leaked from beneath his fingers.

He wrapped his arms around her, and she held him, giving him comfort, instead of the other way around.

"I'm so sorry, Amy," he said weeping, "I'm so sorry."

Tears spilled down her face. "Don't, Jeremy. You did nothing wrong. Now do you believe me?"

He nodded.

When he calmed down, she asked, "Do you want me to continue?"

He nodded again and wiped his eyes, and with the hem of his shirt, he wiped his nose.

She offered him a crooked grin. "Gross," she said, "and not maple."

Jay sputtered a laugh through his tears.

She turned and faced her audience again. "Adam warned me to keep silent. He said if I told anyone he would ruin my reputation. People would consider me the town slut and Jeremy would leave me forever. He left as if he hadn't a care in the world. I waited a minute to be sure he was gone, went into the bathroom, and panicked because there was blood all over my thighs." From the corner of her eye she saw Jay lift his gaze and look at Emma.

"I thought if I had enough time to pull myself together and pretend nothing happened, I'd be okay, but I no sooner got back on the stool when these guys came home."

She used her thumb to gesture at Jay.

Paul's eyes flicked from Amy to Jay and back to Amy.

"Jay was like, 'Hey, Amy,' and he grasped my shoulder. I flipped out. I couldn't...I couldn't..." She swallowed hard.

Jay took her ice-cold hands in his warm ones.

"I freaked out and ran from the house screaming and crying and I never came back. And I am profoundly sorry to all of you." She swallowed and bit back tears.

"Jay tried to catch me at school so many times, but I wouldn't talk to him. I didn't want him to find out what happened. I was young enough to think Adam was right and you would consider me used and wouldn't want me anymore. I was afraid you'd never forgive me. I did the same thing to Emma as well. Adam was your friend," she said to Paul. "I got it into my head you would all think I was trying to ruin him, and you would hate me. I didn't want you to hate me."

She turned to Jay, relentless in her story now. She'd held back for so long, that she couldn't stop talking now. "I was so ashamed. He said I forced him into it and I believed him."

"Your fault?" Alicia said. "Why your fault?"

Amy sighed again. "Because. He said the skirt I was wearing was so short as to be incredibly sexy and he couldn't resist the temptation. Ergo, I was a temptress he was powerless to resist." She huffed. "I haven't worn a skirt since."

"Sounds exactly like something he would say," Paul said, fury lacing his words.

Amy shrugged, finished with her story.

Paul pulled at his lower lip. Charlie drummed his fingers on the arm of his chair.

"Not to add gasoline to the fire," Maya spoke up for the first time, "but Dad, I have a confession to make."

"Oh, Lord," Paul said as he knuckled an eye. "I'm not sure I can take anymore."

"I'm sorry," she said. "I don't want to hurt you, but when I graduated from high school, Adam tried the same thing with me, but in a freak of circumstances, I was able to escape him. I had the presence of mind to warn Emma about him. I wish now I'd said something to Amy."

Amy and Maya exchanged a glance, and Amy understood this was her future sister-in-law's way of asking her forgiveness.

Amy smiled and nodded.

Paul gave Emma a questioning glance. She shook her head no.

Alicia cried and grasped Paul's arm. He patted her hand as he gestured to Maya to tell her story. When she finished, he sat back looking as if he'd witnessed a violent murder and didn't know how to respond.

Jay spoke up. "The reason I wanted Amy to tell you is because this rapist is still out there, and I've often wondered why Adam roams the streets of Burlington at all hours as well."

"That's quite a stretch, Jer," he said.

"Perhaps," Jeremy said, "but something curious happened. Do you recall the night you first broached the topic of my late-night wanderings?"

Dad nodded.

"Well, the night before, we ran into Adam. We were, well, making out, on a bench in front of Lou's. Amy was who I was 'quite involved with,'" Jeremy said, using air quotes.

Amy spoke up. "I work at Lou's Restaurant. Jay comes every night before eleven. He sits at the bar and my boss gives him all the free coffee he wants while he waits for my shift to end and walks me to my car."

The relief on his mother's face was almost comical and if the situation hadn't been so frightening, Amy would have laughed.

32

They talked well into the night. Paul asked Amy questions like a prosecutor building a case and perhaps he was.

She answered with the truth and when he posed questions in a way that she thought questioned her integrity or indicated that she had the details wrong, she said so. If she didn't recall something, she told him, and at times, corrected details for him.

When he was done, Paul sat back. He appeared grieved.

"I'm sorry, Paul," she said. "He's your friend and partner and this is one reason I never wanted to tell anyone, but Jeremy insisted."

She turned to Jeremy. "You understand what I mean, don't you?"

"I do," he said. "Can you help her, Dad? Can she have justice?"

Paul sighed and covered his eyes. "I'm sorry, but no. The statute of limitations in Vermont is six years. This happened at least ten years ago. What I suggest you do is go to the Essex Police because that's where the crime happened and you live in Essex still, right?"

Amy nodded.

"Go to them and make a report. Since no one's been arrested for the so-called Queen City Rapist case, that will give them someone to focus on. They can obtain a DNA sample on Adam and if he's not a match, he's not our guy and if it does..." He broke off unwilling or unable to finish the thought.

Amy was drained. She shared a glance with Jay who raised his eyebrows at her. She nodded.

"We can do that."

"First thing tomorrow," Jay said.

She turned to Paul. "Do you have any more questions?"

He shook his head. "I don't think so."

She nodded once.

Paul rose and grasping her hands, he pulled her to her feet and kissed her cheek before embracing her.

She hugged him back, grateful for his kindness, so much like Jay.

"I'm sorry this happened to you, Amy. I am. You were always like a daughter to me, so you can't begin to understand what emotions are running through me right now."

"I suppose not," she said, "but I have a clear idea of how my dad would react and I like to think you're a lot like him."

She smiled up at him and he released her. Turning he held his arms out to Maya, who went to him.

Paul placed his cheek on her head. "I wish you'd come to me or your mother. I'm sorry you didn't think you could."

Maya shrugged and sniffed. "Like Amy, I didn't think anyone would believe me."

When Amy and Alicia embraced, Alicia held her like a mother comforting her own child. Amy was grateful for their kindness. Perhaps once the shock wore off, things would change, but for now, she'd take what they offered.

Everyone milled about for a few minutes. Emma and Jay hugged each other, and Emma spoke in his ear. He was still in tears, and she let his sister give him comfort.

Charlie approached and she smiled at him. He opened his arms in an unspoken invitation and she accepted.

"I'm so grateful you came, Charlie. Thank you."

He sniffed. "I thought we were coming to rescue Jeremy. If I'd had any idea, we were called here for you, I wouldn't have waited for the summons."

She tightened her embrace. "If I'd understood what love you all had for me back then..."

"Of course we loved you. You were part of the family." He squeezed her. "And now you will be again. I couldn't be happier."

"I'm sorry I hurt all of you. I'm so grateful you don't all hate me." Pulling away, she smiled up at him. "I love you, Charlie. You're the best oldest brother."

"Pshaw," he said with a chuckle. "You will always have a special place in my heart, Amy-Taylor-soon-to-be-Austin. I love you too." He kissed her cheek.

"Yeah, well you can't have her," Jay said, grinning. "She belongs to me, now."

Charlie uttered an exaggerated sigh. "I know, I know. Get my own."

They laughed as Charlie and Jay embraced. Charlie slapped him on the back with a smack that made Amy cringe.

She turned to Paul and lay a hand on his arm. "Are you okay?"

He shook his head and shrugged.

"Are we okay?" Amy held her breath.

Paul glanced at her. "Of course, we're okay," he said. "I'm having a hard time wrapping my head around what you told me, but your story explains things I've long since wondered about." He gestured toward her. "Like you, for one, but so many times, young female interns have quit. No explanations or the only explanation being that they couldn't work with Adam. And always without warning. I'd end up scratching my head."

He gave her a pained glance. "It happened so often I started keeping track of who left. I need to reach out to them and start asking questions." His gaze went over her head to Maya. "I'm pained about her. It's hard on a man to spend your life doing your damnedest to protect your children, especially your daughters, only to discover it's not possible."

The following morning, Jeremy and Amy drove to the Essex Police Station. They sat down with a detective and once again, Amy told her story. They shared their concerns that perhaps Adam might be the Queen City Rapist.

The detective listened and asked questions. Within a few hours, they left.

As they got into the car, Amy glanced at Jeremy. "Well," she said, "what do you think?"

Jeremy shook his head. "I'm not sure." He glanced at her. "I had a hard time reading the guy. I can't tell if he believed you or not."

"So what now?" she asked.

Jeremy shrugged. "As for them, nothing. We let them do what they're gonna do, or not." He started the car. "But for now, we go see Frank."

"Mmm, Frank," Amy said.

"Aim, we talked about this," Jeremy said, misunderstanding her. "I don't want you working at night."

"Jay," she said, laying a hand on his arm. "Relax. I was anticipating having to tell him. Frank is a friend. I'm gonna miss him. Not the job. Him."

He nodded and they pulled out of the parking lot and headed for Burlington.

Amy let them into the restaurant through the back door. Lou's opened in two hours, but after what happened, Frank called to tell her he was giving her the next two weeks off to recuperate.

He must have heard the door open because he popped out of the kitchen and stared in surprise.

"What are you doing here?" He opened his arms, and she went to him.

"I'm going to hug you now before I confess. I'm here to clean out my locker." She showed him her ring. Frank grinned.

"Congratulations, you two!" He shook Jeremy's hand. "I shoulda spiked your coffee."

Jeremy chuckled. "If you'd done that you would've lost out on a catering gig."

After they went into the office and made sure the wedding date was on Frank's calendar, Amy went to her locker and opened the door.

Jeremy pulled the picture of her with her infant son off the door and studied the photo. "If I could turn back time," he said, "I'd be in this." He waved the photo before handing it to her.

She smiled. "I would have made sure of that." She gathered the rest of her things and as Briana and Jason entered, she bid them farewell among tears, hugs, and congratulations.

They drove back to Essex, picked Ricky up from Amy's parents, and headed home. She still needed to call the movers and arrange to pack their belongings. Lindsay had tomorrow off and offered to come and help.

"I meant to tell you." Jeremy turned the car and headed back toward Milton. "Dad called. He confronted Adam this morning about you and Maya. Adam has decided his best course of action is to retire early from the law firm. Dad also said he's contacting every female intern who quit without warning to find out why."

He reached out and turned on the car radio. A song played and Amy tapped her hand on her knee in time to the music.

"I love this song," she said in response to his amused grin.

He started to say something, but the emergency warning sounded, silencing him. "Breaking News," the announcer broke in. "A suspect has been arrested in the case of the Queen City Rapist attacks."

Jeremy and Amy exchanged anxious glances.

"A twenty-two-year-old New Hampshire man, a student at UVM, was taken into custody earlier today. DNA testing reveals him as a match in several of the attacks over the past several months."

Amy switched off the radio. "Thank God," she said. "This may sound crazy, but I'm glad Adam wasn't the guy."

From the back seat, Ricky kicked the back of Jeremy's seat.

"Ricky," he said, "stop kicking Daddy's seat."

He stopped.

From the corner of his eye, he saw Amy grin and turn her face away.

"What? You might as well get used to it."

She chuckled and played with the diamond ring on her finger. "I'm working on it. I can't believe you want to adopt him, but then again, I can believe it. You are an extraordinary man, Jeremy Paul Austin."